PATH TO
NIRVANA

PATH TO NIRVANA

ERIC ANURAG

iUniverse LLC
Bloomington

PATH TO NIRVANA

iUniverse books may be ordered through booksellers or by contacting:

iUniverse LLC
1663 Liberty Drive
Bloomington, IN 47403
www.iuniverse.com
1-800-Authors (1-800-288-4677)

Because of the dynamic nature of the Internet, any web addresses or links contained in this book may have changed since publication and may no longer be valid. The views expressed in this work are solely those of the author and do not necessarily reflect the views of the publisher, and the publisher hereby disclaims any responsibility for them.

Any people depicted in stock imagery provided by Thinkstock are models, and such images are being used for illustrative purposes only. Certain stock imagery © Thinkstock.

ISBN: 978-1-4917-1682-3 (sc)
ISBN: 978-1-4917-1684-7 (hc)
ISBN: 978-1-4917-1683-0 (e)

Library of Congress Control Number: 2013922207

Printed in the United States of America.

iUniverse rev. date: 01/16/2014

CHAPTER 1

When the classroom bell rang, Rahul Sharma reluctantly closed his book, pushed it into his backpack, and stood up to join his friends down the hall at the lockers. He was a freshman in high school, and it was the last day of the school year. All the students showed excitement about the onset of summer, but Rahul was dragging his feet. He loved school and reveled in learning and mental challenges. The end of school also meant that he would be leaving for India soon. He wanted to stay in Boston and participate in all the activities his friends were engaged in.

As he approached the lockers, he noticed that his friends had already emptied their lockers and were ready to take their personal belongings home.

"What's up, Rahul?" Andre asked, flipping his blond hair out of his tanned face. "Aren't you glad school is out?" Andre was kind of an effeminate kid, and almost everyone teased or bullied him.

"Hi, guys!" Rahul replied, looking at Andre and others and grabbing his backpack. "Sure, I am."

Rahul's four friends all lived in an affluent neighborhood in Brookline, Massachusetts. Andre's mother picked up the kids to take them home.

Rahul worked extremely hard during the school year and earned excellent grades. He had remained at the top of his class and made his teachers very proud. Standing at about five feet nine inches tall, he was slim with a light-brown complexion, dark eyes, and black hair. He always wore his shirt neatly tucked into his trousers, and he blended well with his friends, speaking their lingo and maintaining close friendships with them.

After reaching home, he dropped his backpack on his bed and put on his headphones to listen to music while reading a computer magazine.

A little while later, he went to the kitchen and hugged his mother, Asha. "Anything to eat?" Rahul asked.

"What do you want?" she replied. "I'll fix it for you. How was your day at school?"

"Fine, Mom. The first year was a little harder, but I did well."

"Nothing is too difficult for my son," she said proudly, putting the plate down on the dining table in front of him. "Here is your favorite." She patted him and kissed him gently.

"Mom, don't do that! I'm not a child anymore."

"Okay, okay," said his mother while answering a phone call. "It's for you. It's Andre."

"Okay." Rahul picked up the phone. "Hey, dude. What's up?"

"You want to go to the mall?" Andre asked.

"I'd like to, but I have to go out with my folks to get some stuff for India. It's a drag, but I gotta do it. I also want to buy a cassette player and a couple of shirts."

"When are you guys leaving?"

"The day after tomorrow. Listen, we'll have fun when I get back in a month."

"All right. See ya later," said Andre. "Have a good one!" He hung up.

Rahul's father, Vasu Sharma, entered the home and walked into the kitchen. He was slim and of medium height, with dark hair receding from the back of his head. "Hello, everyone!" he said to his family. After sitting down, he spoke to Rahul about his school and upcoming summer vacation.

"Dad, may I ask you something?" Rahul said.

"What's on your mind? How come I don't see any joy on your face about the vacation and our trip?"

"Do we have to go to India? My friends and I had plans for this summer. It was a hard year at school, and we want to unwind and relax."

"You know we are going to attend the wedding ceremony of my sister, *your* aunt," Vasu replied while taking off his jacket and pushing back his glasses. "I had that responsibility after my father passed away. This is the last big occasion in our family, and your grandmother would be upset if we did not go."

"Dad, what am I going to do over there? I don't know anyone."

"This is one of the social obligations we have to fulfill, son. Besides, your cousins will also be attending the wedding. They will take a few days off from school. Listen, we will be at Grandma's house only for a few days. Then we will go to Mumbai, and in three weeks we will be back. You can still enjoy your vacation with your friends." He paused. "Your mom and I have to go. If you do not want to join us, that's fine. But where would you stay? You can't stay here by yourself."

"Okay, Dad," Rahul agreed hesitantly.

"Come on, cheer up. I promise you will have a good time. To make you feel better, next year we may go to Disney World. Okay?"

"That's fine, Dad." Rahul did not care to go to India at this point in time. It would be hot and humid, and his folks would be busy with the wedding preparations.

Rahul was not born in the United States, but he had lived in Boston since his childhood. His parents had come to the United States from India before he was two years old. His father joined the Electrical Engineering Department as a graduate student at the famous Massachusetts Institute of Technology, more commonly known as MIT.

The trip to Delhi and Kanpur was strenuous for the Sharma family, and it took almost twenty hours to reach their final destination. Rahul dozed off and on in his mother's lap and on his father's shoulder.

The wedding of Rahul's aunt was a particularly proud moment for the Sharma household. Although Rahul was not thrilled, he still hoped to meet his cousins, some for the first time. His reluctance to go to India waned with the excitement of the wedding ceremony.

Rahul was proud to be his grandmother's favorite, and she was always delighted to see him. At the same time, Rahul stayed by her and helped her with various chores. "Grammy," as he called his grandmother, was extremely happy to see them and welcomed them wholeheartedly.

Grammy's house was truly an estate. It was a large compound with an enormous backyard and a well-manicured garden, complete with a swing set, a few cane chairs, and a table for relaxation. The house had four floors and a large terrace facing the backyard. A troop of wild monkeys would sometimes come to the terrace, but they never hurt anyone. Rahul had fun watching them, and he would often feed them raw peanuts through the windows.

Kanpur was a popular and important industrial city in the state of Uttar Pradesh, India, with its own historical, religious, and commercial significance. Situated on the banks of the Ganges River, the city was a popular location for religious festivities, fluvial processions, and other celebrations in nearby meadows. And the sights, sounds, and smells of these events delighted the senses.

Guests began to arrive, and within a short time, the house overflowed with people. Rahul met a few of his cousins, but he did not remember many of them. Instead he went to town with his dad, carrying a shopping bag for him. Since Grammy's car wasn't readily available, they usually went by taxi or a motorized rickshaw, simply known as an "auto" or a "three-wheeler." Rahul often had fun playing with the vehicle's meter, much to the driver's objection.

The bazaar was a crowded place, so Rahul's father always made sure that Rahul stayed close to him. One time, Rahul ran over to a crowd of people to watch a juggler perform with his monkeys and his sidekick. His father scolded him for wandering away.

The wedding was still a few days away, and all young boys, mostly his cousins, decided to go to town the following day. Not all of Rahul's cousins were as disciplined as he was. One of them, named Suresh Kumar (a.k.a. Suri), was a very bad influence, and Rahul's mother had always advised Rahul to stay away from him. But kids being kids, they got on a bus to go to town, with Rahul reluctantly agreeing to join them. Unfortunately, however, no one had informed Grammy or their parents.

Rahul's cousins spoke the local language, whereas he barely knew the language or the town. As the crowded bus reached the downtown area, the passengers were pushing others to get on or get off, and Rahul got separated from his cousins in the confusion. When he saw a man dressed in a red shirt, like his cousin Suri, leave the bus, he followed him out to the road, believing it to be his cousin.

"Suri, wait!" Rahul screamed at the man and ran after him.

However, when the man turned around, he was someone else. The red shirt had fooled him. Suri and his cousins were still on the bus, which had long gone. Baffled, Rahul looked around to find only strange faces around him, looking at him with strange curiosity. He was filled with panic and fear. He did not know the bus route back, nor did he have the phone number to call anyone for help. His dad had advised him to keep money and an address slip in his pocket whenever he left home for an errand, but he had neglected to do so. Now he was afraid to take a cab, knowing the dangers of riding one alone. He spoke with many shopkeepers and vendors, but no one would offer any help.

A policeman noticed Rahul's lost and dejected expression and approached him to find out what Rahul was doing alone.

"Kon ho tum? Kya chahiye tuhme?" the policeman asked Rahul in Hindi, which meant "Who are you? What do you need?"

Rahul sensed what he said but could not respond to him in his native tongue.

"I don't speak Hindi," Rahul said. "Do you speak English? I am lost. I need help to get home."

But alas, they could not communicate, since the policeman did not speak a word of English, and Rahul did not quite understand Hindi. A state of anxiety showed on his face, and he looked around for any possible help. Luckily, a police inspector on patrol in the area noticed the confusion on their faces and stopped to help. He listened to Rahul's dilemma, and after inquiring on his police radio, the inspector found out where Rahul's grandmother lived and agreed to bring him there.

"Please listen to what I have to say," the inspector told Rahul's parents and his grandmother in an authoritative tone. "We have one too many cases of child abduction, and we do not want your children's names on the list. You need to be very careful and stop your child from wandering alone. We have a list full of names of children who have been abducted and not yet found. Please see that none of your children becomes a target."

After Rahul's parents expressed great appreciation for his help and judgment, the inspector left, and Rahul went to his room. But as soon as he lay down on his bed, his father called out for him.

"What's wrong with you?" Vasu yelled, clearly enraged at Rahul's lapse in judgment. "How could you be so irresponsible? Do you realize how many young kids are abducted and are never found? Your mom and I do not want to lose our son."

Rahul was unable to speak, and instead he began to cry. He knew he had done something terrible. Grammy came to him and hugged her sobbing grandson.

"It's all right, my son. It's water under the bridge. But we were very worried. I am sure you did the right thing by talking to a police officer. Okay, go and play."

Grammy was not an educated person, but she was remarkably wise. Having been born to a Hindu Brahmin family, and later married into one, she was relatively conservative. Although a caste system was legally obliterated, the society still practiced it, knowingly or unknowingly. In the Hindu caste system, Brahmins were at the top of its hierarchy, and Grammy followed it as a divine order.

A patch of gray hair revealed her age, and she spoke with a stern voice, demanding things to be done satisfactorily. Chewing betel nut almost all day long was her only weakness, but she had taught her children to stay away from the habit.

She was quite religious, and life routines were strictly observed in her household. Everyone knew about her strong views and never tried to offend her.

Every night, Grammy narrated the stories from her books.

"Grammy, do you believe in reincarnation?" Rahul asked her one day.

"Yes, I do. A person is incarnated again according to his or her karma. A person can achieve *moksha* by good karma."

"I don't know what all those words mean, but have you met anyone yet who can give an account of his or her previous life?"

"Do you see the nimbus around Lord Krishna?" Grammy asked. "Doesn't He look fabulous? People say He was reincarnated from God Vishnu. There are many people who speak about their past lives, and their stories may be fictional. But let me tell you one thing that's very important. If you believe in something, then it exists."

Rahul sensed great wisdom in her words.

Grammy was a skillful storyteller. She spoke about various events from the Hindu epics *Ramayana* and *Mahabharata*, and Rahul and his cousins listened to her with considerable interest. They were captivated by the heroics of the characters Arjuna and Lord Krishna, and they would listen to Grammy's stories until they fell asleep, probably dreaming of doing benevolent deeds like the characters did in her tales.

Rahul began to enjoy his trip to India—the wedding ritual, the acceptation of the cultural variations, and meeting with his relatives and cousins. But most of all, reacquaintance with Grammy was very heartwarming.

The wedding was turning out to be a pompous occasion. And why not? The bride was the darling daughter of Grammy and also the baby sister of her two brothers. Rahul curiously watched these ceremonies with keen interest and participated in a few. The groom and his party arrived on a horse beautifully decorated with flowers, garlands, and a colorful saddle. The wedding was performed according to the customs of the Hindu religion, the same way that Grammy and her sons always wanted. When the wedding ceremony was over a few hours later, the bride and the groom departed in a flower-clad automobile.

Rahul was glad that he had taken part in the wedding function, for he did not know when or where in the future he would have the opportunity to witness anything like it again.

The guests departed one by one, and Rahul's cousins got ready to start a new year at the school. Before leaving for Boston, Rahul and his parents decided to visit Rahul's aunt for a few days. She lived in Mumbai on Juhu Beach, an exquisite residential location. Although the days in Mumbai were rainy, Rahul enjoyed his stay on Juhu Beach and took frequent strolls—even though he was occasionally drenched by a sudden rain shower. Camel and Tonga rides thrilled him. Not so adventurous was consuming so-called "junk food" sold by beach vendors, resulting in stomach cramps. But no harm done after proper medication; however, he vowed to stay off such food. Often in the middle of the night, he witnessed large sheets of monsoon rain. Spectacular were the scenes when lightning struck the open water of the gulf. After a few blissful days in Mumbai, Rahul and his family departed to go back to Boston—and back to their routine lives.

CHAPTER 2

Tom Spencer was visiting his father, Robert Spencer, in Boston during the summer vacation. He lived in London with his mother, Barbara, after his parents separated and divorced.

His father was a renowned psychiatrist and a physician at Massachusetts General Hospital, and he lived in the penthouse of a Brookline high-rise. He was tall and handsome with dark-blue eyes.

Although Tom was born in Boston in February in the year 1968, his mother had raised him in London ever since he was eleven. For lack of supervision and guidance from both of his parents, he had turned into a delinquent child and was expelled from a private school.

After Tom and his mother moved to London, Robert missed Tom very much. He visited London as often as possible and always found time to spend with his son.

Robert was very happy to see Tom becoming a young man with a distinct personality, growing tall like him. His body was becoming more filled out, and he was turning into quite the athlete. People were often drawn to his handsome face, framed with beautiful blond hair. On his sixteenth birthday, Robert bought him a moped, in spite of Barbara's dislike. But he was not allowed to take it on busy London streets. This was Tom's ultimate toy and happiness. Moreover, Robert thought a gift of this sort might bring him closer to his son. Tom was very happy to receive these generous gifts from his father.

This was the first time Tom thought that he might have communicated with his father in some sensible manner. On Robert's subsequent visit during the onset of summer, Tom and his father went out to Oxford for a day trip. It was a beautiful day—bright sun, temperatures in the upper sixties, and a light breeze. Tom had opened up a little more, and his animosity toward his father was fading, which made Robert very happy. Robert wanted his son to be his friend and as close to him as possible.

"Can we go to the football[1] game tomorrow, Dad?" Tom asked his father. "Can you get us the tickets? You know that this is a very important game for England—they're playing Germany. If we win, we can go to the finals."

How could he disappoint his son? Getting the tickets for such an important event was almost impossible. But to fulfill his son's desire, he did not mind going all-out. The concierge at his hotel appeared to be very resourceful, and Robert thought perhaps he could help him obtain the tickets. It would make young Tom's dreams come true, he thought. The relationship between father and son had gotten stronger, and Robert thought he also had his son's love and respect. His ex-wife had deprived Robert of his son's love and daily contact by moving away, and he could not afford to lose any affection that Tom was willing to give him now. On Robert's way home, he thought that he would give Barbara a call, inviting Tom to visit him in Boston during summer.

"Certainly, if he wants to," replied Barbara. "But would you have time to spend with him given your busy schedule?"

---

[1]   Outside the United States, "football" usually means "soccer."

Robert sensed that her response was somewhat sarcastic, but he didn't say anything to agitate her. "Well, I have to find some time for him, don't I? Besides, there are many young men he can associate with here. I'm sure he will have fun."

"All right, then." She hung up the phone.

What sort of activities would he be interested in? he thought to himself. Honestly, Robert did not have any clue what Tom liked to do. He considered asking Joyce for her opinion, without knowing about Tom's bitterness toward her.

Tom always thought that Joyce was the reason for his parents' separation. His anguish toward Joyce was ever present. Joyce Briggs was his father's assistant and perhaps confidante. They discussed the patients and their conditions, and they became much closer in the eyes of many coworkers.

It was all set. During his summer vacation, Tom would head to Boston to visit his father and explore a new frontier. He was returning to his birthplace—a place he could not remember and had only heard about from his parents.

Tom was thrilled to travel by himself. He watched movies on the plane, listened to music as loudly as he could, and looked out the window, often wondering if he could recognize anything below. Upon his arrival in Boston, he cleared Immigration and Customs, and then saw his father waiting for him.

CHAPTER 3

Robert threw a party for Tom a few days after his arrival in Boston, complete with pizzas and burgers from a gourmet eatery nearby. He invited young boys and girls from the neighborhood, some of whom only worked there during the summer.

"Tom, let me introduce some of these young men, who live in the neighborhood." Putting his hand on Andre's shoulder, Robert announced, "Tom, this young man is Andre Michot. That tall young man is Joey Leibman. And this young lady is Renee Reibach. Absent is another close friend of the group, Rahul Sharma, who is away from Boston. Have fun!" Robert left the party.

Joey was tall and heavy, had dark curly hair, and was for the most part quiet. Renee was of short to medium height, slim, and brunette.

All the youngsters listened to very loud music, ate some junk food, and drank soda till they were tired and were brought home. Tom had the time of his life. He made instant friendships with all, particularly with Andre. Andre had a timid personality. He drove a '74 Mustang, given to him by his mother, against his father's wishes.

Ever since Tom arrived in Boston and had taken a ride in his father's new-model Jaguar sedan, he wanted to drive his car. He argued with his father about taking his car for a ride, under his supervision, of course. A couple of times, Robert gave in and took Tom for a drive around the block. But Tom had only just turned sixteen, and since he lived in England, he was used to the traffic flowing on the opposite side of the street. But that would not stop Tom from trying.

Tom was inherently a wild kid. One weekday when Robert had gone to Chicago for a meeting, he received an emergency call from his maid, Wynona, that Tom had been slightly injured in a car accident and had been taken to the hospital for stitches.

Tom had been adamant that he drive a car that day, but his father had taken the car to the airport. So when Andre came to meet with him in the afternoon, he asked, "Hey, Andre, you have your car with you?"

"Yes, why?" asked Andre.

"Let's go to a mall."

"Well, Joey is working. Let me call Renee. She lives close by."

After talking to Renee, Andre said, "Okay, let's split."

"Let me drive. I am psyched."

"No, man. My old man will freak out."

"Lighten up! Don't be uptight. It's only a few blocks away from here. I drive a moped in London. Oh, we will be fine." And without asking for Andre's permission, Tom sat in the driver's seat and started the car. "Relax, man!" he told Andre.

He drove with confidence for a while, but then he ran into a pickup truck that was parked on the side of the street. Tom had to get stitches on his forearm, and Andre had bruises on his forehead. Fortunately, no one was seriously hurt, but the car was severely damaged on one side. The police cited Andre for allowing Tom to drive, as he only had a learner's permit, and Andre was not qualified as a driving instructor.

Robert was very upset when he returned that night from Chicago. He made calls to Andre's father to apologize and offered to pay for the damages. But he could not find a way to talk to Tom that night. Knowing the troubles that Tom had at school, Robert felt that Tom was an irresponsible and spoiled brat who needed Robert's help to grow in a well-balanced environment. But how?

"Tom, what do I hear about Andre's car? Luckily no one was badly hurt. You have to act responsibly. If you want to see him or any of your friends again, you have to promise me that you will behave." There was sternness in his voice.

Tom did not say a word but listened to him and stood up. Then he left to his room without any repercussions.

Robert knew he might not be of much help as soon as Tom returned to his mother in London, so he decided that it was in the best interest of all that he did not talk to Barbara at this time. He merely wanted to convince her about the dangers that lay ahead if she continued to allow Tom to behave in this manner.

Andre lost his car for the rest of the summer. Kids would be kids, and they would patch things up. But now, the only way for them to get around was by Boston's public transportation system. Going to the mall was out of the question, unless someone drove them there. It was nearing the end of summer, and all the boys and girls were preparing for a new school year.

At the same time, Tom was packing his bags to return to London. He wasn't looking forward to yet another long, boring year at school. But it was inevitable. He was certainly going to miss his friends in Boston, and he was expecting to come back next summer, if his father wanted him to return. He knew that his father was still upset with him for driving without permission, but next summer was nearly a year away, and that would give Tom plenty of time to patch things up with his dad. He thought that he could be persuasive and sometimes manipulative, like he had been with his mother and grandmother. But he knew that it might not work with his father.

Robert went into Tom's room. "Well, did you enjoy your stay in Boston?"

"I had a wonderful time, Dad. This was indeed the best summer I have ever spent in my life. I am sorry that I behaved badly. But I get sudden impulses off and on, and I do not know what to do."

Robert shook his head and said, "Well, we have to work at that. Don't we?"

"Yes, Dad." And he kept quiet.

"Okay. Get ready. We have to leave for the airport in a couple of hours."

Tom knew for sure that his father loved him dearly. At the same time, his dad was a disciplinarian. Tom also realized that he had to work hard to maintain his father's love and affection.

The trip back to London was uneventful. Since he was traveling at night, there wasn't much to see through the window except for stars and city lights. As Tom approached London in the morning, he ate breakfast and got ready to land. He was happy to see his mother again after being away for a couple of months, the first time he had ever been away from her. He was not sure whether he should tell her that he enjoyed Boston and wanted to go back next summer. He knew that it was premature.

CHAPTER 4

Tom's school started in London, and students talked about their summer vacations. He had much to boast about to his schoolmates regarding his trip to Boston, especially the fact that he had made a few new friends there. He loved bragging to his friends about how he had wrecked a car.

Unfortunately, although he needed to share his feelings about his parents with someone, he had no one he could really confide in, so he drew closer to his rowdy friends.

Tom had no interest in his studies or any other activities, except hanging around in malls, arcades, and movies, and riding on mopeds and bikes.

A couple of months later, his mother asked, "What's this, Tom?" after receiving a complaint letter from his teacher for his absenteeism.

"I hate my school and the teacher. He is too bossy and nerdy."

Popping a couple of Prozac pills, she told her son, "You are going to kill me one day, Tom. I have a massive headache from your behavior. I don't know what to do with you." She left for her room, rubbing her forehead.

Tom did not say anything. He was not bothered too much by her outrage. This was a daily occurrence for him. He became violent at school, and he had roamed around the big city with his raucous friends. He started to use drugs, smoke, and drink alcohol. While painting graffiti and tearing the seats inside the subway compartment, the police apprehended him and his few friends. The kids were released into their parents' custody after being given a strict warning.

After a week or so, Barbara received a note from the school headmaster to see him. It was regarding Tom's reprehensible behavior.

"Mrs. Spencer, I hate to inform you that Tom has become absolutely delinquent. No teacher wants him in his or her class."

"What has he done *this* time, Mr. Jordan?"

"Well . . ." He trailed off and then looked at his teacher.

Reluctantly, the teacher said, "I don't know how to put this delicately, but a girl in Tom's class says that she is pregnant and that Tom is responsible. I questioned Tom, but he refuses to tell me any details."

"Mrs. Spencer, why don't you talk to your son?" Mr. Jordan suggested. "If this is true, we are obligated to remove him from the school, especially if the girl or her parents file a complaint against him."

Very distressed, Barbara left the school, wondering how she was supposed to talk to her son about this.

When she got home, she confronted him. "Tom, I went to see Mr. Jordan and your teacher. They're not happy with your performance and behavior in school. What do I hear about this girl? Did you mess with her?"

"What do you mean, Mom?"

"You know exactly what I mean. Did you have sex with that girl? You know that she is pregnant now. How could you?" She began crying hysterically and took a couple more Prozac tablets from her medicine bottle. "You are driving me crazy."

Looking at the floor, he wondered how he was going to get out of this tight spot. Finally he told her, "Mom, that's a lie. I wouldn't do that."

"And why not?" she asked.

"I'm gay," he said, swayed by impulse.

"Oh, my God!" Barbara replied in a frenzy.

Later, when Barbara conveyed this to Robert, he wasn't surprised. Robert was no stranger to his son's attitude and behavior, but as he already knew, he was helpless to do much about it. When he saw her during his visit to London in the summer, he felt that Barbara looked very tired and frail. He soon realized that looking after a recalcitrant mother, while raising an obstreperous son at the same time, had totally stressed Barbara out. Robert found his visit to London in late September to be a bit shocking. He saw drastic changes in Barbara's physical appearance and personality. She looked pale and anemic. He had not seen Barbara for over three months, and it did not take long for Robert to find out that she had severely deteriorated, both mentally and physically.

"Barbara, what's wrong? You look very different and sick. Are you all right?"

"Well, I . . . don't know how to put it, Robert. I have been diagnosed with cancer, and the doctors say it has spread well beyond the capacity of healing."

"Jesus Christ! Barbara, why didn't you tell me?"

"I didn't know how to put it to you."

She was so markedly weakened that she often could not even complete a sentence without pausing. "Why didn't you let me know as soon as you found out?" Robert exclaimed.

"I don't know," she replied weakly, "but it's too late anyway. What about Tom? Will you take care of him?"

"Of course. He's my son too. But we have to take care of *you* first. Does Tom know that you're sick?"

"No, I haven't told him yet."

"Barbara, this is no time to play hide-and-seek. You and I have a responsibility to Tom. I'll do whatever you want and what is best for him too. Do you agree?"

"Yes. You will take him to Boston with you, won't you?"

"Sure, if you want me to."

Being a physician and after meeting with her doctor, Robert knew that she had only a few weeks to live. Doctors in London told Barbara and Robert that she had to be confined to a clinic or hospital. On the insistence of Robert and her relatives, she checked into a private clinic outside London.

Tom knew that his mother was sick, but not to the extent of a terminal disease. When Robert told him the details of his mom's sickness, Tom started to blame himself for her condition. *Have I brought this on to Mom?* he thought. As a young adult, he did not know how to act and what to do. He was thoroughly saddened. In spite of his mother's consistent outbursts about his behavior, he loved her dearly and did not want to lose her. Even a ruthless and strong Tom shed a few tears when he found out about her health condition.

Tom moved in temporarily with his cousins in Sevenoaks. They bullied him, and he could not do anything about it. Besides being much stronger and older than Tom, they were also street fighters. When they beat him up on occasion, he dared not complain about them, because he knew the consequences if he did. So he paid them bribe money to keep them away from him, and he prayed hard to get out of that place.

Two months after Barbara was confined to the clinic, she passed away in her sleep, with Tom and her cousins by her side. Robert flew into London from Vienna, where he was attending a conference. Tom was heartbroken. Barbara had been the only person he could truly trust. She was always present when Tom wanted someone to talk to, listening to him and advising him to the best of her ability. Tom had hardened over the years, but this might have been the first time anyone ever saw Tom break down. Tom's future was now uncertain. He could not envision it. *Will I stay back with my cousins or move in with my father in*

Boston? he thought. At this time he realized that his irrational behavior might put him in jeopardy. By no means did he want to stay back with his cousins, but the decision was not up to him. He promised himself that if by chance he moved to Boston, he would work very hard to be in good graces with his father—not that he wanted to, but the alternatives were worse.

Barbara was put to rest at her family's cemetery next to her father, at her request. Robert decided that it was the right time to talk about Tom moving to Boston, if Tom was going to be part of his life. He said, "Your mom would like to have you come to Boston for good. You remember Wynona, my maid? She would love to have you in Boston permanently. By the way, have you kept up with your friends there? You probably will be going to school with them."

"Yes, Dad. I did talk to Andre last month, around the time I was leaving Boston. He was still upset about my damaging his car. But he has probably forgotten it by now, I suppose." He paused. "Dad, I'm sorry I drove his car without getting your permission, but I just had the urge to drive a car."

Robert felt better that Tom acknowledged his own wrongdoing. Perhaps he was overreacting. But one thing he did realize was that Tom was very smart to bring it up. He knew that Tom wanted to patch things up with him by admitting his own fault and pushing for his sympathy.

"It's all right," Robert said. I'm glad no one was seriously hurt. But you should always act responsibly. I have a hunch that you have not forgiven your mom and me for our separation. You know, these things do happen, but I wish we'd had a better alternative. We both thought that this was the best answer for us. Anyway, it might not be the right time or place to discuss this, but sometime in the future I'll tell you exactly what happened and why, as I see it. Okay?"

"That's fine, Dad," Tom responded coldly.

~~~

Robert's sister, Elizabeth (Liz, to her friends and relatives), and her husband, Cyril Higgins, had no biological children but had adopted one Vietnamese girl named Dominique, which in French meant "belonging to God." Her biological parents might not have realized that her name would be so appropriate when, as an infant, she was left at an orphanage in Saigon, wrapped in a thin blanket with a handwritten apology for abandoning her at the doorstep. She was likely of Anglo-Vietnamese descent, and she was very young when she was brought to Australia. Now she was in high school. Tom had traveled to Australia once before with his aunt, and he had met her then. But that was a few years ago, and he would only recognize her from the snapshots taken with the family. Liz was very proud of her, and she mentioned many times that she was turning out to be a fine young lady.

After their father, James Spencer's, death, Robert and Liz decided to put the Kensington flat up for sale. As stipulated in James's will, half of the estate money would go to Robert's son, Tom, and the other half would be given to Liz's children. Trustees had to be appointed to look after these assets. Real estate property in the South Kensington area was long sought after by many Londoners and affluent foreigners. The flat was sold quickly, within three months, at a nice profit.

Tom liked his friends in Boston, and he enjoyed living a lifestyle of general comfort, but now he envisioned that he would lose the freedom that he had so enjoyed in London. Before moving to Boston, his father made it perfectly clear to Tom that he would have to abide by his rules.

CHAPTER 5

A few days later, Robert and Tom arrived in Boston. Mounds of mid-December snow blanketed the city. "Perhaps we'll have a white Christmas," Robert said cheerfully as they drove home.

Tom shrugged. "Whatever." He gazed out the Jaguar's window at the streets, buildings, and trees artfully decorated with lights and ornaments.

At home, Wynona had put up a small Christmas tree, which Robert had at first refused but then agreed to. As usual, he had been invited to various Christmas and charity parties. Although he attended a few parties over a few days, there were many that he declined so that he could spend more time with Tom.

"You never have been in Boston during Christmas—well, not after you moved to London. These are very festive holidays. Probably the same as you have observed in London. I realize that you were very close to your mom. Her passing is a sad event for both of us. Life is unpredictable. I am sure she would want you to enjoy the season, and I will do whatever I can to see that you cross that bridge. Here is a cash card for you to enjoy Christmas shopping."

Now he had to enroll Tom in a school in Boston. Fortunately, Andre's mother, Simone, was on the board of the PTA of a private school in the neighborhood. She knew the headmaster very well, someone who could help Tom in his admissions process.

"Hi, Tom. What's up?" asked Andre while walking into Tom's room. "You know, you're going to school with us in January. It's going to be a blast!" He paused. "Hey, man, sorry about your mom."

"That's okay, bro," Tom said. "I miss her. My old man means well, but he comes into my life after all these years and tells me to start a new beginning. Now I'll have to switch over to a new life. Now he tells me, 'I'm your loving father, and let bygones be bygones.'"

"Sorry, pal. I am sure you will be all right," Andre said.

"I'm suffocating. Let's split from here. Is there an arcade or a mall nearby?"

"Yeah. Let's go to the mall. We can get the new Madonna album!" Andre was ready. He picked up the phone and called Joey and Rahul to come along.

"Yeah, I'd like to get that 'Material Girl' by Madonna. That's a cool song, bro."

"Yeah. Let's go!" Andre was ready. He picked up the phone and called Joey and Rahul.

They bundled up and went down to the street. Andre's car was not really a newer model, but it looked nice. It was a GM Buick, spacious and comfortable, complete with a radio and a cassette player, but it was still not as sporty as the Mustang. They went to get Joey, who jumped into the car.

It was cold, but Rahul was still waiting outside his front door. When the Buick pulled up, Rahul got in. Andre drove, and Tom played Andre's tapes, Madonna's *Like a Virgin* and *Thriller* by Michael Jackson, as loudly as he could.

At the mall, parking spots were scarce, but they squeezed the car into a very narrow space. The mall was tastefully decorated, and carolers were singing Christmas songs. A few people were listening to the carolers, admiring their artistic ability, while a man dressed as Santa Claus was cheering up a group of young children.

Andre and his friends went right to the food court, where Tom, Joey, and Andre picked up McDonald's burgers, fries, and Cokes. Rahul got a vegetarian pizza. The court was crowded, and they sat down in a smoking area.

"What's that, buddy?" Tom asked Rahul. "No burger or hot dog?"

Without looking up, Rahul replied, "Well, I'm a vegetarian. I don't eat meat, any meat. Everyone in my family is vegetarian."

"How about eggs, fish, or seafood?" Tom pressed. "Is cheese okay to eat? You mean that you've *never* tried meat or chicken? Boy, you are missing something!"

"No, that's not true," Rahul replied. "I do eat eggs and cheese, but no fish or seafood. There's nothing wrong with being a vegetarian—a large population of India is that way. I have many relatives who are living abroad, and they don't eat meat either. There are several restaurants in London which serve veggie food. I'm surprised that you didn't come across any of them when you lived there."

That was the end of that discussion, at least for the time being. Rahul was sentimental about his habits and values in life.

"Tom, I met you briefly when you were here in the summer," Rahul said. "I recall that you wrecked Andre's Mustang. Hope you're driving better now." He had heard about Tom and his deplorable habits from his friends, and he had no patience for Tom's questions.

Suddenly, Tom lit a cigarette and gave one to Andre.

Bewildered, Rahul looked at both of them. "You smoke, Tom? You too, Andre?"

"No big deal," Andre answered in embarrassment. "Joey knew it. Well, I smoke on occasion when I am fired up or in the company of my friends."

"You know it's an unhealthy habit," Rahul answered. "You shouldn't start if you haven't already."

"Blow it off, Rahul," Andre said while taking a big puff.

Tom jokingly responded, "Okay, Mother. We'll stop it one day. It's only tobacco, not *grass*."

Rahul was now furious, but he didn't say anything. These actions were contrary to his own behavior, and therefore, he hoped to keep a distance from Tom and possibly from Andre, as well.

CHAPTER 6

On Christmas Eve, Robert came home early from the clinic. He had promised Tom that they would go shopping together for a stereo system. They went out to lunch to a decent seafood restaurant in town. Robert realized that it was time to discuss an uncomfortable topic with Tom. He had to be meticulously circumspect so that it would not impede their relationship, which was in the process of mending.

Robert and Barbara's divorce had been a bitter experience for young Tom, but the passing of his mother was even more calamitous. He was a young man who understood why marriages break down.

Robert went to Tom's room and saw he was listening to music on his earphones. Tom did not see his father come in. When his father tapped on his shoulder, he took out the earphones and said, "Oh, Dad, it's you. You are home early today."

"Yes, I thought I could spend some time with you. I'd like to talk about something, which probably has been bothering you for a while. It's about your mom's and my past. You know that your mom and I loved each other. But sometimes people fall out of love. She and I started to view things very differently. Then suddenly, I believe, we were at the threshold of ending the marriage. This does not mean that our love for you had diminished.

"You now have new opportunities to be what you want to be," Robert said. "You may stay with me as long as you wish and enjoy the privacy of having your own room. Finally, when you are ready, we will go shop for your new car. I have money from your grandfather's estate, which can only be used for your education until you graduate or turn twenty-one. Renee's father is a trustee of the estate, and he will explain to you in detail what your responsibilities are. And Joey's father handles the trust fund. I don't want to tell you the size of the fund, but I can assure you that you will be able to get the best education that this, or any other, country has to offer.

"I sincerely hope that you will act wisely and become someone who your mom and I can be proud of," Robert concluded. He softened his voice and looked down for a moment nervously. "I, uh, also want to tell you something. You know that I have been seeing Joyce for a while. I love her. I expect her to be a part of our family soon."

Tom swallowed hard. However, he had expected this to happen sooner or later.

"By the way," Robert added, "I forgot to mention to you that Andre's mom called me and told me that your admission to the high school has been confirmed. After the New Year, you will have a personal interview with the headmaster and teachers to determine which class will be appropriate for you. She has submitted all your necessary paperwork for admission."

Tom listened as Robert kept talking. Then he asked, "How am I going to get to this school? Will someone drop me off?"

"All your friends—Andre, Renee, Rahul, and Joey—will also be going with you. It's easy to get to the T. Go to Copley Station and walk a couple of blocks. If it's too cold, then one of the moms or their maids will take you there. It's not too far from our place."

Robert paused. "Well, are you done with your lunch? Let's go shopping!"

Robert was happy that he'd had a talk with his son. Whether it was fruitful or otherwise, only time would tell.

Tom had fun shopping during the Christmas holidays with his father. At RadioShack, they bought a decent stereo of his choice. It was not hard for Tom to set up the system in his room, by installing tuner and players by his bedside and speakers up high on the wall. He loved doing it. Andre also helped him to set it up.

Over the holidays, they also frequently shopped with Joyce, and she spent a good deal of time with them. Tom's resentment was not as aggressive as it had been during the summer—or possibly he just wasn't openly showing it.

On Christmas Day, gifts were exchanged at the Spencer household. Robert presented Joyce with a diamond ring and proposed to her, which made her ecstatic. Tom nodded mildly with his acceptance, even though he had hoped it would happen under different circumstances. The grief over his mother's demise was still fresh on his mind.

CHAPTER 7

Tom did well in his interview at the school. He knew French well enough to consider it a second language, yet he opted to take it anyway, since he had no desire to assert himself, work hard, and really learn something new. All his friends were taking Spanish classes. Even though they all attended the same school, only Renee and Rahul were in his class.

Tom was disappointed that his good friend Andre would not be in the same class with him. A new school, new friends, and a new environment shook him up a little, but Tom didn't feel uneasy about it. He had learned to master practically every situation that he faced.

On the first day of classes, Robert came along with Andre's mother to introduce Tom to the school, the teachers, and the headmaster. Robert carefully explained to the headmaster about the death of his ex-wife, Barbara, Tom's mother, which was the reason for Tom's change of residence. He left after the introduction.

"Hi, Renee. How are you?" Tom said. In the meantime, Rahul walked in.

"Hi, guys," said Renee. "Did you find everything here? Tom, do you need help?"

"Could you show me where the lockers are, Rahul?" asked Tom.

Unwillingly, Rahul ended up taking care of Tom. Even at the Christmas party hosted by Andre, consisting of their usual friends and some new ones from the neighborhood, Rahul was apprehensive about Tom and purposely stayed away from him. Tom, however, kept butting into Rahul's space. Eventually, Rahul was happy when it was time for everyone to go home.

Most of Tom's classmates were receptive and friendly. Some were aggressive bullies, wanting to show off their haughty manners. But the headmaster did not like any pranks and wouldn't tolerate any reckless behavior by the students.

The classes were less formal than Tom was accustomed to in London, and the teachers addressed students by their first names. He liked it that his English teacher had been educated in England and had a slight British accent.

There was a ton of homework, right from the very first day of school. At first, Tom was not concerned. He had never submitted any homework at school when he was in London. It was different here, and his father expected him to perform at a satisfactory level.

During the winter semester, sports activities were out of the question, at least outdoors. Tom had played basketball while enrolled in school in London, but soccer had always been his passion. He was physically strong and athletic, and he liked to play basketball during his free time. He was a very aggressive and intelligent player, and he spent a great deal of time practicing.

The school had taken pride in his ability to win many games. His position as a guard was well suited for his abilities, and he won trophies at the tournaments over the first two years at the school. Nevertheless, his aggressive nature led to severe condemnation from his teachers and fellow students. Many times, he was warned for inadvertently hitting his fellow players too hard. Without much provocation, he would fight with anyone who was not agreeable to him. Oftentimes his coaches cited him for his abnormal and despicable behavior.

Rahul paused at the lockers outside his gym class, delaying going inside. He hated it. The gym teacher expected every student to work hard on the floor, with no exceptions.

On a cold day in late January in his gym class, it was Rahul's turn to perform on a vault, which he truly detested. When he jumped up to get on the vault, Rahul felt someone push him hard, causing him to miss it completely. It was Hank, a fellow student. He fell, hit his chin on the floor, and started bleeding. The gym teacher turned furious. He warned the students who were toying with Rahul.

The gym teacher was a heavy, homely man with a big belly, graying hair, and yellowing teeth. He was not in control of his students, and he maintained a casual attitude.

As the teacher left to answer a phone call, Tom approached Hank, who had been bullying everyone, especially Rahul. Tom picked him up by his collar. "Lay off, Hank," he said. "This guy is my friend." He pointed to Rahul. "Get off his back. I can take care of you and your friends if you don't listen. Got it?"

"What are you, his mother? Get the hell out of here!" Hank yelled, with his sidekicks laughing in support.

Rahul came over to Tom and said, "It's okay, Tom. Don't get into a fight with them."

Hank pushed Tom to the floor and warned him, pointing a finger in his face, "Keep out of my way, you jerk!"

Tom came charging back and punched Hank hard in the jaw. Hank fell to the floor and started to bleed, and he and his friends stared at Tom in astonishment. He had warned the bullies to keep away from them.

In the meantime, the gym teacher came back and saw Hank bleeding on the floor. "What happened?" he asked.

"Hey, teach!" Tom replied. "He can't do the vault either!"

At the end of the class, Rahul came over to Tom and said, "Thanks for standing up for me. I don't like gym class."

Rahul realized that he had probably misjudged Tom all along, and he thought that Tom might not be as bad as he had first envisioned.

"No one beats up on my friends," Tom said and punched Rahul lightly on one arm. "We stick together, okay?"

"Okay." Rahul nodded and felt better.

~~~

Tom wanted to show his father and his girlfriend that he wasn't going to be rowdy like he had been in London, but he also wasn't about to let go of his contentious nature.

Renee, Joey, and Rahul were school friends, but Andre was his close buddy. They were inseparable during the weekends. Unlike Tom and Andre, Rahul was a brilliant student who excelled in almost all his classes, though computers were his primary interest. His father had a state-of-the-art IBM personal computer. He had installed Microsoft's newly released operating system, Windows, on the computer to develop various applications, and he allowed Rahul to use it for his schoolwork and learning. PCs were not necessarily an expensive item anymore, but Rahul found that they were somewhat limiting to use. "I like the IBM PC over the more sophisticated Macintosh," his father told him. "I've watched Intel's progress and favor their chip over Motorola's processors."

Father and son worked together every day on the hardware and software of the IBM PC. Rahul developed an instant liking for the computer and used the BASIC language to write small programs. At school, he was instrumental in the development of various basic programs, showing fellow students the power of computing. Rahul's expertise in computing rubbed off on Tom, and he became more interested in using the computer.

One March afternoon during a day off from school, Rahul and Tom were drinking Coke and working on the computer at Rahul's house.

"Let me ask you a question," Rahul said. "You like it more here than in London?"

Tom's face saddened when he spoke. "Well, I don't know. I loved my mom. She always treated me like an adult. But I like it here. I have a few friends like you, which I did not have in London. You guys are special. I am trying to know my old man. But he is different. I believe that he is going to marry that broad sometime soon." Tom paused and said, "You know I was the wild one at my school in London. I didn't care then. My mom had no time. I was a delinquent, and maybe I still am. I was almost kicked out of my school a couple of times, but my mom saved me.

"If I were in London, I would still be the same way. But it's different now after my mom's death. My father hasn't said anything, but if I jerk around, he will ship me off to England to stay with my cousins in Sevenoaks. I really hate it there. I would definitely run away from them.

"I'm thinking that if I behave like you or Andre, I might get to stay here. Hey, life is cool here, and I like you guys," Tom said. "In a few years, when I'm old enough, I can do whatever I want to, and no one will be able to stop me. My grandfather has left me a sizable amount of dough—but I'll have to finish school to get it. Can you help me with my classes?"

Bewildered, Rahul looked at him and said, "Yeah, sure. But you have to do *your* part. As I told you, I hate gym class. I would like to learn to play basketball, and you can teach me."

"That's a deal, bro!" Tom answered. "I like to play basketball here. We'll go practice together. But, man, make me a promise— you'll have to teach me math, science, and other stuff."

"You mean . . . *everything*?" Rahul joked. "It's fine. I'll do it if you're serious about it, Tom."

"Thanks, buddy. Tell me about yourself. Where were you born? What are your folks like? I'm just curious. You know, I met many people from your country when I was in London but did not know anyone."

Rahul responded, "Well, it's true that I was born in India, but I'm a citizen of this country. My parents are too. I have very little memory of my childhood in India. I was born in a town called Kanpur." Rahul continued after a brief pause, "My parents are Hindu, and that makes me Hindu too. Whenever possible, they observe it and expect me to do the same. You have asked me before if I am a vegetarian. Yes, I am, but I have a few questions of my own. I have read about, and have even seen, many Hindus who are not necessarily vegetarian. I suppose we belong to the Brahmin caste, and therefore, we observe it strictly. But in today's society, many Hindus, including Brahmins, have departed from being strict vegetarians."

"How did your parents meet?" Tom asked.

"The marriage of my parents was an arranged one," Rahul replied. "My mom's parents and relatives asked my dad's parents if my dad was interested in marrying a girl from the same caste. My dad's parents did some digging and found more information about my mom's family. After exchanging photos of each other, my dad and his family went to visit my mom's family—and that's the first time my dad met my mom."

"Wow!" Tom exclaimed. "That's scary. He must have hardly known your mom before he married her."

"Not quite. Both my parents were college graduates and well educated. They were allowed to go out to the movies, cafés, or restaurants, so they got to know each other before they got married. I was born a year after they were married, and now, here I am."

"Do you think that someone will find a woman for you?" Tom asked curiously.

"It's possible," Rahul replied. "But I make my own decisions. However, it's too early for me to worry about girls and stuff," Rahul continued. "One thing for sure is that I want my bride to be an Indian. It's important to me."

"How often do you visit India?" Tom asked. "When were you there last? I bet it's pretty exciting. Are there elephants and tigers around?"

Rahul laughed. "Elephants and tigers stick to the jungles. We stay in the city. My mom and I used to travel there during the summer almost every other year," Rahul answered. "It's extremely hot during that season. Besides, my cousins are already in school. Lately, we've been there only for special occasions, like my aunt's wedding. This coming July, we'll visit to celebrate my grandmother's seventy-fifth birthday."

"Boy, I could go to India with you one day."

Rahul perceived that Tom was grossly confused. He was good at heart but had very poor judgment, and he had adopted some bad habits from the company he had kept in London. It was hard for Tom to grow up without his mother, and his father was preoccupied with his work and his new fiancée. Rahul felt pity for Tom and wanted to help him cross the bridge between evil and a virtuous life.

CHAPTER 8

Tom was surprised and moved when his friends threw him a surprise birthday party. He got some wonderful gifts, including some crazy ones—but that was fun for Tom, who had not had many birthday celebrations in England, except for the last one before his mother passed away. The biggest surprise gift was from his father and Joyce—a desktop personal computer. Of course, he would have preferred a car, but he realized that his dad would not permit him to drive as of yet.

Rahul and Tom studied together at school and at home. Tom's keystrokes on the computer keyboard became faster and more rhythmic as he learned to type. He also started to learn the BASIC language so that he could write small programs. None of them were useful, but it was a wonderful way to gain confidence.

Things were going well at school. Tom was trying hard to keep passing grades, and he was grateful to his friend Rahul for his persistent help. A long-awaited spring break was just around the corner.

Tom and Rahul were busy on the computer and saw Andre and Joey as they entered the room.

"Hey, Tom. Joey has invited us to go to Florida during the break. Can you go with us? It would be a lot of fun," Andre told Tom, winking at him.

Andre's parents never interfered with whatever decisions he made on his own. His father did not approve of his many activities, but he didn't have the time or courage to confront him because of his wife, who readily gave into Andre's desires.

"Yes, that's right," Joey said. "I go to visit my aunt in Fort Lauderdale every time I get a chance. It has beautiful beaches. And her house is right on the beach."

Tom jumped at the invitation and said, "Yes, sure!" He did not wait to ask his father for his permission. Nevertheless, Robert quickly agreed. He knew Deborah from the Leibmans' Boston parties and was convinced that she'd had a crush on him once. Nevertheless, he trusted her to safeguard the kids.

"How about you, Rahul? Can you come?" Joey asked.

"I have to ask my dad," Rahul replied.

That night, when Rahul asked for permission to go to Florida with his friends, his father hesitated. "But why, Dad?" Rahul pleaded. His father knew of the Leibmans but did not know Deborah well enough to entrust his son to her. He finally let Rahul go, under the condition that he would call home frequently and stay out of trouble.

So, all four friends were on their way to Florida. After their plane landed in Fort Lauderdale, Rahul saw Joey run to hug his aunt, who was waiting in the baggage claim area. Soon they were escorted to their parked van. The temperature was a balmy seventy-six degrees, and it was sunny without a single cloud in the sky. After a brief introduction and thanking their host, they were on their way to Joey's aunt's house.

The Atlantic Ocean opened before them. They marveled at the deep blue water and sporadic white sandy beaches as they drove by.

When they finally reached Deborah's house, they were greeted by a security guard, a gardener, and Rusty, a Labrador Retriever with soft fur and a constantly wagging tail. Joey jumped out of the van and began playing with Rusty, who was quite excited about the new visitors. Tom, Andre, and Rahul petted him, and they became quick friends. All of them played in the grass for a while before his aunt advised them to get in the house.

There were two guest bedrooms adjacent to each other with a shared bathroom on the opposite side of Deborah's bedroom. Both rooms faced the ocean. Tom and Andre chose to bunk together, and Joey ended up with Rahul as his roommate. Rusty was so attached to Joey that he followed him wherever he went.

Rahul noticed that green flags were posted on the beach, indicating calm conditions. The day was not over yet.

"Hey, Joey, can we go to the beach?" Rahul asked.

"Sure, I think it is okay as long as the sea is calm." Rahul and his gang put on their swimsuits, grabbed some towels, and ran toward the water. Rusty also decided to go along, and he was running wildly back and forth with them. Surely he was not allowed on the beach without being on a leash, but that didn't stop him from loudly barking at them from the edge of the water. The water was not necessarily warm, but that didn't stop them. The beach was now getting crowded. A few people played with a beach ball, and others threw Frisbees.

As soon as the kids returned from the beach, Deborah announced, "Listen, there will be a barbecue party for you and other young men and women in our backyard on Sunday at six. We will have some music and games. Is it all right with you?"

No one objected.

Fifteen kids at the party played loud music, and their screams got the attention of many passersby on the beach. Joey knew many of these kids. He had met most of them on his previous visits. Tom and Andre kept to themselves. They were not interested in dancing or mingling with any young kids, especially those of the opposite sex, and a few of them watched their behavior with subtle curiosity. One of the parents was in the diamond business and got into a conversation with Rahul about his trips to India.

Early in the evening, the party ended abruptly. The wind had picked up, and the sky was becoming cloudy. Rain was dropping intermittently to make things uncomfortable, but not too wet. Then, although the forecast had predicted that the rain and thunderstorms would not occur until late in the evening, it started to pour. The activities on the beach were diminishing fast, and the party moved into the house. Eventually the kids departed one by one, with or without their parents.

From his bedroom, Rahul stared out the window as the rain picked up and came down in torrents, making large puddles. The ocean became violent. Lightning flashed above the sea, which reflected in the water, making a spectacular view. Men in yellow raincoats posted flags along the beach, signaling that the beach was closed to the public because of severe currents and the threat of lightning.

Rahul's three friends stood next to him as they all witnessed nature's wonder. When lightning struck a few yards away, they all jumped. Of all his friends, Rahul found himself to be the least astonished by the phenomenon.

"You know, this is similar to what I experienced one time in India," Rahul explained. "Once, on a summer night in July, I saw torrential monsoon rain coming down heavily. My aunt lives on Juhu Beach in the northern area of Mumbai. Severe lightning, approaching from the Arabian Gulf toward the shore, set a small fishing boat on fire and sunk it while I watched. The fishermen were rescued by another boat."

Tom was flabbergasted by the stories. When Rahul told him about India and the people, he said, "Boy, I really want to see this! It seems very exciting. When the time comes, I'll be the first to go there." Looking at Rahul, he asked, "Why don't you get married in India so I can go visit you?"

Rahul simply smiled and brushed him off.

After an hour and a half, it was starting to get quiet, and the rain had virtually stopped. All of them went to bed and fell asleep after watching a late-night movie, which had some power interruptions because of thunderstorms in the area.

In the middle of the night, Rahul awoke to loud voices. Curious, he got up and found Joey in the other bedroom with Tom and Andre. They had a white powdery substance in front of them.

Joey glared at Tom with fury in his voice. "Where did you get that cocaine? That is an illegal drug! Do you know you could get my aunt and us in trouble? I should throw both of you out!"

Rahul shot a look at Tom, who had a smirk on his face. Rahul saw a small bit of white powder near Tom's lip. He had obviously been sniffing the drug.

Andre looked at the floor and shuffled his feet.

Joey gave Tom a hard push on the shoulder. "What the hell do you think you're doing?"

"Calm down," Rahul said, taking control of the situation before Joey awakened his aunt. He saw the white stuff in a small bag on the table. "Is this all of it?"

Tom nodded smugly.

"Okay, let's get rid of it."

Tom reluctantly picked up the bag and followed Rahul to the bathroom, where Rahul pointed sharply to the toilet. With a shrug, Tom dropped the bag into the water and flushed it as the others watched.

Joey turned around and angrily stomped off to his bedroom.

Rahul stared at the backs of Tom and Andre as they wobbled their way to their own room. It greatly disturbed him that his friends used drugs. He hoped it was just a one-time experiment.

Rahul saw that Joey was still furious at the breakfast table the following morning, but on his insistence, they made up. Later in the day, they went to the mall, played video games, and ate at the food arcade. Tom exited the mall, lit a cigarette, and then handed one to Andre. Rahul shot a dirty look at them and walked toward Joey, who didn't seem to care.

Rahul approached Tom. "Quite frankly, I don't know much about you—what you do and what you don't. Do your parents know about your habits?"

"I am over sixteen, and I can do what I want to do," Andre responded in Tom's stead. "They probably don't know that I smoke. Or they don't care. My dad is too busy in his work, and my mom allows me to do what I want, as long as she keeps busy with her social circle. Tom's dad is the same way."

"I don't think that my parents would ever approve if I smoked or drank at this age," Rahul said. "Anyway, that's your choice." He sighed, disconcerted with his friends' new lifestyles. *What next?* he thought. He realized that Joey didn't care if they smoked or occasionally used drugs, but not while they were visiting his aunt. Resentfully, he put this incident behind him.

When they returned to Deborah's home, it was almost seven in the evening. The sun had set and the ocean was a little choppy, but the beach was busy as usual.

Later in the evening when Rahul and Joey were alone in their bedroom, he asked Joey, "Hey, Joey, do you see anything strange about Tom and Andre's friendship?"

"Oh, they are that way. Just forget it!" Joey responded, uncaring while yawning.

Deborah was a hospitable woman, and she wanted the kids to have the best possible time during their vacation. She arranged for them to go to Disney World and Epcot Center in Orlando. She asked her maid, "Yelena, does your cousin Juan come to see you?"

"Si, señora. Do you want to talk to him?"

"Yes, I want him to drive these kids to Disney World, if he is free."

"Okay, I ask him. Juan is good man and good driver."

"Please ask him if he can take them tomorrow."

"Okay."

The visit to Disney World was not so inspiring, as they had hoped to see a basketball game between the Orlando Magic and Boston Celtics. They left very early in the morning, after they were dragged out of bed to make the trip.

When they reached the Disney World gate, Rahul noticed that it was almost ten. They bought their tickets and entered the park.

Fascinated by the live Disney characters, quaint shops, and fun rides, Rahul enjoyed every sight that came into view. As he walked alongside Joey to pick up some food at an outdoor café, he overheard Juan whisper something to Joey.

"Are those two friends of yours *gay*?" Juan asked him. "Do you know what I mean?"

Rahul, along with Joey, looked toward Tom and Andre, who had been lagging behind and keeping to themselves for most of the day. Their two friends walked very close and held hands, like lovers.

Extraordinarily quiet, Rahul stayed behind the others as the day wore on. The somber look on Joey's face told Rahul that Joey was weighing the new information, just like he was. Tom, Andre, and Juan now seemed to be the only ones enjoying the fun at the park, while Rahul and Joey faked smiles at times. Rahul wondered what Tom and Andre talked about and how they could be so engrossed with each other.

"Should we mention anything to them?" Joey asked Rahul.

"I don't know. Let's think about it. Let's wait at least until we get back to Boston."

Joey nodded. "It's not a crime to be gay, you know . . . but still, people don't just openly disclose their sexual preferences like this. Maybe they don't know any better." He shrugged.

Greatly disturbed, Rahul swallowed hard. Although he had lived in the United States for all of his childhood and adolescence, he had never been exposed to anyone who had a different sexual preference, especially someone so close to him. Indian parents usually avoided talking about sex with their children, so he didn't really know how to react. After the discussion with Joey though, he rendered the same opinion, at least for the time being. This was just a lifestyle change. It *shouldn't* affect their friendship.

Rahul was still puzzled about the illegal drug that Tom and Andre had in their possession.

Suddenly, Joey asked Juan, "Hey, Juan, did you get any drugs like cocaine for my friends at the house?"

"Man, I don't do drugs," Juan responded in a clear tone. "I don't have that kind of money. No way! I don't want to go to jail." He looked at them, scowling. "Why are you asking *me*? Go to the beach, and you will find plenty of guys selling it. Man, this is Florida—fun capital of the world."

Rahul, along with Joey, watched Tom and Andre, who were both oblivious to the conversation. They held hands and quietly chatted with each other, steering away from the crowds on the walkways.

Things began normalize after lunch, and by the time they were leaving for home, Rahul had all but forgotten about the striking discovery, if it was even true. Now the question was how to bring it up to Tom and Andre.

Upon their return from their trip to Disney World, they were tired but went to swim. As Deborah returned from her workout at the gym, she called for Andre and said, "Andre, your dad called. Your mom had a freak accident, broke her hip bone by falling down on a slick floor in your home, and she is hospitalized."

"Did he say if she will be all right?"

"She will be fine. She is just sedated to relieve her pain. You may want to call your dad."

"I will do that," he said and left for his room.

Later he called his dad and asked, "Hi, Dad. How is Mom?"

"She had a surgery but she is doing fine. Right now she is sedated. I suggest you take a morning flight back to Boston. She wants you to be by her side."

Andre took the early-morning flight to Boston from Fort Lauderdale.

With Andre gone, Joey and Rahul decided to ask Tom about what had happened between him and Andre. Nervous about the confrontation, Rahul sat on the couch in the living room and let Joey take the lead.

Joey sat in a chair across from Tom. Point-blank, he said, "Let me ask you something personal. Are you gay? How about Andre?"

Tom's face contorted in anger, and his hands balled into fists. "Lay off me, you guys. What if I am? My parents don't care. Why should anyone else? Besides, as far as you know, I'm bisexual." He looked from Joey to Rahul and back. "But who told you? It must be that jerk—what's his name?—Juan, right?"

Joey shrugged. "Well, yeah. He pointed it out when you were walking and holding Andre's hand. He thought you two were lovers."

In a defensive tone, Tom barked, "Of course I like Andre. He's a good friend of mine. He happens to be gay, but that doesn't mean we're lovers."

Rahul remained shocked and quiet. The whole affair disturbed him deeply. Despite the compassion he felt toward Tom for exposing the truth about himself and Andre, Rahul wanted to turn and run in disgust. He didn't know if he could stomach their continuing friendship.

Joey held up his hands to show he was backing off. "Listen, Tom, we don't want to pry into your personal matters. But we were curious about our two good friends. I won't talk about it any further if you feel uneasy about it. Okay? Friends?"

Tom mellowed out, loosening his fists. "You two and Andre are my best pals. But ever since I was a child, I was ordered to do whatever my parents and relatives said. I'm tired of living under constant supervision. I feel suffocated and threatened."

"Listen," Joey said in a conciliatory voice, "I'm sorry that I snapped at you. I didn't mean to. It's all right, but I'm a bit upset too. We're your friends, and you should have let us in on it."

Rahul sat tensely, still not able to fully comprehend the truth that had been revealed. "How do you feel about this, Rahul?" asked Joey.

Reluctantly Rahul said, "Even though I have been raised in a multicultural environment, this event was very shocking for me. I know there may be a few students at the school who are gay or lesbian. But I don't care about them. I am shocked that my close friends like Tom and Andre reveal that they are gay or bisexual and use drugs. I am speechless."

But following advice from Joey, he too put this episode behind him and behaved like nothing happened.

The remainder of their stay in Fort Lauderdale was uneventful. Their week's stay in Florida had been wonderful, but the break was soon to be over. As they briefly glanced at the scenic ocean view from the windows, they could see a few freighters hauling cargo to the ports at a distance. A couple of large yachts were cruising back and forth, making the sailboats wobble. The beach was always busy with people—men and women, young and old. This was a far cry from the winter of the Northeast. The young adults all had a wonderful time, but like everything else, it had to come to an end. Deborah and Yelena were sad to see them go, but once again, it was time for them to go back to school after a wonderful spring break.

On the plane, they all sat together. Rahul and Joey were still curious to find out more about the relationship between Tom and Andre.

Joey said to Tom, "You told us that your dad doesn't know yet that you're gay. How do you plan to break it to him?"

"I don't know about Andre's parents, but I don't intend to tell my father until I move out of the house and go to college. Besides, he must be busy preparing for his wedding. I suggest you both do not bring this up to your parents. I don't intend to give anyone the wrong idea."

"Listen, we will be your friends, no matter what your lifestyle is. Okay?" Joey interjected.

"Thanks, buddies. You both are great friends," Tom said.

Unknown to Tom, his father knew of Tom's affinity when his mother told him in London.

Rahul did not say much. For him, the trip to Fort Lauderdale had been horrifying. He had not expected to find out such deep inner secrets from two of his closest friends. During the entire trip back to Boston, he stayed quiet and wondered if he could bring this up to his mom and dad. If he talked to his parents, they might suggest that he end his friendship with Tom and Andre, so he decided to put the matter to rest.

What a contrast! Florida had been balmy and sunny, whereas Boston was expecting snow late in the afternoon. Rahul's father came to the airport to pick up the boys.

"How was your trip, guys?" he asked them after they had left the airport.

"Very nice," Joey replied. "Thank you for picking us up."

Rahul was unusually quiet, and Tom was listening to the basketball game on his Sony Walkman radio.

After maneuvering through the heavy traffic, they dropped off their friends and reached home.

Tom dropped his suitcase and backpack on his bed and switched on the TV to watch the basketball game. He would occasionally jump up from the sofa and throw his fist into the air when the Celtics scored. Sadly, they fell short to the Lakers in the game, but they never lost their faith that they would win the series.

"Say, you have a nice tan," Robert told his son when he came home. "So how was your trip? Did you have fun? We missed you here."

Handing a small souvenir to his dad, he said, "Fine, Dad. We had a wonderful time. Joey's aunt is very nice and friendly. She has a beautiful house on the beach, and the weather was warm and perfect, except one evening when the rain and thunder disrupted our party. The beach was great, and the water was warm all the time. There were always parties on the beach. We also went to Disney World. It was fun. There is nothing like it in the world that I have seen.

"Dad, by the way, did you know that Andre had to rush home in the middle of the week? His mother had some kind of an accident. I'll call him after dinner."

"Yes, I know that she had a freak accident. I hope she is recovering well. Please ask Andre how she is doing."

Tom nodded.

"What are your plans for the evening?" Robert asked. "Can we go out to dinner? Joyce can't join us since she has gone to Concord to visit her mother." He paused. "By the way, thanks for your postcard from Disney World."

CHAPTER 9

As usual, the Monday after spring break was a busy school day. With hard work and help from his parents, Rahul reached the top of his class, and he was on the honor roll for his scholastic excellence. Rahul had put aside the topic of Tom and Andre's relationship. He had more enigmatic thoughts than Joey had about their friends' mutual attraction because of being raised in a different cultural environment, even though his upbringing was indeed similar to that of any other kid in this country. He let Renee in on this new development, but she did not look surprised. She had probably already guessed, or maybe she simply didn't care.

Rahul didn't waste any time in his preparation for the SAT, and he worked very hard during the school year. He had high hopes of getting admitted to MIT, his father's alma mater, or any other reputable institution of higher learning. It would not be easy to get into these schools unless he was an exceptional student with a high SAT score. Except for physical education, he had performed extraordinarily well at school.

"Hey, Tom, how are your preparations for SAT exams?"

"I guess it is good."

"Listen, Tom. I thought you always wanted to leave this place to be on your own."

"Yes, I do and very much."

"If you do not have a respectable score, you will be staying back in Boston and perhaps alone. This is a gateway to a new place of your choice."

"Please understand, I would hate to be staying at my dad's for long. He loves me, but I hear his fiancée's footsteps. No way, man, I am not staying in that flat with them."

"You mean *penthouse?*"

"Yes, yes. Tell me what I should do to get out of here."

"I have good vibes about it. You have to shape up. Pay attention in school and study hard to get through." Rahul smirked.

Ultimately, Rahul and Tom stayed focused on their studies and the tests. However, it was difficult for Tom to maintain a keen interest in his studies. He had earned well-deserved recognition on the basketball court, but not in the classroom.

As soon as school was out for the summer, Rahul hoped that he would have some wonderful times with all his friends. But Joey had gone to Europe with his parents, while Renee was in San Diego, visiting her cousin. Only Rahul, Tom, and Andre stayed behind in Boston. Rahul worked as a summer intern for a lab at MIT, and Andre's father got his son a clerical job at his clinic. Tom stayed home and occupied himself with his father's wedding.

Robert Spencer and Joyce Briggs were tying the knot in early July. They wanted a small ceremony in the presence of relatives and close friends. His sister, her husband, and their daughter, Dominique, were very excited to come to Boston to attend the wedding.

Dominique was of Asian and European descent, a smart and beautiful girl with dark eyes, dark hair, and a fair complexion. She had no recollection of her biological mother or father in

Vietnam, but she was told early on that she had been adopted. Her parents, Liz and Cyril, worked hard to make her feel that she was a part of their family, and Dominique never felt otherwise. She was extremely bright, maintained high grades in school, and was notably polite.

Rahul, Tom, and Andre spent considerable time together with Dominique and showed her the sights. Rahul realized that she was very observant and did not miss Tom and Andre's affinity for each other. Rahul also perceived that she did not seem to have much in common with Tom or his friends, and hence, Rahul became her primary companion.

Dominique and Rahul were intellectually compatible. She too had performed well in school and thus made her parents very proud. As she grew to know Rahul, they became good friends. They got into many conversations and arguments relating to the cultural variations between America and Australia, East and West, and in unusual circumstances, about the woman's place in Western, as well as Eastern, societies. Rahul often got into serious dialogues with her and then backed off when he realized that he was getting offensive. He was persuasive, but not dominant, which contributed to his fascinating personality. Despite his boyish appearance, he was a mature young man. They both liked each other, but at his age, it was probably just an infatuation.

The marriage of Robert Spencer and Joyce Briggs was performed at a small chapel in Brookline. The bride looked ravishing and was escorted to the altar by her uncle. Her mother, appearing to be ecstatic with joy, sat proudly in the front row with her sister and other family members. Liz and Dominique were beautifully dressed, and Tom donned a tuxedo. There were almost one hundred guests in attendance.

Tom cuddled up to his aunt with a sad look on his face. A strong-willed person like Tom could not easily watch his father marry a stranger. He thought it would further alienate him from his family. Tom perceived this without giving his father a chance to bond with his new family. He thought to himself, *Will Joyce be accommodating or possessive? Will I be lonesome, or will I gain a family? One thing I am sure of is that I am getting out of this household when and if I go to college, which is just about a year away.* His grandfather had left him enough money to last him beyond his college career. Thinking about this eventual but needed planning brought a smile to his face.

The reception was held at the Ritz-Carlton Hotel at the Boston Common. Renee and Joey had returned and were glad to see Tom, Andre, and Rahul. When Dominique arrived, Tom introduced her to Renee and Joey, who was moved by Dominique's beauty and charm—and he nervously started to flirt with her. He asked her to dance at every opportunity. Renee had a crush on Joey, and she tried to ignore his fondness for Dominique by engaging in conversation with other friends. By the time people started to leave, it was past midnight.

~~~

It was Sunday morning, and Tom was sleeping in at the penthouse. Robert and Joyce had spent their honeymoon night at the hotel. Liz and Dominique were getting ready to leave for Sydney, Australia, in the afternoon. While they were packing, Tom came in, rubbing his eyes.

"Don't tell me you're leaving today, Aunt Liz. Dad isn't home yet."

"We have to. Dominique's school is starting, and I have to go back to work. Why don't you get ready, and as soon as we're done with packing, we'll all go get something to eat."

While Tom was tidying up his room, he was listening to music on his headphones and did not hear Liz knocking on his door. All of a sudden, he felt someone tapping him gently on his shoulder, and he turned to see her standing there.

"May I talk to you for a moment, Tom?" she asked.

"Oh, sure. What's up?" Tom said while removing his headphones.

"It's kind of personal, and if you want, you don't have to answer. Okay?" Liz clarified. "It's about you—I mean, about your sexual preference." She paused. "Are you gay?"

Tom didn't utter a word but nodded. He wondered if Dominique had figured it out. He was sure that none of his friends would give him up.

Liz continued, "I can understand that you lost your mother just a short time ago and that you are lonely. I don't know how she would have reacted. But let me assure you that your father loves you very much, and so did your mother. I sincerely hope that you are not doing it to hurt your dad. Are you, Tom?"

"Hurt him?" Tom asked. "No, I wouldn't do that. It's my choice. I'm not doing it to retaliate or hurt anyone. Besides, I'm not gay, but bisexual. You know what I mean?" He had not expected to have such a conversation with his aunt.

Slightly shaken up, she asked, "Do you want me to talk to your dad? I can explain it to him very well. After all, he is a doctor—or rather, a psychiatrist. He would understand and talk to you about the facts of life and, in particular, the physical and mental problems you may need to face."

"No, no, *not* my father. I just need you to be on my side. I'm sure Dominique knows about it too. One more thing—can we keep this just between us? And thanks again for guarding my privacy, Aunt Liz."

"That's fine," Liz said. "You can count on us. We're far away, many thousands of miles, but I am always with you. You can write. Just drop a note, and I will respond quickly. Please remember that I love you, and your mother was one of my best friends. I care for you as I would for Dominique."

Before Liz and Dominique departed Logan Airport for Sydney, Robert and Joyce thanked them for coming to the wedding.

Tom was very saddened by their imminent departure. He thought of being left alone in a strange household headed by his new stepmother, whom he defied without any reasons. All of a sudden, he felt that his space and freedom were to be shrunk and compromised.

CHAPTER 10

That summer, Rahul was interning at MIT, Andre was working for his father, and Joey had gotten a summer job at a local department store. So instead of sitting idly at home, Tom found a job at a bookstore near downtown Boston, close to where Joey worked. Frequently, they went to work at the same time and occasionally had lunch together, spending quite a bit of time at the video arcade and at the movies. Even though they were also receiving an additional weekly allowance, they spent money so extravagantly that they were often out of cash before they even got paid.

The Quincy Market area was ever vibrant, for young and old alike. Joey and Tom worked within walking distance from this place and spent most of their free time there, listening to musicians and watching acrobats and jugglers. Many times, either Rahul or Andre or both of them also came along for lunch or after work to have some fun. They sat on the benches or roamed toward the waterfront. Rahul liked window-shopping, whereas Tom and Andre smoked discreetly. Joey mainly watched the crowd while sipping soda from a can.

Summer vacation was almost over, and the group began pondering their post-graduation plans.

"Hey, Rahul, what are your plans after school is over?" asked Tom.

"Well, I am trying hard to get into MIT; at least that's what my parents want. I may look to move out of Boston. Frankly, I don't know yet."

"I am going to La Jolla to UCSD. My cousin and I plan to bunk together. Hey, guys, it's cool out there. Around-the-year sunshine! I will leave my heavy coats for you guys if you want them," Renee japed.

"Joey, have you planned anything yet?"

"No. I believe that I may go to a community college. I do have my dad's office to look after, especially when he is out of town. He wants me to work with him in his business. I like it, and that's the best experience I can ever get."

Andre said while biting his nail, "You guys will be gone, so I am leaving too. I will be lonely though."

"Where are you going?" everybody asked.

"Well, I might as well tell you. My father is thinking of joining Columbia University in New York, and we might move there. I don't like it, but I don't have a choice. I am not as bright as you guys, and besides, I am not interested in going to college anyway."

"That's a shame, Andre. I hope you are happy, whatever you do," Rahul interjected. "By the way, Tom, you are not staying in Boston in your lovely penthouse?" he jokingly asked Tom.

"Screw you, man! Not in a million years! I don't know yet. I probably need some help in selecting the college if I should attend one. I am not as bright as you all, but I have money to spend from my grandfather's estate. If I don't go to college, I might lose it."

"That's not a reason to go to school, Tom. You are in school to learn."

"Well, that's the difference between you and me, bro," Tom mumbled.

Contrary to everyone's beliefs, Tom was a bright young man but was just severely misguided. He could have easily gotten back on the right track, if he had ever put his mind to it.

Like most kids of Indian heritage who were brought up in reasonably well-educated families, Rahul had a high regard for his parents. He would not want to disappoint either his father or his mother. The father was the ultimate decision maker for children who had been brought up in a truly traditional Indian environment. Mothers usually did not participate in planning for their kids' future. These families were hoping that their children would grow up to be professionals, such as medical doctors, engineers, and, most recently, computer engineers. The decisions were not based on the child's aptitude, but on social and economic well-being.

The Sharmas were different from many other Indian families who had emigrated in pursuit of higher education and standard of living. They didn't impose dos and don'ts on their son but simply kept an eye on him to guide him in the right direction. This made Rahul an independent thinker.

Rahul's mother had always kept an eye open for an appropriate bride for her son, but Rahul was a teenager, so courting and marriage were hardly priorities in his life. However, Indian mothers had the cherished desire for their sons— arranged marriage—but Rahul's father strongly opposed it. He thought that their son was still too young, and he felt it was up to Rahul to choose his own partner. They were not going to interfere with his life. They had groomed him well, so one day he might make the right decision for himself. His father had full faith in Rahul, and would strongly stand by him, no matter what he chose. And that was the end of the discussion between his parents.

Having scored very high on his SATs, Rahul began looking at the curricula of the choice colleges and universities. School was not over yet, and Rahul needed some guidance from Tom in his extracurricular activities and sports. They both signed up for soccer and community service, counseling underprivileged kids in math, science, and computers. In fact, both of them pleaded to their parents to donate their old computers so that other kids had the means to learn. They got remarkable recommendations from their peers for their dedicated service.

In sports, Tom was an excellent basketball and soccer player, and he taught Rahul some fine tricks of the games. Tom was an irreplaceable team player who had shown his ability to win big games during interschool tournaments. Local newspapers flashed headlines and photos showing Tom leading his team to a victory, and his friends were proud of him. He had a great cheerleader in Rahul, who never missed one of his games. However, because of Tom's competitive but violent temperament, he was often fouled out. In a championship game, the referee sidelined him for punching a player on the opposite team. He complained to his coach and the referee that his opponents had constantly harassed him during the game. But all was in vain. His school lost the game by a point.

Rahul and Tom were not that much alike, and they didn't have very much in common. Their thoughts were different, their ideas were unusual, and their aims in life were diverse. Yet there was an unparalleled bond of friendship—a friendship based on dedication and respect.

When Tom scored a little over one thousand on his SATs, he was extremely happy. But since his score was about average, he expected that he would never be able to get into the same caliber of school that Rahul would be able to attend. He just hoped that he would end up in the same town as his friend and mentor, Rahul—as long as that town was not Boston. Tom was happy about what he achieved and was thrilled to move somewhere else—like a bird eager to get out of his cage. He knew very well that his performance was well below that of Rahul and Renee. Nonetheless, he was grateful to his friend Rahul, whose persistent help and encouragement had gotten him this far.

The time had come for them to apply to college. This was a hard task for school graduates, and the choices were unlimited. Selecting a handful of colleges from the maze of potential schools and universities was difficult. Rahul's father suggested a few good schools, which included Rice University in Houston. Houston weather was warm, and it was a good chance to escape the frigid cold of the Northeast. And during the blistering hot days of summer in Texas, he would be cool and cozy in Boston. This seemed to be a perfect plan. Rahul and Tom both applied to Rice University for admission immediately and planned to visit the campus together. Rahul knew that the only chance that Tom had to get into Rice was on his athletic abilities.

Late in the fall, the cold wind was blowing from the north, and the weather was turning miserable. Flocks of birds were flying to the warm South. But Rahul and Tom were excited. They were going to Houston to visit the Rice University campus. The university was not an Ivy League school, but it was considered one of the best institutions in the Southwest by the media and teachers alike. Located close to downtown, the campus was adjacent to the famous medical center, where pioneers in the medical field and famous specialists in heart disease treatments and cancer research were located just a few steps away. But Rahul had no interest in pursuing a career in medicine, and Tom had no aptitude for it.

Rice University had a cozy little campus. Rahul liked what he saw, including its academic programs, which were what he was mainly interested in. Jimmy, a senior student, guided and escorted them and other visiting prospective students through the campus. "Rice is comprised of several colleges," he said, "one of which you may be admitted to. Each college has separate dorms and a cafeteria. You may decide to stay off campus, but it is mandated that you stay on campus during the first year at the school. When you move off campus, you will still belong to the same college."

"I believe that the Rice Owls are the basketball team, right?" Tom asked. "Are the players any good?"

"Well, they're okay," Jimmy answered. "They try their best to stand up against the Houston Cougars and other collegiate teams in the conference. But the Cougars are a very strong and powerful team. Rice needs to draft some good athletes. Do you play basketball? If you're good at it, you would probably have a good chance of getting admitted to Rice and being on the team."

Tom knew very well that it would be difficult for him to be admitted to Rice, even on his sports ability. But he vowed that he must try very hard, if he was to become independent and get away from the Spencer household, especially after Joyce's arrival. Besides, he wanted to stay close to his friend Rahul. When Jimmy mentioned the Cougars, Tom also decided to apply across town for admission to the University of Houston. He might not be able to stay with Rahul on campus, but he would at least be close to him. The tuition was higher for out-of-state students, but money was hardly an issue for Tom.

After an educational and meaningful stay in Houston, they headed back early the next morning for Boston.

~~~

"How was your trip, Rahul?" asked his father.

"I'm thrilled about the campus. I intend to apply to Rice for admission."

In Boston, Rahul lived in a comfortable household, with loving parents. Yet he was searching for his own identity. Moving to Houston and living at the dorm might offer him the self-confidence he needed.

"I am happy for you, Rahul," his father said. "I don't know how your mother feels about it."

However, his father was adamant about Rahul leaving his hometown in order for him to grow up. He debated this point many times with his wife, telling her how he had left India alone and come to a strange country almost ten thousand miles away.

"We will see," Rahul responded and left the room.

Later Rahul's mother said, "Why don't you suggest Rahul try for admission at MIT? Why does he have to go that far?"

"Why don't you ask him?" replied his father. "You do remember that I left India to come here, and don't forget that you were the first one to encourage me to do so. What's wrong with him going to Houston? Besides, he is old enough to take care of himself. And if not, he needs to grow up."

On the other hand, Tom was utterly excited about his trip and called his friend the following day.

"What's up this time?" Rahul asked.

"Hey, dude. Ready to go to Houston?"

"Take it easy, Tom. By this time next year, I may be gone to another town, if I can't get admitted to MIT. You probably will too. Am I right?"

"You are right, my friend. Under no circumstances am I staying behind."

Rahul felt that Tom was very stern about leaving Boston, in spite of the fact that he lived with his father and stepmother in an elegant penthouse in comfort. Yet he missed the warmth of a family.

"I just heard that Andre and his family are going to New York. His father has a groovy job offer from a medical college," Tom said with sadness in his voice. "You know I . . . er . . . *we* will lose a good friend."

Andre was not going to any college in New York. Unlike Rahul and his other friends, Andre was totally confused. Both of his parents knew of his shortcomings, but his father stayed busy at the clinic and hospital, and his mother spent more time socializing with her friends than confronting her son about his school, money, and other extravagant habits. She was concerned about the move to New York, but then again, the notion of living in Manhattan, possibly in a penthouse, had always been at the top of her wish list. Life in the fast lane had always excited her.

Before very long, Christmas arrived. It was a lonely time for Tom. His father and Joyce were spending most of the holidays with her folks in Concord, New Hampshire, and Andre and his family were spending the holiday in New York, finalizing their move. Rahul and his family did not celebrate Christmas, but they were certainly enjoying the festive days—and, as everyone had hoped, it was a white Christmas in New England. Church bells rang, and people listened to Christmas carols. Shopkeepers were selling and wrapping presents. The streets were crowded with shoppers. Children were playing on the snow-covered playground. It looked like a Norman Rockwell painting came to life.

The Christmas and New Year holidays passed without too much excitement for Tom. He met Andre, who had come to Boston with his mother over the holidays to finalize the sale of their home.

"How is life in the Big Apple, bro?" Tom asked.

"I don't like it, but I have to try. I have no friends in New York, and it will be lonely without you all. I'll have to give up my car too!"

"Don't worry," Tom said. "I'm leaving Boston too, and if I'm lucky, I'll go to Houston with Rahul. Come to visit us, buddy." He tried to console Andre.

"You like Rahul, don't you?" Andre asked. "He is a good man. He'll always help you when you need it. I really liked him. Wish I had more time to know him better."

"What's troubling you, Andre?" Tom asked anxiously. "Are you sick or something?" Deep down, he was worried that Andre might be ill from HIV.

"I am fine. I just feel lonely," Andre responded, evading his question.

Where, when, and how Tom and his friends would see each other again were unknowns, but at that moment, they were busy getting ready for the remainder of the school year. Teachers were giving the final pitch to their students about life in college and citing the main differences between the high school environment and campus life. Students were waiting to hear from the college admissions offices. Some were happy that they had been accepted to the college of their choice, whereas others were disappointed. Students and friends were dispersing, going away in different directions like flocks of birds—and many of them might never see each other again.

When Tom learned that Rahul had been admitted to Rice University in Houston, he was happy for him. But he wondered what would happen to him if he stayed behind in Boston in an undesirable household without his friends. Throughout his childhood and adolescence, he had seen plenty of adversity in his life. He shivered thinking about it all, feeling that he had grown up almost like a desolate child. His parents were divorced and lived in different towns, not to mention other countries. His mother never guided him until her death, and his father had virtually no time for him. Although he and his friend Rahul had their differences in lifestyles, values, and upbringing, Tom found a common bond with him. Rahul was his true friend, and he could always count on him for proper advice. Rahul's maturity at a young age made him respectable. Tom's innermost feelings for Rahul made him restless, thinking of being left behind if he could not go with him.

Rahul exultantly showed his father a letter of acceptance from Rice University. Although he was still waiting to hear from other colleges about their decisions, they were no longer important to him. He was determined to go to Houston to join Rice University.

"Dad, should I accept my admission at Rice?" Rahul asked his father, who had more insight about the admissions process at the colleges.

"Don't you want to wait to hear from the other colleges?"

"Well, I sent applications to MIT, Rice, and a few others."

"I would be curious to hear from all of them. Then you can decide which one suits you the best."

Rahul was headstrong but not disobedient. He reasoned with himself to listen to his father, but he wanted to accept the admission at Rice immediately. He too was hoping for Tom to join him, but that was still up in the air. After pleading with his father to let him take the early admission offer from Rice, his father commented that he certainly should attend the school if he felt that compelled to do so.

When MIT deferred his admission for a later semester, Rahul was even more determined to leave Boston for Rice University. All he wished was for Tom to be admitted to a college in Houston too. Even though it was almost six months or more before he had to leave for college, Rahul was putting things together. On one Saturday evening at about midnight, the telephone rang at Rahul's house. It was Tom, and he urgently wanted to talk to Rahul.

"What's up, Tom?" Rahul said, sounding a little annoyed. "Couldn't you have waited till tomorrow to call? I was fast asleep."

"No, man, no!" Tom shouted from other end of the phone. "Guess what? I am going to Houston with you! Yes, yes, I got in at the University of Houston, and I'm on the Cougar basketball team too. Thanks to you, buddy. I was out the whole day. When I came home, I got the letter and could not wait to call you. I called you late last night, but you must have been out. I am so happy. Listen, I'll let you go now. This calls for a party. Okay?"

Rahul was stunned but said nothing.

"I had started to feel like a schlemiel," Tom continued. "Nothing worked out for me, and I thought I was going to be left behind."

"Wait!" Rahul piped up. "I thought you wanted to go where I was going. Why are you so excited to get admitted to the University of Houston?"

"I'll talk to you later. Bye!" Tom said, hanging up the phone.

Rahul thought that Tom probably wanted his freedom at any cost. Now Rahul couldn't go to sleep. He was too perplexed.

Tom, who loved to sleep till noon on weekends, was at his friend's doorstep at about nine in the morning. As soon as Rahul's mother opened the door, he greeted her and asked her if his friend was up. Before she could respond, Tom ran up to his room. Rahul was still asleep, but Tom woke him up.

"Rahul, wake up, man!" Tom said. "We need to plan our life in Houston." Rahul groaned. "What time is it?" After looking at his clock, he said, "It's only nine o'clock! What are you doing up so early? Let me sleep. Go away!"

"Wake up, bro," said Tom in an excited voice.

"Relax, man. There's still time. Why are you so upbeat? Scram! You are going bananas. I'll call you later." Rahul was now getting mad.

Jubilant, Tom said, "Man, I am all fired up, and I am crazy about leaving. Can you believe it? I hate living here. I was choking. From the day my mother died, I've been alone."

"Get a grip. It is not so," Rahul said, rubbing his eyes. "I'm sure both your father and your stepmother love you."

"Thanks, pal. You know, if I didn't have you all as my friends, it would have been a shit hole to live here. Joyce is no friend of mine and no stepmother either. We don't see eye to eye. She's just a woman who married my father for his dough. My mom was different. I feel so good that I am gonna be out of here. No bickering from no one." He paused. "You know, Rahul, you are my best friend. I would do anything for you."

"You are a piece of work! Let me ask you, Tom. Are you and Andre lovers?"

The blunt question from Rahul surprised Tom. "Hell no! I told you and Joey so. We are just friends. I guess he has a friend. Listen, that's all I can tell you. I don't want to talk about him."

A minute later, Tom said, "Hey, you guys have anything to eat? I'm starving."

Rahul's parents had already finished their breakfast, and his father was on the phone talking to his relatives in India. His mom made buttered pancakes for them.

Tom was no stranger to the Sharma household, and they were pleased that he was going to Houston with their son. But it was unclear if Rahul's parents knew about his sexual orientation and his unworthy addictions.

Tom left as hurriedly as he had come that morning.

Soon after Tom left, Rahul's father came to his room and asked if he could speak to him.

"Sure, Dad," Rahul answered. "What's on your mind?"

His father was bashful talking to his son and put his arm around Rahul's shoulder. "Young people like you might feel that we have outgrown your generation and do not understand you. Well, it may be so. But when I see Tom, I have a strange feeling. I do not understand his mood, his interests, and often his behavior. Do you feel . . . I don't know how to put it, son . . . but is he a homosexual?"

"How can you tell, Dad?" Rahul said, surprised. "So what if he is?"

"I am not sure. In that case, let me ask you frankly. How do *you* feel about it?"

"Dad, you are asking if I'm like him, aren't you?"

"Well, I would like to know."

"No, Dad! I am not. Tom is a good friend—that's all! We knew all along about his lifestyle. But he has his life, and I have mine. We do not influence each other in any way."

"While I come from a different cultural background, I do not approve of it, but at the same time, I do not strongly object to it either. Let it be, and be careful while you are in Houston. I hope we have brought you up well. You have always made us very proud." He paused. "One more thing, son: please do not bring it up to your mom. She will never understand it."

"Will do, Dad."

His father left the room with wistful thoughts. All he wanted was to warn Rahul of the consequences. He was concerned, but he realized that Rahul was a very mature person for his age and would understand what was good and bad for him. At the same time, he was afraid to have a preemptive discussion with his wife about their son.

CHAPTER 11

Robert felt it would do Tom good to not be under the parental shield, as he was old enough to take care of himself. However, whether Tom was actually mature or not was another point entirely. He also requested the trustees of Tom's funds to set up an educational fund withdrawal for Tom while he was attending college in Houston.

A week later, Tom came running up to Rahul, showing him his letter of admission to the University of Houston, as well as a conditional admission letter to Rice, based on his athletic ability.

"What should I do now?" Tom asked Rahul. "Here I have a definite admission to the University of Houston, and if I go to Rice on my athletic ability, we may bunk together. What do you say?"

"It's all up to you, Tom," Rahul replied. "You decide."

"You are no help, man. Let me see! I am not cut out for hard work, you know. And I like playing basketball for the Cougars. I need to find a pad between these schools. What do you say?"

"Get real, man! But let me warn you, if you think college life at Houston will be easy, you are wrong. You are smart. Why don't you work a little harder to get ahead in your life? I'll help you, but you have to help yourself, bro."

"Well, I've made up my mind," Tom said. "Cougars, here I come. That does it! I am going to the University of Houston. And I am sure you will help me in my classes," Tom added after a brief pause.

"That's utterly impossible, and you know it," Rahul said.

Rahul shook his head in disbelief. He knew that Tom had no idea about what lay ahead. But Rahul did not want to be his guardian, and he knew very well that Tom had always wanted to be an independent person. Tom was very determined to go his own way, and this was well-known in his circle of friends.

Houston was a widespread town, and a car was necessary to get around. Tom would need a car if he did not stay on campus, and the University of Houston did not have an adequate number of dorm rooms for the freshman class. Robert had hesitantly suggested that Tom should attend driving school before they would consider buying him a car. He had to practice his driving first. Soon after he obtained his driver's permit, he bought a 1983 Toyota Corolla with most of the necessary accessories.

Tom did not know the difference between one car and another, but owning any car, new or used, was a proud moment for him. Tom was a high-risk insured because of his age, plus the accident a few years ago. He had already wrecked a car, and that was while driving without a valid driver's permit or insurance. The paperwork for his Toyota did not take any time. Within four days, he picked up his car.

Tom and Rahul went out for a long drive. Tom was still not familiar with the roads but managed to drive well without getting lost. A typical teen, Tom raced the car with the radio on full volume. At times, he passed police patrol cars. They simply ignored him. *Probably this was my lucky day,* he thought.

There was no overnight parking on the street, but fortunately he got one of the spots that were reserved for residents at his father's penthouse. His car was visible from his bedroom window. Many times during the night, he woke up and glanced out the window to make sure that his car was doing fine. This was one of the most restless nights for Tom, but also one of the most exciting ones.

Rahul's mother was coming to terms with her son leaving for Houston, and she was lost with dejection. She wanted so badly for her son to stay at home, or at least in town, so she could see him frequently.

The time had come for all these friends to leave their homes. For Rahul and Tom, the semester began in late August. They decided to drive to Houston. Tom's father was a little worried, but with Rahul as a copassenger, he was more relaxed. Rahul's parents argued a little about them driving to Houston, but they finally gave up.

"Listen, Tom, we need to go to an AAA office to get maps and the best route to drive to Houston. You know it's about two thousand miles. It may take a couple of days to get there. Will you be all right?"

"No problem, man! I only need four hours' sleep. Besides, I am going to buy a fuzz buster, so no problem."

"I was of afraid of that. Don't you have to sit down with your dad before we leave? My dad is cool, but I will get a big sermon from my mom. She is very emotional, but hey, that's Mother all right."

Tom winked at him and said, "Yeah, I will sit down with Joyce and ask for her advice. Get real, man! My dad talked to me about all that shit. *Study hard, don't spend too much money, etc.* Sure, Dad."

They were boundlessly excited, and they packed the car with the bare minimum of luggage, shipping the rest through a freight company. But Tom was more than just excited. He was very happy to leave Boston for obvious reasons.

When Tom arrived at Rahul's home on the day of their departure, Rahul's father asked him, "Are you ready to leave for Houston, Tom?"

"Ready as ever, Dr. Sharma." After a brief pause, he continued, "At least I'll be happy to miss the frigid winter of Boston."

He did not utter a word about his problems at his father's home. But he could not hide his joyous face.

With tears in their eyes, Rahul's parents were very emotional on their parting. "Be sure to take care of your health, son. We have faith in you, and you will do fine."

"Write and call us frequently, you hear?" Only these words came out of his father's mouth. His mother had not stopped crying. Rahul was consoling her.

"Mom, I'll be fine," Rahul said. "I will call you. Anyway, I'll be back in a few months during the break. You and Dad can visit me anytime you want to. Please don't make me more nervous than I already am."

Rahul hugged her very tightly, and his eyes turned moist with tears. He did not want to show his emotions to Tom and his dad. After giving his father a hug, they drove off.

His mother stood at the doorstep, waving good-bye until their car disappeared over the horizon.

~~~

After winding through the plains of New Jersey, the Appalachians in Maryland, scenic Virginia, the Smokies in Tennessee, historic southern Alabama, and French-influenced Louisiana, as it turned dark, they stopped overnight in a motel in New Orleans.

"Hey, where have you been?" Rahul asked. "Why didn't you tell me you went out?" He was a bit upset when Tom went missing in New Orleans.

"Hey, man, we are in New Orleans!" Tom replied. "I went to the French Quarter, met a few guys, and we had a lot of fun. The food was great too. I don't know how I got back. I must be pickled. By the way, can I borrow some cash? I'll give it back to you in Houston."

"I thought you were loaded."

"Well, so? I spent it."

"All of it?"

"Yes, *Mother!*" Tom snapped.

"On what?"

"On food and drink, among other things."

"How could you get a drink?" Rahul asked incredulously. "You're too young."

"Hey, man! That's New Orleans, and when your pockets are full, *anything* is possible. You know what I mean." He winked at Rahul.

Rahul shook his head and said to himself, "Here we go again!"

Tom came over to Rahul, hugged him gently, and said, "Sorry, pal. I should have told you. Look, I can't help it. I get impulses now and then."

They finally crossed over the eastern border of Texas. By the time they reached Houston, it was a sweltering afternoon in the scorching heat of August, and they were both totally exhausted. In fact, it was one of the hottest days on record in Houston, and it was a unique experience for both. They checked into a small motel close to the Rice campus. The next day they would be busy getting started at the schools with registration, etc.

~~~

"Your parents care for you, Rahul. I'm touched," said Tom. "My dad left a good-bye note on my table. Joyce was already gone and told Wynona to convey her good wishes to me and to tell me that she will miss me. Ha! That's a laugh! That's *my* family, bro. And a while ago, when I called, I had to leave a message with the maid. Earlier it was that stupid machine."

"I'm sure your dad loves you, Tom," Rahul replied. "Or else he wouldn't have brought you from London, put you through school, and now through college."

"Well, it's not his money I'm spending. His old man left sizable dough as education funds for me and Dominique. I have to go through my trustees to get my own money. Crap! I could simply withdraw from my account without going through them. It's ridiculous. Not a big problem, but I need no more guardians."

Remarkably, the car held up well during the trip, except for a flat tire and a small windshield crack. There were no other major problems on the road.

As soon as Rahul completed the formalities, he headed to Brown College, one of the colleges at Rice University, to meet with other students and his college master, who provided guidance for incoming students regarding college and campus life, and who also assisted them in making an easy transition to college. The room at the dorm was small but quite functional. It did not take much time for Rahul to arrange his stuff, not counting the additional boxes that were expected to arrive by freight. Rahul understood that no one would assign him his classes the way it had been done in high school. So almost his entire day consisted of signing up for classes, and, in the end, he felt he had done a good job.

Rahul's father had briefed him about college life, so his parents had no reason to worry about their son. He was a gem, the kind of person that all parents hoped their sons or daughters would turn out to be. Rahul's strong will was his virtue, so he would never be drawn into doing improper things. Rahul's family was very close to him. He was well protected and pampered, and many predicted that he would never grow up. However, contrary to popular opinion, Rahul was actually a very mature young man.

Tom, on the other hand, was carefree, but lately he had shown signs of improvement. He had obtained his admission to the University of Houston on his own merit.

Unlike his friend Rahul, Tom was reckless in his behavior. He did not take most matters in life very seriously, and he never listened to anyone, except for his aunt Liz and Rahul. College gave him freedom, something that he did not have in London or Boston.

After Tom's admission to college, he was somewhat attentive, but his attention and concentration waned as time passed. By midterm, he started to miss classes. Had it not been for Rahul, he would have quit.

It was late October, when one weekend evening, Tom came to see Rahul.

"Hey, buddy. How have you been?"

"Don't worry about me. I called you many times yesterday and today," Rahul said to Tom in slight anger. "Where were you? Are you attending your classes? You'll be in trouble when you have unannounced tests."

"Listen, I'll be all right," Tom answered. "Besides, you know all these subjects backward and forward. You can teach me before the test," Tom added in his usual careless manner.

This angered Rahul. "Get real, Tom! This is not our high school homework. Besides, we're not at the same institution. We don't have the same curriculum, and I don't have any extra time to tutor you."

"But you can help me, buddy," Tom toyed with Rahul.

"Don't 'buddy' me, Tom. You have to prepare for classes by yourself. Well, I can help you as much as I can. But if you continue to miss your classes, you will never get through college. You know you're my friend, and I want you to have a good education too."

"Hey, don't get mad. I met this friend, and we went out. I'll be good. I promise. Okay?" Tom responded humorously.

"What, you have a *girlfriend?*" Rahul joked. "I'd like to meet her!"

"Maybe! Why can't I have a girlfriend *or* a boyfriend?" Tom shot back. "Look, I'm leaving and will see you soon. Let's grab a bite. I need to study, and this will be an all-nighter. See ya." He turned to leave.

Suddenly, Rahul said, "Tom, I have a thought. I suggest you get some help with your classwork."

"What do you mean? What kind of help? You know someone who can help me?"

"Not really. I meant a private tutor," Rahul explained. "But not at Rice. I suggest you talk to one of your professors or his assistants. For a price, I'm sure they'll help you. I strongly recommend that. If you like, I'll go with you to talk to your tutor. Okay?"

"That's great! I love it."

It was late October, and Rahul's suggestion seemed to be working. Tom started paying better attention in his classes with his tutor's help, and with Rahul's occasional assistance he performed satisfactorily on his tests. As an ardent and dedicated basketball player, Tom made his mark on the basketball court, which made his coach very happy and proud. With on-court practices and games, along with Rahul's constant attention to Tom's classes and studies, Tom was exhausted and spent a good deal of time unwinding by drinking and gambling. Rahul spent many hours on the computer and in the library. He dragged Tom frequently to his library, despite his grumbling, and made him work hard on his class projects.

"I wish you were attending Rice," Rahul said. "I could help you more. But I'm helpless to do more for you, Tom."

"That's all right," Tom said. "You're doing the best you can. I wouldn't even be here if you hadn't helped me with school. I can't imagine how I can ever repay you for your advice and help."

"You don't have to pay me anything. Just complete your studies, and you're on your own." Rahul sighed.

A couple of weeks before the Thanksgiving holiday, Rahul spent weekends studying or unwinding by going to movies with friends. Tom was surprisingly absent. He was nowhere to be seen. On Sunday evening when Rahul went to Tom's apartment, he found him fast asleep. He woke Tom up for dinner.

"Where have you been the entire weekend, Tom?" he asked.

Tom reluctantly admitted that he was with his new friends, who lived about a mile away off campus in an apartment. He was unsure if they were even college students.

"Oh, it was merely a card game we were playing."

"Say what?" asserted Rahul.

"Oh. We were playing poker. But the stake was very small to make the game interesting."

"Tom, did you waste time playing poker? How could you?"

After strong persuasion by Rahul, Tom put his destructive habits on hold and started to concentrate on his studies.

Over the Thanksgiving holiday, Tom told Rahul and his father that he was preparing for tests and would like to stay back in Houston.

Rahul was delighted to see a change in Tom's attitude, but he had his doubts about Tom and suspected there was something strange going on with him; however, he could not quite figure it out.

Tom's father, on the contrary, was pleased that his son was becoming more responsible. Besides, Robert was going to be spending time with his in-laws in Concord, New Hampshire, anyway.

Tom was in a jovial mood when Rahul returned from Boston after the Thanksgiving holiday. In Tom's apartment, there was a brand-new expensive music system, and the refrigerator was filled with soda, hard liquor, and several beers, hidden deep in the corner.

"Where in the hell did all this come from, Tom?" asked Rahul.

"I bought most of it, and my friends bought some, as well. Do you like it? I don't live in a dorm, and I hate going out for food in the middle of the night."

"I hardly see any food in here, Tom. And I don't believe that you're the kind of person who would go out for food at night. I've never met anyone who has consumed as many pizzas and burgers as you have."

"Did you see my new music collection?" Tom asked. "I bought it over the weekend."

Rahul gazed at it. "What will your roommates say? You hardly have any room to walk in here."

"Oh, they're never here. They wouldn't mind. In fact, they'll thank me for all these comforts."

"I know where they are. Probably in the library, studying." Rahul sighed and looked at Tom. "You are a piece of work. Come on, Tom. Give yourself a break and finish school. Get a degree, and make your father happy and proud! You know he may be feeling guilty for not taking care of you while you were in London. But now you have a chance to really show him something. A whole life is in front of you. Make the best out of it!"

Tom didn't respond.

Rahul did not say anything more and started to wonder if Tom had any more surprises coming his way. He, however, sensed that Tom must have had a sudden surge in his cash flow, either from his inheritance or gambling, but he couldn't quite figure it out.

"I meant to ask you—where did you get the money to buy these things?" asked Rahul.

"Okay, I have money," Tom replied. "I have large amount of dough in the bank, and more is coming every time I need it."

"You should stop getting this quick buck."

"Come on, loosen up! I know what I'm doing."

"Do you?" Rahul asked and then sighed.

After the Thanksgiving holiday, classes started with a bang. There was hardly a month left before classes would take a break once again for the Christmas holiday. The final tests were right before that, and everyone was preparing to do their best. To Rahul's wonder and delight, Tom started to spend quite a bit of time on his classes and studies in preparation for his finals.

The months passed by quickly, and the time for final exams had come. Amid last-minute cramming, students were planning their upcoming vacations. Most out-of-town students were going home for the holidays.

A phone rang at Tom's, and it was his father. "How is it going, Tom?"

"Fine, Dad."

"I'd like you to come to Boston over the holidays and spend some time with the family. It is lovely this time of the year."

Family. He laughed to himself.

"Okay, Dad. I will be glad to come."

CHAPTER 12

Rahul was happy to be in Boston during Christmas. He noticed that it had snowed a few days earlier, but the streets in Boston were clear. The whole town was in a celebratory mood. And why not? The economy was good. The world was at peace. Thanks to President Reagan and Secretary Gorbachev, the USSR was on the brink of dissolution. Youngsters were glued to MTV. Boston was thriving with financial prosperity. People had more disposable income, and shopping never seemed to be complete until the final hour of Christmas Eve. Of all, he made his mother the happiest person, for he was staying with them for a whole month.

"You look pale," his mother said. "You are neglecting your health." His mother was jabbering at him while putting some snacks on the table.

"Mom, this is college, and it's hard work. I *have* to work hard. Besides, I just finished my final tests last week. I'm fine. Don't worry!"

His father smiled at him, indicating to his son to just ignore her fussing.

Robert was happy to see Tom, but he was very cordial and maintained his coolness. At dinner, Robert decided to bring something up. "Tom, we have a surprise for you. Joyce is expecting a child."

Tom looked at his dad and then at Joyce, smiling and gently congratulating both of them. His poker face did not reveal any emotions. He was faking a smile. He was happy though that he was no longer staying in this household.

"When is the big day?" he asked.

"In about six months."

"Oh, that's great!"

Neither of them could judge if Tom was happy or not. He finished his dinner quietly and went to his room. He was listening to music when his father came in, inquiring how it was going at college. Tom described the campus and how Rahul had assisted him in his studies.

"How do you feel about your new brother or sister?" Robert asked his son.

"Dad, how did Mom feel when I was born?" Tom asked.

"She was ecstatic and elated. I was thrilled too. Why do you ask?"

"Don't you see?" Tom whined. "Joyce enters this home at the cost of your and Mom's marriage. How do you expect me to feel?"

"Stop it, Tom. I have reasoned with you many times. These things do happen. You will have to learn to forget about it and move on. Listen, Joyce is a very sensitive person. If you can't be part of our happiness, then don't. But please don't agitate her even more. It is senseless to tell you over and over again that she cares for you."

Tom saw Joyce at the doorstep, knowing that she probably heard the entire conversation. His father didn't say anything further and left for his study.

Late that night, Tom lay motionless in his bed, feeling breathless and wanting badly to get out of that house. He had no reason to feel that way, but he despised Joyce's presence. In the past, he knew that Joyce had objected to his expensive lifestyle and careless attitude, and hence, Robert had confronted Tom for not being a responsible person. Tom remembered that his father tried to constrain his extravagant habits, but he could not do much about them. Tom probably knew that he was on the wrong path, but he was strongly convinced that his father's and Joyce's happiness had come at the cost of his parents' marriage and, ultimately, his mother's life.

He spent Christmas Day with his folks and the day after with Rahul, Joey, and Renee.

"Hey, Renee, how is life in sunny California?"

"Oh, great! We go to the beach, listen to music, and party. But that's on the weekend only. The school curriculum is tough, and we have to maintain our grades and do our homework."

"So what are you majoring in?" asked Rahul.

"I haven't decided yet. I might major in English or psychology."

"Well, here is Tom, your first sample in psychology," Rahul cracked.

"Screw you!" Tom yelled.

"How are you guys doing in Houston?" she asked, looking at Rahul and Tom.

"I'd like to major in computer science. Rice is tough, though I am doing well."

"I knew you would. I am sure Tom is busy on the basketball court."

"Well, he tries a lot. But if we had poker on our curriculum, I am sure he would do great."

"Why are you guys picking on me?" he asked and stomped out of the room.

"Oh, come on, Tom. We are just pulling your leg. Be a sport!"

"By the way, does anyone know about Andre?" asked Renee.

"No, not really. His physical, as well as mental, health has deteriorated, and he was often treated for depression at the local clinic."

Andre's friends felt sorry for him, especially Tom, since he had been so close to Andre at one time.

Tom did not wait for the Christmas vacation to be over. He told his friends that he wished to return to Houston early. Quite often, he spent nights at his friends' houses. They persuaded him to stay at least until the holidays were over, to which he reluctantly agreed.

Rahul looked at the calendar of the New Year. Ten days had passed, and he started packing to go back to Houston. His dad walked in right as he was about to close his suitcase. Then Rahul remembered something that he had wanted to convey to his father.

"Dad, this summer I would like to work in my field. I don't know where I will find a summer job, but that's irrelevant. I may not get back to Boston for the holidays. Could you please convince Mom that I have to work hard to get ahead in my life? I could always work at MIT as an intern and stay at home, but that would not be fair to me. Do you agree?"

"I agree with you 100 percent," Vasu said. "But let's not tell your mom right now. I will fill her in later, and if you keep calling as regularly as you do, it will soothe her immensely."

Nevertheless, his mother did not take his leaving lightly. She broke down several times and hoped that her son would be back in the summer for a longer stay.

On the other hand, Tom could not have been more delighted that the holidays were over and he was back in Houston.

Joyce was also happy to see Tom leave.

When school began, students were hustling and running around to get to their respective classes or labs. Rahul and Tom had heavy workloads, but Rahul took it as a challenge to excel in his classes.

Classes resumed at their normal pace, and students became very busy in their studies and projects. The library started buzzing with the murmurs of students discussing diverse topics.

Rahul had enrolled in computer science as a major and had influenced Tom to do the same, but at a different institution. Rahul had his doubts as to whether Tom could follow the courses, get a degree, and eventually be gainfully employed. Moreover, Rahul was unable to monitor Tom's progress regularly, but he helped him when Tom lagged behind in his studies and surrendered to other temptations.

Rahul was overjoyed when, during the spring semester, he was selected for the president's honor roll. His perception in the field of computer science was amazing. On the whole, Rahul was among the top 10 percent of students who excelled in their studies and received teachers' commendations.

For the summer, Rahul had an interview with a company called Robotechnique, Inc., specializing in robotics and artificial intelligence. The interviewer knew of Rahul's father, who had a reputation of his own in the field of electronics.

"Hello, Rahul, I am Mark Garcia. I am the head of this department." Shuffling his paper, he said, "I know of your father. How is he?"

"He is fine. Thank you," Rahul responded.

"I see you are at Rice. I am also a Rice graduate. Why do you choose to work for us? Do you have any special interest in what we do?"

"First of all, you have an exceptional reputation in the field of robotics and automation. My professor speaks highly of your company. I am majoring in computer science, and your company seems to be a perfect fit for my education."

"Very well. You have a great recommendation from your professor too. Besides, I know of Rice's program. I like it. Well, do you have any questions, Rahul?"

"Not now."

He left after shaking hands with Mark Garcia.

The company offered him a job as a summer intern at their laboratory in southwest Houston. Rahul met about eight to ten interns from different schools at work, and he was assigned to the Design and Development Department under Dr. Mark Garcia, who was also the head. During the course of training, they were told to implement the software they had designed. Rahul was quite delighted that he was going to spend considerable time on their newest Sun SPARC workstations. He knew how to program using the UNIX operating system, but he needed to learn a lot more about the system and the work flow. His sincere efforts almost guaranteed him employment during the following summer and beyond. Dr. Garcia was very pleased with Rahul's performance and contributions.

Tom, on the other hand, found a summer job at one of the department stores as a sales intern in their TV and stereo department. He was good at it and helped the customers with enthusiasm and vigor. Basically, he was happy to be able to stay back in Houston with his friend and mentor. He felt that he owed his life to his friend Rahul. Tom was very irregular at his workplace, but he managed to keep his job, despite some dissatisfaction from his supervisors.

It was mid-June when Tom's father called to tell him that Joyce had delivered a baby girl named Jessica. He invited him to Boston so that he could meet her. In reality, Tom had mixed feelings about the birth of his half sister.

The first two years of college passed without any big surprises, and Rahul excelled, while Tom was barely able to stay in college. Tom and Rahul, along with two of their close friends from school, rented an apartment with two bedrooms, a kitchen, and a bathroom. Rahul would have continued to stay at the dorm, but Rice University had mandated that many students vacate for a year because of a shortage of living quarters on the campus. Hence, Tom was more than happy to share an apartment with Rahul.

In February 1989, Tom's roommates and friends threw him a surprise party. Tom went out on an errand, and when he returned, his place was dark. He flipped on the light switch and saw that the living room was decorated with balloons and a banner reading, "Happy 21st Birthday."

Finally, Tom was a legal adult. He ordered pizza for all and drove out with Rahul to buy a couple of six-packs of beer. Presumptuously and proudly, he took out his driver's license to show the storekeeper that he was old enough to legally buy alcohol. Although the manager carefully studied Tom's driver's license to verify his age, he was not much interested in Tom's strange behavior. For the first time, Tom felt as if he now owned the world.

"You know, folks, I am so happy today. I am an independent person. We should celebrate this with a bang. Why don't we drive to New Orleans for Mardi Gras? I will drive. How's that?"

They waited for Tom on Friday evening, but there was no sign of him anywhere, and his car was not in the parking lot. Rahul started to worry that something might have happened to Tom. Something did happen, but not what Rahul was worried about.

One of their roommates said, "I think he is in Las Vegas. He told my friend Marty."

Unfortunately, gambling had become his obsession. When Rahul found out, he was raving mad that Tom had left town without telling him. Rahul was agitated about Tom's erratic behavior and irresponsibility, but when he calmed down, he sympathized with him. Tom's life was in a state of extreme confusion and disorder.

During spring break, the school was off for a week. Having this break was a sigh of relief for many students on campus, and Rahul decided to fly to Boston to be with his parents.

"Aren't you going to Boston for the week?" Rahul asked.

"No, I'll stay here and do some work on school reports," Tom answered.

"Yeah, right! Come on, get real! I don't think that's the actual reason."

"Okay, you got me. I don't believe anybody will miss me there."

"Don't say that!" Rahul exclaimed. "Your dad loves you. And you need to visit your sister. Aren't you excited to meet her?"

"I'd like to meet her. But I'm not in the mood right now."

"Okay. Whatever pleases you, Tom. But stay out of trouble." It seemed to Rahul that Tom had a plan of his own.

Tom dropped Rahul at the airport and told him that he would pick him up when he returned.

~~~

About a week later, Tom picked Rahul up at the airport.

"Hi, Rahul. How was your trip?" asked Tom. "Did you have fun in Boston?"

"It was nice to see my folks," Rahul replied. "I met your dad in an elevator, and he inquired about you. You should have come. Anyway, how have you been? You look a little worried."

Tom looked very perplexed, dismayed, and jumpy, but he did not show his discomfort. Upon reaching their apartment, Tom suddenly told Rahul that he was in trouble.

"What kind of trouble, Tom?"

"I was in Las Vegas last week. It was going well, but then I lost some money at a casino. They extended me credit. I was very careful, but I ran into some bad luck."

"How much did you lose?"

Tom did not respond.

"How much, Tom?" Rahul asked again.

Tom hesitated before answering. "Fifty thousand dollars."

Rahul screamed, "*Shit!* How could you, Tom? How did you get that much money? How are you going to pay it back? And what happens if you don't?"

"They got me the credit with the casino. I have to pay them back within a month, or else they'll hurt me bad. These people are rough. They know where I live, where my parents live, and all about me. When I drink, I can't think straight." He paused, trying to collect himself. "Rahul, I fucked up," he said with a shiver in his voice.

"You know, Tom, you really are a piece of work. You have become a compulsive gambler. Jeez! What a mess!"

Tom stared at the ground in shame.

"How are you going to explain this to your dad?" Rahul asked. "He is going to be very mad. He is a wonderful man. Don't play games with him. Okay, so your parents didn't stay married and got a divorce. Don't punish him for that. Be sensible! I'm sure he cares for you."

Tom was withdrawn in his thoughts, and he said, "I am gonna hit the sack."

Rahul was now certain that there was no restitution of normalcy for Tom. He was getting deeper and deeper in the hole. If he didn't watch out, his days might be numbered.

Tom's croupier friend arranged for him to pay his creditors in Las Vegas in installments over three months—if he also agreed to pay exorbitant interest. Tom somehow stayed sober for a while. Rahul organized Tom's weekend chores and studies so that he would not get a chance to escape to Las Vegas.

But the real reason for Tom to stay away from Las Vegas was different. Not only was he afraid of these loan sharks, he was also afraid of his father, who had no knowledge of his monetary trouble. At least, not yet.

CHAPTER 13

Robert was home on the eve of Memorial Day. Joyce said, "Remember, we are going out for dinner?"

"I know," he replied and poured himself a scotch. He picked up the day's edition of the *Boston Globe*, and a telephone call disrupted his reading.

"Robert Spencer here. May I help you?"

"This is George, Renee's father. How are you, Robert?"

"I am fine. It's a surprise to hear from you. How may I help you?"

"I need to talk to you about Tom. By the way, how is Tom doing in school?"

"I guess he is fine. But I do not suppose you called me to find out how he is doing. What's the matter, George?"

"I have Karl, Joey's father, with me on speakerphone. You know we are trustees of Tom's funds, allocated by your father."

"Yes, what about it?"

Karl interrupted and said, "Robert, I have some news for you. I don't know quite how to put this. I'm not aware if you know how Tom is doing financially."

Robert stared at the phone. "My father left a good amount of money for both of his grandkids. He should be all set until he graduates, and he should have a good amount of funds left for him after his graduation." As George and Karl exchanged glances, he added, "I don't understand. You should know the size of his portfolio. You both are the trustees and handle his money matters."

"Precisely," Karl answered. "There is one problem, and in your position, you can cope with it much better than we can."

Robert listened to them with some astonishment.

"This may come as a shock to you," Karl said, "but last year he withdrew over eighty thousand dollars from his account. I know what his annual expenses are. He usually draws around thirty thousand dollars per year, but this is well beyond what he needs. I hope you are aware of his sudden surge in expenditures at school. We also know that he is an adult now and we have no right to interrogate him about his decisions, but the will stipulates that he can't have his money from the trust fund if he doesn't graduate."

Robert sat there, motionless. "I know he has many extravagant habits. But this is outrageous. To answer your question, no, I did *not* know. I don't think he made any major purchases. I certainly will have to talk to him. He still has one more year to go, and I hope he does not exhaust his trust fund." He continued, "You both know that I have a young daughter, and I can only spare a limited amount of money for him to complete his studies. I want him to be more responsible and accountable for what he does."

"The account has plenty of money to carry him through the final year at college without any major expenses," said Karl.

"Of course, I was hoping that he would utilize the balance of the fund to pursue his studies beyond his college education or to start a new life after he graduates," Robert said.

"Robert, do you know *why* he needed that much money in a single year?" George asked.

Robert shook his head. "No. In a few days, his semester will be over, and he will be coming here. I want to give him a chance to explain this to me."

Karl said, "Robert, this is Karl. Let me go to the library. I want to talk to you in private. Hang on." After a brief moment, Karl said, "Robert, you know Andre Michot, Henry's son. I believe that you treated Andre upon his father, Henry's, request. You do know that he is gay—or, say, homosexual?"

"What does that have to do with Tom? You surely aren't suggesting that Tom is one too." Robert was playing ignorant.

"Robert, there may be some connection to his extravagant expenses," Karl said. "But if he is experimenting with illicit drugs," Karl continued, "you do know that the costs could be prohibitive. This is only my assumption and a possible explanation. I am not suggesting that he does drugs, but you may have to ask Tom, in all honesty."

Robert was now totally disgusted. "This was indeed a surprise, all right," he said. "I will talk to him when he comes back. I need another drink though."

Robert was not an ultraconservative like his father, but he wasn't a liberal either. He did not like what Karl had to say. He remembered that his wife, Barbara, had spoken to him about Tom's affinity, but he ignored it at that time.

Little Jessica was over two years old now and was growing up to be a pretty girl. She was beautiful, and her father adored her. On several occasions, Joyce played Jessica to her advantage to extract information out of Robert if something was bothering him.

Robert had hoped that Tom could have confided in him as a father and a psychiatrist—it should have been the proper solution for Tom. Robert kept thinking about why Tom needed such a big chunk of money. *Is there a woman in his life? No, it can't be. He is supposedly gay. Did he let his friends borrow from him?* He had no other idea what exorbitant habits he might have. Flashing back over Tom's life in London, he thought that he might have a drinking problem. *Or is he into drugs? Yes, it must be it!* This was an expensive habit, and it could run up a huge price tag.

CHAPTER 14

As the school year ended, Tom knew that Rahul was assured a summer job at his former employer. The company also promised Rahul employment after he graduated. Tom was unable to land any job, primarily because he was a sloth. He requested that Rahul help him locate employment at Robotechnique, where Rahul worked. After Rahul persuaded Dr. Garcia, Tom ended up at Robotechnique.

The job dealt with the more prosaic aspects of computer operation. But it didn't matter to Tom; he preferred to stay back in Houston rather than be in Boston with his father and Joyce. Meanwhile, both of them took a small break before they commenced their summer internship and flew to Boston to be with their families.

Tom was astounded to see his father waiting for him when he arrived in Boston. He was awestruck and ran toward him, hugging him like a little kid. Tom wasn't emotional, but seeing his father at the airport was overwhelming. At that moment, he felt that his father truly cared for him. Realizing that he had essentially grown up without his dad, their father-son relationship had never blossomed the way it should have. So the moment bewildered him, and he felt like crying. But he was tough and hid his emotions. Robert smiled back at him and asked him how he was doing in general.

They drove quietly home.

The penthouse looked the same as he remembered it. Joyce was at the entrance of the condominium when they arrived. She welcomed them while holding Jessica in her arms. Tom thought his half sister was cute and lovable. Even though Tom did not see eye to eye with Joyce, he became considerably fond of little Jessica. He picked her up and started to play with her.

"I have a little toy for you. Would you like it?" Tom asked Jessica.

"What is it? Can I have it?"

He had brought her a present from Houston, a toy spaceship from NASA.

He gave it to her and said, "I will help you put it together, okay?"

"Okay," Jessica responded in a sweet tone.

His room had not changed much except that the arrangement of furniture was slightly different and the new wallpaper was not his taste. But the pictures of his mother, friends, and others were still on his night table.

Settling in his room, he called his friends to see how they were doing. He also called Joey, realizing that both Joey and Renee were still at school.

Tom mentioned college to his father and what lay ahead after graduation.

"What are your plans after school?" asked his father.

"Rahul and I will be working over the summer at one electronic company. They offered us a job. They specialize in robotics. I am staying in Houston this summer, and we have to report within a week's time."

He also told his father that Rahul was his best pal and had helped him throughout his college career, especially when he was in crisis.

At this opportune time, his father asked Tom, "Can you come meet me at my office one day? Then we will go out for lunch."

Robert did not invite Joyce to join them, and she realized that he wanted to talk to his son privately and that it would be best for her to keep out of their discussions. Tom probably got the hint that his father may have already learned about his gambling debt. It was for the best that these things came out into the open, and besides, he had to face this fact sooner or later. Very soon, he would graduate and be on his own. Then there would be no one to stop him for his cravings. However, he owed it to his father to disclose his gambling and other unusual habits.

"Yes, sure, Dad," Tom answered. "When do you want me to come to your office?"

Robert looked at his calendar and said, "Let's meet for lunch on Wednesday."

On Wednesday they arrived at the Doctor's Club, which was rather exclusive and maintained strict privacy for its members. Robert ordered a dry martini and asked Tom what he would like to drink. Tom was reluctant but asked his father if he could have a beer.

"Why not?" Robert asked. "You are an adult now."

As soon as the drinks arrived, Robert did not waste any time in starting the conversation. "Tom, you knew that your grandfather left a large sum of money, which your aunt and I allocated to your and her daughter's education." He paused momentarily before continuing. "What I hear is that you have run into sudden large expenses. Of course, I do care for you, and I would like to know how you are doing. I want you to finish your studies and at least graduate from college. You are an adult, and I certainly hope that you behave like one. Is there anything I should know?"

Tom meant to prevaricate but found no opportunity to do so. The truth had to come out. He took a sip from his glass of beer and hesitated before speaking. "Dad, I am not cut out to be an educated person like you. I don't like school. Had it not been for Rahul, I would have quit. Anyway, we are here, and likely I will graduate next year. It was and still is hard for me to keep my head above water." He continued after a brief pause, "Well, I made some friends. They worked during the day, drank, and horsed around most of the time. I found out later that they were high school dropouts and not even college students. Occasionally I used to buy pizzas and beer for them, so I got to drink once in a while. It was life on easy street, and I got hooked on it. During the weekends, they played cards, mostly poker with money, and I enjoyed spending time with them. Many times, I drove them to Lake Charles in Louisiana for gambling so that I could get in.

"After my birthday last year I had a wild impulse to go to Las Vegas. It was like a dream. I enjoyed every minute of it. I made money—and spent it too. Last spring break, I did not come here. Instead, I went to Las Vegas."

Tom continued with his story of Las Vegas gambling and loss. "The casino manager meant business. I had no choice but to pay it before I got into any more serious trouble. You have to believe me when I say that I was going to tell you as soon as it happened. But I thought that it might be better to bring this up to you in person. Besides, Rahul insisted that I tell you the truth.

"Next year is my final year in college, and I believe that the company where Rahul has worked during the summers may offer regular jobs to us. I understand that I have more than enough money to graduate. I wish I had more, but I hope to save some money from the job so that I will be comfortable.

"Dad, I'm sorry I have to tell you this. I never wanted to be the black sheep of the family, but I can't resist these temptations. I hope that this incident has taught me a lesson."

Robert listened to Tom very attentively, though he doubted the sincerity of Tom's soul searching. But he didn't want to give Tom the impression that he was uncaring at any point.

"I'm glad you are asserting self-discipline," Robert said. "But you have to be strong. Mere words do not mean much. You are an adult, and I cannot dictate how you conduct your life, but hopefully it will be in your best interest. I am a physician and a psychiatrist, but I am still a father. It hurts me a great deal when any of my kin is in misery. I may or may not be able to help you cross over the bridge, but I can certainly listen to you, and perhaps we can find a way out of your problems." Robert continued, "I didn't know about your gambling problems. I was drawn to the conclusion that you may be taking illicit drugs. Are you?"

Tom kept quiet for a while and said, "Yes, Dad. I did it occasionally in the past, when I was in London and while I was here. But I don't do drugs now. I'm on the college sports team." He paused. "I know, Dad, it's a nasty habit. It's easy to get hooked on but very hard to come off it."

Robert was disgusted with what Tom had to say. He did not fully believe that Tom was remorseful. He listened to Tom without any emotion, expecting to hear more from his son about other nasty habits that he had. But he didn't. It did not take Robert long to figure out that Tom was a delinquent individual.

"Oh! One last thing," Robert said. "I don't want to pry into your private matters, but your mom had told me that you are gay. Is it so?"

Tom was stunned and did not quite comprehend how to respond, yet he said, "Yes, it's true, but I'm bisexual. I don't know how to explain it, but I strongly feel that way. I hope that it doesn't bother you."

Robert responded, "I didn't want to believe it. To tell you the truth, it *does* bother me. It would be wrong for me to say that it's all right. Generally, if one of my patients tells me that he is gay, I may not have any adverse opinion about it. But when my *son* tells me that he's homosexual, yes, it hurts me. I don't want to be hypocritical and tell you that it's okay when that's not how I honestly feel. But I can't do anything about that, can I?" Robert paused before continuing. "I am primarily concerned about your well-being. There are deadly illnesses resulting from sexual activity if you're not careful."

"Dad, I am very careful. And by the way, Andre and I are not lovers, and we never have been. We are very good friends who happen to have similar interests."

"I never mentioned Andre, did I?" Robert said. "Anyway, let's forget it."

Robert was now worried about what other surprises Tom might have to offer. He realized and hoped that Tom's association with Rahul was the only recourse for Tom's improvement. Robert did not want to hear any more about Tom's shocking personal life.

"Let's change the subject," said Robert. "Now, getting back to your money woes, I can't give you very much. The money from the trust—whatever is left of it—is yours, and you should use it wisely. You have wasted a lot of it, but that's water under the bridge. I also have a responsibility to raise Jessica and afford her the same opportunities that you and Dominique had. I may not be able to spare much money to dig you out of any trouble if you don't watch your step. Just think of the consequences before you follow your impulsive habits. Okay, let's put this incident to rest for now.

"Oh, I have some good news for you. We will be at your graduation in Houston. Your aunt and Dominique also plan to be with us. You know that Dominique graduates in a year's time. She plans to come here for further studies. She is a bright young lady."

Tom was glad to get the monkey off his back. His stay in Boston was short but exactly the amount of time he wanted to spend with his dad and his family.

CHAPTER 15

After Rahul and Tom returned to Houston, they started their summer jobs. They soon made many friends at work. At a company picnic, the president of Robotechnique, Clarence Marshall, took Rahul aside and spoke to him about the inner workings of the company and its background. His sales pitch seemed to help Rahul decide to join the firm after he graduated from Rice.

In spite of many interviews from giants like Microsoft, Intel, Sun, and other high-tech companies in Silicon Valley and the Northeast, Rahul was keen on joining Robotechnique.

Tom, on the other hand, tried very hard to get a job after his graduation—*any* job to stay with his friend in Houston. He attended several on-campus interviews, but most of the potential jobs would take him away from Houston, and he wasn't willing to consider them. After many unproductive attempts, he asked Rahul if he could again request that Dr. Garcia offer him employment. Tom knew full well that Mark Garcia would definitely entertain Rahul's request. And thus, Tom was hired by the company in their computer programming department.

It was by accident that the dates for graduation fell during the same week for both Rice and University of Houston graduates. Parents, relatives, and friends of the graduating students were present at the ceremony. And so were Rahul's and Tom's parents and Tom's aunt, along with Dominique.

Dominique was very impressed with the Rice University campus and its programs. But she had already enrolled at Stanford University in Palo Alto for further studies in anthropology.

While Tom was entertaining his aunt, Rahul saw an opportunity to invite Dominique.

At the Rice campus, Rahul was busily showing Dominique his department, as well as the type of work he and Tom would be doing in their new jobs. Dominique had grown up to be a bright young woman. She was slim and looked pretty and perfect in her black trousers and pink blouse, with the top two buttons open and barely showing her cleavage. Rahul perceived that she was trying to impress him with her charm. He sensed this and bashfully observed her with interest and admiration.

During lunchtime, Rahul asked her if she would like to try Indian cuisine.

"I would love to," answered Dominique.

They ended up at an Indian restaurant near the campus. The maître d' recognized Rahul from his previous visits and seated them in a corner booth. They decided on the buffet.

"Are you still a vegetarian, Rahul?" asked Dominique.

"Yes, I am and will probably stay that way, but I don't mind if you're nonvegetarian. They have excellent tandoori chicken and other meat dishes. I hope you like the buffet. Are you familiar with Indian dishes?"

"We have many Indian restaurants in Sydney, as well as in London. Do you come here often?"

"No, not really. We didn't have much time to go off campus. Besides, I needed a ride to come here. Tom and I have been to this place a few times, but he isn't fond of spices. My food habits are completely different from his."

Dominique studied him intently and was captivated by his manners and courtesy. From the beginning, she had always been impressed with him during their previous encounters. But now, things were different. Both of them were now adults, and they could make their own decisions.

Dominique delicately sampled various dishes from the buffet. Some she recognized, and others she wanted to try. Sitting back down at their table, she asked gently, "Rahul, now that you have completed school, what are your objectives in life?"

Rahul realized where this question was leading, so he responded with utmost care. "I would like to go to graduate school one day, but not right away. I need experience first. This job is perfect for me, and I may not get a chance like this in the future. I have discussed this with my father, and he and I are of the same opinion. Anyway, I'm only twenty-two and have a long way to go."

"Are you thinking of settling down?" she asked. "Are you in a relationship with any of your female friends?"

Bingo! He was not expecting an abrupt question like this. "No, I don't have any such relationship with anyone. But I'm not ready yet."

"What is an ideal woman for you?"

In a careless tone he responded, "I don't know. I haven't really thought about it!"

Dominique asked bluntly, "Do I appeal to you?"

Rahul said gently, "You are a young, beautiful, and intelligent person, and I'm sure you will find the one you are looking for. Any sensible person would be flattered to be with you. If I were looking for a bride right now, you would be at the top of my list. But I'm not ready yet."

"You mean to say that I should keep trying?" Dominique asked, smiling. "Is there a possibility?"

"But of course. There is always a possibility. My parents are open about my relationships. You are coming to the West Coast for further education, so it is very likely that we will meet each other often."

"What is an ideal mate for you, Rahul?"

"Seriously?"

"Yes, sure!"

"I'm leaning toward finding an Indian girl, but I'm not hung up on that. I feel that it would be the most suitable choice for me. I was brought up in this country, amid Western culture. Even then I strongly feel that an Indian would be more ideal for my personality and emotional makeup."

"I'm glad to hear that. I'm part Asian too! Do you plan to go to India in search of your bride? Or will your parents find one for you?"

"No, there is a large Indian community in the United States, particularly in Boston and Houston," Rahul answered. "I'm sure I will come across someone who has similar interests to mine. My parents have never insisted on what I should and shouldn't do, although they do hope that I make all my decisions responsibly. They know our community well, and should I need an introduction to a particular person, they will definitely provide it." He paused. "But let's not talk about me. What are your plans for the future? I'm sure you've thought about it."

Nodding her head, Dominique said, "I'm not giving up on you though." She smiled. "I'm planning to attend Stanford in the fall. I've heard nice things about its program in anthropology, and I've always wanted to go there. I'm still too young to think about settling down, which is the same way you feel about the matter."

"So, how about your friends or acquaintances? You did not tell me about them."

"Oh, well, I did have a friend or two. But nothing serious! You know that there is a large population of your countrymen in Australia."

"Do you mind going on a date with me?" Rahul tempted her.

"Of course not! Seems like a good idea. When do you want to start—now or later when I am in Palo Alto?" Dominique snapped.

They laughed.

CHAPTER 16

That evening, Rahul and Tom invited their guests for dinner. Tom stood up with a glass of wine in his hand and said, "Cheers, everyone! Thanks for coming. I would like to take this moment to acknowledge my gratitude to my pal Rahul. Without his help and guidance, I might not have ever graduated from college. Thanks, buddy."

Tom did not truly care for anyone else in the room, but he had great admiration and respect for his friend. Robert could not have been happier about what Tom had said and hoped to return the favor, if Rahul or his family ever needed his assistance.

On Monday morning, when they reported to their jobs, they were inspired by their new opportunities. The pay and benefits were excellent, and most importantly, Rahul found that the work environment was very friendly. He started his training in the R&D Department, and Tom was assigned to work under the assistant manager of the Programming Department. The company had an impressive list of clients, comprised of oil companies, NASA, and various other government agencies, including the Department of Defense. The R&D Department was maintained with utmost security.

Rahul soon realized that life on the job was quite challenging compared to what he was used to on campus. He did not mind and loved the challenge. They moved into their new apartment and bought new furniture from a local superstore. Their living habits at the apartment resembled those of the characters portrayed in Neil Simon's play, *The Odd Couple*. Rahul was meticulously clean and maintained his routines in a conventional manner, whereas Tom was wild, sloppy, and easygoing. Nevertheless, both liked each other, and they never exasperated each other, except for minor altercations due to their different cultural views.

Tom's cousin Dominique was admitted to Stanford University, which gave Tom an instant opportunity to escape to the West Coast—whether it was to Palo Alto or Las Vegas, no one knew for sure. She also visited her cousin in Houston over long weekends and thoroughly enjoyed the company of these young men. Domino, as Tom always called her, had grown up to be a beautiful, responsible, and intellectual individual. She still had a crush on Rahul, and Tom knew it. Rahul had a great deal of respect for her, but he was not sincere about her.

"You want to go to a movie tonight, Dominique?" asked Rahul.

"Okay, it's a date."

"Why can't we go to a movie without a date?"

"But it sounds very romantic," Dominique joked.

"Which movie do you want to see?"

"I don't know what you like. If it was Tom, I am sure he would choose *Naked Gun* or *Terminator*.

"You like *JFK*? I'd like to find out if there was a conspiracy in his assassination."

"Okay, let's go!" Rahul said.

She gave him a kiss on his cheek. "What is that for?" Rahul asked bashfully.

"Just to show my appreciation."

"In that case, I should have taken you to a Broadway-type show."

"Don't push your luck!"

After the movie and a quick bite, before entering his apartment, he kissed her with her acquiescence.

"Now, that's what I call a *date*," Dominique said.

On Sunday evening, after Dominique left for Palo Alto, Tom said to Rahul, "You know, I can't help noticing that Domino likes you. What do you think of her? She is a nice girl."

"Are you playing Cupid, Tom? If you are, then please don't. She is a very nice person, and we are fond of each other. She is also very intelligent and affectionate. But I'm not ready for any serious relationship. And I don't believe that she is either."

"Let me be frank with you," Tom said. "You mentioned earlier that you would like to find a suitable match whose characteristics include being well educated, being from a good family background, and being beautiful. Well, she is all that. So why don't you have any interest in her?"

"Tom, don't make me repeat it. She is a very sensible, sensitive, and beautiful woman. I like her. But I don't want to hurt her feelings if things don't work out. And if something should work out, we will handle it at that time."

CHAPTER 17

Rahul was very pleased to be working in the Research Department, developing software modules for automation. Almost a year and a half later, Rahul enrolled in the school for a master's degree program and took a leave of absence from his work. Dr. Garcia was very pleased with Rahul's performance and granted leave without any hesitation. He requested that he return to his previous job, of course, with the appropriate raise in salary and possibly a promotion.

While enrolled for his graduate work, Rahul came to know another fellow countryman, Madhu Marve, who was also admitted into the same department for a master's degree program. He was a computer science graduate from the Indian Institute of Technology in Mumbai, India, an affiliate of Rahul's father's alma mater in India.

"Madhu, I understand you worked in India before coming here."

"Yes, after my graduation, I worked for a computer company in Mumbai. I am on leave until I graduate. A friend of my father's has a small software company that offers services to various countries. Software engineers are in short supply, and it was a perfect opportunity for our company to expand the business, but we need technological expertise. This was the principal reason why I ended up at Rice to further my education."

These two students, Rahul and Madhu, were always at the top of their classes, racing toward perfection. Rahul admired Madhu's knowledge and talent, and he introduced Tom to Madhu. All three of them became friends.

Although the group was inseparable, Madhu was never comfortable in Tom's company. Madhu couldn't tolerate Tom's abrupt and inquisitive nature.

"Hi, Madhu," Tom said. "How come you're still single? Haven't you found a girl you like yet?"

"Yes, I have," Madhu replied, "but it's somewhat complicated."

Rahul asked gently, "I don't want to pry, but is it a social problem?"

"Yes and no. I told you that I live with my mother, who is critically ill. I have a sister who's married and has her family in Mumbai too. She and I take care of our mother. We thought of putting her in a nursing home, but she's very frail and refuses to move out of her old apartment. So I stay with her. Due to her dominant nature, I feel uneasy entertaining any female friends at our dilapidated house.

"We lost our dad when we were kids," Madhu continued. "My mother worked in a school, brought us up, and got us well educated. She even helped my sister get married. For twenty-five years, she sacrificed her life for us, and I hate to drive her out of her own home. Now she cannot be left alone in the house and feels threatened if the maids or nurses look after her."

Tom said in disbelief, "That's a shame. So don't you know any girls that you like?"

"I know many, but there is one that my heart is set on. However, I haven't told her yet."

"Why not? Doesn't she like you?"

"Yes, of course. She likes me very much, but I haven't gotten a chance to talk to her." Madhu paused. "You see, I'm hoping that one day I'll move into a reasonably decent apartment, and I can ask her then. My sister knows her, and she insists that I ask her, but I'm not ready yet. I have other social responsibilities that I can't ignore."

"So you're telling me that you have never been with a girl?" Tom asked. "Are you still a virgin, like my friend Rahul?"

His gaffe caused Madhu to walk out of the room.

Tom's comments also infuriated Rahul, and knowing Tom's indiscreet and abrupt questioning, he left in disgust, as well, before Tom could start with him.

Tom was confused and asked loudly, "*What?* What did I say?"

~~~

For Rahul and Madhu, graduate school was about to end. They worked diligently for their postgraduate degree, and they were often honored by their peers. Soon after completion, Rahul was to return to work and Madhu would return to India to implement his plans for the future growth of his company.

Rahul was greeted warmly by his superiors and colleagues. He was also promoted to the position of assistant manager of software development.

To his dismay, the company was not able to recruit qualified software personnel for his projects, and their clients were getting edgy and impatient for the delivery of the finished goods. He approached Mark Garcia, who was now director of project engineering.

"Mark, I have to give some thought on how to raise the production and cut the cost at the same time. I think we may have a solution."

This was music to Mark Garcia's ears.

"All right, I will be pleased to hear about it. What do you have in mind?"

"Our strength remains in our technical expertise and our talented staff pool. But we are beat at our resources. We cannot commit more than we can digest, and we've had to let go of some very rewarding projects. If our management keeps an open mind, we can outsource some work."

"Who and where do you have in mind?" Mark asked.

"I was thinking about my friend Madhu. I have been in touch with him, and he keeps reminding me that if we would consider shifting some of our mundane work to him, we could concentrate on the high-tech end of jobs. I told you that he is in charge of technical development for a small software company in India—Mumbai, to be precise—and in a duty-free zone. We would not only increase out technical output, we would also increase our profitability for the routine workload."

"How is that?" asked Mark.

"The cost of technical help is still low in India, so our unit cost reduces for far less than what we have allocated. Subsequently, we would also raise the output of our high-tech work."

Mark scratched his head and said, "Why don't you prepare a report for my review, and later we may submit it to our management committee."

Rahul ran to his office and within a week he meticulously and painstakingly prepared a report, detailing the technical and economical advantages of his proposed solution, as he had discussed with Mark.

Mark Garcia was so impressed with Rahul's proposal that he read it over many times and finally took it to the president of the company.

"Excuse me," said Mark, "Clarence, may I talk to you for a moment?"

"Of course," said Clarence. "What's on your mind, Mark?"

Mark handed the project report to Clarence Marshall. "At my request, this is a report prepared by one of our junior executives.

It outlines how we can effectively carry out our work to keep our clients happy by timely deliveries *and* cut costs to our benefit, as well. I will leave the report with you, and if you have any questions or feel this proposal has any merit, I would be glad to meet with you at your convenience."

"Will do, Mark. Thanks!" Clarence replied.

A week later, Mark came in to see Rahul in his office with his head hung low. "Listen, Rahul," he said. "Often we don't get what we want. The chief wants to postpone your proposal for the time being. I'm led to believe that from the beginning, the management was not in favor of your proposal. They were mostly concerned about the reduction in our workforce and the security of our work."

"Oh, well. Next time, hopefully I'll present my case better."

"That has nothing to do with it, Rahul," Mark said. "One of these days, you will understand office politics."

"What do you mean?"

"I can't talk about it, Rahul. Let's put a lid on it for now."

CHAPTER 18

Even though summer had come to an end, the weather in Houston was still hot. Labor Day was a week away, and Tom insisted that Rahul go to Las Vegas with him. He assured him that he could enjoy the shows and the city.

After much persuasion, Rahul and Tom were on their way to Las Vegas, for very different reasons. Las Vegas was quiet when they reached their destination midmorning. Tom was very familiar with the scene, so he guided his friend into a cab and they went to his favorite casino hotel.

At the casino, there were a few people gambling at the slot machines, shooting craps, and playing blackjack and other games. Maintenance personnel were cleaning and vacuuming the floor, and the restaurants were packed.

Rahul noticed that Tom appeared to be very visible, and the staff greeted him warmly. Soon after they checked into their rooms, Rahul came down to eat and saw that Tom was already on the floor, gambling. Rahul realized that Tom didn't want to be disturbed, so he went to the pool for a swim and met a couple of guys from Midland, Texas, who bragged about their win at the blackjack table, explaining to Rahul about the system.

It was late afternoon when he returned from his swim, and the casino was buzzing with people. The city came alive at dusk, and the lights illuminated it beyond imagination. The streets were crowded, and large limos whisked by, carrying VIPs. Inside the casinos, people were speaking loudly and cheering to welcome their momentary wins. Half-clad bar girls were serving drinks to their customers of all ethnicities. Americans, Chinese, Japanese, Arabs, and many others were here, all on a quest for fortune. People were intense and serious about their gambling and hopeful winning. Rahul was no exception. He wasn't a gambler, and it was actually his first time he had ever been tempted to try his luck at the slot machines.

After losing all the change in his pocket, he left to look for his friend. Tom was at a poker table with other players, jumping with excitement. But his unruliness at the craps and blackjack tables did not seem to bother anyone. Rahul walked behind him and watched him play his game with high intensity.

"Have a drink, Rahul," Tom said.

"Thanks, but I don't need any more stimulation."

"What have you been doing?"

"I ate, went swimming, and now I'm going to a show by Wayne Newton at eight."

"Good for you. I'm sure you'll enjoy it." He paused, removing something from his pocket. "Here, keep it," he said, handing Rahul a pack of condoms.

Rahul could not believe his eyes.

"Keep it," Tom said again. "Keep it. You never know when you'll need one in Las Vegas."

Wayne Newton, also known as "Mr. Las Vegas," had numerous fans, and Rahul was one of them.

Tom was waiting at the bar when Rahul returned from the show. Just as Rahul anticipated, Tom was drunk, but he wasn't distracted from his losses in gambling. He ordered a drink for Rahul, and to be social, Rahul did not object.

When Rahul came to, he was in the arms of a strange woman in his room. Her name was Erika, or that's what she told him. Rahul realized that they'd had sex. He was in shock and ashamed of himself.

"Who are you? What are you doing here?" Rahul asked her, blushing.

"Hey, man! You brought me here. Don't you remember? Okay, lover boy, get up. Give me my money," said the girl as she was still dressing.

Rahul was disturbed that he had spent the night with a hooker. He didn't say anything, but he pointed his finger at his wallet, which was laying on his night table. She picked it up and took out some cash.

"That's kind of pricey," he complained, noticing how much she had taken.

"Tutoring ain't cheap, honey. See ya later!" With that, she left the room.

Somewhat embarrassed, Rahul got up and went to the bathroom. He felt cheap. He had hoped that his first sexual encounter would be a special moment—a hooker was the last thing on his mind. He had no idea how he ended up with her and did not recall what happened after he had the drink with Tom. Somehow he felt that Tom might have had something to do with it.

Downstairs in the lobby, he ran into Tom outside the restaurant.

"Where were you, man?" asked Tom.

"I ended up with a girl . . . a hooker. Her name was Erika."

"Oh, yeah. That's *Erotic* Erika. Everybody here knows her by that name. She's very naughty. Did she clean you out?"

"Yes, I believe so. Did you have anything to do with it? Did you spike my drink?"

"No, I wouldn't do that. But the bartender told me that you left with a girl after you had a couple of drinks together." He smiled. "In fact, she was looking for *me*. I had a fling with her for a while."

"I thought you were gay. You don't look at women."

"I go either way. I told you guys that." Tom paused. "Oh, what the heck! Forget it! Didn't you have a good time? Remember, this *is* Las Vegas, and anything can and *will* happen."

CHAPTER 19

Ever since Rahul had returned from Las Vegas, he was reticent.

"What's wrong, Rahul?" Tom asked one day.

"Nothing. I'm all right."

"No, you're not. Why don't you tell me what's wrong? I'm your friend."

Rahul then talked to Tom about his rejected proposal to the committee and how he was somewhat disturbed by his encounter with the hooker in Las Vegas.

"Why are you uptight about what happened in Las Vegas? Everyone else has forgotten it. Why do you keep thinking about it?"

"It's probably due to my upbringing," Rahul replied. "My idea of a good time does not include having sex with promiscuous women. Anyway, I've already forgotten about it."

"So what's the problem with your proposal?"

"Well, nothing much, but we will face a severe shortage in production unless we get serious help. My concept is to get extra professional help, but a few in the management committee were opposed to the idea of outsourcing. Well, let's see what happens."

~~~

The second-quarter profit for Robotechnique was well below expectations, which infuriated the chief. The projection, which was prepared by his accounting department, was way off. He summoned his staff, including the controller of the company, Ms. Rhodes, for the explanation and solution to the problem.

"I have an idea, Russell. Talk to your clients, and see if they will allow us to subcontract a portion of the jobs," the chief told his marketing manager. He then told his secretary to ask Mark to come in.

"Mark, I would like to go ahead with the outsourcing idea that you presented during the last meeting," he said, undermining his vice president of technical development, Dr. German.

"Will do, sir. What next?"

"Please give me a spreadsheet to look at. When you're finished with it, I'd like to see you and . . ."

"Rahul."

"Yes, I'd like for you and *Rahul* to come and see me. Pronto! Thank you, Mark."

Mark and Rahul entered the boardroom, which was connected to the chief's office. It was well decorated with nice pictures of patriotic landmarks. In the middle was a large photograph of a NASA shuttle at liftoff, which was autographed by all the mission's astronauts. It was an eye-catching conversation piece. Everyone was highly impressed with a couple of pictures of the chief—in one, he was chatting with President Reagan, and in the other, he was playing golf with President George H. W. Bush. The room had a small overhead projector for a slideshow, and a whiteboard with colored pens. The room was large and bright. Rahul sat down at one end of the table, while Mark notified the chief's secretary that they were ready.

As the chief entered the boardroom with Ms. Rhodes, he asked Mark to close the door. After discussing a few points from the report, he said, "Gentlemen, I need for you to initiate the outsourcing project and give me another realistic spreadsheet for me and Ms. Rhodes to look at."

Rahul and Mark left as hurriedly as they had come in. Rahul began to prepare the cost estimate, as well as administrative planning, for the potential project in India. Although Rahul was a novice in such administrative and financial matters, he expected a lot of input from Mark and Madhu.

Even though it was late evening in India, Rahul picked up his phone and dialed Madhu.

"Hi, Madhu. This is Rahul from Houston. How are you? Sorry to bother you at home and at a late hour."

"That's no problem, Rahul. I am glad to hear from you. How may I help you?" asked Madhu.

"I need your help on a matter, what we had talked about earlier. I am preparing a report for our management to outsource some of our work to you. I need some input from you."

"That's great. I will try to answer your questions to the best of my knowledge. Let me suggest a better way to handle it. Why don't you send me an e-mail message comprising your questions, and I can answer precisely. Besides, I will have my staff to assist me."

"That's a great idea. Please wait for my message, and respond to me accurately as soon as possible. I will call again if I have any questions."

"Anytime, my friend!"

"Bye! Have a good night!" Rahul said and ended the conversation.

Over the next few days, Rahul stayed focused on getting detailed information about the operation from Madhu. Rahul prepared a draft of the labor and logistic costs and submitted it to Ms. Rhodes. There were other unknown problems that might crop up unexpectedly, so it was almost like shooting in the dark to undertake a venture over tens of thousands of miles away. But Rahul was extremely optimistic that he could overcome any obstacles and could expect full cooperation and assistance from his friend Madhu.

Another meeting with the chief was set to recapitulate the plan. He looked in detail at the spreadsheet, which yielded a decent profit while increasing production. He suggested that Rahul and Mark make an exploratory trip to India to get a more rational picture. Rahul was thrilled. He talked to his parents to see if they could offer more suggestions. They did so, of course, but did not offer many pertaining to the purpose of his trip.

For a few large companies such as IBM, Microsoft, and Citibank, outsourcing was not a unique idea. But for a private enterprise like Robotechnique, it was something new. Taking precautions against security lapses and a lack of control was very important to the chief, and Rahul and Mark explained that the expansion of their office in Houston was impractical, if not impossible, because of the unavailability of a trained technical staff. On the other hand, the Indian company could avail themselves of a highly technical staff in India, at a fraction of the cost.

"There is, however, one issue we need not ignore," Rahul interjected. "Although they will have well-qualified staff at our disposal, we have to have constant training and supervision of our work. This has to be controlled by Robotechnique. That means that it will be necessary to post a full-time resident agent in Mumbai. Hence, the work will be performed at the skill level required by Robotechnique, and security will be maintained to the chief's satisfaction."

"Can we afford this by allocating extra manpower?" the chief asked.

"Afford or not, sir, this is vitally important to us, and we simply cannot ignore it. Besides, the trainer will have to be relocated every three to six months to satisfy the statutory tax laws of India."

The chief agreed to that, in principle, after reviewing the costs and the advantages of doing so.

"Get going, boys," the chief ordered and ended the meeting.

~~~

"What do I need to do to prepare for our trip to India?" Mark asked Rahul while entering his office.

"Nothing in particular—the same that you have done before for a trip to any foreign country. However, we do need a visa, and that's the easy part. Carry cash in the form of traveler's checks. Credit cards are widely accepted, but cash is king. And most importantly, carry all your medications, if any. It will be warm there, so I suggest that you take light clothes with you. That's all!"

"Okay, that's good enough for me," Mark said. "By the way, how well do you know Madhu? Tell me about him, his family background, etc."

He narrated to Mark about Madhu; his mother, who had been sick for a long time and whom he was taking care of; and his boss, who helped Madhu and his sister.

Mark listened quietly.

"Mark, may I ask you a favor?" asked Rahul.

"Yes, of course."

"I haven't been to India in over four years," Rahul said. "Can I take a leave of absence for a month after we're done with our work? I would like to spend more time in India on this trip."

"I can't see why not," Mark answered. "But let me find out."

"Thanks."

Rahul wanted to spend some time in India with his relatives in Mumbai.

CHAPTER 20

It was October when Rahul and Mark landed in Mumbai. The weather was warm and humid in spite of the fact that it was well past midnight. Even the airplane windows were fogged up. After getting through Immigration, they waited for their luggage to arrive. People were clustering at the entry of the luggage belt, perhaps anticipating that their luggage would arrive first or safeguarding their valuable cargo. In any case, it created a chaotic scene.

The exit doors were clogged with people waiting to receive their guests. Barely able to exit the airport facility, Mark and Rahul finally spotted Madhu, who was driving them to a hotel in Juhu Beach, Mumbai's exquisite suburban area.

Even at this late hour, Mumbai was in a festive mood. The streets were sporadically full of people, celebrating the upcoming holidays.

"I see people are having fun. Is it a special occasion of some kind?" asked Mark.

"Well, we are approaching *Diwali*, widely known as the Festival of Lights. The people are in a state of euphoria, depending upon if we have a good rain in the monsoon. You see, rain is the lifeline of most people, especially for farmers. As such, people do not observe time strictly, but our rainfall does. If we have a dry season, then they have to wait the whole year for the rain, and it brings tremendous hardship on the lives of people," Madhu said.

"It seems that you had a good rain this year," Mark said.

"Well, Mumbaites do not need any reason to celebrate. But you are right. The rainy season was quite satisfactory."

The hotel was right across from the beach on the Arabian Gulf. It was a couple of days after the full moon, and its reflection in the water and splashing waves made for a splendid view from their hotel room windows.

They rested and got ready to start the day at Madhu's office. After fighting unruly traffic, they finally reached his office in the morning. The office was spacious and neat, with visible computer terminals all over the floor within a secured area. The administrative area was on the left, and its personnel were busily shuffling papers and talking on the phone. Rahul and Mark were escorted to a large conference room, which was nicely illuminated and furnished. Madhu introduced them to his staff and Mr. Sethia, the CEO of the company.

"Gentlemen, I have very sketchy information about your visit here, but would you please explain to me, if possible, in detail?" Madhu asked both of them.

Rahul answered, "You have met Mark before and know him well, I presume. Let me begin by telling you that our company is facing an acute production problem. After our recent discussions on the phone and via e-mail messages, I took it upon myself to inform my management that there may be an alternate way to fight the problem. I'm seeking your help in closing a severe production gap."

"Rahul, you know that I'll help you in any way that I can. But I'm completely unaware of the work that you do at your company.

Unless I know the type and scope of the work, I'm unable to talk about it. Why don't we start with what you want us to do?"

"Mark, may I?" asked Rahul.

"Yes, by all means."

Rahul explained what kind of help they were seeking, as well as other administrative and maintenance issues that they needed to cover in order to come to a fruitful conclusion. There were many details and intense discussions about the business, operational logistics, and economic aspects of the project.

Madhu said, "What we should do now is write a memorandum of understanding for our collective management teams. Then we can go from there."

As Mark and Rahul agreed, he picked up the phone and called his legal counsel for a meeting.

Shortly thereafter, a young, svelte woman in her mid- to late twenties entered the room and greeted them. Rahul could not take his eyes off her shapely body, which was clothed in a beautiful navy-blue dress. She was slim and tall, and she walked with excellent posture. Her hair was stylishly brushed, and her perfume filled the room with a pleasant aroma.

"This is Ms. Julie Anand, our legal counsel," Madhu said. "She has been with the company for over a year." Madhu introduced her to his guests.

"Good morning, gentlemen," Julie said. "I hope you had a pleasant flight. How do you like India so far? You probably know that we refer to Bombay as 'Mumbai' now." Her voice had an elegant accent that was like a nightingale singing. Rahul was dazed into silence.

"Very well, Ms. Anand," Mark responded. "We have not had much time to explore your wonderful city. I'm sure we will do that before we leave. Rahul has been here before, so he probably knows more."

"Call me Julie, Dr. Garcia. I like it that way. So shall we start? What do you want me to do, Madhu?" she asked in a cordial voice.

Madhu explained the business proposition on hand to her. Their discussions continued for a couple of hours.

Madhu asked, "Why don't we break for lunch? Julie, we would be very happy if you could join us. Say we leave in about fifteen minutes?"

"That's fine with me, if it's all right with you, gentlemen."

Everyone nodded, and she left the room to go to her office, while Mark excused himself to go to the washroom. That left Madhu and Rahul alone in the room.

Rahul could not resist his next question. "Madhu, what do you know about Julie? She is very charming."

Madhu grinned and responded, "She is not only beautiful, but also very intelligent. She is a close friend of my sister. We went to the same school, but she was my sister's classmate. My sister is now married, and she recommended that we hire her."

"What does her husband do?" asked Rahul.

"Whose? My sister's?" Madhu asked. "He manages the marketing department of a large company here in Mumbai."

"No, I meant Julie," Rahul said.

"She is single, but there is something you should know," Madhu responded. "I'll tell you later."

They stopped their conversation abruptly as Mark entered the room. Julie came in, wearing designer sunglasses and carrying a black purse. She was smiling.

"I'm ready when you are," she replied. "Madhu, do you want me to drive?"

"No, we will have the cab take us to the restaurant. I don't want to fight the traffic and parking."

A deluxe five-star hotel was in the vicinity, overlooking Juhu Beach. They were seated in a restaurant overlooking the gulf. People strolled on the beach, and hawkers busily sold their items. Food stalls were buzzing with lunch traffic. This was the life in Mumbai—there was never a dull moment!

At the restaurant, Madhu explained to Mark what each dish in the buffet contained, while Rahul was busy chatting with Julie. He told her that his aunt, his mother's sister, lived close to the hotel, but unfortunately she was out of town with her family. He explained how he had a faint memory of the neighborhood when he visited before, and then he continued with his small talk.

Julie explained that she lived with her mother in a suburb called Santa Cruz, and that she had no siblings. Although Rahul had many questions, he didn't want to pry into her private and social life.

"Try this fish," Julie offered. "It is a specialty of the Mumbai region and is cooked in a *tandoor* oven."

Mark took a piece of it, but Rahul passed.

"Don't you like fish, Rahul?" Julie asked with curiosity.

"I'm a vegetarian," Rahul answered. "I don't eat meat or fish."

"Oh, I understand. There are many dishes which you may like, Rahul. And I am sure that you must be very well acquainted with them."

In a discreet way, Rahul kept up his conversation with Julie. He was simply captivated by her charm and beauty.

Back at the office, they discussed a few more points of business. Then Mark and Rahul got ready to drive back to the hotel by late afternoon. Jet lag was something they were not accustomed to, so Madhu finally suggested that they go to their hotel and rest.

"In the evening, I'll come by your hotel so that we might go out for a drink or two," Madhu said. "Then, if you like, we will go out to dinner. Is that okay with you?"

"That's fine," Rahul said. "We will be waiting."

When they were finally alone, Rahul asked Mark, "How do you think the meeting went?"

"I think we can do business with them. They seem to be ethical and, of course, you know Madhu well enough to confide in him about our concerns. I still have a few questions, and I would like to see the commercial aspects of the projects, as we have indicated in our spreadsheet. I believe their accountant is preparing one for us. By the way, their legal counsel is very cute," Mark added. "I noticed that you like her."

Rahul remained silent for a couple of seconds before he answered warily, "Yes, she is pretty and also has a wonderful personality." He paused. "Sure, I like her. But I don't know her. I could possibly ask Madhu to find out what he thinks of her, and whether she has a boyfriend, etc. I'm inept in the art of courting a girl, any girl, whether here or in the States."

"Let me assure you of one thing—she is very pretty and smart too," Mark told Rahul. "I've only known her for a few hours, but she has already made a wonderful impression on me."

When Madhu came to pick them up that evening, Mark passed on the invitation, so Rahul was the only person Madhu had to entertain.

"Did you rest well, Rahul? It's hard to fly straight from the States to India. You should try to take a day off in Europe before commencing your journey. You can ease your jet lag that way. I do it all the time."

"Yes, we could have done that," Rahul said, "but we're short on time. Besides, Mark has other commitments at the office." Gathering his courage, he finally asked Madhu, "May I ask you a question in confidence? I can understand if you don't want to respond to it."

Madhu did not seem surprised. "Yes, sure," he replied soberly. "Listen, we're friends. You can ask me anything. What's on your mind?"

"You were going to tell me something about Julie at the office," Rahul said gingerly. "Can you tell me what it is now?"

"I told you that Julie is a close friend of my sister," Madhu said. "But there is something more. She was married once before, but her husband got killed in an accident. She is a very private person now." Madhu paused. "Why are you asking these questions? You aren't interested in her, are you?"

"Shouldn't I be?" Rahul asked. "Do you think she's seeing anyone or interested in anyone?"

Madhu replied hesitantly, "Not that I know of."

"Why don't *you* have any interest in her?" Rahul asked with curiosity. "I know you like her. She respects you. Is there anything you want to tell me?"

"There is nothing more to tell. I like her as a friend. She is a very warm and good-hearted person. As I already told you, she is a close friend of ours. My sister and I are a year and a half apart in age. Julie, my sister, and I all went to the same school. My sister thinks that I had a crush on her back then. But I believe it was simply an infatuation."

"What else can you tell me about her?" Rahul asked.

"You sound so interested in her."

"I'm simply curious. But if I'm interested, is there any objection?"

"Not that I can think of," Madhu responded

"What else can you tell me about her?"

"Nothing in particular. But let me tell you, if you are interested in her, you should approach her with caution. She is a widow and may be reluctant to commit to anything. Otherwise, she is a wonderful person."

"This is my sister, Aarti's, residence," Madhu said, pointing at a building. "We have to give her a ride to the restaurant. I hope you have no objection."

"No, none at all," Rahul replied.

They drove into the parking lot of a tall skyscraper. Many Mumbaites preferred living in high-rise buildings because of the lack of space on the island. The building was located en route to downtown Mumbai from the north. Parking for the residents and visitors was on the ground floor and was guarded by a watchman. Even at that evening hour, the elevator was run by a liftman in a uniform.

Soon after Madhu rang the bell on an apartment door, they were greeted by a slender, pretty young lady, who was introduced by Madhu as "my lovely sister, Aarti Bole." The living room had a balcony with a view of the Arabian Gulf at a distance. The household servant brought some snacks, but Rahul preferred a glass of wine, which was fruity in taste and had supposedly been vinted locally.

Aarti joined them and said, "I'm sorry that my husband will not be joining us this evening. He is out of town."

"You have a lovely place," Rahul said.

"Thank you. We like it, especially its close proximity to my mother. You know she is not well, so she likes the fact that I visit her frequently and spend a good deal of time with her."

"I know, and I understand," Rahul said.

Aarti said to Rahul, "By the way, I've requested one of my friends to join us for the evening. I hope that is okay with you."

"That's perfectly all right," Rahul replied.

As they were sipping their drinks and talking about their likes and dislikes regarding the big city, Julie came in and sat on a chair near Rahul. Madhu offered her a glass of wine from her native town of Goa.

"Are you familiar with Mumbai, Rahul?" Julie asked, trying to start a conversation.

"Well, somewhat," Rahul answered. "I've been here before, but that was a few years ago. I can see so many changes since then. New buildings, more traffic, and, of course, very crowded streets. As I said, my aunt lives in Juhu Beach. I hope it hasn't changed much. I haven't been to see her yet, but I'm sure she has many stories to tell."

The restaurant was located at the Worli Sea Face.

"By the way, if you and Mark are free over the weekend, you can go to town," Madhu said. "I can suggest some places to shop. And if you are not keen on shopping, you can go to the Elephanta Caves. Unfortunately, I have a previous engagement. I'll tell you a short story about Hindu mythology. The famous *trimurti* of Elephanta, which shows the three faces of Shiva, almost looks like the trinity of Brahma, Vishnu, and Mahesh. You know, the name 'Elephanta' has a funny history. The word is supposed to have been derived from a Portuguese word regarding the violent storms that occur at the onset and at the end of the monsoon season. Furthermore, the elephant is the symbol of the Hindu thirteenth lunar mansion, or *nakshatras*."

"I've heard about it, but I'm not good at the religious chronicle," Rahul said. "Furthermore, you may recall that Mark is leaving for the States late on Friday night. I'm here for a month and would love to explore."

Julie said, "Excuse me for interrupting, but I have to go to town on Saturday to pick up an item for my mom. Why don't you go with me? It will be fun!"

"That's all right with me," Rahul said. "But I don't wish to impose on you."

"No, that's okay," Julie said. "I can pick you up at your hotel on Saturday morning."

"That's wonderful. But I'll be going to my aunt's place in the evening."

Julie was glad to hear that he was free and was willing to go with her. "That's fine," she replied. "I would be happy to be your guide. I trust you would enjoy more sightseeing in the city rather than spending time at the shopping malls. I don't think you are the kind of person who is fond of visiting boutique stores." She paused. "By the way, have you ever been to the Elephanta Caves?"

"No, not that I remember," he answered. But even if he had, he would not have admitted it anyway, since he wanted to spend time with Julie.

"They are across from Mumbai Island. People take a ferry to reach the caves. Wear light clothing—it might get warm in the afternoon. Well, it's all set. I will pick you up on Saturday, early in the morning." Julie was confident that Rahul would really enjoy a trip to the Elephanta Caves.

But Rahul had other reasons to be elated. Spending time with her was the highlight of his trip to India.

It was a long drive back to the hotel, and it was almost midnight when his hosts dropped him off. He was fast asleep within a few minutes, with a smile on his face. When he woke up, it was close to three in the morning. He tried to go back to sleep, but he lay in his bed and stared at the ceiling, his mind wandering to Julie. He was very attracted to her and wanted to get to know her better. He could not wait for the weekend, and it was only Wednesday morning. Three more days to go—an eternity.

By the time he went back to sleep, it was after four. A phone call from Mark at seven woke him up. "Meet me downstairs for breakfast," Mark said. He was already eager to start the day and finish the job at hand.

CHAPTER 21

Waiting till Saturday was simply torture for Rahul. To overcome his boredom, he watched TV and found nothing interesting, except local MTV. He packed his luggage and got ready to check out of the hotel in the evening to move to his aunt's residence. He attempted to sleep but had a restless night.

When Rahul opened his eyes Saturday morning, it was still dark outside. He heard birds chirping. It was five fifteen. He stayed awake, got ready, flipped TV channels to pass time, and waited in the hotel lobby for Julie to arrive.

She was at his hotel at seven o'clock sharp, dressed casually in designer jeans and a crimson silk blouse. She looked ravishing— but then again, she always did. Soon after breakfast, they were on their way to catch the ferry to the Elephanta Caves. It was a bright day with a light breeze. The ferry to take them to the Elephanta Caves was small and cramped, but it was stable and cozy.

Julie said, "Hope you are enjoying this so far. We will be there shortly. Look at the Gateway of India. It looks gorgeous from the sea. Behind it, you can see the famous Taj Mahal Palace hotel. If we make good time, we can have lunch there on our return."

"Julie, I really appreciate your taking time out of your schedule to spend time with me," Rahul said.

"It's my pleasure. I don't get to spend much time with friends and acquaintances."

The waves splashed across the side of the ferry, making some passengers wet. But everyone seemed to think it was fun.

"Please tell me more about your family and friends," Rahul said to Julie. "What do you generally do with your time off? I'm sure you have friends you go out with."

Julie realized what this conversation was leading to, but she responded anyway. "I was born in Goa and live with my mother. My father died when I was about ten years old, and I only have a faint memory of him. He was a very loving person and enjoyed eating and drinking. After his death, my mother brought me up. She is the principal at one of the convent schools. I believe I have had a very good education, and I graduated from law school about three years ago. Then Mr. Sethia and Madhu asked me to join their firm. Well, that's all about me," she added. "How about you? I have heard a good deal about you from Madhu."

"Madhu and I had a great time during our graduate work," Rahul said, smiling. "My parents came from Kanpur. My father graduated from the Indian Institute of Technology, simply known as IIT, and then joined MIT. Currently, he is a staff member at MIT, after working for many years in the industry. He is a brilliant man, and I hope to measure up to him one day.

"My mother studied in India to be a teacher, but never worked in the States," Rahul continued. "Instead, she decided to stay home, educate me, and help me during my school years. She is very loving but is a typical traditional Hindu woman.

"I was born in Kanpur, but now I'm a naturalized US citizen. I spent my childhood and school days in Boston and then moved to Houston, where I attended Rice University. I have a wonderful and respectable job in Houston." Rahul smiled and looked at

Julie. "And today, I'm having a wonderful time with an attractive young lady."

Julie blushed. "Thanks for the compliment. I am enjoying your company too. Madhu told me about your friend Tom. Tell me more about him."

"Well, Tom and I are friends from high school in Boston. I attended Rice University, whereas he joined the University of Houston. He is a great athlete and played basketball for the college team." Rahul paused. "He is different. How can I put it? He likes male company."

"So he is gay. Is that right?"

"Yes."

"And he does not mingle with women."

"Right again." Rahul realized that he wasn't telling her the entire truth about Tom, that he was not just gay, but bisexual. But that was unimportant.

"Madhu also tells me that he has many bad vices."

"Let's not delve into his personal life, please," Rahul said uncomfortably.

"I won't. Do you have any female friends?" she asked.

That was an abrupt question, he thought. But he liked it because it gave him an opportunity to ask her other direct questions, some of which he already knew the answers to, and some he didn't.

He answered her with a laugh. "I have many friends who are female, but I haven't had a girlfriend so far. I just haven't found one yet. Maybe it's because I was too busy at school before, and now I'm too tied up at work." He wanted to say he was already working on it, but held his tongue.

"Madhu tells me that you knew Tom's cousin well. What's her name . . . Dominique?"

"Well, well. Madhu told you a lot about me. She is at Stanford and comes often to Houston. I find her bright and intelligent. We are good friends, but not serious about marriage."

"Yes, Madhu keeps talking about you. He finds you very challenging and compatible."

"I did not know I had such a wonderful well-wisher. What else did he say about me?"

"Nothing much. You are a good person and have a bright future with the company you are working for, etc. But he does not have a high opinion about Tom."

"Yes, I could gather that. But he never told me about you. I wish he had."

"There is nothing to tell."

"He could have told me, 'A gorgeous girl works for my company, and you should meet her.'"

She laughed loudly. "You are funny."

Rahul looked at her. "Julie, I'm wondering why a girl as beautiful as you does not have a close friend. Perhaps you already have one."

Julie suddenly looked sad. "I did have a wonderful childhood and school days," she answered, looking down. "Then I went through a dark period for a short time, but I think I shouldn't bring it up right now. We are having a lovely time, so let's enjoy it."

"Julie, please tell me!" Rahul insisted. "I would like to know. While we're having friendly conversations to get to know each other, you shouldn't be afraid to tell me deeper and darker things."

Julie hesitated before replying. "I had a friend in college. His name was Vikram Anand. We got married when we turned twenty-one. We did not get his parents' approval because I was not from his caste. They lived in a small town in Punjab and were very conservative. Vikram was an air force pilot, and we moved into an officer's residence near Delhi. One day, he went on a mission and never came back."

Rahul looked at Julie in sympathy.

"We were very much in love," Julie continued. "It was a total disaster for me, and I could not cope with the loss. Vikram's parents never called me to allay the grief of losing my husband, but my mother came to visit me as soon as she heard the news. We packed up the house in Delhi and returned to Mumbai. I enrolled in law school, and after getting my degree, I got a job and began working. I wanted to close that part of my life, except for my close relationships with Madhu and his sister. It has only been about five years, and I'm still trying to get over the pain. My dreams were shattered, and I don't have the strength and courage to build another relationship like that again. I am simply too afraid to lose it. Initially, I hated Vikram for leaving me alone in this world. But now, when I think about it, I am very proud of his conviction and sacrifice for the country."

"I'm sure you are," Rahul asserted.

Rahul saw anguish in her eyes. She was a lively and vibrant woman, yet she simply broke down in front of him. He understood her pain and hated to bring it up. He put his arm around her shoulder and tried to console her, offering her a handkerchief. She wiped her tears and gave him a smile, as if nothing had happened.

"I'm so sorry," Rahul said.

After a few brief moments of silence, Rahul gathered his courage to open his mind to her. "Julie, you have to get on with your life. You are still very young, and your whole life is ahead of you. I understand that you have had a horrid incident in your life, but that doesn't mean that you should curb your enthusiasm about the future."

Julie looked at him skeptically.

"Let me be frank with you," Rahul said. "I like you—and if you like me, I would love to be your friend, or perhaps even more than a friend. We should be able to find common ground between us. I'm sorry that you had to experience the social disparity inflicted by his parents. We cannot change such things overnight, but there is always hope." He paused. "If this project with Madhu goes through, then I'll be back here soon for a longer stay. Otherwise, I can always come and visit you."

With these comforting thoughts, Julie again smiled. "You are different, Rahul. I like you a lot. But we are not a couple of teenagers. We can't get emotional about how we feel about each other. Surely you can understand that. I would certainly like to be your friend, and I hope you will do the same. You have my e-mail address, and I will respond promptly, I promise. Okay, let's go to the caves!"

They were approaching the pier and got off the ferry. Elephanta was a beautiful sight, depicting ancient Indian history. Weatherwise, it was very warm, as it was almost noon.

They returned to the Gateway of India and headed straight for the Taj Mahal Palace hotel, which was buzzing with tourists and businessmen. The cafés and restaurants were crowded, so they decided to wait at the Sea Lounge to grab a sandwich.

"If you like, we can go and see a Bollywood movie," Julie suggested.

"No, I don't follow Hindi very well, and the stories in those movies are never all that clear. But I guess among several paeans in the Bollywood movies, there might be a story somewhere."

"You don't like movies?"

"Of course I do. My favorites are action movies, especially ones featuring James Bond."

Later that afternoon, they returned to the hotel, slightly exhausted.

"Why don't you come in for a moment?" Rahul asked. "We can have a cup of coffee or tea."

She looked at her watch and replied, "Only if it doesn't take much time. I need to go home."

"It shouldn't take long." Rahul wanted to be with her as long as he possibly could. "Any plans for tomorrow?"

Julie looked at Rahul with a naughty grin. "You want me with you all the time, don't you? I enjoy being with you too. But my mother will start wondering what I am doing all day." She smiled. "Tell you what. Tomorrow after the church sermon, my mother and I will go to the cemetery where my father was buried. It is the fifteenth anniversary of his death. Why don't we have lunch at my place at one o'clock? Or, if you want, you can come to church with us, and then we will have lunch after that. I will cook something special for you—a Goan dish."

Rahul said it was fine with him to go to church with them, as long as he wasn't intruding on their privacy.

"You don't mind going to church? I had a friend once who followed a different religion, and she bashfully opposed going to church with me. She always told me that her family would never approve. I didn't mind. Everyone is different, and some cannot have an open mind."

Rahul did not know what to say. "Well, people follow various paths and beliefs. But to answer your question, I would be happy to go to church with you, if I'm not taking up your time. It's your day off, and you may want to spend time with your family."

"That's no problem," Julie said. "My mother may probably know about you by now, and she would be delighted to meet with you. Every mother wishes that her daughter would bring a charming prince home," she joked.

"In that case, I'll be good and try not to disappoint her," Rahul affirmed. "By the way, I'm checking out of this hotel soon, and I move in with my aunt today. They should have returned from their trip. I have to call my cousin to come and pick me up.

"Julie, you have been a perfect hostess. I believe you need a raise from Madhu. I'll tell him that." He was smiling.

"I could use it," Julie said, smiling too. "So call me when you get settled, and give me directions so I can pick you up tomorrow." Julie waved and left.

When Rahul checked his messages at the front desk of the hotel, he saw that his cousin Vic had called, so he picked up the phone and dialed Vic's number.

"Hi, Vic. How are you?" Rahul said. "I'm back at the hotel and will check out. What? No, I'll wait for you in the lobby. You don't need to park your car. I'll see you in an hour. Bye."

Rahul returned to his room. His mind kept wandering about his time with Julie. *Was it a love at first sight?* All his life, he had never experienced anything like this. He felt like a teenager who was fascinated by the girl of his dreams.

Over the years, he'd had a few female friends, but he had never felt any attraction for them. He felt something different for Julie. The closest he had come to liking a girl in the United States was Tom's cousin, Dominique, barring his encounter with a hooker in Las Vegas.

He hoped that Julie liked him, but there were minor inequalities between them. She was a Catholic, devout or not, and he was Hindu, albeit not a conservative one. His pondering mind had now built big castles of hope that soon started to shatter at the thought of Julie's possible denial.

As far as his parents were concerned, it would be easy to convince his father, but his mother's response might be unfavorable. In the past, he never had any occasion to talk to them about this, and he did not know how they would react. Nevertheless, he was sure that his parents were not going to go against his will and happiness.

He gave a last glance at the room and left to go to the lobby to wait for his cousin.

CHAPTER 22

Rahul had not seen his cousin in almost four years. As soon as Vic arrived, Rahul greeted him and jumped in his car to go to his aunt's home.

She was happy to see Rahul and gave him a big hug.

"Let me look at you, Rahul," she said. "You really have grown up to be a gentleman." Introducing her children, she said, "You have met your cousin Vic. This is Sonja. You probably remember them from your last visit to Mumbai."

Rahul said, "Oh, that little Sonja has grown up a lot. I liked it when she always kept her mouth shut to hide her braces. Does she still talk much?" he teased.

"You will find out soon," his aunt said, smiling. "You may know that Vic works for a multinational company in their marketing department. Sonja just started a new job at an insurance company. Vic is happy in his work, but I don't like it. He is always on the road. He should stay in one place so that he can settle down one day."

His aunt was in her late fifties and about five years older than Rahul's mother, and she closely resembled her. She was a strong-willed woman, and after the death of her husband, she raised her two children and educated them well.

Vic and Sonja were in their twenties. Vic was tall, had a ponytail, and wore glasses. Sonja, on the other hand, was of medium height, slim, and followed the Bollywood fashion well.

"Why don't you go to your room?" his aunt asked. "We will plan for the remainder of your stay in India. I'm sorry that we had to go out of town to attend a wedding before you came. But we are here now, and I'm so happy to see you." She paused. "So how are my sister and your dad? I heard that she had a minor heart problem."

"She's fine," Rahul replied. "I haven't been to Boston for over six months. But I still talk to them frequently." He started to narrate the family gossip and broke off the conversation at an opportune time, asking his cousin to bring him to the guest room.

After leaving his aunt behind, Rahul went to his room, escorted by his cousins. When he looked out the window, he could see the sea under a hazy sky. It was breezy but moderately pleasant.

"This room looks different than I remember."

"Yes, we have remodeled the entire space. It's more functional than before."

"That's great. I like it."

Unpacking his luggage, he gave each of his cousins nicely wrapped packages. "I know you had a birthday last week," he said to Vic. "Here is a small belated birthday gift for you. Hey, Sonja, I haven't forgotten about you. Here is something for you too. Hope you like it."

"That's interesting. You remembered that we were both born in October."

"You know my mom," Rahul said. "She has a daily calendar and reminds me of every occasion."

While they were unwrapping their gifts, Rahul said, "Vic, I need a favor. Can you give directions to someone over the phone and tell them how to get here?"

"Sure, no problem! It's very simple. Where is he coming from?"

"First of all, it's not a *he*. It's a *she*. I don't know where she's coming from."

"Hey, cuz!" interrupted Sonja. "Who is she? Where did you meet her?" She then left the room to answer her mother's call.

"Hold on just a minute! She's just an acquaintance. I met her at my friend's office. Listen, Vic, I'll call her, and you can tell her how to get here."

Rahul picked up the phone and called Julie. She answered and said, "Hi, Rahul! Can I pick you up tomorrow at ten in the morning?"

"That's fine. Here's my cousin Vic. He'll explain to you how to get here, okay?"

Vic gave her the directions in detail and hung up. Rahul told Vic how and where he had met her and what he thought about her, without yielding further details. He also explained that he was spending Sunday morning and early afternoon with her and her mother.

Sonja asked sharply as she walked in, "So, cuz, what's going on? Who is she? Where did you meet her?"

"Listen! I told you that she's just a friend. Nothing more! I met her only a few days ago." He paused. "Hey, are there are any florists around here?"

"I'll get you a bouquet of flowers from a shop across the street," Sonja said sweetly. "You have to make a good impression with her folks, don't you?" Sonja kept kidding around with Rahul.

Leaving the room, Sonja smiled and said, "Mom, Rahul won't be here for tomorrow's lunch. He has a *date*."

"Oh!" Rahul's aunt said. "I was planning a get-together in the evening with our relatives and friends. You will be free in the evening, won't you?"

"I'll be here," Rahul answered.

"This girl . . . is she someone we know?"

"No, Auntie, she works at my friend Madhu's office. She took me to the Elephanta Caves yesterday."

Rahul's visit to Mumbai coincided with the *Diwali* festivals, a Hindu festival in which everyone—male or female, young or old—was in great euphoria. At dusk, houses and trees were brightly illuminated. Although lighting firecrackers was prohibited in the city, they were heard with loud intensity at a distance, and often very nearby. Even at dawn, they were still heard sporadically.

Rahul woke up early, got ready, ate breakfast, and used his cousin's computer to send e-mail messages. Julie arrived at about nine thirty, and he invited her into the living room. She was dressed up in a nice dark suit with a matching purse and shoes.

After a brief introduction, she said, "Rahul, we should get going. I still have to pick up my mother."

Her charm and charisma were overwhelming, and she instantly received admiration from his aunt and cousins for her manners, style, and beauty.

Sonja was not ready to let them go. She wanted to get to know Julie better and said, "You have to promise that you will spend more time with us on your *next* visit."

"I sure will," Julie assured her. "But right now, we have to go, or else we will be late."

Vic winked at Rahul and gave him a thumbs-up, admiring his choice in women. They soon left to take Julie's mother to church.

Rahul was a Hindu by birth. He went to Hindu temples on occasion with his parents, but never got an opportunity to attend any Christian churches or masses except for weddings or other special events. However, ever since he was young, he had been curious to find out about other cultures and religions. A Sunday mass was not something new to him, but he wanted to find out more about Julie, her family, habits, hobbies, and religious convictions.

Within thirty minutes, Julie pulled up in front of an old, traditional building, and Rahul got out of the car to greet her mother. People from this building and those surrounding it were walking down the street toward the church. He assumed that most of them were of a Christian faith. Her mother was already waiting outside, chatting with an elderly couple. Julie introduced Rahul to her mother, Mary D'Silva. He presented her with the bouquet of flowers, thanking her for inviting him.

Mary was in her fifties and was graciously attractive like her daughter. She spoke perfect English, and her command of the language was stunning. But then again, she had been an English teacher for over twenty years. Weariness was apparent on her face. The untimely death of her son-in-law had saddened her, and on several occasions, she had tried to convince Julie to start her life over. But there was finally a glimpse of hope in her eyes today.

Mary started the conversation. "Usually Julie does not go to church with me every week. My late husband passed away fifteen years ago today, and we think about him a lot. Julie doesn't have much recollection of her father, as she was barely ten years old when he died. He loved her very much. My husband drank a lot, but he never was abusive or intolerable," Mary continued. "Julie used to go to the bar, wait for him, and bring him home. God bless him!"

When mass started, the priest began to narrate verses from the Bible. The chapel was full of parishioners, who were humming along with the padre's preaching.

Rahul got lost in his thoughts. Here were two ladies, a mother and a daughter. Both had tragic events in their young lives, one in the twilight of her life and the other while she was just beginning to blossom into womanhood. In spite of their losses, they had not lost any respect for their religion or fellow human beings. Rahul sat quietly and observed the church service. It ended sharply an hour later, and they left to go to the car, leaving her mother chatting with fellow church members.

Many acquaintances looked at Julie and Rahul with curiosity. A few inquisitive friends asked Mary about them, but she avoided their questions with her usual charm.

"Did you like the service?" Julie asked Rahul. "The priest is very well-known in this community."

"It was nice. I've been to services before with my friends, especially for weddings. But I don't think I was ever up this early on a Sunday to go to a church or a temple."

"I also don't go to church as often as my mother wants," Julie said. "After Vikram's death, I started going to church more frequently than ever before. It just gives me strength to continue with my life. By the way, I am sorry to have awakened you this early on a Sunday."

"I was the one who wanted to go to your church and the cemetery to pay respect to your father," Rahul assured her. *Maybe I should just pop the question and ask for his daughter's hand in marriage*, he thought to himself.

As soon as her mother joined them, they were on their way to the cemetery, where Julie and Mary cleaned the grave, laid out fresh flowers, lit a candle, and quietly prayed for a few minutes.

Rahul observed this ritual with interest and realized how much they must have loved him.

They arrived at Julie's residence a little after noon. The place was small, but neat and clean with no signs of extravagance. It had a living room, balcony, kitchen, and a couple of bedrooms. In the corner, he could see a small dining table that had been nicely decorated. Julie offered him a drink and brought out light snacks. She sat next to him and asked if he was nervous.

"Why should I be?" Rahul said. "I'm with you."

"Well, if I were going to meet *your* parents, I would be!"

"No, not really. I haven't come here today for you to introduce me as your groom. Your mother seems to be a very affectionate person, and charming too. But I'm selfish and would rather be with you alone." He smiled.

Mary entered the living room. Rahul took the opportunity to say, "Thanks for inviting me, Mrs. D'Silva. I didn't want to impose on you like this. Julie has been very hospitable since I've been here. And when she invited me, I couldn't refuse a chance to be with you both."

Mary grinned and said, "We're happy to have you with us. We will eat shortly. I understand from Julie that you're a vegetarian. She cooked especially for you. Goan dishes are very popular, but they tend to be hot and spicy. I certainly hope you can take spicy food."

Rahul's mother cooked at home, and he often complained to her that the food was too hot or spicy. But today it was neither. The food had a distinct flavor and aroma that he had not experienced before.

"I have prepared everything vegetarian for all of us," Julie said. "Hope you like it."

"It's wonderful," Rahul said. "I cannot pinpoint where this taste comes from. It must be typical of Goan food."

She nodded.

After having a wonderful time, Rahul returned to his aunt's residence late in the afternoon. Julie did not feel it was fit to meet his aunt now and told him that she would call him later.

"Is it okay for me to infringe on your time for a few more days? You know that I'm leaving in a month, and I don't know when we will meet again. I wish I didn't have to go." He had become so fond of her that he couldn't resist asking.

"Of course I will see you again. Just call me either at the office or at home." Julie smiled gently.

"Julie, may I ask you something personal?"

She hesitated and asked, "What's on your mind, Rahul?"

"Are you seeing anyone now? I mean, do you have any friend you go out with?"

"You mean to ask whether I have a prospective boyfriend, is that it? The answer to that is no. I don't know why. My mother wants me to go out with a young group of friends. But I am not ready yet."

He spoke again somewhat warily. "After knowing you, I feel lonely without you, and I've known you for only a few days." After a brief pause, he added, "I hope I'm not out of line. This is how I perceive things, without even knowing how you feel about me."

Julie sighed and responded in a gentle tone, "Rahul, aren't we moving too fast for a relationship?"

"I simply hope this isn't a dream. I like you a lot. You're different from many people I've met. As I look into your eyes, I believe that you are a sensitive and sincere person."

"To be honest with you, I like you too," Julie said. "But my life is here. I have my relatives, friends, and other responsibilities. I can't just quit and move on. You and I live almost ten thousand miles apart. We hardly know each other. I think we both need time to think about us. We simply can't jump to any conclusions—we are not teenagers anymore."

"I like you, and you like me," Rahul replied. "Isn't that enough? Everything else will fall into place once we start to know each other well." Rahul was pleading.

Julie smiled and said, "You have the perfect argument for an arranged marriage. But you have to understand me. I am afraid, scared stiff."

"You know my feelings for you. I like you, and I hope you like me. I'm not suggesting anything yet. When I'm with you, it gives me enormous strength and the courage to go out and take on challenges in my life."

"Listen, I can't give you an answer yet. I need some more time to think it over. I need to run, but I will call you later." Her car sped away down the street.

But Rahul had seen the sadness in her eyes, and the last thing he wanted to do was to make her unhappy. He felt bad about it and decided to call her and apologize for making her feel so dismal.

CHAPTER 23

Rahul's aunt and cousins were waiting for his arrival. They had invited a few relatives and friends for the evening, some he knew personally and a few whom he only knew by name.

His cousins swarmed him as soon as he entered the residence. When his aunt left to go to the other room, Vic and Sonja began inquiring about his relationship with Julie, asking how he had spent his time with her and her mother, and what they talked about.

"Nothing serious," Rahul said to them. "We just had a good time." He retreated to his room, with Vic following him.

Rahul reluctantly started to tell Vic the details as Sonja entered the room. "You know, I haven't known Julie for long, but I like her a lot. I hope she likes me too. During our short courtship, I've become serious about her. I hope our family supports me in my decision, whatever it may be—provided, of course, Julie agrees to my proposal, and I hope she does."

"Isn't it too soon for you to feel this way?" Vic asked.

"What is an appropriate time for courting, Vic?"

"There is no hard-and-fast rule about it," he said. "But I'm sure that you will hear this from many people."

"I don't care about them," Rahul said. "Listen, I don't have the luxury of staying here longer and spending more time with her. Within a month, I am gone. Then what?"

"You know what?" Vic interrupted. "You should do what your heart says. I guess that even after a long courtship, people still make mistakes. It all depends upon your compromising and indulging nature."

While thinking out loud, Rahul said, "The problem may arise with my grandmother. She is very conservative and may not even consent to my marrying Julie. I don't care, but at the same time, I don't want to hurt her feelings either."

"Cuz, why are you putting the cart before the horse?" Vic asked. "Why don't you and Julie decide what you have in mind, and then the rest can be worked out? Don't try to build castles in the air."

"You're right. I'll do just that. Julie and I need to sit down and talk it over with each other." Rahul paused and smiled. "Julie is a breath of fresh air. She instills an extra confidence in me. She gives me strength. I've only met her recently, but it seems that we have known each other for a long time. We appear to have many common interests. She respectfully listens to me, and I do the same. When I'm with her, I don't see or hear anything else. I simply feel her."

"That's wonderful," Vic replied. "I agree with you that she is really a beautiful and stunning person. I wish I would meet one just like her. Do you have any other reservations about her or her family?"

"No. None whatsoever!" Rahul answered. "And she isn't seeing anyone else at this time either. I've rarely seen a combination of beauty and brains. She has it all. She is very compassionate, emotional, and open-minded." He became lost in his thoughts. "I need to think about how I should approach my mom and grandmother."

"You mean to say that you never had any discussions with your mom about your girlfriends or who you like?"

"This topic never came up before. But I'm sure they'll bring it up as soon as I go to Boston next time."

There was a distinct silence for a moment.

"Well," Rahul said, "I should invite Julie out for dinner to reciprocate her hospitality."

Vic said, "It's *Diwali* time, and I suggest you invite her to our home. That way, we all may have a chance to meet her. Listen, I know my mom. She will definitely welcome her. I'm pretty sure that Julie made a good impression on her when they met briefly."

"Isn't it too early for me to invite her to meet my folks?"

"Well, she did take you to meet her mother."

"I think that was different."

Rahul said after a brief pause, "All right, I agree with you. But I have to find out if she is serious about our relationship before I leave for the States in a few weeks."

"I envy you," Vic replied. "I've been here all my life, and I've yet to come across a beautiful and talented girl like Julie. You come here for a few days and catch a gorgeous nymphet. Just how did you do it?" Vic obviously admired Julie's beauty.

"You will meet one someday, Vic. The thing is, you can't really look for her. You'll simply meet her out of the blue." He paused. "All right, then I'll talk to Julie and we will plan an evening here with her accordingly."

As they left the guest room, Auntie was coming toward them. "So, Rahul," she said, "did you have a good time today with your friend?"

"Yes, thanks!" Rahul answered. "She prepared wonderful Goan vegetarian dishes for lunch. She's a good cook."

Vic interrupted and asked, "Mom, why don't we invite her for an evening with us? It's *Diwali*, and we will have a nice dinner.

What do you think? Maybe Rahul *Bhaiya*[2] will get serious about getting hitched."

Amid her curiosity and exhilaration, Auntie looked at Rahul and asked, "Are you both serious?"

"No, Auntie," Rahul said. "Vic is just kidding. I like her, and I believe she likes me too."

"Then why don't you invite her to visit us on Thursday evening, Rahul? You might as well also invite your friend Madhu and his sister."

Rahul's aunt had met Madhu earlier when he came to visit Rahul and had gotten to know him and his family.

"I'll certainly do that. Auntie, you don't think I'm simply rushing into a relationship or something?"

"That perception you will have to judge for yourself, Rahul. She appears to be a decent and nice person. It's up to you to decide what's important in your life. Time will tell whether you will be happy together under one roof. But we in Asia have learned to be more tolerant and compromising."

"Thanks, Auntie," Rahul said, admiring her wisdom.

---

[2] *Bhaiya* is a typical suffix in many Indian languages to address an older brother or to show respect for another person. Here, it was humorously applied to the same age group. Indians have learned to respect their elders and usually address them as "uncle" and "auntie" in suffix form, unlike Western languages. This guideline may apply in general even to strangers.

Chapter 24

The following Monday, Julie saw Madhu in his office, talking on the phone. She knocked on his door and sat down in front of him.

"You seem to have something on your mind," Madhu told her after finishing his conversation on the phone. "What is it?"

"Madhu, I need your advice," Julie said. "I have a dilemma."

"I could guess that. I was just talking to Rahul. He explained everything to me and asked for my opinion. I believe that's what you're going to ask me about. Am I right?"

"It appears that I am an open book. Yes, Madhu. I am confused, very confused. He proposed to me yesterday. Not in so many words, but he indicated that he wanted to further our friendship into a relationship."

"How do you feel about him?" Madhu asked her in a steady tone.

Gulping her coffee, she said, "I like him. He seems to be an honest and sincere person. But I have only known him for a few days. Madhu, I can't build a relationship over a short encounter. I have failed once before, and I am afraid now."

"What do you want me to say?" Madhu asked. "All I can give you is my candid opinion." He paused a moment. "You know he is a good friend of mine. He is a decent human being, and he is moral and deeply compassionate. It's now up to you to decide about this relationship. If you have any reservations about it, tell him openly. He is a very emotional individual, so please don't play games with him. But he is also persistent and tries hard to get what he wants. He is rarely excited or mad unless he has a reason."

"Anything else?" Julie paused. "Madhu, I don't know what I should do."

"I am hardly in any position to advise you. This is a very personal matter. Looking at all the circumstances, you have to do what is best for you."

"Thanks for your advice, Madhu," she said, leaving his office.

CHAPTER 25

"Hey, how are you, Madhu?" Rahul said to his friend on the phone later on Monday. He asked if there had been any response from Mark about the progress with the project initiation from Houston.

"No, not yet. It's only been just over a week since Mark left. You know things don't move quickly in the corporate world. However, I've received a few changes for the memorandum. Julie is looking at them now."

"That's fine," Rahul said. "I was just curious. By the way, my aunt wants to invite you and Aarti on Thursday evening for the *Diwali* function. I hope you can make it. I need to call Aarti, but I don't have her telephone number. Could you please give it to me?"

Jotting down the number, Rahul said, "Thanks."

"Anything else?"

"No, not that I can think of."

"Okay, I'll see you on Thursday."

~~~

After finishing Madhu's call, Rahul called Julie.

"Hi! How are you?" asked Julie.

"I'm fine. Lonely though."

"You're among your relatives," she said. "How can you be alone?"

"Nevertheless, are you busy?"

"Well, I've been working on your contract. And I can tell you that your people in Houston are demanding. I hope they appreciate my suggestions." She was referring to his employers, who were known to drive a hard bargain.

Ignoring what she said about the contract, Rahul asked, "Julie, do you have some time to have lunch or dinner with me?"

"When?"

"How about tomorrow?"

"Let me see," Julie said, looking at her calendar. "Tomorrow I'm free for lunch and, as a matter of fact, for the whole afternoon. What did you have in mind?"

"I just want to talk to you and be with you. You may also help me buy a few gifts and curios for my colleagues in Houston, if you like."

Hesitantly, Julie said, "All right. I'll pick you up at your aunt's residence at eleven thirty in the morning. Is that okay?" She remembered Madhu's words that Rahul was quite persistent.

"That's perfect," said Rahul. "See you tomorrow."

~~~

She arrived at eleven thirty in the morning to pick up Rahul at his aunt's place.

"Hi, how are you?" Rahul asked. "How was the rest of your weekend?" He paused. "So did you have a chance to think about us?"

"What is there to think about?" Julie replied. "I hope you are not proposing. Are you?"

149

"Do you want me to? I'll do it right now. I'll get down on my knees and ask for your hand, if that suits you." Rahul tried to act like he was joking, but deep down he really wasn't.

"Well, I can't let you propose to me without a ring, and it had better be a diamond one," she joked. "You know what people say—diamonds are a girl's best friend."

"Okay, let's buy one. Why waste time?"

"You are out of this world, aren't you? Are you trying to take advantage of me?"

"I'm simply trying to help you to make up your mind," Rahul said patiently. "You know I'm going to pop the question, sooner or later."

Staring at him, she seemed to struggle for words.

"Listen, Julie! I came here, met you, and got to know you a little better. I did *not* come here to fall in love. It just happened. I'm very fond of you, and you know that. Unquestionably, you are a beautiful woman. Anyone can see that. But what really amazes me is your wit and wisdom. You are full of energy, and I am convinced that you will make someone very happy, so let that someone be *me*! So help me God, I'll do my best to make you a happy woman. My utmost wish is to spend my entire life with you."

"It had better be when we are truly ready," she said. "There's no rush to get to the altar." Julie was avoiding his flattery.

"Well, we have a few days left, and anything can happen. I wish I were staying here, but I'm not. I don't want to lose you."

"You won't, Rahul. At the same time, we cannot afford to make a mistake." Julie paused. "We know very little about each other. Don't you think we need to take some more time? What would your parents say about the short courtship? Actually, if they're moderate to conservative, as you say, what makes you think that they haven't selected a bride for you already?"

"That, I don't believe. I don't think they would do anything without consulting me. To tell you the truth, my dad is quite open-minded. It's my mother who may have dreams of her own. We are the ones who should decide whether we know and like each other or not. I wish I had known you for a long time. Unfortunately, I didn't have that privilege, but I don't regret it. We are mature enough to speak out now if we need a longer courtship. People still make mistakes. We could be making a bad move, but we will never know unless we try. You are exactly the type of person I've been looking for, the kind I have always hoped to comfortably spend my life with, being her best friend.

"I don't remember whether I told you already what I like about you. Okay, here it is. You are an intelligent, decisive, and stunningly attractive person. You have all the womanly qualities that every man dreams of. Most of all, I realize that, in addition to your beauty, you are a considerably brilliant person. I know that I'm not making a mistake," Rahul assured her. "I hope you feel the same."

Julie was undoubtedly moved by Rahul's remarks and was gaining confidence in him.

They drove for a few miles until they came across a small shopping mall. There were boutiques selling wooden and metal artifacts, clothing, bangles, and other local and imported items to attract local shoppers and tourists.

"What do you think I should get for my mother and aunt?" asked Rahul.

She laughed and said, "I don't know them, so I don't know what they like. If you have an idea, I can suggest some items."

"Well, that's a start. You can help me buy something for Sonja. She and you might have similar tastes."

After some carefree purchases, she drove him to his aunt's home.

"By the way," Rahul said, "my aunt and cousins wish to have an evening together. If you have no objections, would you come for dinner at her house on Thursday? You know it's *Diwali* on that day."

"Why are they inviting me for dinner at your aunt's place on *Diwali*?"

"It's just a courtesy for inviting me to your place last Sunday. Besides, it just happens to be a holiday. My aunt is a lovable person. On her behalf, I've invited Madhu and his sister. I presume it's simply a social evening." He paused. "Well, I may warn you. She has a peculiar way of asking personal questions, and it's up to you to respond the way you see fit."

Julie asked, "Do you think your aunt wants to know about me? It makes me nervous, and I'm quite a novice in such social gatherings."

"Well, I'm not sure. But I'm going to introduce you as my friend, like Madhu and his sister. But she may judge that you are more than a friend."

"Are you serious?" Julie said. "Shouldn't we talk more before we let people jump to any conclusions?"

"I thought I made it very clear to you what my thoughts are. All I need is for you to agree. Julie, I like you very much and I want to develop our relationship into more than a simple friendship. I hope you don't have any objections."

"No, I don't. But that's not the point. I think we had better not make any hasty decisions. Shouldn't we wait for a while?"

"Time, I don't have. All right, let me suggest something. I'm leaving in a few days. We'll stay in touch until my next visit. We will have enough time to think about each other, and I hope it will give us some more time for our relationship to mature. But we will remain friends and be honest and open with each other. Is that all right?"

Julie thought to herself. *He really is persistent, as Madhu said he is.*

"I like that and think it's worth a try," Julie answered. "I will certainly miss you and your company."

"I know that I'll miss you too." Rahul looked at his watch. "It's getting late. We should go home."

CHAPTER 26

By nature, Rahul was a hardworking man, and sitting idly at his aunt's home was not something that he enjoyed. Vic and Sonja had gone to work, but he didn't feel like disturbing Madhu and Julie. His aunt was hardly any company for him. Suddenly, he thought of his cousin Suresh Kumar, a.k.a. Suri. His not-so-reliable and nonchalant cousin was probably free.

Rahul wasn't familiar with the city of Mumbai. Nevertheless, he took it as a challenge and decided to go see Suri in South Mumbai, which was in the busy downtown area.

After catching a taxi, Rahul was on his way to town. When he reached their meeting point, he didn't see his cousin. He would have to wait for him, just as he expected.

Waving his hand out of a taxicab, Rahul's cousin Suri glanced at him and said, "Is that you, Rahul Sharma?"

"Yes. Are you . . . Suri?"

Suri nodded. "All right. Get in the cab."

"You are looking good, Suri," Rahul said as he slid into the taxi. "We haven't seen each other since we met in Kanpur at the wedding. You remember how we were naughty and went to town on a bus?"

"How can I forget?" Suri said, laughing. "You got me a spanking by Grammy."

Rahul kept looking at Suri. He had grown tall and robust since Rahul had seen him last at his father's sister's wedding. His flashy attire was reprehensible. He wore a Versace shirt, Ralph Lauren sunglasses, and Gucci shoes. And he showed off by wearing a Rolex watch and cologne that had a pleasant fragrance. It looked like he was walking out of a mall in Dubai.

"I have a small import/export business."

"I would have guessed you would have driven your own car here instead of taking a cab."

"Well, my Benz is at the shop today," Suri answered.

After a brief chat about the family and various friends, Rahul asked, "Where are we going?"

"I have a place in mind. It's too early to eat. I have to run an errand. Let me finish that. Okay?"

Rahul was somewhat uncomfortable as they entered a bar. Its inadequate lighting, loud music, and foul smell made him a little nauseated. Even at that early hour, a few drunken customers were making rude remarks about the half-clad waitresses.

"Suri, this place is kind of crappy. Why don't we go someplace else?"

"Sure, in time! I have an appointment here." Before he finished his sentence, two rough, dark, and heavy guys joined them.

"Hi, Suri," one of the men said. "Where in the hell were you? We were looking for you."

The other guy addressed him as "Aftab."

Suri got up and grabbed him by his collar. "*What* did I tell you?" he yelled angrily. "My name is Suri. What? *Suri!*"

"Okay, okay, I'm sorry, boss."

The other guy said, "Let it go, Suri. I will see to it that it won't happen again."

Rahul just watched this drama unfold and was somewhat shaken up. Suri got up and said, "Rahul, let me take care of some small business, and then we will leave." He signaled to the waitress to take care of Rahul.

When Suri came back, he had a bundle of rupee bills hidden in his hand, which he shoved into his pocket.

"What are all those?" Rahul asked.

With a roguish smile, Suri said, "That's income from my business."

Rahul lost his appetite. But just to be social, he and Suri had lunch in a restaurant near the Churchgate area.

"I have to run after lunch," Suri said. "Can you make it to Juhu on your own? Don't get lost like you did in Kanpur."

Rahul got in a cab, but his mind was on Suri. There was something peculiar about him. He was not only secretive but also authoritative. He had heard from his mother and his aunt that Suri was the black sheep of his family, and now he believed that it might be true. But eventually, Rahul put these thoughts to rest.

~~~

Suri grabbed a cab and asked the driver to go to an address that made the taxi driver shudder. As soon as he got out of the cab, he went into a dark alley and walked to a dark, shabby house, which appeared to be heavily guarded.

"Hello, Saleem. Is *Bhai*[3] here?"

"*Assalamu alaikum! Bhai* is waiting for you."

Suri was well-known in the area and in that circle.

A bearded person let him in. Suri saw a person sitting on a sofa, sipping his tea and talking on his cell phone. He asked Suri to sit beside him on a chair.

"Welcome, Aftab-*miya!*" To his colleagues in the underworld, Suri was known as "Aftab Ali."

---

[3] A don or a leader of a gang is known as *Bhai*. This term also means "brother."

"Greetings, Ismail-*bhai*. Welcome to India."

Ismail Peshawari was a notorious criminal and a terrorist. He was on the wanted list of criminals. Yet there was no bounty on his head. He was accused of having a hand in murdering Western visitors and diplomats in Pakistan, and he had a close tie with the Taliban in Afghanistan. He was a very hard-hearted and vicious criminal, yet no Western agency had any proof of his illegal activities in their countries. The Central Bureau of Investigation (CBI) of India was on a constant lookout for him. But he had escaped very swiftly every time.

"Did Suleiman explain to you why I want to see you?"

"Yes, he did, *Bhai*."

"We have found out that your cousin Rahul Sharma works for a company whose detail and design of—what they call—yes, ZRQ, we are very much after," Ismail said after reading from a dirty chit of paper from his pocket. "I heard you had lunch with him today. Can he get it for us?" Ismail's voice was stern.

Suri hesitated and said, "No, Bhai, I don't think so. He is very naive and dedicated to his company and the country, so there is no chance. We have to find an alternative way to get it."

"What do you have in mind?" asked Ismail.

"I can't entice Rahul to do anything illegal. But I've found out that one of his close friends, Tom Spencer, is a loose cannon. We have a very good chance of tapping him. Rahul trusts him and listens to him. If we get Tom to work with Rahul in his department, Tom can steal the data for us. But we have to spend a good deal of money."

"That's no problem," Ismail said.

"Tom has a nasty habit of gambling and is usually in debt. Currently he is heavily indebted to a casino in Las Vegas. We can lure him to work for us by paying off his debt. He also enjoys drinking, fast women, and drugs."

"So what do we do now?"

"I'm already ahead of the game," Suri answered. "I made a point to meet this Tom Spencer in Las Vegas. I used our contact, Andy Waters, to introduce me to him, and then I started working on Tom—I bought him a few drinks, gambled with him, and chased women with him. In other words, we were with him in the fast lane. Then I urged him to get Rahul to Las Vegas with him. I asked Andy to spike his drink and get him with a hooker."

Handing over an envelope with indecent pictures of Rahul and a hooker, Suri said, "This is just in case we ever want to blackmail Rahul into doing something. But I strongly believe that we will have a better chance of working through Tom."

"Wonderful!" Ismail said. "Can you go to Las Vegas and arrange all of this? I will go with Mohammed Johri and Syed Akbari and meet you there when you say so. I hope we will get what we want."

"One more thing, Bhai. Please don't hurt Rahul. He is my cousin. We will get what we want, one way or the other."

"Don't worry about it. Your cousin is my cousin," said Ismail pretentiously. "Here," he added, handing Suri a stack of bills. "Keep the fifty thousand dollars. You will need it in Las Vegas. I'll get more. Tell Suleiman about your plans. *Khuda Hafiz!*"

Suri left.

"You know what, Saleem? We fight for a cause. These Hindus, like Christians in the West, do it for money. They don't have any morals and would sell their mother for money. We will win ultimately. You know what our mullah said? We must eliminate anyone without any remorse who gets in the way of the fight for our cause, whether he is our brother, father, or friend.

"They have a democracy—that's their weakness. They fight among themselves, and no one has time to worry about us and what we are up to. As long as the money keeps coming in, we can do what we want. Before too long, believe me, Saleem, we will have a man in the White House. Our Saudi brothers will definitely help us. Then we will turn their world into an Islamic nation. *Insha'Allah!*"

"*Bhai*, can we trust this Aftab?" Saleem asked. "After all, he is a Hindu."

"No, we can't. But right now, we need him. When the time comes, I will personally deliver him to the CBI."

CHAPTER 27

Dressed in a classy solferino Indian sari, Julie entered Rahul's aunt's house at eight on Thursday evening. She brought a box of sweets for the family, a gift that was appropriate for the occasion of *Diwali*. Rahul didn't notice when Madhu and his sister, Aarti, arrived to join them for the evening. Julie artfully started her conversation with them, and as far as Rahul could figure, her beauty, charm, and finesse overwhelmed his aunt.

They had eaten their food and were now relaxing comfortably, enjoying the cool evening breeze from the gulf.

"What did you do today, Rahul?" asked Madhu.

Before Rahul responded, Auntie said, "He went to see his cousin Suri this morning."

Rahul told them about his meeting and Suri's flashy look and flamboyancy. "It was funny," he said, "one of his associates called him 'Aftab' or something, and he got raving mad. I don't know why."

As everyone was engrossed in conversation and gossip, Madhu signaled to Rahul to go with him to the balcony.

"Rahul, how well do you know your cousin Suri?"

"This is the first time I've seen him in fifteen or twenty years. Why do you ask?"

"You mentioned that his associate called him Aftab and he got mad."

"What's wrong with that?"

"The local CBI is looking for a big-time criminal named Aftab Ali. No one has seen him, but his network is large—his business empire encompasses the entire neighboring region. The way you described him . . . well, are you sure that he isn't involved in any illegal activities?"

"Madhu, are you pessimistic, or is something else bothering you?"

"Rahul, it seems that you are too naive. The world is not as simple as you see it."

"You also warned me about Tom, didn't you?"

"Yes, I did, but please watch out for Suri. His association could be extremely dangerous and deadly, but I can't prove anything right now. Be careful, and watch your back."

"I probably won't see him again before I leave for Houston anyway," Rahul said.

They left to go inside to join the conversation while Rahul shook his head in disbelief.

When they returned from the balcony, Auntie asked, "How is your mother, Madhu?"

"She is all right, but she has her on and off days. We have a full-time nanny helping at home and looking after her."

"I assume that you are still not married."

Aarti replied hastily for Madhu, "No, he is *still* available. In spite of several of my requests, he is still alone and staying with my mom. I wish I could help him more, but he refuses."

Madhu ignored his sister and said, "By the way, I have an announcement to make. Rahul's company has accepted our proposal in its entirety, and it's likely that Rahul's trips to Mumbai will be more frequent."

Rahul and Julie knew about this and weren't surprised, but his aunt and cousins were boundlessly happy.

Auntie said, "Well, that's great! It gives us a chance to meet with him often. Well, Madhu, you have to help find a suitable bride for yourself. I hope our Rahul does the same." She seemed to be clueless about the attraction between Rahul and Julie.

"He may have already *found* one," Vic said in a barely audible voice, referring to Julie.

"My nephew is very shy and docile," Rahul's aunt continued, not picking up on Vic's comment. "His mother wishes that he find someone, and she is ready to help if he hasn't yet."

The wonderful evening came to an end, and everyone dispersed.

Rahul went with Julie to her car and said, "You did well. I'm proud of you. If all goes well, I would like to propose to you on my next trip, and we can get engaged to be married, if you are willing."

Julie said, "I guess your aunt doesn't know that you are courting me and trying to propose to me."

"I'm sure she does, but I'll bring her up to date." He gently squeezed her hand, which he had been holding in his, and gave her a nod of approval and affection.

She tapped on his cheek gently and said, "You'll be all right." She blew him a kiss and drove off.

There were some anxious folks at his aunt's place. Everyone wanted to know about Julie and if Rahul was serious about her. There was a moment of silence before Auntie asked, "You are very fond of her, aren't you, Rahul?"

"Yes, Auntie, I am. Very much so, in fact! We like each other a lot," Rahul admitted openly. "But I need your help to convince my mom that she is the right one for me. She may object, since Julie is not a Hindu. But I doubt it."

"Is that all?" Auntie asked. "Well, that's no problem. She is, after all, an Indian, and you both like each other. Don't you?"

"Yes, we do," Rahul said. "But there is one other problem."

"What's that?"

"She was married before. Her husband was killed in an accident."

Auntie sat quietly for a moment before she spoke. "Your mom may object that she is a widow. But it's not the girl's fault that her husband was killed. She can't just waste her life because of one little mishap. She is a very nice and cultured girl, and I'm sure she will make you very happy. Of course, your mom and I care about your happiness and joy. You have my blessing, son!"

Speechless, Vic and Sonja looked at their mother with great pride. They had never experienced this tender side of their mother, and they realized that she really cared about their well-being.

Rahul could not help wondering about how his aunt, who was not an educated person, had more wisdom than many other relatives he had encountered, including his own mother.

CHAPTER 28

After bidding farewell to his aunt, cousins, and friends, Rahul was ready to leave Mumbai after his wonderful monthlong stay—but not before he had intimate moments with Julie. They were sad to part but happy with an anticipation that he would be back soon.

The journey back to Houston was an exhausting one. After a long and tedious journey, he was about to land in Houston. Clearing Immigration and Customs, he exited and saw Tom waiting for him and waving to get his attention. It was Sunday afternoon, and the traffic was light.

"How was your trip?" Tom asked as soon as they were seated in the car. "How did it go?"

"Very well. I enjoyed it very much. I met my relatives and cousins after not seeing them for a long time."

"So who's this girl Mark keeps telling me about?" Tom asked abruptly.

Rahul was astounded at his question. "So! Mark has been talking," Rahul said. "Why am I not surprised? It's very premature for me to talk about it yet. I just wanted to break it to you personally. Julie D'Silva Anand works for Madhu," Rahul continued. "She is a legal counsel for them. She's a slender and beautiful girl, the kind you fall in love with at first sight. We spent a wonderful month together, and they were the most amazing hours of my life. Tom, I am in love."

Tom said loudly, "I am glad for you, my friend."

When they reached their apartment, Rahul handed Tom a token gift he had brought for him and showed him Julie's picture.

"Wow! She's beautiful," Tom said. "I can understand why you fell in love so fast. Tell me more about her. I'm sure she must be a fascinating person."

Rahul filled in the details about her, her family, and his visit to India. "Every time I went to India in the past, I spent time with relatives and friends. But this time, it was different. I wish I could jump right in and go back. I hope she can be with me soon. Tom, I miss her already."

Rahul called his parents as soon as he returned to Houston and told them he was coming to Boston over the weekend. He also told them that he had a very important matter to discuss, and he left them guessing. Then he called Julie in Mumbai.

"Hi! How are you?" Rahul said. "I miss you very much."

Julie had the same response. She sounded happy that he called but sad because he wasn't with her. Rahul said, "I'm going to see my parents over the weekend, and I'm going to tell them about us. I hope you're ready for the commitment."

There was only silence on the other end of the line.

"Are you still there, Julie?"

"Yes, I'm here. I hope we're doing the right thing. Our relationship grew so quickly that I'm afraid. Are you sure we're doing this right?"

"Julie, please don't start that again! I can't show my sincerity any more than I've already done. You'll have to believe in me. I love you so much that I will protect you at any cost."

"Yes, Rahul. I know. I do trust you. But I don't trust myself."

"Listen, let it be," Rahul said. "Whatever will happen will happen! We'll tackle it at that time. Please put these thoughts behind you, and have faith in me."

"I'm all right," Julie said. "Please call me and tell me what your parents say after you see them."

"Be brave! I'll talk to you soon. Good night. Love you!"

And he hung up the phone.

~~~

Mary D'Silva knocked on her daughter's door and entered to see if she was awake.

"I thought you might be asleep," Mary said.

"I'm reading a book. Can't sleep yet."

"Julie, may I ask you a question?"

"Yes, of course."

"I noticed that you like your friend Rahul. Are you serious about him?"

Julie looked at her mom. "Why do you ask? We hardly know each other."

"He is a good boy."

"Mom, are you trying to fix me up?" Slightly annoyed by her mother's statement, she said, "Yes, I like him a lot. I liked my first husband too. What's your point?"

"Don't be mad at me, dear. I am your mother, and I like to know how you feel about all these things. You were very relaxed and happy in Rahul's company. You brought him home to be with us, and you spent a good deal of time with him during his visit to India."

"Sorry, Mom." Moving her head into her mother's lap, she said, "I'm lost. I don't know what to do."

"You can tell me. Maybe I can be of some help." She gently rubbed her fingers along her daughter's cheeks.

"He asked me to marry him. As I said, I like him a lot, but I don't know him. What should I do?" She paused. "He is sincere and honest. He is very bright and will make his bride very happy.

His parents will most probably support his decision. I can't decide what I should do."

"Don't promise Rahul on the rebound," Julie's mother said. "You must love him and be certain that's what you want to do. But let me remind you of one thing. In their Hindu society, marriage to a Christian widow is not universally accepted. It's a bitter truth, but a reality." She paused. "Rahul appears to be a person of good character and judgment. You should go with the choice you feel the most strongly about. However, Rahul may eventually want you to move to the States. It may be good for you—you need a break from this place and your horrifying past. Of course, I would hate for you to leave me, but you must get on with your life. Now go to sleep. It's very late."

CHAPTER 29

A couple of days later, Mark knocked on Rahul's door at the Houston office. "Hello! Wake up, Rahul!" he said jokingly.

Rahul, a little embarrassed, looked at him and answered, "Oh, it's you, Mark. I was busy looking at my mail. Plus, I'm fighting jet leg."

"I'm kidding," Mark said, drawing a chair close to his desk. "What's new in Mumbai? Are Madhu and his team ready to accept our workload? In the beginning, and even later, we'll have to be very careful. Our continuation depends on their performance."

"I think they'll be ready when we are. I'm now collecting data to see how much work we can deliver."

"That's great. I've also compiled a list, which you should go over carefully." He paused. "By the way, how did you do with Julie?"

Bashfully, but with a sparkle in his eyes, Rahul responded, "We had a great time. She conveys her best wishes to you." Smiling, he added, "Mark, I'm in love. I love her so much that I almost proposed to her. I find it hard to be without her. It's up to her to make up her mind. Is that what happens when you're in love?"

Mark smiled and patted him on the back. "It's normal. Well, if you work on our list, you can be with her shortly."

"Thanks. By the way, I'm leaving early on Friday for Boston to see my parents."

~~~

That evening, Rahul called Julie at her office. "How are you, Julie?

"I'm fine. How was your trip back?"

"Fine, but I miss you very much."

"I feel lonely too, Rahul."

"I'm leaving for Boston on Friday. May I have your permission to ask my parents about us?"

There was a break in the conversation.

"Julie, are you there?"

"Yes, I am here, Rahul. You asked me the same question just two days ago. But don't you think we're rushing into a decision?"

"No, I don't think so. Well, my question still remains. Do you want me to ask my parents?"

"I am willing to accept it if you promise never to leave me. Never! I'm scared."

"Not in your lifetime! As long as I'm alive, I will never abandon you. I love you, Julie. Can't you see that?"

"I love you too, Rahul."

"Is there anything else you want to tell me?"

"I can't think of anything else at the moment. Please call me from Boston, all right?"

"Okay. Sit tight and enjoy the day. By the way, Mark told me that I'll be with you very soon. I'm short-listing the project. My regards to Mama! Say hello to Madhu."

As they hung up, Rahul felt relieved that a big monkey was off his back.

The cold and wintry Friday did not prevent Rahul's dad from picking him up at Logan Airport, even with the increased traffic because of the upcoming weekend. He had come to the airport directly after work. On the way home, he asked Rahul how his trip to India was, and Rahul replied that it was very enchanting. Rahul decided that this was a good time to bring up the subject of Julie, as he wanted some time to chat with his father alone first before bringing up the topic with his mother.

"Dad, I need to talk to you before we get home. Can we stop somewhere for a cup of coffee?"

Curious, his father agreed and stopped his car at a newly opened café on the way. Usually calm and collected, his father was extremely eager to find out what his son had to say. He parked the car, and they were seated at a table in the corner.

"So what's on your mind?" asked his father.

"Dad, you are more of a friend than a father to me."

"Yes, I know," replied his father.

"I'm in love, Dad," Rahul said bashfully.

"Someone we know?"

"No, she works at my friend Madhu's office in Mumbai. Something unusual and sensational happened. I met her and found her very enchanting. It just happened. So I wanted to talk to you both before we take the next step."

"That's nice," his father anxiously interrupted. "Please tell me more about her."

Rahul was now losing his shyness. "Her name is Julie D'Silva Anand. She's twenty-five years old, a Catholic, and her family is from Goa, but she lives in Mumbai with her mother. Her father died when she was ten years old. She is a law graduate and is currently working as a legal counsel at Madhu's office."

"Son, I have confidence in you. I realize that she is not a Hindu. But that does not matter to me. You have to lead your life in the best way you see fit. The only thing that matters to me is that she can and will be a part of our family." He paused. "But one thing that puzzles me is what you mentioned a while ago. You said her name is Julie D'Silva Anand. I don't understand that. I do recognize D'Silva as a Christian name, but Anand is a Hindu name. What is the connection?"

Rahul was stunned by his father's perception. "Dad, there is something else I need to tell you. There was a pilot in the Indian Air Force whose last name was Anand. While fighting the insurgents at the border, he was shot down and presumably killed. This happened about four or five years ago. Julie was formerly married to this Captain Anand."

"Does she have any children?"

"No."

His father kept sipping the coffee without lifting his eyes. He looked around, and after a while he said, "I truly am sorry that she had such a tragic incident in her early life. That's terrible! I hope she has found comfort despite her grief." He looked at Rahul. "You know that I have faith in you and trust your decisions. Do you love this girl? Do you think that you are making the right move?"

"Yes, Dad, I do—on both counts."

"Rahul, I'm sure she is a wonderful girl. How about her? Does she have the same feelings for you as you have for her?

Rahul smiled. "Yes, she does."

"Son, I have not met her. Nor do I know much about her. Your mother and I want you to be happy, and we will be more than happy to welcome her into our family. Ideally, we would have loved to have met her before you propose to her, but under the circumstances, I can understand."

"She is a really nice girl, and we are very honest about our relationship. Madhu and his sister know her well. Besides, Auntie, Vic, and Sonja have met her too and speak highly of her. Of course, I have not had a long courtship with her, but I'm very confident that she and I will be very happy together. Actually, it was her idea, and I hope to get your and Mom's permission and blessing before we go ahead with our plans."

Vasu realized the magnitude of his son's affection for this girl of his dreams. He was not going to disappoint him in any way. "Mothers are different, and she may have many questions when you get home. But she will be with you all the way. She may be disappointed that she did not have a chance to meet Julie before you proposed to her. All we want is for you both to be happy."

"I have not officially proposed to her yet—well, not directly, but in a roundabout way. But I plan to do it the next time I visit India. All we want now is your blessing to go ahead with our plans. But I'm very concerned about Grammy. You and I know that she is very conservative. She still follows old Hindu creed and caste systems. When I go and tell her that my wife-to-be is a Christian, that will be hard for her to chew, but when I further tell her that she is a widow, I think all hell will break loose."

"You may be right, son. But we will have to face it one way or the other. She loves you very much, and you may use it to your advantage. Don't cross the bridge until you come to it."

"If Julie is agreeable, then we will get married without any reservations. But Julie wants our wedding to be harmonious and peaceful. She knows that there may be a few hurdles, but we will have to cross them together. Julie really wants a wedding where she can wear her wedding gown and walk down the aisle on the arm of her uncle."

His father smiled and winked at him, expressing his full support.

Rahul was glad that he'd had this chat with his father, and as soon as they finished the coffee, they headed off to his parents' home. His mother was waiting anxiously at the door.

"Was the flight on time?" asked his mother as soon as they entered the house. "Why are you late?"

"Everything is fine, Asha," Vasu assured her. "It was just the Friday evening traffic."

She hugged her son affectionately. As most mothers do, she looked at him from head to toe.

As they were seated in the family room after dinner, Rahul started to describe his trip to India. His aunt and other relatives, his work, and his friend Madhu were the major topics of his story. Then he casually brought up the subject of Julie. Suddenly his mother's eyes twinkled, and the anxiety on her face eased, but it was replaced with intense curiosity. She now wanted to know all the detailed accounts of this girl, and any other topic was unimportant to her. It was a delicate moment for her son to reveal the full truth to her in a single instant, which was prudent.

"Mom," Rahul said, "I met a girl in Mumbai, and I'd like to marry her."

"What is her name? Please tell me more about her."

"Her name is Julie—Julie D'Silva. She works as an attorney in Madhu's office. We went out frequently and got to know each other well. On *Diwali* day, she came for dinner at Auntie's house, and I introduced her to them." He retrieved a picture of Julie. "Here is a recent picture of her. Would you like to see it?"

Asha said, "Yes, of course." She put on her reading glasses.

Rahul gave the picture to them. Both his parents cuddled up together and looked at it with great interest. Asha viewed Julie's photo many times over.

"*Beta,* she is very pretty," Asha finally said with a smile on her face. "I hope you two will be very happy." Tears of joy were dripping down her cheeks, but she did not try to wipe them off. "Please tell us more about her."

Rahul told his mother everything that he had mentioned earlier to his father, but in more detail.

Asha said, "She seems so cute. I am sorry that she had such turbulence in her young life. But I am sure she has overcome that. Is she prepared to come here soon after your wedding?"

Rahul said, "I haven't asked her that question yet. But I assume that it should not pose any problems." Running to his room, he said, "I should call Julie before she leaves for the office."

Rahul quickly dialed Julie's number to tell her the news.

"Hello?" Julie said on the other end of the phone.

"This is Rahul. How are you? Are you ready to go to the office?"

"Yes. I am glad you called. So what did your parents say?"

"What do you expect? They were very happy. My mom saw your picture and fell in love with you."

"I am so glad. I told my mom about it last night, and she was extremely happy for two reasons. One, to get a son-in-law like you, who will take care of his bride, and two, for me to move on with my life." She paused. "Rahul, you don't know how happy I feel."

"How do you think I feel? Hold on for a minute, please." He walked into the dining room with the phone. "Julie, can you say hello to my mom? She would like very much to talk to you."

"What should I say?" Julie asked nervously.

"Just a few words! Okay, I'm giving the phone to her."

Asha took the phone and answered, "Hello, Julie, is that you?"

Julie answered, "Yes, Mrs. Sharma. I am Julie. How are you? I am very happy to make your acquaintance on the phone. I hope we will meet soon."

"My son is very proud of you. He is also very fond of you. Although I have not met you yet, I would like to welcome you into our family. My husband conveys his best wishes too. We are now no longer strangers and you can call us here in Boston anytime you like. All right?"

"Thank you very much," Julie replied. "I will definitely do that. It was my pleasure talking with you. May I please talk to Rahul?"

"Here he is," Asha said. "Bye!"

"My parents gave their blessing for our wedding," Rahul said. "Aren't you happy? I'm thrilled. I can't wait to be with you."

After Rahul finished talking to Julie, Asha said, "She sounds very sweet. I like her and can't wait to meet her. Maybe we can go shopping together."

~~~

Marriage was such a big social obligation. It was important that none of their relatives or friends be left out. But the number of wedding invitees easily could have climbed into the hundreds.

Rahul indicated to his parents that he hoped to go to India within a short time, and if the time was right, he would like to propose to Julie and possible marry her.

The wedding was to take place in India, and Rahul's aunt took it upon herself to make all the arrangements according to the preferences of Rahul and Julie, which were yet to be determined.

Having nothing to do over the weekend, Rahul went out to meet with his friends Joey and Renee. They were happy for him and promised that they would attend his wedding, even if it was held in India. He ran into Dr. Spencer and his family in an elevator at their condominium. When he told Dr. Spencer about his matrimonial plans, the doctor wished him well with the wedding and married life. He suggested that he keep in touch with him and his family.

Dr. Spencer very much appreciated what Rahul had done for his son and was forever indebted to him. He asked Rahul if he thought that his daughter, Jessica, looked like his half sister.

Rahul said, "There is a slight resemblance to Tom. He will be happy to know that."

Joyce was as lovely as ever. Rahul thought that Tom would be happy to know that he had met Tom's father and his family, even though the meeting was short and sweet.

A young man was launching a life of responsibility and commitment. But he was looking forward to the challenge. His dreams were becoming a reality. He could not leave Julie out of his mind for a single moment; he was so much in love. He kept thinking, *Can anything go wrong? Certainly not!* Otherwise, it would destroy him emotionally. He was sure of their mutual commitments. She was not the kind of girl to walk away from the altar. Besides, Madhu and his sister spoke highly of her. Auntie and his cousins liked her even though they had only met her briefly.

Rahul's parents were making plans for the wedding in India, which was a huge responsibility. They were located almost ten thousand miles away from where the wedding was to be held, and they quickly began calling around Mumbai to get the ball rolling.

"Dad, hold off for a while," Rahul interrupted. "I have yet to propose to Julie. She and I have agreed to get married, but I have to be honest in our relationship and diligently ask for her hand in marriage. I'll call you when we are ready. The company has assigned me to work temporarily in India, and they'll set the date of my departure. From there, we can plan accordingly. Eventually, I'll have to delegate my authority to someone else, as the company may want me to work on other major projects in Houston. When that happens, I may not have as many chances to visit India as I do now."

~~~

As Rahul's parents were driving him to Logan Airport for his flight back to Houston, he said, "When we decide on a wedding date and rituals, I hope you will be ready to leave for India. I can't keep going to India that frequently, so I believe that we should take this opportunity to be in India at the same time."

"Don't worry about a thing," his mother said. "We will handle everything. We were going to take our vacation in India during the upcoming winter, but it would be our pleasure to be there to facilitate this wonderful occasion. I talked to my sister yesterday, and she is so excited about our trip that she wants us to arrive at least a couple of months earlier. We might do that, unless, of course, you want us to be here."

"No, you do what suits you the best," Rahul suggested.

The flight to Houston took a little over four hours, and as usual, Tom was at the airport to pick him up.

"So how did it go?" asked Tom.

Rahul jokingly said, "It seems that either you or I will have to look for a new apartment."

"Hey!" Tom said excitedly. "Listen, I'm so happy for you. When is the big day? I'll be at your wedding, wherever it is. I'm sure you're going to invite me."

"Of course! You know what? I met Joey and Renee, and both of them agreed to attend my wedding, even if it's in India. And it likely will be. You're going to be my best man, so you have to be there."

"Man, it will be fun. Tell me more about Mumbai. I have never been in that part of the world. Yes, I was in Australia, but that's different."

"I will, I will. Later! Oh, by the way, I talked to Andre. Man, he is very incoherent. I don't know what's wrong with him," he said.

"Yes, I know. He is not happy in New York."

"I met your dad in the elevator. Jessica is growing up to be a doll. I thought she looked a bit like you. Believe me, I'm not kidding."

"I have been told that," Tom said. "She's very nice, and I'm fond of her. Not like her mother!" He paused. "I want to tell you about Andre in strict confidence. Please don't tell anyone what I'm about to say. I talked to him only last week, and he's very sick. He's suffering from AIDS, and he might not even make it. That was the primary reason that they moved to New York. Since I've known about it, I've been very devastated and careful about whom I hang around with. It's a dangerous game for homosexuals, and for heterosexuals, as well. You never know when the disease will strike you. You just have to be careful. He's one of my best friends, like you and Joey. I like him very much, and I still talk to him on occasion. I truly feel sorry for him."

"I'm truly sorry for him too," Rahul said. "I sincerely hope he makes it. It must be hard for his parents though." He was deeply saddened by the news.

As soon as they reached their apartment, Rahul checked his mail and paid the bills, which had been piling up for some time. They ordered pizza to go, and Rahul hit the hay, whereas Tom left to meet with his friends. Lately, Rahul did not know where

Tom was going or who his friends were. Rahul was busy with his daily routines, and now he was even more so. He had to plan his trip, and most importantly, he would shortly have a partner in his life.

CHAPTER 30

Monday at the office was a busy day. Collecting and gathering data took longer than anticipated. Logistics were harder than usual. But Rahul took time to respond to Julie's loving e-mail. Another e-mail message was from Madhu, indicating that they had installed a broadband Internet connection, which meant that Rahul could make a video call to Julie and Madhu. He just wanted to see her smiling face. It was very comforting to him.

Later in the summer, Andre passed away, and Rahul and Tom made a weekend trip to New York. Tom was shocked and dismayed by his friend's death, but everyone close to him knew that his premature death was inevitable.

In the meantime, he made a couple of trips to Boston to meet with his parents. He noticed his mother's failing health.

"You have to take care of your health, Mom!" Rahul said.

"Don't you worry, my son! I am going nowhere without seeing you married."

He laughed and said, "I hope it will be soon."

~~~

Soon after Labor Day, Mark Garcia brought in a stack of files that contained the project layouts and program descriptions.

"Get going, Rahul," Mark said. "I hope you're not reminiscing about your time in India, especially with your friend Julie. By the way, how is she doing?"

Rahul quietly explained what their plans were. Ever since he had started working with Mark, Mark had become very fond of him and treated him as his kin.

"I'm so happy for you, Rahul," Mark said. "Now start the ball rolling with the project so that you can be with her shortly. We are aiming for you to leave for Mumbai during the upcoming month. Three of our junior staff members will join you on this trip and report to you. They will probably stay until the first phase of the project is completed. We will want a progress report once a week. I suggest you get going on this now."

"Yes, sir!" Rahul answered with excitement. "Is there any chance for Tom to join our team?"

"No, not at this time," Mark replied. "He isn't familiar with this project. Probably sometime in the future." He hurriedly left the room.

Now Rahul was counting the days when he would get a chance to meet his love again. He called his parents to inform them of his timetable. Then he called Julie that evening and talked to her for a long time.

Things were going so smoothly that Rahul wondered if everything was a dream. Time passed by quickly without any further incidents or interruptions. He called his team for an introduction and quick update on India. Mark was present, as well.

"Listen, guys, you all know me well. As you probably know, we are heading to India very shortly. It's a different culture and system. Things are as different as day and night. People are sensitive and proud of their heritage. Please back off if you feel you are offending them. Food will be different. I am sure you will get what you want but not always. Stay away from hawkers, and do not—I repeat do *not*—try any food or drink from them. It's okay to buy from the shops. And finally, keep an open mind and be bar-sensible."

"Should I carry any food item such as peanut butter, a Twinkie, or any snack food?" asked Jeff, one of the trainers.

"Yes, if you want to. But I don't find it necessary. You get almost everything in Mumbai at a cost. Oh, one important thing: carry your medicine, if you take any. Lastly, let me warn you. I want you all to be team players. If you have a problem with it, you will definitely be sent back. This project is vital to us. That's all, folks. Anything else, Mark?"

"I fully concur with Rahul, and good luck to you all!" Mark said before leaving the room.

All of them were young but mature enough to understand the job and its responsibilities.

~~~

Late in the evening in mid-October, they reached Mumbai International Airport, which was highly disorganized because of the heavy traffic passing through it. People were rushing to get through Immigration and Customs.

Somewhere nearby, Rahul heard a European tourist calling for a luggage porter.

"Hey, coolie, come here!" the man said.

Rahul went over to him and said respectfully, "Excuse me, sir, he is a *porter*, not a *coolie*. The word *coolie* is derogatory, given by the British when they ruled India. They are gone, and it is not proper to use it now. Thank you."

The tourist stood there, aghast, looking at Rahul, but did not say anything. A few people who were standing nearby looked at Rahul with amazement and smiled.

Clearing their way through an unruly and somewhat disorganized crowd, Rahul and his colleagues exited the airport.

It was a little past midnight. He saw Madhu waiting for them. The place was brimming with other people who had flocked to the arrival area of the airport to pick up their respective guests.

As Madhu was helping the porters load his car, Rahul came up to him and said, "Hi, Madhu, how are you?"

Rahul introduced all his colleagues to Madhu, and they took off for the hotel.

"Julie wanted to come, but I told her that it was very late in the evening and suggested she meet you at the office or your hotel. Hope you don't mind."

"No, that's all right. It's quite chaotic at the airport."

"She will see you in the morning at your hotel."

These Houstonians were not strangers to warm, balmy weather like Mumbai's, but the fatigue of travel was apparent on their faces. It was a mild cultural shock for a couple of his colleagues. Even at that late hour, the traffic was flowing slowly.

Jeff, one of Rahul's colleagues, asked Madhu, "Why do these drivers honk all the time? Is it some kind of ritual?"

Madhu smiled and said, "No, nothing of that sort. They're just used to it. The traffic moves at the same speed even if they don't do it. Noise pollution doesn't mean much here."

A strange-looking vehicle passed their car, and Jeff asked, "What's that? A three-wheeled, motorized rickshaw? I've never seen anything like that."

"Yes, that's the most economical and polluting mode of transportation for short distances. You will see it in most of the cities in India, as well as in the neighboring countries. The local government is about to enforce the use of cleaner fuel, such as CNG or LPG, rather than conventional gasoline."

"Amazing!" Jeff remarked.

People were crossing streets randomly, without obstructing the slow-moving traffic. Traffic was not restricted to motorized vehicles in Mumbai. There were peddlers moving their four-wheeled manually drawn carts, selling food or other consumable items; motorized rickshaws maneuvering through the traffic while exhausting fumes from loud engines; and bicyclists cruising the streets with ease. One wondered how the traffic even flowed at all. But they all managed well and had very few fatal accidents. There must have been some traffic laws in effect, but to many, they were not readily visible.

The American visitors observed the cultural, social, and economic variety around them. Elegant residences and shops indicated prosperity on one hand, while half-clad, barefoot children and adults exhibited extreme poverty. The country seemed perfectly indifferent to the people who were a part of its system. However, the country was striving hard to achieve economic freedom and welfare for all its citizens.

After Rahul checked in at the hotel, Madhu told him, "Listen, Rahul, I have rented a van for you all to move around. It comes with a driver. He will report to you in the morning and wait for you to get ready and come to the office."

"Thanks, Madhu. You better go home. You look tired."

"See ya in the morning." And Madhu left.

In the morning, when Julie came in to meet Rahul, they hugged each other and he introduced her to his colleagues. They all left to go to the office.

When Rahul was alone in Julie's car, he said, "I'm so glad to see you, Julie. You don't know how lonely it gets when I'm not with you. I missed you every single day I was in Houston."

She smiled and affirmed that she felt the same way. "I am happy that you will be happy here for a long time."

"No, I have come here to take you home with me to Houston. Are you ready?"

"By all means! But do you think we can accomplish all the formalities while you are here?"

"We have to try. But I am not leaving without you though."

"You are impossible, you know?" Julie said.

They reached their destination.

Lost in the time difference and cultural contrasts, the visitors tried to focus on their important assignments.

Meanwhile, Rahul remained preoccupied with his thoughts of Julie and life beyond. Nevertheless, he was an intelligent human being and demanded that the work begin, and he continued as quickly and efficiently as required. He noticed that Madhu had prepared a small area equipped with local staff and computer terminals in order for them to get acquainted with the work at hand. After a brief introduction, all of them got busy with their assignments.

In the evening, when Julie dropped Rahul off at his hotel, he insisted that they have dinner together. She hesitantly agreed. Today was a big day for Rahul. He was going to propose to her and get the monkey off his back. When she arrived at 6:00 p.m. sharp, he was waiting in the reception area. He asked her if she would mind going up with him to his room.

"Rahul, what's on your mind?" Julie asked in surprise. "You know that it isn't proper for me to go to your room."

"No! It's nothing of that sort," he assured her. "It is for a truly honorable reason. I want to talk to you in private, and that's the only place I can think of right now. Listen, you can trust me. We are both adults. You may walk out if you think I'm making any uncalled-for advances."

"No, that's all right. I trust you. I was hoping that I would enter your room only when you carried me over the threshold," Julie joked.

"If you wish, I'm ready to do so."

They entered his room, which Rahul had decorated with several flower arrangements. He seated her on the sofa and drew a chair near her with his fist closed. "Julie, I want to ask you a very personal question, if you'll let me."

"I can assume what you are going to say. But I want to hear it from you." Julie was now in a state of anticipation.

Rahul got on his knees, opened his fist, and presented her with the diamond ring in his hand. "Julie, will you marry me?"

It was a ring fitted with a large oval-shaped diamond, almost flawless, shining in the light coming through the window. She sat there motionless, looking at Rahul with moist eyes, and then extended her hand for him to put the ring on her finger.

She stared at the ring for several moments. "You have made me very happy today," she said. "I'm still scared of the future, but we need to take chances. Rahul, I love you so much, and I'll make you very happy." She hugged him passionately and kept holding him tight.

"I've chilled a small champagne bottle, which I've saved for this occasion," Rahul said, bringing out two tall glasses filled with the golden liquid.

"Cheers!" she said, raising the glass. "I like it already. *Mrs. Julie Sharma!*"

"You know what? I still have not asked your mother for your hand in marriage. I'll come by your home and do it soon. I should have done it before, but I couldn't avoid the temptation to hold you close to me. Is tomorrow evening okay?"

"Tomorrow is fine, and we'll go to my place straight from work," Julie confirmed.

"By the way, I hope you have not forgotten about joining me for dinner. I have invited my friends to be present," Rahul said.

Julie said reluctantly, "Well, it is okay. I need to call my mother to tell her that I will be late."

He then told her about the plans that were already laid out, and if she and her mother were agreeable, he intended to ask his parents and his aunt to proceed with the wedding ceremony. He explained to her that he naturally had limited time before he had to return home. Julie consented without any hesitation.

At around eight in the evening, when they went downstairs toward the restaurants, she saw familiar faces. In addition to his coworkers, Madhu and his sister Aarti, and Rahul's cousins Vic and Sonja were seated at one large table, waiting for the couple. Although Rahul had not told them about his proposal to Julie, they all seemed anxious to know the news of the day.

Before they reached the table, Julie said, "I thought I was the first to know."

"Of course you are," Rahul answered. "They don't know yet. They're simply here to join us for dinner. I'm sure they will be surprised when we tell them the good news." They approached the table.

The waiter brought drinks and menus. It was still too early for many Indians to have dinner, but they all accommodated their guests from abroad.

Shortly after Julie and Rahul were seated, he interrupted the conversation among his guests and said, "Friends, Julie has something to tell you." He turned the attention over to Julie with a wink. "Julie?"

With a gracious smile, Julie extended her hand, displaying a twinkling diamond ring on her finger. The rest was self-explanatory. Both the girls, Aarti and Sonja, screamed with joy and excitement, and all of them congratulated the new couple and wished them well.

This was like a dream come true for Rahul. Now he had to get the ball rolling by calling his parents and his aunt. He knew that time was limited, and he had to plan the wedding if his parents and relatives intended to have the ceremony in India.

Is this happening too soon? he thought to himself. *What if Julie isn't convinced that I'll make her happy? Will she ever get over her emotional attachments to her past?* He thought about these things for a while and then decided to discuss them with Julie in order to give her confidence.

~~~

Julie was more than happy to bring Rahul home to meet her mother. But today was special. She was bringing her Prince Charming home.

"Mrs. D'Silva, may I talk to you, please?" Rahul asked.

"Yes, of course, by all means."

"Julie and I love each other. May I please ask you for her hand in marriage?"

Mary looked at both of them for a moment and said, "Oh, this is wonderful. There is nothing more gratifying than seeing my daughter happy. I am so delighted to give you both my blessing." Mary was really pleased. She truly wanted Julie to put her dreadful past behind her by accepting Rahul. "I am certain she will make you very happy. On the other hand, I am sorry that she will leave me so soon. She was my sole emotional support and companion. But marrying you is the best for her, and that's what parents wish for." Latent grief showed on Mary's smiling face.

It was going to be a marriage between two people who had different faiths but insurmountable confidence. Mary had always dreamed of seeing her daughter in a wedding gown and felt that her wish was about to come true.

"Rahul, you know it breaks my heart to say that I can't afford an elaborate wedding," Mary confessed. "Julie's first wedding was in a court, and I was hoping to give her a church wedding. She's a good girl, and I am proud of her. She's turned into a responsible and virtuous woman. I wish I could offer more than just a small wedding and my good wishes."

"Mrs. D'Silva, that's not important," Rahul affirmed. "My only joy is to be a part of your family and spend my life with Julie. She means so much to me that I really don't care if we marry in a court, a church, or a temple. But my parents may want an extravagant wedding." Rahul continued, "They will probably want to show off, and I can't stop them. Our relatives and friends expect it. I don't believe that you need to reciprocate in any way. Besides, they will feel very grateful if you allow them do so.

"Logistically, it is ideal if the Hindu wedding follows the church wedding on the same day," Rahul continued. "I hope both locations are not far apart. I suspect that my parents will suggest a Hindu wedding in the afternoon and the reception in the evening at the same hotel where I'm currently staying. How does that sound?"

"That sounds like a perfect plan," Mary answered. "You know, Julie calls me 'Mama.' Now that you are going be a part of the family, why don't you call me that too? I would like it very much."

Julie was listening to this conversation and frequently staring at her ring, admiring it. It wasn't the size of the ring that mattered; it was the token of profound affection that was bestowed upon her by her lover.

Julie said, "We can ask Father Rodriguez if he will perform the wedding. I would like to invite a few of my friends and relatives for the wedding and reception. We will have a wonderful wedding. You've always wanted that, Mama."

"Yes, dear. I wish your father could have been alive to see you in a wedding gown. He would have been so proud of you." Wiping away her tears of happiness, she said, "I'll certainly talk to Reverend Rodriguez. I am sure he will be very happy. We can fix the dates after that. Is that all right?"

"Mama, that's understandable," Rahul said. "When you have the dates in mind, I'll talk to my parents. It's also important that you meet them." Rahul said this last phrase with emphasis to Mary.

~~~

Rahul called his parents in Boston later that day. "Mom! Dad! Are you listening? I proposed to Julie, and she accepted! I believe you should leave immediately for Mumbai and plan the wedding. As I already told you, I can't keep coming to India very often. So I urge you to arrange all the ceremonies you have in mind while I'm here for the next couple of months."

"First of all," Vasu said, "congratulations, son. I hope that you two will be very happy together. We'll leave as soon as possible to start planning the wedding. Is there anything else you need?"

"No," Rahul said. "Oh, one more thing. There will be a church wedding too. Please bring my tux. I'll see you both soon." And he hung up the phone.

Rahul was thinking happy thoughts about his upcoming marriage, wondering how his life would change. He called his office to tell Mark about the wedding. Then he called Tom. Luckily he got him in the apartment. He was still sleeping. Rahul said, "Wake up, man. Rahul here. Are you ready to come to India?"

"When? I am ready to jump on the plane right now."

"Hold your horses, Tom. We still have to fix the dates. But it should be soon. You get prepared. I will let you know. By the way, I talked to Joey and Renee. Can you also invite them on my behalf? It would be fun for all of us to be together."

"Will do, dude." And he hung up the phone.

CHAPTER 31

Rahul had promised Mark that he would oversee the work in Mumbai. Work progressed at Madhu's office, but Rahul's attention and supervision were sporadically absent. Fortunately, Madhu and his assistants took care of Rahul's leftover workload.

He invited Julie and her mother for an evening to meet his folks. Julie was a bit nervous to meet her future in-laws. But she had full faith in herself, and most importantly, she had faith in Rahul.

His aunt and cousins welcomed Julie and her mother. Julie was stunningly dressed in an Indian sari. It was simple, but it matched the rest of her attire perfectly. His parents watched her in awe and realized why their son admired her and was so much in love with her. Mary was also dressed in an Indian sari. Rahul introduced them to his parents.

Vasu broke the silence, saying, "I have to commend my son for his choice."

Julie replied calmly, "On the contrary! I am fortunate to have come to know Rahul. He is very gentle and caring, and my boss tells me that he is also very bright. Rahul says it must be in his genes." She smiled at Vasu and Asha.

Vasu was quite amused by her answer, and after a few conversational moments, he realized that she was an extremely bright person. "So he tells me that you are an attorney," he said. "Are you planning to be a corporate lawyer?"

"I like corporate law and its intricacies," Julie responded politely. "It presents a multitude of challenges."

Julie, Rahul, and his cousins retreated to the next room while the elders were busy discussing the plans for the marriage ceremony and other formalities.

In order to expedite the visa process at the US Consulate, the immigration lawyer suggested that Julie and Rahul get married in court and submit an application so that the process would not stall. The lawyer helped them to complete other formalities, which were time-consuming under the bureaucratic process of the Indian government. They did. It was a very hard day, shuffling papers and completing all formalities under the Indian bureaucratic system.

Totally exhausted when they reached Rahul's hotel, he suggested that Julie go up to his room to freshen up.

She had been in his room a few days earlier, so she entered with no hesitation. She was a part of his life now, and he was a part of hers. When she came out of the bathroom, he presented her with a small package.

"What's that?" she asked.

"Open it! I brought it just for you."

She opened the package. It was a bottle of Chanel No.5 perfume.

"I could not find your brand, but I hope you like it," Rahul added.

"Thank you very much! It's great. I love it." She looked at him seductively.

"You know what? I haven't kissed my bride." Expressing his affection, he grabbed her and kissed her passionately. She kissed him back. He was now aroused by lust.

She didn't mind, but she mildly hesitated and said, "Shouldn't we wait for our wedding night?"

"No! We are legally married, and nothing we're doing here is wrong, honey," Rahul insisted.

They lay on his bed, and she unzipped her clothes. They made sensuous love, clinging to each other and kissing wildly. She met his sexual appetite, and they were elated.

The sun was about to set while they both lay in bed, caressing each other. Rahul admired her well-toned and proportioned figure, which was slender but strong.

While kissing him, Julie said, "You've made me very happy, Rahul. Please don't ever leave me! I don't want to lose you."

"I have no need to. I love you now and forever. No one can take you away from me." Rahul moved to the edge of the bed. "Well, I don't know about you, but I need a cup of coffee. Would you join me?" He stood and picked up the phone to call room service.

"Yes, I'll have one," Julie said. "But I must leave soon. You also have to go to your aunt's house to meet your parents. I'll drop you there." She entered the bathroom.

"Boy, you are an extraordinarily beautiful woman. You should be on the silver screen."

"No, I wouldn't qualify," Julie said. "I'm not one of those bimbos. They don't allow anyone who has a brain. I don't want my beauty to master my personality. They go hand in hand."

"Well, I thought they needed talent."

"Talent? What talent? The only talent they need is to find the right bed!"

Rahul's father was anxiously waiting for him to arrive at his aunt's place. It was evening when Rahul returned.

"Sorry, I got delayed," Rahul said. "I had to go to the court with Julie for our marriage license, and then on to the American Consulate for her visa."

"Well, no harm done. Actually, we were planning your wedding."

"Oh, that's good."

Rahul wasn't keen on listening to the conversation. He kept thinking about the intimate moments he had just spent with Julie. Suddenly, a thought occurred to him that made him feel awful—the time he had spent with the hooker in Las Vegas. He brushed that meaningless incident from his mind and hoped never to encounter it again.

Mary was a dedicated church supporter, and the reverend was more than happy to marry the couple the morning of the Hindu wedding.

Indian families pride themselves on the wedding ceremonies of their children. They are quite elaborate in India. A decorator may be hired to coordinate the event. Additionally, the hotel management may organize the event, but at an exorbitant cost. The Sharmas accepted the hotel's offer. They also hired a wedding planner. The hotel grand ballroom was set up to accommodate the Hindu wedding, and then later in the evening the room was transformed for the reception. The hotel also was to provide food and drink at appropriate times.

Rahul's mother, along with her relatives and friends, busied themselves while shopping for various saris and clothing for different rituals. Buying jewelry for the bride and themselves was a joyous and proud event. It was no exception for the Sharma family. Rahul was their only son, and his parents could afford to perform the ceremony with grandeur, as they wanted.

For Rahul, it did not matter, but he did not object to his parents' enthusiasm and extravagance. All he wanted was to have his bride, with their parents and friends by their side.

Mark, Tom, and Joey decided to come to Mumbai to facilitate the wedding event of their friend, who was very precious to all of them. Rahul could not have been more thrilled to be surrounded by his friends. Tom and Joey were happy to see Rahul, and it was their first visit to India. After the wedding, Tom would head to Australia to be with his aunt, and Joey would travel to Japan to help his father in a business transaction.

At a dinner with his friends and colleagues, Rahul introduced Julie to them. All of them were overwhelmed by her charm and beauty.

As usual, Tom was partly drunk and abrupt. "Hello, Julie," he said. "Nice to know you. I'm not surprised that he fell for you. You are ravishing. So please tell me, how did you meet my friend Rahul . . . or, more accurately, Mr. Felix Unger?" Tom referred to Rahul as the character in Neil Simon's play.

"Well, I believe that I am just lucky," Julie replied.

"Well, good for him! We have to celebrate your wedding, Rahul. How about a bachelor party? Remember Las Vegas? We had a lot of fun."

Rahul knew that Tom never cared for discretion, especially when he was under the influence of alcohol.

~~~

Madhu was shocked to hear from Rahul late that evening.

"What's the problem, Rahul?" asked Madhu.

"Can you do me a favor, please?" Rahul asked wearily. "Joey returned from a bar a while ago. He's alone. Tom was arrested for fighting with a customer at the bar. It appears that Tom hit this person with a glass bottle and sent him to the hospital. Madhu, I don't like it either. But can you please help?"

Placing his palm over his forehead, Madhu said in disgust, "Why do you associate with such friends, Rahul? Let me see what I can do. Does Joey know where Tom is being held?"

Undoubtedly, Julie and Madhu were largely uncomfortable with Tom. Julie had heard from Madhu about Tom and his nasty and outrageous behavior. Nevertheless, she remained graceful and affable. Everyone put this incident to rest, and requested that Joey watch over Tom.

One of the most important guests yet to arrive was Rahul's grandmother, who was notably conservative. As far as Rahul knew, she was not going to compromise on the fact that he was marrying someone from another caste, let alone a different religion. Rahul had a hunch that she would exclude herself from the wedding ceremonies, which would be very inappropriate. Rahul knew that, in her orthodox world, she would not listen to her sons. But Rahul was her favorite. He was the oldest grandchild, and he knew that she loved him very much. In order to persuade Grammy, Rahul and his parents arrived in Kanpur on an early-morning flight on Wednesday.

"Hello, Grammy," said Rahul.

She put on her glasses and looked at him, squinting. "Oh, my Rahul. What a surprise! What brings you here?" She hugged him affectionately.

"I've come to invite you to come to my wedding in Mumbai. I'm sure Mom and Dad have told you about it."

"Yes, yes. I know. Now come and sit by me. Tell me about the girl and her family. Where are they from? Why did you rush into a marriage without conferring with us?"

Rahul's dad barged in. "It was done in a hurry, Ma. He did not have much time to spend in India."

Grammy said, "All of you nowadays are in a hurry. Well, we will talk about it after lunch."

After lunch and her nap, they assembled to discuss the wedding. Vasu asked, "Ma, what's on your mind? If you do not come to your grandson's wedding, you know he will be heartbroken."

Grammy was chewing the betel nut and tobacco. "What do I hear about my Rahul's bride? She is not from our caste. How could you allow that?"

Vasu said, "Ma, she is his choice. We are not going to interfere with his wishes. He is now an adult, and he's a very responsible young man. We, as parents, have to cross over the hurdles of religious and caste barriers. He has been brought up in a different environment, and I can't let him withdraw from the path of independence." Vasu paused briefly. "Ma, why don't you ask him what he has to say?"

Grammy looked at Rahul and waited for his response.

"Grammy, Dad's right. Times were different when Mom and Dad got engaged and married. They brought me up in the best way they could. For practical purposes, I am an American."

"But you don't look like an American," she said.

"What do you think Americans look like, Grammy? They are white, black, and brown. They are Christians, Jews, Muslims, Hindus, and others. They speak English, Spanish, Chinese, Italian, Hindi, etc. I am happy to be associated with them. We have friends who are male, and we have friends who are female. I like this society. For the most part, we are friendly and united.

"I came to Mumbai last year and met this girl. She is very cultured, highly educated, and well mannered. On top of that, she isn't Hindu—she is Christian—but I don't have any objections to it. I've made her a promise, and I'm going to keep it. By the way, Grammy, if you meet her, you will surely love her.

"Now, it's your choice whether you'll have faith in me and be part of my happiness or decide to dampen my hopes of contentment. Even after my appeal to you to attend my wedding, if you wish to be firm with your decision, I can understand that. But I'm going to marry her, by all means, and it would then be unfair to you if she and I visited you again in the future."

Not to ostracize herself from her grandson's family, she said, "I do not totally agree with your marriage, but I love you very much," she said gently. "Your grandfather, my husband, would have accepted her as your bride, if you had insisted. So I cannot and will not refuse you." She looked at her grandson. "Come here, my child! If you love each other, then you should marry her. You both have a full life ahead of you. Do you have a picture of her?"

Rahul jumped up from the chair and showed her Julie's picture. "Here she is, Grammy."

She gazed at the picture eagerly. "She is beautiful. What's her name?"

"Julie," Rahul said. "Julie D'Silva. She is from Goa but lives in Mumbai with her mother."

Grammy gave her picture back to Rahul and said, "Listen, I don't know what your plans are for the rest of the day, but I need to pack and get ready to go to my grandson's wedding."

Rahul hugged his grandmother.

Vasu looked at him and nodded. "You know, you still do have one more bomb to drop by telling Grammy that Julie is a widow."

"I'll do it in due course," Rahul said. "I don't think Grammy will object after meeting Julie."

~~~

In spite of Julie's Christian faith, she participated in all parts of the Hindu wedding, preceding the Christian ceremonies. She knew of all the functions, but she found *Mehndi* to be an interesting celebration. *Mehndi* is a typical reddish-brown dye obtained from the leaves of the henna plant, which is used in making designs on the hands, feet, and forearms. The bride is usually decorated well.

At the church wedding, Rahul and his friends wore tuxedos, and the bride wore a white chiffon wedding gown. This was the first time Rahul got to see Julie in a wedding dress. Her uncle walked her to the altar. After his homily, Father Rodriguez blessed the couple. At the end of the ceremony, Sonja caught the bouquet thrown by the newlywed bride. This was a joyous occasion for both the Sharma and D'Silva families.

It was November, and the weather was pleasant. The Sharmas decided to perform the wedding ceremony outdoors on the lawn, and the reception was to be held in the grand ballroom of the hotel. The food also was prepared with the typical North Indian flavors.

A *Mandap* was erected outdoors on the lawn with chairs for the guests to witness the ceremony. The *Mandap* often came as a set that included pillars supporting a frame, royal chairs for the bride and the groom, side chairs for parents, and a pedestal for the sacred fire. The priest conducted the marriage. No Hindu marriage was binding and complete unless the ritual of seven steps and vows in the presence of fire (*Saptapadi*) was completed by the bride and the groom together.

Finally, Rahul, Julie, and Madhu retreated from their group of friends so that they could be alone.

"I like your watch," said Madhu. "Where did you get it, Rahul?"

"It's a Patek Philippe watch. My cousin Suri gave it to me as a wedding gift."

"*What?* You know this watch costs over twenty thousand dollars. Are you sure he's not up to something?"

"Madhu, why are you so distrustful of him? He is rolling in money, and I imagine he likes me. He even lent me his Mercedes to use during the wedding."

"Rahul, whatever you say—but I don't like it." Madhu walked away.

Julie, confused by this conversation, asked, "What was that all about, Rahul?"

"I don't understand Madhu's strange behavior. He believes that my cousin is a big-time smuggler and criminal."

"By the way, where is he? I'd like to meet him," Julie said.

"He could not make it for the wedding. He is out of the country," Rahul said.

CHAPTER 32

After returning to Mumbai from their honeymoon in Rajasthan, a state in India, Rahul found that Mumbai was as muggy and warm as ever. Tom and Joey had left for their destinations. Mark was still working on his project with Madhu and filling in for Rahul while he was away. Many wedding guests had already gone home, and some were just about to depart. His parents, along with his grandmother, were leaving for Kanpur in a day or two. In the meantime, Julie had become a lovable daughter-in-law to Rahul's parents, as well as one of his grandmother's favorite people.

As soon as Julie was granted a US visa, Rahul and Julie decided to take a flight out of Mumbai for Houston via the German airline Lufthansa.

Mary D'Silva was getting nervous as the day her daughter would part from her approached. Julie made regular trips to her home to pack her things. Her mother was jittery, realizing that she was leaving for an unknown land far away, where she may not have a shoulder to lean on. In a way, Mary was happy. She had full faith in Rahul and strongly believed that he was Julie's true love and friend, now and forever. She also liked Rahul's family. But mostly, she had full confidence in her daughter. Still, the time was coming close for Julie's departure, and Mary's heart ached with anxiety.

Rahul tried to wrap up his work at Madhu's office, and he thanked his coworkers and other colleagues.

One day, when Madhu was alone with Julie, he said, "One more thing, Julie. I have to warn you about Rahul's friend Tom. Please be very careful. I know Rahul likes him a lot, but I found him to be somewhat dubious. I may be overreacting, but there is no harm in being watchful and alert."

"I understand, Madhu, and I know that," she replied. "But I don't want to offend Rahul over his friendship with Tom. I have to watch that Tom never comes between Rahul and me. Madhu, you know that I look up to you, and I always will. I'll ask for help if I ever need it."

When Rahul entered Madhu's office, they chatted for a while and then left the office for the day.

While waiting for the confirmation from Lufthansa, Rahul asked his wife, "Should we stop in Europe? It may be very cold this time of year. I am used to the weather, but after staying in Houston for the last several years, I am beginning to dislike it." Rahul realized that they had to get home. "Well, I promise you that I will take you to Europe one day, anyway. A few cities there are my favorites."

"One of these days, I would like to visit Rome and the Vatican," Julie said. "My mother would like it very much. I am not a religious person, but being a Christian, I would like to pay my respects to it."

Rahul was very excited about leaving Mumbai for Houston and starting a new chapter in his life. For Julie, it was the beginning of a brand-new life—a new world with new friends and a new family. She would have been extremely uncomfortable if she did not have Rahul to lean on.

"Are you okay?" Rahul asked. "You look tense." Rahul noticed that Julie was somewhat restless.

"I had a fear of flying after Vikram died, but I am all right now."

"He must have taken you up in the air with him."

"Yes, he did a couple of times," Julie replied. "But I was scared stiff."

"Don't worry. I'm with you." He held her hand tight.

The flight to Houston was comfortable but long. The time difference of almost eleven and a half hours, in addition to a long journey, took its toll on the body. It was afternoon when they landed in Houston. This was Julie's first trip abroad, and she was impressed by the cleanliness of the facilities and the efficiency of the people handling their affairs. Mark came to the airport to pick them up and drive them to their hotel. After they arrived at the Westin Galleria Hotel and checked into their room, Rahul left with Mark to retrieve his car, which was parked at the apartment complex.

CHAPTER 33

Houston was so large, it would have been impossible to move around town without an automobile. Public transportation had improved immensely over the previous few years, but a denser network was needed to cover many points around town. Besides, Houstonians were not used to commuting by public transportation.

They were excited to move into a furnished condo. They cuddled together, talked to each other, and got lost in their dreams. Rahul wanted nothing more than to be with her, talk to her, and listen to her. Often she sounded like Cinderella, who had found her prince, and she was the happiest person on earth.

"Are you comfortable here?" asked Rahul one day.

"Yes, very much so. I am so happy to be here with you. You are my husband and my love. I have nothing more important to do than to make this place our home."

Our home—how sweet! He knew instantly that it was home wherever she was. *A man builds a house, but it is a woman who makes it a home with her tender love and care.* She had made a tremendous difference in his life, and he was now a contented person.

"May I ask you a very personal question?" Julie asked Rahul.

"Yes, what is it?"

"Why is Tom so critical about you and so contrary to what you are?"

When Rahul kept quiet, she asked, "What are you thinking? Did I say something wrong?"

"No, it's not that. I have a feeling you don't like Tom. But I've known Tom since we were in high school in Boston. In our friendship, I don't consider his criticism to be an insult. I'm sure he is only trying to be funny."

Rahul knew that a question about Tom would come up, but he evaded it by changing the subject. But he did not know how long he would be able to do so.

"Well, it's getting very late, and I am tired," said Julie. "I am going to bed. Good night!"

~~~

Julie started to pick up the local lingo, in spite of the fact that her command of the English language was perfect. She was now the lady of the house, and she enjoyed every moment of it. The Indian community in Houston was very large. Not even Rahul had realized it. Not far from their townhouse was an Indian market, Mahatma Gandhi District, where they shopped on occasion and ate some fast food. Julie was the kind of person who made friends very quickly and possessed the power to attract them through her candor. She met another Indian girl at the market named Tina, and they became good friends. With Julie's beauty and charm, she was always the center of attention at the parties that they attended, and they were invited quite frequently. At Indian parties and functions, she loved to dance, especially to bhangra music from North India, which had gained popularity and had driven many youngsters and adults crazy.

Julie was a vivacious host; therefore, a party at her home was always a bash. This also allowed her to keep Tom at arm's length. However, she missed being a professional, and she badly wanted to find a suitable job. Many of her new friends were working men and women, and she was filled with boredom whenever she was alone. To keep busy, she read books, wrote letters and e-mails, and talked to her friends about any leads they had for work.

Then one evening, Mark Garcia and his wife came over for drinks, and they all went out for dinner.

"Well, Julie, how do you like Houston?" asked Mark.

"I would like it better if I had something to do, like a job," Julie responded with mild displeasure.

After a brief pause, Mark said, "Julie, why don't you talk to Joann Armour, who is a partner at the law firm of Monk and Abernathy? She also handles our legal business. They are in downtown Houston. I hope Rahul is agreeable to my suggestion."

"No, that's fine with me if that's what she wants to do," Rahul responded quickly.

After Mark and his wife left, Julie decided that she would talk to Joann anyway, take her chances, and get her advice on how to move forward.

On Monday, after getting an appointment to see Joann on Thursday, she was excited to tell her husband about it. "Guess what? I'm seeing Joann Armour in about four days."

Weatherwise, it was overcast, but no rain was in the forecast on Thursday. The temperature was in the seventies when Julie prepared to leave for her interview. She was dressed in a beautiful dark suit with a white silk blouse and colorful scarf. Her designer sunglasses and purse added to her beauty, and she looked very much like a professional. People were busy and rushing to go somewhere.

She entered the building and got into the elevator to go to the twentieth floor, where a receptionist greeted her. Within a few minutes, Joann appeared.

"Julie Sharma? I'm Joann Armour. Please come in." She continued talking while they walked to her office. "So did you find the place all right? Don't we have wonderful weather today? We don't have many days like these in Houston. The summer is too hot, and winter is sometimes too cold. I'm a West Coast girl myself."

Joann was a well-dressed brunette in her late thirties or early forties. She kept chewing gum at her desk and offered a piece to Julie.

"No, I don't chew gum."

"Actually, I don't do it either. But right now, I'm trying to kick my smoking habit."

Her office was a large room with many open books laying around.

"Please sit down," she instructed. "Would you like a coffee or a Coke?"

"No, thank you, I'm fine."

Joann continued, "As you know, I represent Robotechnique in their corporate matters. I've had a chance to review the contract, which your former company had sent to me. It was very well done. I was impressed. Did you work on these documents?"

"Yes, I prepared them, and then they were reviewed by another law firm."

"I see. Well, you have done an excellent job on this document."

"Thank you, Ms. Armour."

"Call me Joann. Now, tell me what's on your mind."

"Okay, Joann," Julie said. "I have a law degree from a university in India. Again, I worked as a corporate lawyer for a firm in Mumbai where Robotechnique is a valuable client. I got to know Rahul Sharma when he visited our office. One thing led to another, we got married, and here I am. I'm looking for a job where I can utilize my knowledge and experience. Since I've worked all my life, I hate to sit at home doing nothing."

Joann listened to her attentively and said, "I've had a chance to see your work. It was very well done. You have talent, but you may need some real-life experience. Let me be frank with you. Before we appoint anyone as an attorney or a lawyer, we require the candidates to have a law degree and to have completed the bar exam. Corporations work differently here compared to what you are familiar with, but that's not the sticky part. For you to represent a client, you have to have proper credentials.

"I don't want to hurt your feelings. What may be appropriate for our firm and a real help to me is for you to assist me as a paralegal. You would prepare the cases and do the research. In the meantime, I suggest you go to school, complete all the necessary course work, then take the bar exam. How does that sound to you?"

"That sounds wonderful. I'll have to be advised by my husband."

"Okay, then. I'll put in the letter what we normally do around here. I think you will make a good attorney." Joann kept talking. "You know, Julie, I've never had a chance to visit your country. I am sure it must be fascinating. Maybe one day I'll get there when I have some spare time." Joann looked at her watch and said, "I have another appointment at two o'clock. Why don't you join me for lunch? There is a small restaurant around the corner. The service will be quick."

"I would love to," Julie said. "But only if I am not imposing on your time."

"No, not at all! But first, let me introduce to you our company's cofounder, Mr. Abernathy."

She led the way to his office, with Julie quietly following her. "Walter, do you have a moment?"

"But of course, my dear!" Mr. Abernathy responded with a smile and a pipe in his hand. He was an attractive, well-built, and well-dressed African American man, standing over six feet tall. *He must have been an athlete in his youth,* Julie thought as she looked at his imposing form.

"This is Mrs. Julie Sharma, Walter. Her husband works for Robotechnique. I am inviting her to work for me, assisting me on corporate details until she gets her license."

"How do you do, young lady?" said Walter. "I hope Joann was friendly." His handshake was firm, and Julie's petite hand was well hidden in his large palm.

"Yes, Joann has been extremely courteous," Julie replied. "I would be delighted to work for her. Since I am not very familiar with the local customs, I would like to confer with my husband before I say anything."

"Well, I hope you will make the right decision. Good to have you aboard, should you decide to work for us."

The elevators were busy as lunchtime was approaching. It was good that Joann had asked her secretary to make reservations at the restaurant.

Joann ordered lunch for both of them.

As they left the restaurant, Julie said, "Thanks, Joann. It was very nice of you to invite me for such a lovely lunch."

"You are very welcome. I hope to see you soon. My offer could be a stepping stone in your career. Think about it!"

For Julie, the interview was a novel experience. However, she knew how to appear for a job interview. The idea of going to school and completing her other academic requirements appealed to her so much that she was almost tempted to accept the job instantly.

It was almost three o'clock when she reached home, and she called Rahul to give him the good news. Rahul was happy about the job offer, not only because she would bring in extra income, but because the job would keep her occupied and content.

At dinner, Rahul said, "Now, please tell me about your interview in detail."

"I have a lot to tell." She told him about the job and people in the firm.

"That's wonderful. As far as the pay is concerned, I have no idea what the norm is for your position, but I can ask around and let you know. In the meantime, why don't you wait to see what they are willing to offer in Joann's letter? Then you can decide whether to accept the job or not."

Julie nodded. "The thing I like the most is that I can go to school and take the bar exam at the same time."

"That's excellent. I like it too."

Almost every weekend, they had friends come over or they visited them and kept their social calendar busy. Julie especially kept this social schedule going. She wanted her husband to keep away from Tom.

One Friday evening, Tom came in with Rahul and poured himself a drink.

"How are you, Julie?" Tom asked. "You must be getting used to Houston."

"I'm fine, Tom. How are you doing? Are you staying for dinner?" Julie was usually very polite, but it was clear that she disliked Tom.

"We will go out, if you don't mind," Rahul said. "Did I forget to tell you that Tom was coming over?"

Julie said coldly, "Yes, you did. Anyway, I'll get ready."

Julie did not really enjoy this conversation. She was slightly annoyed by Rahul's response. But she was smart not to reveal her mood in the presence of Tom.

She had lately come to the realization that whenever Tom was around, Rahul acted strange. He was probably trying to convey some message, but it did not come across clearly. This could be one of the reasons that Julie was never fond of Tom's company.

She hadn't liked Tom from the first day she met him. Madhu had warned her about Tom's personality. He was abrupt, indiscreet, and vulgar. She did not care for how Tom behaved in private, but when he influenced and began to intrude in Rahul's life, she was infuriated.

Tom said, "You're so quiet today, Julie."

"I'm all right," Julie said. "But I had planned for a quiet dinner at home, and I didn't know we would have company. We'll go out instead."

Later in the evening, Rahul noticed Julie's discomfort and apologized to her, saying that in the future he would check with her first to see if she wanted to spend the evening with his friends.

CHAPTER 34

Julie had been in Houston for over three months and was now an expert driver. They got a car on Saturday. This was one item Houstonians couldn't do without.

The following morning, Rahul said, "By the way, I forgot to mention something to you. I am shifting myself from the Indian project. They have very important work here that I have to personally supervise and monitor, and it requires a very high security clearance. Madhu is a great help with the project in India, and he handles it very well. I am training one of my associates to take up my assignment in India, and therefore, I may have to go to India with him for a week or two. You can come if you want to."

Julie was a bit disappointed. "Well, if I start this job or school, it would be impossible for me to leave. But we will see at that time. I would hate to be here alone without you."

"Don't worry! I'll ask Tom to look after you."

"Not Tom," she murmured. She would be just fine without him around.

A few days later, a courier brought a letter for Julie from the firm of Monk and Abernathy, making her an offer of employment. The letter detailed her duties, her salary, and the company policy, and she read the letter over and over again. Holding it to her heart, she kissed it with pleasure and excitement. She could not wait for her husband to come home.

Rahul read the letter and said with surprise, "Wow! Nice starting salary. That's great. You really must have worked on them."

"No, we just like each other. I will go to meet her next week."

Julie was very excited about her job, feeling happy that she was headed in the right direction. She called her friend Tina, and they planned for lunch at a nearby delicatessen.

Something about Julie fascinated her friends, male and female, and they all wanted to be around her, including Rahul and his friends. They talked about social, economic, and political issues with anyone who dared to listen, and they liked to discuss these topics with her. In spite of her popularity, she had maintained utmost humility and made everyone around her feel welcome and important. There was never a trace of arrogance or annoyance in her voice. She never left her husband alone at any party or gathering, and she made it very clear that he was the most important person in her life.

Over lunch, she talked to Tina about her job and the car they had bought over the weekend.

Julie said to Tina, "Let me ask you something. May I?"

"Oh, sure!" Tina answered.

"Did you ever meet Rahul at any gathering before? Or know about him?"

"No, not that I can think of. I wish I had. I would have tried to grab him first," Tina joked. "But we have a large Indian community here, and it's hard to know someone unless you're in school or college together. We probably didn't move around in the same social circles. Why do you ask, Julie?"

"Just thinking out loud. We had a brief encounter in India and decided to get married. Sometimes it makes me wonder if we took the right steps. Don't misunderstand me, please. I love him very much and always will. But intimacy comes with time. And that, we did not have."

"Julie, you are so ravishing, and all men are attracted to you. Besides, you are very intelligent and caring. I am not surprised that Rahul did not let the chance get away."

"I am happy with how it has happened," Julie answered. "Luckily, we like each other, and that is all that matters to us. Let's eat before it gets cold." Julie tried to avoid any further conversation about her husband.

After lunch, Tina went back to work, and Julie returned home and found that her new car was ready to be picked up.

CHAPTER 35

Julie needed a good cup of coffee when she arrived home after meeting with Joann. She wasn't physically tired, but she was mentally exhausted. She fell asleep on the sofa while watching television, but the telephone woke her up. It was Rahul's dad. He told her that his wife, Rahul's mother, had been hospitalized because of chest pains. She had suffered a mild myocardial infarction, but she was resting and doing fine.

The news prompted them to visit Boston in a hurry.

While they were in Boston, Julie met with Renee, one of Rahul's friends who lived in the city. Joey was also there.

While Julie was alone with Renee, she reluctantly said to her, "Renee, I have a personal question to ask you. It's kind of silly for me to ask, but what do you think of Tom?"

Renee hesitated. "I don't want to tell you, since he is Rahul's best friend, but I will. He is basically all right, but too flaky. You know that he is bisexual. That doesn't bother me, but his excessive drinking, gambling, mingling with hookers, and possibly using drugs make me very nervous to be around him. I wanted to come to your wedding, but I was afraid to be with him most of the time. You know something else? Joey doesn't feel the same way I do. Probably Joey and Rahul look at things differently."

"Why am I not surprised to hear this?" Julie said. "I wish Rahul would keep him at arm's length."

Julie and Rahul returned home on Sunday evening and decided to go out for dinner. As they were approaching the restaurant, Rahul told her, "By the way, I have asked Tom to join us for dinner. I hope you don't mind."

Julie did not appreciate this, but didn't say anything.

As soon as they were seated at the table, she saw Tom approaching them with a drink in his hand.

"Good evening! How are you, Julie? I haven't seen you in a while. So I hear that you were in Boston and met our friends. That was nice! So how is your mom, Rahul?"

"She is fine and recuperating," Rahul answered. "I've asked them to visit us as soon as we finalize on a house. We will start looking very soon. I wish Julie could come to India with me, but she has a new job to attend to."

"Certainly she will go with you!" Tom said. "I can't believe she would refuse you. Or if she decides to stay back, I'll keep her company. Don't you worry, my friend."

After they ordered dinner and drinks, Rahul talked about his trip to Boston, as well as Joey and Renee. But Tom seemed to have had one drink too many. He was incoherent in his speech and wasn't listening to what others were saying.

Julie was not enjoying a moment of it. She wished she had fixed dinner at home instead of spending an evening with Tom. And Tom keeping her company in Rahul's absence was absolutely not acceptable to her. Tom's response gave her all the more reason to go with Rahul, provided she could work out some arrangement with Joann.

"Thanks for inviting me, Rahul. I am flat broke," Tom said, calling the waiter for another drink. "Scotch and water, double, easy on the water!"

"Go slow, Tom," Rahul said, slightly annoyed. "How come you're broke? You won't get paid until midweek."

"Let me tell you. I had two pairs and an ace on top. This guy had a flush. I thought he was bluffing. But they took my money and threw me out. I am not going there again, trust me!"

"Here, have a hundred bucks," Rahul said. "Pay me back when you can, okay?"

Tom accepted the money without any hesitation, as he always did. At this point, Rahul realized that it had been a bad idea to invite Tom. Rahul didn't know what shape Tom would be in when he showed up.

They ate dinner quietly and were ready to leave. "Julie, I'll have to take him home," Rahul said. "He is in no condition to drive. I'll drive his car. Can you please follow us? Is that okay? I'm sorry."

Julie was furious but kept her cool and said, "Of course. You ought to help your friend. How far does he live from here?"

"Not too far. We'll be there in ten to fifteen minutes. Thanks, Julie."

They brought him to his apartment, parked his car, and left. *Silence is golden*, both thought to themselves while driving back. Rahul was slightly embarrassed, because he knew how she felt about Tom, and tonight Tom had proven her right.

Julie finally found the courage to approach the subject. "I don't find anything in common between you and Tom. I can't understand your friendship with him."

Somehow, Rahul had anticipated a conversation like this. He told her in detail about Tom and his family, his mother who was dead and his father who was remarried.

"You see, he has no family to speak of. He is my friend, and I am pretty sure that I mean everything to him. He would not be afraid to lay down his life to protect me, if I ever needed it. I know you have a different opinion about him, and you are entitled to it, barring the fact that you don't know him as well as I do."

Julie felt somewhat withdrawn. It wasn't that she had started to like Tom, but she was now very proud of her husband and felt a newfound respect for him. He was a man of character and compassion, and he did what he believed was right.

~~~

When Joann called the next morning, Julie was excited to hear from her.

"Julie, the admissions office at the college has received copies of all your papers. Mr. Abernathy talked to the dean, and after consulting with his staff, he has a few suggestions for you about your courses. The college will guide you on how and when you can appear for the bar exam, etc. He also recommends that you begin at the office soon to gain some legal experience before you start school. I agree with him. So what do you think?"

Julie said, "That's wonderful. You know I was going to start work today, but I got delayed in Boston. I am now coming to work next Monday."

"That's fine," Joann said. "But before I continue, let me tell you what I've been up to. I got married over the weekend. My husband, Charles Rowenta, is also an attorney. This is a second marriage for both of us. No one knows about our wedding except a few at the office. He has one son who lives with his mother in California. I haven't taken a vacation for a long time. So tonight, Charlie and I plan to leave town for a couple of weeks or so. I suggest that you have Mr. Abernathy guide you when you come in."

"That's great, Joann!" Julie said excitedly. "Let me congratulate you on your wedding. I hope you both will be very happy. I'll be fine working with Mr. Abernathy. Don't worry. Once again, Joann, please accept my thanks for giving me an opportunity to work with you and your firm. Have a good time on your honeymoon."

She couldn't wait for Rahul to come home that evening. When she called him, he was in a meeting, and she had to wait for his call. She then called Tina, and they decided to go out for lunch.

Tina showed up at the café with a friend. "Julie, meet my friend Seema Nair. We work at the same place. She is also single, like me. Do you have anyone in mind for her?"

CHAPTER 36

L ater that day, after a couple of telephone calls, Julie could not track down Rahul at his office.

"So what's all the commotion?" asked Rahul when he came home that evening. "I hope you're not pregnant."

"Come on, you know me better than that," Julie said. "I talked to Joann. I have some good news and some bad news. Which one do you want to hear first?"

"Tell me the good news."

"After I talk to Mr. Abernathy next week, I'll visit the admissions office at the law school and get the details about what courses to attend, etc. The new class doesn't start until the summer, and then I can take the bar exam when and if I am ready. By the way, I start my job next Monday. That's the good news. The bad news is that I cannot go with you to India. But I'll be fine. You will be gone for only a week or two."

"That's a shame. But I'll be back before you know it."

Julie started her work at the firm of Monk and Abernathy promptly the following Monday.

On the first day of work, she was very presentable. Joann's secretary, Becky, took her to her office, which was small and cozy. It had a small desk, a couple of chairs, and a desktop computer connected to a printer. She reviewed the old cases and noted the comments.

She finished her first day at five o'clock. Exhausted, she ran to catch her bus to go home. It had been a fulfilling day for her.

At home, she washed up and waited for her husband to arrive. Relaxing on the sofa, she flipped through the pages of *Better Homes and Gardens* while waiting.

As soon as Rahul entered the house, she hugged him and said, "I missed you a lot. Did you miss me?"

"But of course! I got your new e-mail address. I'll send you a message every day from India."

"I thought you loved me more than that. I expect you to call. I always want to hear your voice."

"I'll do that too. By the way, I need to start packing for my trip, honey."

"I'm a bit tired," Julie replied. "Can we order Chinese or something?"

"Sure," Rahul said. "What do you have in mind? Why don't you order? Then I'll pick it up."

He left to wash and change, and she ordered food at a nearby restaurant.

On the day of his departure, Rahul told Julie, "I have a colleague going with me who is taking over the Indian assignment from me. Since it's a workday, we'll get a limousine to drop us at the airport."

"That's great!" Julie said.

Before she left for work, she clung to him for a long time, kissing him intermittently but very affectionately. Finally, Rahul had to let her go.

"You're going to be late, and so am I," said Rahul. "But I'll be back in two weeks or so. Please call Mark or Tom if you need anything. You can call your friend Tina to come over too. Before you know it, I'll be back."

~~~

Back at the office, Julie's mind was wandering. She could not concentrate on her job. Although she had almost completed her synopsis of the case, she wanted to be thorough. Joann was not due for at least a week, and she was going to catch up with her final submission.

In the meantime, Mr. Abernathy called Julie into his office. When she went in, there was a young man in the office with him.

"Julie, this is Mr. Jason Brookfield. He's an attorney, and he'll be working with you on your current project. All right?"

Looking at Jason, Julie said, "Hello, how are you?" She shook his hand. As soon as they got acquainted, she left to go to her office.

That day, she decided to have lunch at the café. As she was going down the hall, she saw Jason waiting by the elevator.

"Are you going out for lunch, Julie?"

"I am," she replied, getting into the elevator with him.

When they reached the lobby, he asked, "Can you join me for lunch if you're going that way?"

Julie nodded.

"I'm sorry to intrude," Jason said. "But your last name is familiar to me. Are you related to Rahul Sharma?"

"Yes, I am. He is my husband. How do you know him?"

"We were together at Rice University and were good friends. After my studies were over, I left for Austin to pursue my law degree and lost contact with him. He and I exchanged a few e-mail messages, and last year I came to find out that he was getting married in India." He smiled at Julie. "So how is he?"

"He is fine. Right now he's on his way to India for work."

"Son of a gun! I don't know much about what he does or what he's up to. But I can tell you one thing—he must have very good taste if he married you."

Julie smiled sheepishly.

~~~

Julie and Jason reached the café and got seated.

Jason asked, "What will you have, Julie?"

"A salad is fine. I don't eat much for lunch."

"Neither do I," he replied.

"Jason, please tell me more about you."

"I'm a law graduate from the University of Texas. Now I work at Monk and Abernathy. But I guess you already know that." He blushed.

Julie smiled. "It sounds like we will be working on the same project. Am I right?"

"Yes, for the time being—until my boss, Joann Armour, returns."

"I work for her too. I only started a few days ago."

"Are you a lawyer?" Jason asked.

"Yes and no. I got my degree and experience in India. I met Rahul, got married, and came here. I now work at this firm, and Joann has arranged for me to go to law school so that I can pass the bar exam. I guess I will be an attorney then."

Jason said, "That's great. We'll see a lot of each other. Joann may assign you to help me on my case."

"Yes, it's a possibility."

During lunch, she told him more about Rahul and his friends, and they exchanged addresses and phone numbers, planning to get together as soon as Rahul returned home.

"Jason, can I ask you a personal question?" Julie asked.

"Yes, sure."

"While you were at Rice, did you recall meeting Rahul's friend by the name of Tom Spencer?"

"Sure. I knew Tom through Rahul. He wasn't at Rice, but he hung around Rahul and his friends. He was kind of weird though—and he did a lot of things we wouldn't do. He smoked, gambled, and drank heavily, except when concentrating on his studies. Had it not been for Rahul, he would have never gotten through college. His behavior didn't make him any new friends, but Rahul always stood by him. Do you know where he is now?"

"He's right here, working at the same place as Rahul."

"Why am I not surprised?" Jason said. "He owes Rahul a lot. We used to joke at college that he was Rahul's twin brother, even though they didn't look alike. We thought he was gay. Sometimes we wondered if Rahul was too. But it's now confirmed that Rahul is *not* gay, because he married you."

"Tom is still the same," Julie said. "You may want to see him again one day. I'll tell him that I met you."

"Please, no! I can live without his company. I'm sure one day I'll meet him again through Rahul." He looked at his watch. "Well, time to go back. If you're finished, we can leave."

Julie kept wondering why everyone else had the same opinion of Tom except her husband. Rahul had, in fact, discussed with Julie how special his relationship with Tom was that very day, but since she did not want to agitate him any more than she had, she decided to lay low and not tell Rahul what Jason had told her. She wasn't in much of a hurry to go back home, but she couldn't miss the bus.

When she finally reached her home, she felt as if the ghosts of loneliness surrounded her. Normally, Rahul's presence gave her added security, but tonight she was spending the night alone in their bed. After tossing and turning from loneliness, she finally went to sleep.

Over the weekend, she spent time with Tina and her friend Seema. After shopping at the nearby Galleria shopping arcade, they decided to meet at Julie's home in the evening and go out for dinner. When the doorbell rang, she rushed to open the door, expecting Tina or Seema. Instead, it was Tom, smiling with a bottle of wine in his hand.

"Hi, Julie! How are you? I thought I might cheer you up while Rahul isn't here."

She stood there like a statue.

"May I come in?" Tom asked. "You look like you've seen a ghost."

"Come on in, Tom," she said reluctantly.

"Here, I brought you a bottle of wine. It's Bordeaux, the one Rahul likes. I hope you do too. Shall I pour?"

Even though Julie didn't respond, he got up, opened the bottle, poured a couple of glasses, and gave one to her. "Cheers," he said.

She took a sip and put the glass aside. This was an awkward moment. Even though Tom had said he would keep her company while Rahul was away, Julie didn't really expect Tom to keep that promise.

"Have you had your dinner yet?" Tom asked. "I'd like to take you out."

Julie was not at all comfortable with Tom's vexatious company. She had handled many situations like this before, but tonight she thought that it was going to be very difficult.

"Not tonight," Julie answered. "I am expecting a couple of my friends to come over, and then we are going out. Maybe some other time."

Suddenly, the doorbell rang, and she opened the door to let Tina and Seema in. This was a dose of fresh air for Julie, who was almost drowning in awkwardness.

"Come in!" Julie said to her guests. "This is Rahul's friend Tom. Tom, these ladies are Tina and Seema."

"Nice to meet you, ladies," he said. Tom could not resist adding, "But I thought I was your friend too, Julie." She avoided responding to him, as usual.

"Well, ladies, you'll have to try this wine." He poured wine into two more glasses and gave them to her visitors. "Cheers!" he said, holding up his glass.

"Tom, we have plans to go out to eat tonight. Can we meet some other time?" Julie asked, hoping that Tom would leave.

"All right, let me suggest something to you all. Ladies, you don't mind having dinner with me, do you?"

Hesitantly, they said it was all right with them before Julie had any chance to decline. He could not have been more charming and charismatic. Tina and Seema loved his company, but Julie kept quiet most of the time. It was a lovely evening for all except Julie, who felt suffocated. Tom left after Tina and Seema thanked him for a wonderful time.

Julie was angry at Tom for ruining her evening. The fact that her friends seemed to have enjoyed his company made Julie even more furious, since they did not perceive the way she felt about Tom. Both Tina and Seema wanted to know about Tom in a little more detail.

After Tom left, Tina said, "Tom is kind of a likable person. Is he single?"

"You want to know about Tom?" Julie asked. "I'll tell you." She told both of them about Tom and his shortcomings.

"He is a really bad seed," she concluded. "Keep away from him."

"You're not telling us everything, Julie," Tina said. "Something tells me that he isn't straight. Am I right?"

"Well, I heard from Rahul that he is gay."

"What a shame!" Seema said. "I thought he was rather handsome, charming, and fun to go out with. Well, you can't win them all!"

With that, all of them retired for the evening.

CHAPTER 37

After spending a quiet Sunday doing her house chores, Julie had a busy Monday at the office. Joann had returned from her vacation and appeared to be relaxed. She had a nice tan, which indicated that she had spent a good deal of time in the sun. During her absence, Julie had prepared the case for their client. Joann talked to her for a while to inquire if she liked her new job in general and the environment. After the formalities were over, Joann asked Julie how she personally felt about the case.

"I think we have a good chance of winning," Julie said. "All of the details are in my report."

"Wonderful work," Joann said. "Julie, I'm proud of you. Let me bring this to my legal team and see where we go from here." She paused. "By the way, I understand that Mr. Abernathy has assigned you to help one of our attorneys. Are you aware of it?"

"Yes. I've met Jason Brookfield. He was Rahul's classmate at Rice. He is a very kind person," she added.

"Isn't that nice?" Joann said. "You might help us in this case. The report you just finished is for his clients. Since you are now familiar with the case, can you work with Jason and his colleagues?"

"Oh, sure," Julie answered. "I'd love to."

Handing over another large portfolio, Joann said, "In the meantime, you might be more familiar with this case. It involves the laws of India and an Indian company. This will take you a while. We are in a time crunch, but not in a panic yet, because the Indian government takes its time. By the way, if you want a new edition of the Companies Act, 1956, please order it immediately. I hope you still remember the laws of the Reserve Bank of India. Also, there are copies of the memorandum and articles of the association and its amendments. Good luck!"

Julie was very pleased to work with Jason and his clients. But nothing was more pleasing than her new assignment, with which she had more familiarity and experience. She withdrew to her office and glanced at her new project. There were a couple of e-mail messages. One was from Rahul, saying that he was really busy with his work, but he was fine. The other one was from Tina, thanking her and Tom for a wonderful evening, adding that she was looking forward to seeing her over the upcoming weekend.

Julie invited Joann to have lunch with her, and Joann readily accepted. On their way to the restaurant, they saw Jason.

Jason came up to them and said, "How are you, ladies? How was your vacation, Joann?"

"It was lovely. Thank you. Jason, you know Julie. We have assigned her to work with you on your case. I am also available to work with you, whenever you need me."

"That's wonderful," Jason said and left.

"That's a gentleman," Joann said. "Very charming, indeed!"

Julie was totally engrossed in her work and did not think of Rahul that much. Nevertheless, she missed him a lot. *Only a handful of days left before Rahul returns*, she thought. *No real chance for Tom to be a party crasher.*

It was Thursday, and Rahul was to return in four days. Julie went to work, as usual, and by the time she got home, she was exhausted. Her projects at the office were very involved. She worked on the project with Jason for the time being while the case was being reviewed by other team members. She then did some research through the maze of Indian legal documents, which was painstaking. At home she showered and was about to eat, when she heard the doorbell.

When she opened the door, she saw that it was Tom.

"I thought you might want to go out to eat," Tom said after coming in. "I know you're tired, and I am too." And without her permission, he poured himself a drink. "Can I get you a drink, Julie?"

"No. I'm really tired today. Why don't we do it some other time?"

"Are you trying to get rid of me? I know you haven't eaten yet, and I haven't either. We can have a quick bite, and that's all."

"Tom, I am not in the mood to go out, and I would like to call it an evening soon. Please go."

"Julie, I didn't come here to scare you. I was only being friendly. Let me ask you one thing, please. You don't like me, do you?"

Julie preferred not to respond to his question, and said nothing.

Tom continued in a grieved tone, "Let me tell you something. Maybe I'm not a perfect person in the minds of many people. My parents didn't like me either. Rahul is the only one I can lean on now and while we were growing up too. He's my only family. He has done more for me than anyone else in my life. He gave me reasons to live." He paused to take a sip of his drink. "Okay, I have my weaknesses. I agree that I am not a normal person. I'm bisexual. I drink a lot. I gamble, smoke, and often spend time with some wild men and women. But I am *not* a bad person. I don't know whether you believe me or not, but if my friend Rahul ever needs me, I will lay down my life for him. He means a lot to me, and I was hoping that you would recognize that too." With those words, he left his half-empty glass on the table and left in a hurry.

Julie went after him, but he was gone.

She came back, closed the door, and sat stoically on the sofa. She regretted the incident, and now she was greatly confused. Were Madhu, Jason, and even Renee wrong about him? One thing was for sure—Tom was indeed a complicated individual.

The next day, Jason, his clients, Joann, and Julie remained very busy for the whole day, working on the case. They had a quick lunch, and the work continued until late in the evening.

When everyone left, Jason said, "Julie, I'll drop you off at home in my car."

Julie said, "Thanks, that's very nice of you, but you don't have to. I'll take a taxi."

"Where would you find a cab now?" Jason asked. "You and I also haven't eaten yet. Can we stop to get a bite?"

Julie hesitated, but then she thought of Tom, who could drop in at any moment. So she agreed to go to dinner with Jason.

"Let me go to my office. Then I'll meet you out front," she said.

In her office she saw that she had a few missed calls. Two calls were from nondiscernible sources, and a few others were from Tom. She ignored them, happy that she had missed Tom's calls.

When Jason dropped Julie off at her house, it was almost eleven. Jason drove off, and Julie walked toward her front door. There she found Tom, sitting on her doorstep with a bottle of beer in his hand. Julie was now very annoyed and wished that she had a back door to use so that she could just avoid him.

"What's this, Tom?" Julie said. She did not want to confront him.

"Where were you? I've been trying to get in touch with you for the last four hours. Why didn't you answer your cell phone? And who was that guy who dropped you off here?" Tom's voice was assertive.

Julie did not enjoy Tom's questions. She remained calm but said in a stern voice, "Tom, I don't like your tone. I am a professional, and I have my own hours and assignments. Rahul would never interrogate me like this."

"Well, I'm sorry. I didn't mean to hurt your feelings, but Rahul had called a couple of times and wanted to convey a message to you that he may be delayed in his return. He wants you to call him so he can talk to you about it."

He left her quickly without coming into her house. Julie realized that this relationship was going to be trouble, and she would have to handle it as delicately as she could until Rahul arrived.

She went into the house and called Rahul immediately.

When Rahul answered the phone, she said, "Hi, dear, how are you? Did you call me?"

"Hi. Yes, I tried a few times on both your cell and the home phone. You weren't available. You know I get worried, so you should at least answer your cell phone."

"It has been a hectic week at the office," she replied. "We had a meeting the whole day today with the client, and you know that Joann doesn't like anyone to answer the phone while we're having a meeting."

"I can understand that. But I was worried, so I asked Tom to come to our house to check on you, to see if you were all right. I left a message on your voice mail at the office and at home. I also wrote you an e-mail, but there was no reply."

Julie struggled with how to answer. Before she could say anything, Rahul said, "Well, I'm glad that you're fine. Listen, I have to stay here for a week more. I'll let you know the exact date of my arrival. But please stay in touch every day. Promise?"

"I will. I'm okay. Don't worry."

"Okay. Listen, I need to run. I'll talk to you later. Love you! Bye!"

Julie kissed the phone and said, "Bye, dear!" She hung up.

~~~

There was no doubt that Jason was a charming young man. His wavy groomed hair, physically strong body, and mentally sharp mind were of keen interest to the female staff at his office. Many looked at him and Julie with suspicious eyes, and rumors could take their toll. But Julie was utterly professional and brushed away any such hearsay.

While Rahul was away, Julie did not object to working late in the evening, primarily to avoid Tom's unexpected and uninvited company. On top of that, the work she handled for Jason was approaching the deadline, and it mandated that many colleagues work late. They ate at the office, coffee shops, and cafeterias. Often Jason accompanied Julie to her house.

"Want a bite, Julie?" asked Jason as he stood at the door to her office.

"You know what?" she said. "I'm tired of eating out, day after day. I've prepared some food and would like to eat at home."

"Won't you invite a friend?"

"I didn't prepare very fancy food. But you are welcome, if it isn't too late."

"Well, give me a minute, please. I'll get a few files from my office, and then we can leave. Do you have your car with you?"

"No, it's in the shop. I was expecting to hop in a cab and go home."

"I'll drop you off, and then I'll eat with you. That way, we're even."

The office building was totally empty and frightening. Julie was glad that Jason had accompanied her home.

"Jason, do you mind opening a bottle of wine?" Julie said while setting the dining table. "The glasses should be in the cupboard." She lit a candle and said, "The food is served."

Holding two glasses of red wine, Jason entered the dining area and sat on a chair. "You have a lovely home."

"We're currently leasing it. But we plan to buy another home as soon as Rahul returns."

When they finished dinner, she asked, "How about coffee?"

"I'll have some, if you'll have some too."

"Sure."

Jason was holding a picture of Rahul and Julie, studying it. "Rahul hasn't changed much from his college days," he said. "Oh well, he has put on some weight, but it looks like he's matured."

Julie brought the coffee to the living room. She saw Jason shuffling papers from his files when the doorbell rang. Julie looked through the peephole and saw Tom, waiting for her to open the door.

"What brings you here, Tom?"

"Oh, you have company?"

Jason saw him entering and said, "Say, aren't you Tom Spencer?"

"Yes, I am," Tom said, puzzled. "I don't recognize you. Have we met before?"

"Of course, I'm Jason Brookfield. I was with Rahul at Rice University. We met several times in his dorm room and then once at your apartment."

Julie was apprehensive about Tom's visit in Jason's presence. She thought of Tom being cynical and feared that he might convey some fallacious tales to Rahul.

Jason stood up and said, "Thanks, Julie, for a lovely dinner. You'll have to give me a chance to reciprocate it one day. I should be going. We have a lot of work to do tomorrow. Tom, are you staying or leaving?"

Julie realized that Jason was trying to drag Tom out of her house.

"Thanks for dropping me at home, Jason," Julie said. "I'm going to bed as soon as you both leave."

Tom got the hint and left her house along with Jason, but there was a trace of anger in his eyes.

CHAPTER 38

Julie was anxious for Rahul's arrival. Even at a public place like the airport, she could not delay her warm embrace for him. She had missed him very much, and he had missed her too.

They drove off as soon as he packed the car. On the way, Julie told him about meeting with his friend Jason and how she had made a new friend, Seema. She also said that Joann was back and had given her a new and interesting project. When Rahul didn't respond, she looked over at him and saw that he was fast asleep. She patted him gently and continued driving toward their home.

The next morning, both of them left for their own workplaces.

"Call me," Julie said.

When she got to work, Mr. Abernathy and Joann called Julie into Mr. Abernathy's office, congratulating her for her thorough research on their client's pending case. He briefed her on how he expected her to approach their clients in India.

"One more thing, young lady," he said. "Here is a list of courses which are recommended for you. I suggest that you take those and appear for your bar exam. Joann will help you adjust your schedule at the office. Good luck!"

After work, when she reached home, she found Rahul had already returned from his office. She saw him going through the mail. He was in somewhat of a foul mood.

"Oh, you are already home. Is something wrong?" Julie asked.

Rahul said, "Nothing, just tired. By the way, who is the guy who has been accompanying you home? Tom thinks that he knows him or of him."

That's it. The question did not surprise Julie. She had expected it, and she answered calmly, "You mean Jason Brookfield? He and I work on the same project. It is difficult and takes much of our time. He brought me home, thinking that it would be unsafe for me to go alone. He seems to know you from your college days. He graduated the same time you did."

"Tom tells me that you were very friendly with him."

Julie burst out with anger, "What is *that* supposed to mean? Are you questioning my fidelity? You can't trust me, but you trust Tom. Don't you understand? He tries to come between us."

Rahul had never seen Julie upset like this before. "It's not his fault. He acted on my behalf. I was worried when I could not locate you late one night."

"It seemed like Tom was checking up on me. I also didn't like the tone of his voice one night. I am married to you, not to him, and he has no right to offend me. He keeps barging in whenever he feels like it. I like privacy too. Tom is an egregious liar. Jason has been here more than once, and to tell you frankly, he is a good friend." With anger in her voice, she added, "You should have waited to propose to me. At least you might have found out what my likes and dislikes are. I like to make friends, but not necessarily lovers. Do you understand, Mr. Sharma?"

"All the time I was in India, I thought you were lonely. Instead, you were having a lovely time here," Rahul snapped.

She frowned and said sternly, "I am really hurt now. Listen, we have to trust and respect each other. Don't you think that

Tom is the root of our problems? This is our first fight, and it's due to Tom's insensitivity. It looks like you trust him more than you trust me."

"All right! I guess you're misinterpreting my concern. I have work piled up to my neck at the office, and I need to attend to it." And he left.

Frowning, Julie slammed the door of the bedroom and lay in bed crying. After a few moments, she got up, realizing what she had done. She felt sorry for herself. Her thoughts turned to Madhu's warning about Tom, and she needed someone very badly to comfort her. She went to sleep, lamenting Rahul's absence.

Julie tried to call Rahul, but there was no answer. Finally, she called Mark and asked about her husband. "Mark, this is Julie. I can't get Rahul on the phone. Has he gone somewhere?"

"He should be here. I'll tell him to call you. Are you at your office?"

"Yes."

"Julie, what's wrong?" Mark asked. "Why are you both mad at each other?"

Julie didn't answer.

"Julie, are you there? Listen, I know you both. I like you, and sometimes there is a simple explanation which can be cleared by just talking with a cool mind."

"I am sure you're right. But the root of our problem is something else, and I'll tell you about it one day when we can get together."

"Julie, I'll bring him home tonight. You know, my wife and Anika are visiting her folks in the Netherlands, so I would love to take you both out for dinner."

"I would be glad to join you," Julie said. "Why don't we have a drink at our house and then go out for dinner?"

"That's fine," Mark answered and then hung up the phone.

~~~

"Hi, honey. I'm home. Mark is with me," Rahul said as he entered their home, handing Julie a bouquet of flowers.

Julie smiled, shook hands with Mark, and kissed Rahul. "Are you all right?"

"Nice to see you, Julie," Mark said. "I haven't seen you in a while. How is your job?"

"I enjoy it. Thanks, Mark," she said. "It's quite challenging. I'm also going to law school to get my license to practice law."

"That's great."

Rahul changed his clothes and returned with three glasses of wine.

"Welcome back, Rahul," Mark said. "You must have missed her when you were away."

"Yes, I did."

"Julie, Rahul, I consider you both very close friends of mine. What's the problem? Rahul, why are you behaving like a child? Don't you realize that she was lonely without you?"

"Mark, we don't have any problems," Julie said. "I believe that Tom's insensitive remarks and misinterpreted information screwed him up. I overreacted and made Rahul mad."

"Why am I not surprised?" Mark said. "One thing you should learn is to ignore his baseless statements. Okay, are we ready to go eat?"

They left to go to a Chinese restaurant and had a quick dinner. They ended the evening in order to be ready for a hard day of work the next day.

Julie wrapped her arms around Rahul and said, "I'm sorry, dear. I shouldn't have behaved as I did yesterday. I know you love me and care for me. Can you forgive me, please?"

Rahul said, "That's all right. It's mainly my fault. I believe Tom had no right to interrogate you like he did that night. And I should be more sensitive. I love you."

They cuddled up together and went to sleep.

~~~

After Rahul's return from India, Julie and Rahul bought a townhome near the Galleria and moved into their new home. As promised, Rahul carried her over the threshold. The house looked fantastic, especially with her feminine touch. Of course, she had some help from her friends Tina and Seema, but she mostly managed everything by herself.

"What is in these boxes, Rahul?" Julie asked with surprise.

"Open them! They're housewarming gifts from my cousin Suri."

Opening the large boxes, she exclaimed, "Oh, these are Tiffany floor lamps. How sweet! I love those."

As Julie admired the beautiful and expensive presents, she began to question Suri's motives. "These are very pricey. What have you done for him that has inspired him to shower you with these expensive gifts?"

"I don't know. I must have done something."

"But how did he know that we're moving into our new home?"

"Oh, I met him briefly in India, and I must have told him. He got them shipped to my office a week ago." Rahul paused. "Funny," he said, scratching his head, "I never gave him my office address."

Later in the spring, Rahul's parents arrived from Boston to visit them. His mother appeared very frail because of her heart trouble. She did not opt for any surgical procedures, in spite of recommendations from many cardiologists. Upon Rahul's insistence, she visited a cardiologist in Houston, but the diagnosis remained the same. She was kept on a strict diet and constant medication, and she kept nitro pills in her purse.

Joey and Renee decided to get married, which made their families and friends very happy. They had not set the wedding date yet.

Houston was hot and humid in July, and even Julie started to complain about the heat. Her job was going remarkably well, and she prepared for her courses and exam with all her energy. She was doing a wonderful job at her work, and the senior partners had promised to make her a full staff member once she passed her bar exam.

Rahul was extremely busy. In the meantime, Madhu visited his office and spent a good deal of time with Rahul and Julie. Madhu was delighted to see them both in good spirits.

Tina and Seema were still single and looking for a perfect match. The same went for Tom. Apparently, he was in some trouble for his gambling debt, but he was still receiving his inheritance check from his grandfather's estate.

One evening, he came running to Rahul. "My dad and Joyce have separated. I knew she was married to him for his money." Rahul heard the distinct tone of disgust in his voice.

"You are terrible, Tom," Rahul said. "Your dad loves you very much. At least you could wish him well. There's no joy in his misery."

"I'm sorry. You're right. He loves me too, but I never trusted his wife. She married him for his money, and he married her for her looks. If he wanted to have a happy home, he should have stayed married to my mom."

"These things do happen," Rahul said. "No one has any control over it, Tom."

"No, I'm right. She has wiped him out. At least I get money from my grandfather." Tom was as happy as a child. He was getting revenge on his father for abandoning his mother.

As time passed, he became totally inconsiderate toward his friends and work, and he rarely visited Rahul and Julie, which suited Julie just fine. Mostly, he hung around with his so-called friends from Vegas and at his apartment, gambling, drinking a lot, and using illicit drugs with them. A few times, he was arrested for getting into fights in bars and getting caught with hookers, but Rahul was too busy to look after him.

After a couple of years at Monk and Abernathy, Julie finally completed her Texas bar exam. Rahul was eagerly waiting for her exam to be over so that they could have their normal lives back. After the tests, she was exhausted. She had never worked so hard in her life. Everyone told her that she had lost some weight and looked a little pale. All she wanted was to sleep for a few days.

Rahul said to Julie, "By the way, I forgot to mention that Madhu's mother passed away a few days ago. He told me on the phone and asked me to convey it to you."

"I believe that she was very sick for a long time," Julie replied. "How well did you know him?"

"We have been very good friends since our school days. He and his sister mean a lot to me. They helped me after my first husband was gone."

Rahul watched Julie go to the kitchen to make dinner.

At about half past ten in the evening, a phone call abruptly halted their conversation. Rahul answered it.

Rahul looked concerned. "What? Where? Okay, let me see what I can do." He hung up the phone.

Turning to Julie, he said, "Honey, can I ask you a favor?"

"What is it?"

"Tom has been arrested, and he's in jail. He has been denied bail. He'll need an attorney. Can you or someone you know help?"

"Rahul, you know that I haven't officially passed my bar exam yet. The results are still pending. If you want, I can call Jason and see if he will help."

In reality, Julie did not like the thought of getting Tom out of jail. And although Rahul did not want any favors from Jason, he was helpless to do otherwise if he wanted to help Tom.

"Could you, please?" he asked reluctantly.

She got Jason on his cell phone and asked if he would get Tom out. Jason agreed on the condition that she would have dinner with him—with or without Rahul.

A couple of hours later, Jason called and said, "Julie, I got Tom out of jail. It seems that no one here likes him either. He has been in jail before for a DUI and other charges. Today the police caught him drunk and in possession of cocaine. His trial is set up for next week. Anything else you want me to do?"

"No. Thank you very much. It means a lot to me. One more request—Jason, can you please sweep this under the rug for the time being? I don't want to embarrass Rahul at work. I really appreciate it."

"Julie, I'll try—for your sake."

Julie hung up the phone in agony and anger. Dejected, she went to the bathroom and refrained from talking to Rahul, in order to avoid any emotional outbursts.

CHAPTER 39

Playing poker was Tom's passion. But today in Las Vegas, he was losing badly. Cursing and screaming, he watched his cards when the manager came over and asked him to calm down.

He went to the cashier and tried to cash his personal check. The manager called him into his office and said, "Tom, you're already in debt to the casino for over a quarter of a million dollars. I can't cash any check of yours."

"Listen, George, I am a good customer. Besides, I am good in paying you money every month."

"I appreciate your loyalty toward our casino, but my boss has put a limit on your spending. You clear our debt substantially, and I will personally vouch for you."

Dejected, Tom came back to his table.

Next to him was Aftab Ali from Mumbai. He was none other than Suri, Rahul's cousin. Tom did not recognize him as Rahul's cousin. Luckily (or purposely), he was out of town during Rahul's wedding and Tom never got to meet him in Mumbai. And Suri had never come to Boston or Houston to meet his cousin. Suri (a.k.a. Aftab) and Tom had met earlier in the same casino a few months back. He dragged Tom to another table so he could entice him into their plan.

"Hello, Tom. How are you doing?" Aftab asked Tom while patting his back.

"Hi, Aftab," said Tom. "Man, I am losing badly. I think they're cheating," he added very quietly.

At an opportune time Aftab handed him $10,000 in cash and said, "Here, my friend. Take this."

Although tempted, Tom said, "Thanks, but I can't. I hardly know you."

"You know me," Aftab said. "This is only a loan. We both are gamblers and aim to win. It perhaps isn't your day today. But I've been blessed and had a big win earlier. I can only share it with you."

As expected, Tom lost it all. Suri and Tom went to the bar and ordered drinks. Tom was already under the influence of alcohol.

"Aftab, I believe that you are a Muslim, aren't you?"

"Well, yes. My name says so."

"Then why are you drinking? Isn't it forbidden in your religion?"

"Oh, well. I am in Las Vegas, and everything is forgotten here. Tom, you are a good player, and it seems that you are a regular too. Why are you losing so much?"

Tom pulled him close and spoke into his ear. "It's all a conspiracy. I've been coming here for over ten years. They were nice before, but now they won't even cash my check." Tom paused. "You see, I owe them over a quarter of a million dollars. I think they cheated, but I can't prove anything."

"Why don't you play in another casino?" Suri asked.

"They know each other, and all of them know now that I'm a bad risk. These people treat me fairly and let me play when I have cash. Also, I have a croupier friend here. He loans me money now and then."

"Listen, Tom. I am here with a few friends. They're not gamblers, but they come here to enjoy themselves. Wine, women, etc. You know what I mean? You know any girls?"

"Do I know any girls?" Tom said, laughing. "*Hello*, I know plenty—some very intimately! What did you have in mind?"

"These guys like to throw parties," Suri said. "They have a penthouse suite here. Would you like to meet them?"

"Sure! When?"

"Right now! Let me call them first and see if they're there."

When Suri returned, he was smiling. "They will be glad to meet with you. Why don't you arrange for a party with a few women, Tom?"

"It costs a pretty penny, you know?"

"It's no problem," Suri said. "Tell me how much."

~~~

Tom, along with Suri, entered an elegant penthouse suite, which was occupied by Ismail Peshawari and his henchmen.

"Hello, my friend," said Ismail. "Come in, come in! So this is your friend, Mr. Tom."

"Yes, I am Tom, Mr. . . ."

"Ismail Peshawari, but please call me Ismail. These are my friends, Mohammed Johri and Syed Akbari. And you know Aftab Ali. So tell me, Tom, what brings you here?" He laughed out loud. "What am I saying? Why would anyone come to Las Vegas if he did not want gambling and a good time?"

Suri brought drinks in tall glasses for Tom and himself.

"You guys won't have one?" Tom asked Ismail and his associates.

"No, not today," said Ismail. "Perhaps some other time. So do you gamble, Tom?"

Suri answered for him. "Of course he does, Ismail. But he has run into some bad luck. He has been losing since the morning. Otherwise, he is a very good player. He has been coming here for ten years and has never lost to this extent."

Even though Ismail already knew all about Tom's debt with the casino, he played innocent. "Oh, what a shame," he said.

"Ismail, may I ask you a question?" Suri asked.

"Sure, what is it?"

"Can you let Tom borrow some money so he can continue to play here? In return, he will arrange some girls for the evening."

"Of course," Ismail said. "Your friend is my friend." Calling one of his goons, he said, "Syed, please give me my briefcase."

Ismail opened the case, pulled out a large stack of bills, and gave them to Suri. It was $100,000.

"More?" Ismail asked.

"Why don't you make it two hundred and fifty, and he will pay you back quickly, as soon as he wins," Suri said. "Let's go, Tom. We have a party to organize for tonight." He handed Tom the cash.

"Don't you worry about it," Ismail said. "Hope you win a lot of money, Tom." As they were leaving, Ismail handed Tom another $150,000. "Good luck, Tom. Aftab, are you coming back?"

"Yes, I'll bc back shortly."

Tom was now holding tight the stacks of dollar bills, some in his pockets and some in plastic bags. He did not care to find out if the money was hot, laundered, or stolen. He was now obsessed with getting even with the casino and winning a lot more.

As expected, Tom gambled heavily for the next four hours and lost everything. Now he was indebted to Ismail for an additional quarter of a million dollars, in addition to the casino—half a million dollars in total.

A party was going on in Ismail's penthouse suite. Tom ran to his croupier friend, Andy Waters, and told him the whole story.

"Andy, can you help me to talk to Aftab and his friends? I will return their money as soon as I have some."

"Tommie, I like you. But my hands are tied. You are already in trouble with the casino, and now this. This dirty laundry you will have to wash yourself. And watch out for these guys. They are not as considerate as the casino managers. So watch your steps. I shouldn't be saying so." Andy left, shaking his head.

Ignoring the fact that Tom was getting involved in a vicious charade, Andy couldn't warn Tom of the possible outcome. He himself had been blackmailed by his Middle Eastern buddies to help lure Tom into their trap. These goons simply wanted Tom to steal the secrets of Robotechnique for them, especially the projects on which Rahul had worked.

Tom hesitantly got in the elevator with Andy to meet with Aftab and Ismail.

"Come on in, Tom," Ismail said in a loud voice, and he told his friends, "Hey, guys, look who's here." Ismail looked at Tom squarely. "So did you break the bank?"

"No, my luck didn't favor me today, Ismail," Tom said, looking at the floor.

"Never mind that," Ismail said. "It's only money. Come and have a drink. Enjoy!"

For the first time, Tom was extremely quiet. Suri blinked a signal at Andy.

"Ismail, I have to go back to work," Andy said. "I'll see you later." He left, along with the girls, thus ending the party.

Suri came over to Tom and put his arm around his shoulder. "Tom, how do you plan to pay us back the money?"

Tom was silent.

"Okay, forget the ten thousand I gave you. But how about the quarter of a million dollars?"

"I don't have it," Tom replied meekly.

In a thunderous voice, Ismail said from across the room, "What do we have here, a charity show? It's *money*, and you have to pay it back."

"I don't have it, Ismail. How can we work this out?" Tom responded with a shiver in his voice.

"We need some collateral if we let you walk out of here," Suri said. "Perhaps there is something you can offer? Some bit of knowledge, some insider information?"

Tom shook his head. "I don't know anything special."

"I know you work for a company called Robotechnique in Houston. We want details and drawings of a few projects. Here is a list."

Tom skimmed through it and said, "I have no access to many of these."

"Precisely! But I know you have a good friend, Rahul Sharma. You will have to gain his confidence and work with him closely."

"I can't jeopardize his future at the company," Tom said. "And secondly, he would never do it, even if his life depended on it."

"We know that," said Suri. "You will work with him and will get the details for us. Without his knowledge and consent, of course."

"That's *stealing*," Tom said incredulously.

"Bingo!"

"You know I can go to jail for this."

"It's better than losing your life," said Ismail.

"By the way, don't try to run," Suri warned. "We have Houston and other cities well covered."

Tom realized that he was now in deep shit. For the first time, he hated his gambling habits for putting his and his friends' lives in danger.

Suri continued, "You will not see us in Houston unless you give us any trouble. Deliver these items to us here in Las Vegas. Our man will contact you in this casino."

"They will not let me play for long. You see, I owe them some money too."

"We know," Suri said with a smile.

Ismail came over and interjected, "We will take care of your old debts and give them strict instructions not to give you any more credit. You will come here and play whenever you have cash."

Suri said, "That makes half a million dollars to you, Tom. Start working! You have a long way to go." With that, he opened the suite door and let Tom walk out.

Tom dragged his feet and took the elevator down to the lobby. He needed a drink. He called Andy and told him about the conversation he had with Aftab.

"Yes, I know. I could not tell you earlier," Andy said.

"How could you, Andy? You are my friend."

"I could not help it. Now, I am your contact man here. You deliver the CDs to me, and I will pass them on to them."

Rubbing his forehead, Tom said, "I don't know how I am going to get this done."

"Listen, Tom. You and I are both in trouble if we don't do what they have asked us to do. You can't skip town or even the country. You can't go to the police, because you do not have any proof. The risk is all yours. And if you gather money, they would not want it either. They want what they have asked for. Nothing less! You understand?"

"That's mean. I do not have any other choice."

"None!"

"It's late, and I am going to my room. I am catching a flight tomorrow morning. I will see you," Tom said.

"Go ahead! I will take care of these drinks. Remember, call me on this number," Andy said, handing over a small piece of paper.

"And don't be a stranger—for your sake." Andy waved and left.

CHAPTER 40

Ever since Julie had come to Houston, she never had a chance to return to Mumbai, even for a few days.

Vic, Rahul's cousin, had set his wedding date for the second week in September. It was an excellent opportunity for Rahul and Julie to visit India. On the return trip, Rahul wanted to surprise his wife with a visit to the Vatican. He knew that Julie was not a staunch Catholic, but visiting the Vatican would be a dream for anyone of the Christian faith.

On their way back to the United States, they stopped in Rome and checked into a hotel near downtown.

"Why are we stopping in Rome?" Julie asked.

"We're staying just for a few days before we fly to the States."

"How wonderful!" she squealed. "What a great surprise! I would love to."

After checking into a hotel, Rahul and Julie arrived at St. Peter's Basilica in the Vatican. The square was packed with tourists and worshippers. She visited each and every chapel in the cathedral, and its elegance and magnificence stunned her.

In spite of his Hindu faith, Rahul, an avid aesthete, admired the work by Michelangelo and Raphael at the Sistine Chapel.

They took a short flight to Venice and arrived at the Marco Polo Airport. Venice was a unique city, and Rahul had always wanted to go there, ever since he was a young teen. This was the perfect time to visit with his wife, who was the love of his life.

Most of the attractions were along the canals and were approachable by water taxis and boats. They had made reservations to stay at Hotel Danieli at the Piazza San Marcos. To sit down at one of the restaurants at the Piazza San Marco was fulfilling and the ultimate luxury. They had seen these places only in pictures or at the movies, but when they witnessed them in person, they were overwhelmed.

During a gondola ride, Julie said, "This is by far the happiest day of my life. I like it here. It's alive and romantic. You cannot comprehend the beauty unless you are in this place. Thanks for bringing me here and showing me a good time. I love you!"

Her happiness made Rahul feel absolute contentment.

"There is something more I would like to tell you," Julie said, smiling. "Are you ready?"

Curiously, Rahul asked, "Yes, what is it?"

"You are going to be a father. I am pregnant."

Rahul was pleasantly in shock. Feeling jubilant, he hugged his wife and kissed her passionately. "Really?" he exclaimed excitedly. "Wonderful! I am so happy. Are you feeling okay?"

"I am fine. I'll find out more when we get to Houston."

The gondolier looked at them and gently smiled while uttering, *"Amore! Amore!"*

While giving him a cute smile, Julie bashfully hid her face.

This was the ultimate goal in her life. She thought about her past, and she shivered. But all that was forgotten now.

When Rahul realized she was crying tears of joy, he let her rest in his arms. "What now? You are not sad, are you?"

"I am not sad," she said. "On the contrary, I am overjoyed. These tears are from my happiness and gratitude for you. You have made me very happy, especially today. This was my dream. Thank you for being part of my world."

"No wonder people call Venice 'a city for lovers.'"

"You are right," Julie said. "There is no better place in the world than this to share the news of my love with you. Don't you agree, Mr. Sharma?"

He just smiled.

~~~

Julie, unlike everyone else, was eager to go to the office on Monday and continue with her project. She had passed her bar exam and was now promoted to a full attorney at her office.

Rahul tried to spend as much time at home as he could, but the new client, the Department of Defense, had a strict timetable. The DOD also required very tight security. Although Mark had always trusted Rahul's work, sincerity, and judgment, he warned Rahul when he said he wanted Tom to join his team. Rahul assured him that Tom would be of great assistance to the project. After Rahul's promise to keep an eye on Tom, he was cleared by the DOD on a very limited basis.

CHAPTER 41

Rahul wasn't too happy to be absent from home, because his wife needed him the most right now. But Julie understood his responsibilities and knew very well that Rahul would never abandon his duties, whether they were at work or at home.

Upon recommendations by Joann, they hired Lupe Izquierdo, a nanny with a long list of credentials. Regular medical checkups kept them informed that the baby was fine and growing normally.

On the twelfth of May, a little princess was born to Julie and Rahul Sharma. They named her Rachel. The mother was exhausted, but very much elated, and the young father was delirious. The grandparents held the little princess with ebullience. Within a month, Rahul's parents left for Boston, and Mama was preparing to return to her home in Mumbai. The nanny had already started work and was getting acquainted with her new assignments. Things were getting back to normal at their household, and Julie was now ready to go back to work. Lupe was already attached to their young princess.

Rachel was growing into a little girl who demanded more attention from both her parents, as well as her nanny. Rahul and Julie's social life came to an abrupt halt with the arrival of little Rachel. But Tina and Seema, in addition to Tom, were still frequent visitors to their house. Rachel was attached to their friends, especially to Tom, who loved her very much and showered her with toys and various gifts at every possible occasion.

Time and tide wait for no man. There were ups and downs in Rachel's young life, but nothing serious. Often, when she was sick, her parents became hysterical. But overall, she was a healthy child. With immunization, teething, and digestive disorders, it was not uncommon for a child to become sick. With Lupe's help and comfort, they remained calm.

Within a year, Rahul was promoted to the role of vice president of program development, whereas Julie was on her way to becoming a junior partner at Monk and Abernathy.

On Rachel's first birthday, Rahul and Julie hosted a big party. They invited local children and a few friends from their workplaces. Regretfully, Rahul's parents could not be present at their granddaughter's first birthday party. His mother was very sick and was hospitalized. Immediately after Rachel's birthday celebration, Rahul, Julie, and Rachel left to go to Boston to visit his parents, at his father's request. Rahul had been told by the doctors that his mother was very sick. All of them visited her at the hospital only to find that she had turned pale and very frail. But she was very pleased to see Rahul and Julie, and she was especially happy to see Rachel. That night was very critical for her, and both Rahul and his father stayed with her. Julie left with Rachel to stay at Rahul's parents' home in order to keep her daughter's routine.

Very early the next morning, Rahul rushed to his mother to find out that she was getting very uncomfortable, and by dawn, she was unable to breathe. With her family at her bedside that morning, she passed away.

The family mourned her death, especially her husband, who was lost without her. Rahul and Julie had to extend their stay and called their respective offices to notify them. Every Hindu man's and woman's sincere desire is to have their funerary pyre ignited by their offspring. Fortunately, Rahul was present at his mother's bedside at the time of her death, and he could fulfill her last wish. Rahul watched the cremation with deep sadness. She had died happily with her husband, her son, and her son's family by her side, and she was eternally grateful that her beatitude had been granted.

Rahul was mournful on his trip back to Houston. He reflected on his mother's life and his childhood, all those years he spent growing up by her side. Her immense love for him, and now for his family, was a true illustration of herself. She was extremely fond of her granddaughter, and she always affectionately called her *Titlee*, a Hindi word for "butterfly," an appropriate name for a cute child. He was forever indebted to her for what he was today. His father was traumatized, but he had endured it well.

Rahul and Julie happily raised their daughter with great care and affection. Rachel was now almost four and learning fast. She rarely went to sleep without her dad reading her bedtime stories. Ever since she was an infant, her favorite book had been *Baby Faces* by Margaret Miller. Her dad read it with sincerity and always explained to her that each and every child was charming and precious, no matter the color of their skin or their ethnicity.

CHAPTER 42

One cold day in January, it was cloudy and drizzling. Rahul started a fire in their fireplace, which went mostly unused throughout the year.

Just before they were about to go to bed, the phone rang. It was Tom. He was in a panic, and he was stranded at a gas station. He begged Rahul to give him a ride to his apartment since his car had broken down. Rahul told Julie about the call from Tom and suggested that she should go to sleep while he left to take care of his friend.

Rahul left in a hurry. As soon as Rahul entered the gas station, he saw Tom waiting in a dark corner, waving to him.

"What happened to you? Where have you been?" Rahul was a little annoyed.

"I am in trouble. Can you please quickly take me to my apartment?"

"What kind of trouble?" Rahul asked Tom.

"I'll tell you later. Right now, I have to go home. I need to do something in a hurry."

"What is so important that it can't wait until later?" Rahul asked.

"No, please! Drive! Hurry!" Tom was drenched in rain and was now shivering more from fear than from cold.

Rahul did not remember having seen Tom this horrified before. He was actually fleeing from this place.

~~~

In the middle of the night, a phone call woke Julie up. Rahul's side of the bed was empty. She looked at the clock. It was a little after two o'clock in the morning. *Who could it be?* Julie wondered. *Where's Rahul?* She picked up the phone.

"May I please talk to Mrs. Sharma?" said the voice at the other end of the phone.

In a heavy, sleepy voice, she answered, "Yes, who is it?"

"This is Sergeant O'Malley of the Houston Police Department. I am afraid I have to inform you that your husband and his friend have had a bad car accident, and we are at Memorial Hospital. Can you come through the emergency entrance of the hospital, please?"

She was now fully awake and trembling from the news. She could not hold on to the phone and dropped it. She held a pillow over her mouth and stared at the walls aimlessly. She grimaced as she sat at the edge of the bed, wondering what to do next. She picked up the phone and heard the same voice again.

"Are you all right, Mrs. Sharma?"

"How is my husband? Is he okay? Which hospital did you say?"

"Why don't you come as soon as you can?" the sergeant said softly. "He is at Memorial Hospital. Do you know where it is?"

"Yes, I'll leave right now and will be there soon."

She woke up Lupe and explained to her that she had to leave for the hospital. It was late at night, but she called her friend Tina, who arrived at the hospital at the same time Julie did.

This cannot be true, she kept thinking. She was in no condition to drive, but she managed to reach the hospital. She parked the car and ran over to find out what had happened. The hospital was filled with waiting patients, and doctors and nurses were busily hurrying around from room to room. She heard the screeching sounds of ambulance sirens, both from a distance and nearby. She saw new patients being brought in on gurneys, and some were severely bleeding. *They must have brought in Rahul the same way*, she thought. *How dreadful!*

Tina came running to her. In the middle of a large room, Julie saw a man talking to uniformed police officers. As soon as he saw Julie and Tina coming in, he came over and asked if one of them was Julie Sharma.

"I'm Julie Sharma. Did you call me? Where is my husband? Can you please tell me what happened?"

"Yes, ma'am. I am Sergeant O'Malley." The police officer was in his forties, of medium height, balding, and very muscular. "Your husband had a bad car accident. An ambulance brought them here. It appears that there were gunshots, and he lost control of the car and smashed it into a concrete barrier on the freeway. The impact was great. The car was totaled."

Julie's mouth hung open. She was in shock. Tears streamed down her cheeks as Tina put her arms around Julie's shoulders.

"Do you know if your husband or his friend had any fights with anyone earlier? That would explain the situation."

Julie simply shook her head, at a loss for words.

O'Malley said, "The doctors are still with him, and we should know his status very shortly. His friend is also being treated here."

Mark came in when he heard the news. On Rahul's ID card, Rahul had requested that Julie and Mark be notified in case of emergency. Mark called Joann, since Julie was in extreme shock, so she also came in as soon as she heard the news. They all asked Julie what happened, and she told them about the call from Sergeant O'Malley.

Now they were all waiting to hear any good news from the doctor. After half an hour, a doctor walked out of the emergency area, removing his surgical gloves. His mask still hung from his neck. Walking over to Sergeant O'Malley, the doctor talked to him for a while. Then he came over to the area where everyone was waiting and asked for Julie.

"Mrs. Sharma, I have some very bad news for you."

She didn't hear anything else that he said. A painful scream came out of her mouth, and she almost fainted. Tina and Joann held her tight and tried to console her. She was dejected and speechless with this horrendous news.

A little while later, she heard Sergeant O'Malley, who was still speaking to her. "Mrs. Sharma, I don't want to disturb you in your moments of grief, but you will have to identify the body. Can you come by tomorrow when you feel able?"

"I'm her attorney," Joann interrupted. "Please tell me what you need, and I'll instruct her about what she should do."

O'Malley spoke to Joann briefly and left. Julie was shaking terribly, and Tina held her up for support, taking her back to her car. Mark and Joann saw her off. Mark told Julie that although he wasn't looking forward to it, he would inform Rahul's father of the news.

Tina stayed at Julie's house to console her and keep her company in her grief. Tina stayed awake for some time, but eventually she was fast asleep on the sofa, and Julie sat beside her, wondering what had happened to her life.

A few years ago, she lost her first husband in a tragic accident, and now Rahul was gone. She was left all alone in the world again, with no one to lean on, no one to comfort her in her moments of need. Her wicked fate had struck again—not just once, but *twice* in her young lifetime. But this time, her beloved husband had left her with a memento of his love. She had to be brave. At least, that's what her husband would have wanted. Uncontrollable tears were rushing out of her as the reality began to strike: she was alone once again. Finally, she dozed off, and Tina put her to bed gently, sleeping by her side.

Early in the morning, Rachel ran to her parents' bedroom and found Julie lying on her bed with Tina. "Where's Dad?" she asked.

Julie got up quickly and hugged and held her daughter. She was trying to find a way to talk to Rachel about what happened, but she couldn't think of anything.

"Honey, Dad has gone to the office early today." She tried to say more but could not speak. Restraining her tears in front of her daughter, she went to the bathroom.

~~~

On his mobile phone, Mark called the Sharma residence in Boston to break the news to Rahul's father.

"Hello?" answered Rahul's father.

"Dr. Sharma, I am Mark Garcia from Houston." He paused. "I have some very bad news for you." Then he conveyed the heartbreaking message.

Heartbroken, he flew to Houston and went straight to his daughter-in law's house.

The presence of Rahul's father gave Julie a little more strength. The identification of the body at the morgue and arranging for the funeral were terrible jobs, but they were necessary and unavoidable. Julie consented that Rahul was to be cremated, per Hindu ritual.

During this ordeal, Rachel was very confused. She wondered where her dad was and why he wasn't there to be with her, to read her stories and tuck her into bed at night. She kept asking everyone, but no one would tell her.

Finally, she asked her grandfather, "Where is my daddy, Grandpa?"

Tears burst from his eyes, as if he were a child, and he held his granddaughter, crying and sobbing.

Still suffering from unbearable pain, Julie was seeking a little refuge by visiting the church, which she and her mother often did during her mother's visits. Julie was looking for salvation from the misery that had struck her once again. Life was momentarily halted for her, and her future was bleak. The glimpses of hope and happiness she had once were fading fast. Was it karma? It was possible. Right now, she was looking for some indisputable answers. How? From where? Turning to religion might not be the solution, she thought, but the tranquility of church gave her courage to seek her inner peace and strength.

CHAPTER 43

At the same hospital, Tom's life was hanging by a thread. He had been unconscious for five days, but his vital signs were improving and the doctors believed that he had a fifty-fifty chance of survival.

Dr. Spencer, who flew in from Boston, went to see his son at the hospital. He paid a visit to the Sharma family to console them in their grief. After all, Rahul had been his son's best friend and confidant.

In the meantime, at Rahul's office, Mark received a phone call from an FBI agent who wanted to have a talk with him. Mark went to receive him and his colleague at the reception area. Then he brought them to his office.

"Dr. Garcia, I am Agent Stuart Turner, and this is Agent Ira Kaminski. Can we close the door? What I am about to tell you is a sensitive issue."

Puzzled, Mark did what they asked and settled back in his chair. "What can I do for you, gentlemen?"

"You had Tom Spencer working for you. I guess he has been here for some years now. We also understand that he had security clearance to work for the Department of Defense."

"Well, he had the clearance, but I doubt that he ever had any confidential information. You see, Rahul, Mr. Sharma, was in charge, and he kept Tom at a distance, as far as confidentiality was concerned. But, gentlemen, what is this about?" Mark was now getting curious.

"Let me start from the beginning," Agent Turner said. "We have been following Tom for a long time, especially his gambling debts. He borrowed in excess of half a million dollars over a period of two to three years. But he has made some powerful enemies. His so-called 'buddies' who lent him the money introduced themselves as Middle Eastern businessmen. The CIA and the FBI, in fact, identified them as hard-nosed criminals and spies. We couldn't nab them officially until we had some proof."

"But what does this have to do with us?" Mark asked inquisitively.

"Hold on, Dr. Garcia. I am coming to that," Turner responded and continued. "Look at these photos taken last month in Las Vegas by our field office. This one is Ismail Peshawari. He is the leader, and the other two are his associates. There is a fourth person, an Indian, who is not seen in this picture. His name is Aftab Ali, and he orchestrated the entire operation. We don't know whether Peshawari is an Iranian or Afghan national, though he holds a Pakistani passport.

"Peshawari is a dangerous criminal who is wanted for murder and stealing several secret documents. We have reason to believe that they belong to Al-Qaida, a militant Islamist terrorist group. Peshawari knew that Tom was working on a DOD project with you. They asked him to steal the design and architecture of a product named ZRQ."

"Oh, my God!" Mark exclaimed. "How do you know about ZRQ? It's supposed to be classified information!" He was astonished.

"Dr. Garcia, if we all guarded our secrets as they were meant to be, our job would be a lot simpler," said Agent Kaminski. "There is always a leak somewhere. By the way, what is this ZRQ?"

"You know I can't discuss any of our secret projects with an outsider. But in short, it's a government project."

"Does it have to do with the Department of Defense?" Agent Turner asked.

"It has something to do with the missile deterrent system," Mark said reluctantly. "But how is Tom involved with it?"

"They planted Tom to work closely with Mr. Sharma and steal designs of several projects, which Tom has been supplying to them for the last couple of years. Tom apparently knew that he had no access to ZRQ and its confidential information. We have no knowledge if he ever got any access to these documents. Do you believe that he stole from the Department?"

"That's very unlikely," Mark said. "It is very well guarded and stored in our safe, which we believe to be foolproof. Only a handful of people have access."

"Do you and Mr. Sharma have access, Dr. Garcia?" Agent Turner asked.

"Both of us have access," Mark answered. "But what are you trying to imply?"

"Nothing, sir," Turner said. "We are simply trying to cover all our bases. Anyway, coming back to Tom Spencer, we planned to use him as a patsy. We'd pay off his debt and drop any charges if he cooperated with us and we were able to arrest and convict these criminals. He had no choice but to play along.

"We believe that these crooks flew in to Houston, and the meeting was to take place on the night of the accident with Tom. We wired him, and he went off to see these goons. But these guys were smarter than he thought. They smelled a rat, and when he arranged a meeting in a bar, they told him to hand over the documents. Tom said that he left the papers and disk in his car. They kept him under their gun, and one of their associates went to his car to look for it and apparently found nothing."

"How did Rahul get into all this?" Mark asked impatiently.

Ignoring the question, Turner continued. "In the meantime, Tom escaped somehow and went to a nearby gas station. He then called his friend, Rahul Sharma, and asked him to give him a ride to his apartment. When Rahul came to pick him up, these people must have chased him. We have an eyewitness who happened to be driving in the vicinity at the same time and told us that the cars were going at a very high speed and there was a shooting. We have a reason to believe that these criminals were shooting at Rahul's car. Remember that it was not a clear night, and visibility was very poor.

"Evidently, Rahul Sharma was hit by a bullet in his shoulder, and the car went out of control and hit the side barrier, killing the driver and also seriously injuring Tom. We have kept quiet about the cause of Rahul's death, and we suggest you do the same. By the way, Rahul was clean and had nothing to do with this charade. He didn't even know what was going on. He just became a victim of circumstances. Now, if Tom survives, he could be in grave danger.

"We went to the hospital and talked to the doctors and Sergeant O'Malley. He briefed us about the victims, and we came here to see you." Agent Turner concluded, "We thought you might shed some more light on these two men."

Mark was sitting in his chair, expressionless. Then he suddenly lashed out, "That's great! You guys have killed one of my very best friends and a dedicated husband. You should be ashamed of yourselves that you have no guilt."

"Dr. Garcia, I can understand that you feel that way," Agent Kaminski replied. "Everything would have been under control if Tom had not panicked. He put not only himself in danger, but the life of his good friend. Tom was the one they were after, and he brought this on himself. Please keep in mind we were not a party to his gambling habits and his debts."

"We'll keep you informed if something new develops," Agent Turner said. "Good day."

Mark was horrified when the agents left. After gaining his composure, he went to the chief's office to explain the whole episode and discuss how the DOD project should be handled from now on.

The chief was shocked and terrified. A somber mood had set among the people who knew Rahul or had worked with him. The company had operated like a family, and they felt as if they had lost one of their loved ones.

CHAPTER 44

Back at the hospital, Dr. Robert Spencer had spent a good deal of time watching his son fight for his life. Still, Tom was in no condition to talk to anyone. Even now, his head was covered with bandages, and only his eyes and nose were visible. He tried to shake off the tubes that fed him fluid intravenously.

Once Tom identified Robert, he waved his fingers. A short time later, he fell asleep, and the doctor asked Robert to take a break and come back the following morning. The doctors were glad to inform him that the patient was still in serious condition but recuperating well.

The next day, the doctor was talking to Tom as he and the nurses were removing his bandages.

"What happened?" Tom asked. "Where am I?"

"You are in the emergency room. You were in a serious accident, and you had to fight to survive."

"Where is my friend?"

"You are very lucky to have come out of this alive. Unfortunately, your friend did not make it. I'm very sorry about him."

Tom looked around and did not see anything remotely familiar. "What? You mean to say that my friend is dead?"

"Yes. He has been moved to the morgue."

"There!" the doctor said while the nurses were still cleaning his forehead and forearm. "There are a few cuts and bruises, but they will heal soon. You will be all right."

He lifted his hands and gazed at them. In addition to the tubes, his forearms were blotchy. *It must be from the injury*, he thought.

The nurses cleaned his face and forearms with water and alcohol.

"There you go, Tom. You are clean. After we remove the IV, you can walk around if you like," the doctor said.

He looked around and asked in a faint voice, "Tom? Why are you calling me Tom? You said that my friend had been killed. So where is he?"

The doctor and nurse looked at the identification tag on his forearm, and it indicated that the patient was "Tom Spencer." The doctor looked at his colleagues, perplexed. "Why, aren't you Tom Spencer?" he asked his patient.

"No, my name is Rahul Sharma."

They called for the chief of staff and told him what the patient just said.

"So what's wrong?" he asked.

"I am not Tom Spencer. My name is Rahul Sharma."

The chief of staff looked at his tag tied to his arm, and his chart, and called the admitting office.

"We have a problem. The patient is not who you say he is. What's going on?" he shouted into the phone. "Please come here and explain it to me."

The chief of staff gathered all the physicians on the call and asked them if they knew what was going on with the patient and why he was unable to identify himself. In the meantime, the nurse came in and said, "Doctor, we have the patient's father here. Why don't we talk to him?"

"Where is he? Can someone call him here? God damn it!" He was furious.

When Robert approached the patient, the chief of staff asked him, "Are you the patient's father?"

Apparently, he had not met Dr. Robert Spencer and did not know him.

"Yes. My name is Robert Spencer. I am a psychiatrist and a physician in Boston."

"No, he is not my father!" shouted the patient from his bed.

"What's going on?" Robert asked.

"We'd like to know, Doctor."

In the meantime, the patient tried to get out of bed but was held tight by other doctors and nurses. "Don't! Don't! You cannot get out of bed yet!" the doctors and nurses were yelling.

He moved his hand over his face, rubbed it, and then moved his hand over his hair. He felt a sudden, strange uneasiness about himself. "Could you please get me a mirror?" he asked a nurse.

Everyone was confused, and one of the nurses went out of the room to get a mirror. She could only find a palm-sized mirror, which she gave to him after the doctor allowed her to do so.

As the patient looked in the mirror and saw Tom's face, he said in a low, jittery voice, "Who am I? What has happened to me? What have you done to me? I want to see my family. Where is my wife?"

No one had an answer.

"Dr. Spencer, what have they done to me?"

The chief of staff took Robert out of the room and told him what the patient had expressed.

"Is he your son, Doctor?"

"Yes, I am sure he is."

"Then why doesn't he recall his name? He is physically fit."

"Well, he may have had a traumatic episode. I can't say without examining him. I could talk to Dr. Albert, if he is available."

Dr. Albert was a fellow psychiatrist associated with Memorial Hospital.

"Let me see what I can do." He left, shaking his head in disbelief.

Robert went to the patient's room and asked him, "So what's the problem, son?"

"Dr. Spencer, they're calling me Tom. I'm Rahul, not Tom. Something is wrong. I even look like him in the mirror. What have they done to me? Why is this happening? Is Tom dead?"

"It's all right," said Dr. Spencer. "Calm down, and take it easy. You've been under severe stress. Why don't you tell Dr. Albert? He's a friend of mine and is associated with this hospital. He should be here soon."

"Is he a psychiatrist like you?"

"Yes, he is."

"Why do I need to talk to one?" Tom asked. "Is there anything wrong with me? I feel all right. I feel strong enough to get up and walk. Please don't stall! I want to go home to my wife and my daughter. They need me. You know Rachel waits every night for me to read her books before she goes to sleep. And where is my wife, anyway? Why isn't she here?"

The doctor had to restrain him. The nurse gave him a shot of a strong sedative, and he went to sleep soon after.

Dr. Albert showed up a little later and greeted Dr. Spencer. After all, Dr. Spencer was an authority on psychiatry. He explained to Dr. Albert what the patient was going through. "I would like to help, Dr. Albert, but he's my son. I would like you to treat him."

"That's fine. I would like you to be available for advice and consultation."

Robert nodded and went to Tom's room. He was resting peacefully. Robert left the room and made calls to his office. In the meantime, the doctor and nurses were running back and forth from Tom's room.

"What's happening, Nurse?" asked Robert.

"He's getting very restless. He's talking loudly in his sleep, and his movements are so severe and violent that we had to strap him down. We don't understand what he's saying. He is very incoherent."

"Don't wake him up," Robert said. "Let him settle down by himself. I can see what might be happening. I'll call Dr. Albert."

Impetuously, Tom woke up and screamed for the doctor. Robert and Dr. Albert came rushing in. "What's wrong, son?" asked Robert.

"Where am I?" Tom asked. "It was very frightening. No, it couldn't have been a dream. It was all too real. I can't imagine that it happened to me. Can it be true?" Stuttering, he continued, "I don't know what I'm doing here. Please help me."

"What's happening?" Dr. Albert said as he came in. "Tell me more, Tom."

"I remember now. It all looked so real. I heard voices, and they were really loud. It seems that I was drawn through a noisy, dark tunnel. I saw people there. They all looked like strangers, but they helped me cross through it. They were drawing me through the darkness. At the end, there was a shiny light, and I saw an angel, or it looked like one at first. It appeared to be Tom. He was very affectionate and loving.

"Then he said to me, 'Rahul, I'm sorry for causing you all this trouble. You helped me over the years, and you really mean a lot to me. It's time for me to repay you. I want you to go back, and that is the gift I want to give you and your wife. You have your family. I have no one waiting for me. Please do me a favor and accept what I'm offering. It will make me very happy, and I will have a peaceful death. I will always remember you and thank you for all you've done for me in my life. You cannot live in your body, and therefore, you will have to return in mine. Please hurry!'

"All of a sudden, everything became dark, and I didn't know where I was or what I was doing." Tom was shaking from this experience and wondered what was happening to him.

Seeing some grief on Tom's face, Robert said, "That's all right. Dr. Albert is here to help and will explain things to you."

Was it possible for Robert to believe in such an incident? Could it be that the person he thought was his son was not his son at all, but instead his son's friend, Rahul, who had come back in his son's body? How were they going to explain this to other people, especially to Rahul's family? This was certainly a mystifying event.

After giving the patient another dose of sedative, both doctors went out of the room while the nurses prepared the patient to take him from the emergency ward to another room. "What do you think, Doctor?" Robert asked Dr. Albert.

"How does his voice sound to you, Dr. Spencer?"

"Well, he sounds like Tom," Robert said. "His body parts, fingerprints, and even his DNA should match Tom's. The only thing that seems to have changed is his mind. And I cannot say for sure who he is—at least, not yet."

Dr. Albert shook his head. "I don't know what to say. We have to analyze him. As you say, Rahul and Tom had different personalities, and if we can identify them, we can come to some possible conclusion. Is this some kind of schizophrenic behavior?"

"I don't know, Doctor," Robert said. "But I agree with you completely. I know about your expertise in hypnotic induction. Why don't we try that as a last resort? I am aware that it has the danger of provoking further disruptions."

In the afternoon, Agent Turner showed up and asked to see Tom—or whoever he was. He entered Tom's room. The patient was looking healthy and was able to talk and walk slowly.

"How are you, Tom? Nice to see you again. I'm glad you're looking all right." Agent Turner was trying to be friendly.

"Who are you?" the patient asked. "I'm not Tom."

Confused, Turner looked at Tom with a certain curiosity and requested to see his doctor. The nurse referred him to Dr. Albert, and in a short while, he entered Dr. Albert's office and saw Robert Spencer sitting in a chair. He showed his credentials to him and asked to speak to him in private.

"That's all right," Dr. Albert said. "This is Dr. Robert Spencer, Tom's father and my confrere. What can I do for you, Mr.—"

"Turner. I came here from Tom's room. He refuses to identify me. I've known him for well over six months, so I'm confused. Can you please tell me what's happening?"

Both the doctors looked at each other with subtle curiosity.

"I'm not allowed to disclose any particulars about my patient, but I can make an exception because you're an officer of the law, and it could help us in identifying his problems." Dr. Albert explained the entire incident to him.

"Oh, my God," Mr. Turner said. "That's amazing. Could you please keep me posted?" He passed his business card to Dr. Albert.

"Why does the FBI have any interest in this case?" Robert asked. "I'm puzzled."

Reluctantly, Turner told them the entire history of the event, except that Tom was used as bait to catch the criminals.

Robert was furious. "Why has no one told me that this was not merely a traffic accident, but the murder of an innocent human being? Mr. Turner, I have a few friends in high places in Washington, and I can make enough waves to force you to stop playing your games with innocent people."

"Hold off, Doctor!" Agent Turner said. "It was not our doing. You may or may not know that Tom had a severe gambling problem, and he came in contact with some very bad people. He got high off his instant wins in gambling, and he borrowed and spent money without any remorse. May I talk to Dr. Spencer alone, please?" Agent Turner asked Dr. Albert.

Dr. Albert said, "Yes, of course. You can talk here. It's quite safe." And he left the room.

Agent Turner continued after Dr. Albert left. "I came here to give the patient an option. I talked to my supervisor, and he has consented for me to talk to Tom. We will protect him, and he is safe now." He continued after a slight hesitation. "However, these terrorists do have various cells, and they might have a few here in the States. They can act on the terrorists' behalf. The best solution is to help Tom and get him into the witness protection program. But now it has turned out to be a very complicated matter, if what you say is true."

When Agent Turner left, Dr. Spencer stayed in his chair, wondering what was next. Things were getting more and more confounding as time went by.

~~~

Rahul's apparent demise left Julie desolate. She loved Rahul and Rachel so much that she often broke down while holding her daughter. After a couple of days, Mark called and requested that Rahul's father collect Rahul's personal belongings at the office. Julie did not have any objections, but she was not ready to do it herself. Rahul's memory was still too fresh in her mind. She kept a couple of photos and a handful of files. The rest she gave to her father-in-law, requesting he keep them as mementos.

One day, Vasu Sharma received a surprise phone call from Robert Spencer.

"I want to talk about something very important," Robert said. "It concerns us both. Can I talk to you in private? I don't wish to disturb Rahul's wife until Dr. Albert and I are confident about what I'm going to tell you."

They agreed to meet at Dr. Albert's office. Rahul's father was very distracted by Robert's call, but he didn't say anything to Julie yet. She was still in a state of trepidation, and she often woke up in the middle of the night, possibly because of dreadful nightmares. Vasu did not feel that it was fitting for her to get involved at this time.

The next day when Vasu reached the hospital, he found Dr. Spencer with Dr. Albert, discussing Tom and Rahul. They introduced each other and continued to talk.

"Dr. Sharma, what I have to tell you may come as a shock," said Dr. Albert. "We are not sure what we are looking at, but we would like to keep you informed."

"I am listening," Vasu replied. "What's going on?"

"The best thing is to go visit the patient and see how he is," Dr. Albert suggested.

As soon as they entered his room, the patient said in a loud voice, "Hey, Dad! Nice to see you! When did you come to Houston?"

Vasu looked at Robert, assuming that the patient was talking to him, since he was Tom's father.

Dr. Albert said, "He is talking to *you*, Dr. Sharma."

Vasu took a step back and looked at Tom, bewildered, trying to figure out what was going on. He was absolutely dumbfounded.

"Is this some kind of a joke?" he asked angrily, leaving the room.

When Robert saw Vasu Sharma exiting the room, Vasu said, "Robert, I like Tom, but I've lost my son. I don't find this amusing."

"Neither do I, Vasu," Dr. Spencer responded. "Neither do I."

"Then can you please explain to me what is going on?"

"Why don't we ask Dr. Albert?" Dr. Spencer suggested.

"What is going on here?" Vasu asked Dr. Albert. "Can you please give me a simple explanation?"

"Please sit down, Dr. Sharma," Dr. Albert said, closing the door. "This may come as a shock to you, but I have to tell you what's happening here." He looked at Vasu a moment before continuing. "Physically, the patient is Tom Spencer. His reflexes, blood group, DNA, etc., belong to Tom. We ran numerous tests, and they all tell us that he is Tom Spencer."

Vasu asked, "So what's the problem?"

Dr. Albert said, "The patient insists that he is Rahul Sharma, your son. He tells a story about Tom passing his body to dying Rahul. So he has returned as Rahul and not as Tom."

"How could this be?" Vasu asked. "He may be lying. Excuse me, Robert, but Tom did not have high morals. He will do anything to conceal the truth."

"I'm sorry about how you feel, Vasu," said Robert. "I can understand what's happening here. But let's analyze something."

"Does he do it for—"

"Money?" Robert interrupted. "No, I doubt it. He had some from his grandfather's estate. But he always had the temptation to get more. He has a good job, I suppose. I know he has a nasty habit of gambling and possibly using drugs. But that can't be his motive.

"Family? I don't think that could be his motive. As I am told, he is gay or bisexual. He could have gotten any girl he wanted, since he is so handsome and athletic. And I am confident that under no circumstances would he ever hurt his friend, Rahul. So let's ask ourselves why? What could be his other motives?"

"I am no psychiatrist," Vasu said. "But could it be a delusion or some form of amnesia?"

"Delusion? Yes, it's possible," Dr. Albert replied. "But we have to find out for sure. Amnesia? No. He distinctly remembers his life as Rahul and whatever he knows of Tom. And we will conduct tests to prove that.

"Gentlemen, let's address him by whatever name he chooses. Hopefully, soon we will find out the truth, one way or the other. Otherwise, we are facing an unforeseen and troublesome complexity."

On top of that, Vasu was very upset with what Turner had to say. He got even more disgusted with Tom, who had orchestrated the whole episode, which had cost Rahul his life. Vasu Sharma had lost the most of anyone, except Julie.

"I am not asking you to do it for Tom," Dr. Albert reasoned. "But what if you are turning away from your own son, Dr. Sharma?"

How could Vasu face Tom, or whoever he was claiming to be, the person who had knowingly or unknowingly killed his son? It was a difficult task for a father. How could he encounter his daughter-in-law, who had lost her husband and the father of their child? No, it was not possible for him to accept this outcome.

But, Vasu thought for a moment, *if, by chance, he is who he says he is, am I ready to lose my son again forever? This is so confusing!* He decided that there was no harm in talking to the patient to find out the truth, if anyone could ever decipher it.

They arrived at the patient's room. Dr. Albert checked in with the nurse to see how he was doing, and he was displeased to find that the patient had not eaten.

"What about his food?" Dr. Albert asked. "Why hasn't he eaten anything, Nurse?"

"He says he is a vegetarian. We got him soup and a cheese sandwich on short notice."

Vasu heard what she had to say and wondered if it was true. He entered the patient's room reluctantly. "So Tom, tell me, how are you?" he asked him purposefully.

"What? You called me Tom," the patient said. "Dad, why did you call me Tom? I am still your son, Rahul. I may look like Tom, but I really *am* Rahul. Please don't abandon me! It seems my family and friends have already done that. I don't blame them. I don't look like who I say I am. But it's not my fault! My friend Tom gave me the gift of his own life. Please help me regain it."

"I can't believe it," Vasu said. "But let's assume what you told me is true; you know it will be an uphill battle. Your job is mainly to convince one person—and that is Julie."

"Listen, son," said Dr. Albert, "I can't say for sure who you are. You say you are Rahul in Tom's body, and that is quite a mystifying story." He smiled. "Suppose you are who you say you are. Can you convince us of what you have experienced? You, Dr. Sharma, Dr. Spencer, and I are all scientists, so we don't believe in this unnatural abnormality. Do you agree?"

The patient nodded, "Yes, Doctor. I agree with what you say. But there is always a fine line between faith and reality. We all believe in super beings, but no one claims to have seen them— well, except for a few extremists. What I've gone through is not real, I agree. But it did happen. And it may never happen again." He paused. "I am Rahul, and only Rahul knows him the best. You may put me under the microscope, and if there is any question about who I am afterward, I'll withdraw my claim that I've returned.

"Yes, physically I am Tom, but my soul and my mind belong to Rahul, and that's the only thing that matters to me at this time."

All of them left the room with a promise to return the next day.

"So do you believe that he is actually Rahul, Dr. Albert?" Vasu asked. "Has he returned in Tom's body?"

"Dr. Sharma, you are a Hindu, and it seems that you do believe in reincarnation," Dr. Albert replied. "But I am a physician, and I need hard evidence. I will call him whatever he wants me to call him for now, since I don't want to agitate him. I need an open line of communication between my patient and me."

Vasu was not a devout Hindu like his mother, and therefore he was not a staunch believer in religious miracles. For him, reincarnation was like a fairy tale, and to believe in such a phenomenon, he needed scientific proof. For all practical purposes he had cremated his son, and that was the end of it. Nevertheless, he decided to keep his mind open.

Vasu was very quiet on the way to his daughter-in-law's home. He and other friends realized that Julie had become extremely hateful toward Tom and Rahul's past friendship with him. Hence, they became her savior. In her state of ambivalence, Vasu did not find a suitable occasion to talk about what he had experienced at the hospital. Nevertheless, he would have to find a way to convey the message to her and possibly have her meet with the patient.

Julie was to resume her work the following week. She was still in a somber mood and isolated from her friends and relatives. The agony of her separation from her husband was deeply rooted, and she felt betrayed. It had happened again! Brutal events had shattered her dreams, even much more this time. In another country, with no one who could comfort or console her, Julie wished sorely that her mother was by her side.

After meeting with Tom (or Rahul), Vasu returned home. Reluctantly, he approached Julie and asked her in the most persuasive tone, "Julie, may I talk to you for a moment, please?"

"Sure." She came to the living room and settled in a chair. "Please tell me why Dr. Spencer called you earlier."

"I'm glad you have brought that up. I went to the hospital and saw Dr. Spencer and Dr. Albert, who were discussing something very curious and also extremely important." Then he told her the whole story about what he had gone through.

Julie cried hysterically. "Are you trying to insinuate that Tom is my Rahul?"

"It's possible, but you have to decide, Julie," Vasu replied in a gentle tone. "I don't know what to believe."

"So you are saying that this son of a bitch is *not* Tom but my husband Rahul? This can't be true. He has *killed* my Rahul! How can I ever forgive him? Please tell me it isn't so!"

"We are not sure," Vasu answered. "But can you trust the doctors? If they come up with a diagnosis that confirms what he says, are you ready to change your opinion? Don't you want to keep an open mind? Don't you want a chance to get your husband back?"

"I will do whatever possible in my power to get him back," Julie said. "But I have lost him. It's a false hope, and it is nightmarish for me to think about a terrible wolf trying to disguise himself in sheep's clothing. Tom is a very conniving and deceitful person, and you should not believe what he says.

"Ever since Rahul left us on that dreadful night, I have been suffering from fear of the dark," Julie continued. "I keep thinking about him and me. I could not accept or love him because he looks like Tom, even though he may actually be Rahul. I don't want to talk about it. Can I go now?" She did not mean to be disrespectful, but she could not stand any further discussion about it. She was profoundly opposed to Tom or anyone who looked like him, and there was hardly any chance of reconciliation.

Soon after she left, Vasu sighed. "God help us," he said and went to the guest bedroom.

Back at the hospital, the patient was moved to a psychiatry ward at the request of Dr. Albert. He was physically fit to walk around.

CHAPTER 45

Tom's aunt Liz had asked her daughter, Dominique, to go to Houston and see how her cousin was doing. In spite of the fact that Dominique was extremely busy with her classes, she took time to visit him over the weekend. Fortunately, she had a key to Tom's apartment. She went straight to his apartment from the airport.

The bachelor pad was a real mess. She cleaned it to make it more livable. Then she got hold of his car and drove it to the hospital. There, she met with her uncle Robert, who was waiting in the hallway for Dr. Albert. They greeted each other, and he asked her to go in and talk to the patient.

"Hi, how are you, Tom?"

"Oh, it's you! I'm fine, Dominique. How are you?"

"Come on! You never called me Dominique before. I'm Domino, remember? What's wrong with you?"

"Well, something is very wrong, and I'm trying to convince you and everyone else out there." He told her about the accident and the life-after-death experience he had encountered.

"Oh, my God! So you're telling me that you're Rahul and not Tom? That's weird." She was in a state of shock.

The more she talked to him, the more she was becoming convinced that the bodies might actually have been switched, as Rahul claimed. Mentally, the patient was possibly Rahul, the one she knew all along as the bright and cheerful one. He could not possibly be Tom, whose personality was completely different.

She hugged him before leaving and told him that she would be back the next day before leaving for Palo Alto.

Both doctors were planning a set of tests to identify the patient and what really was happening. They requested Vasu to be present, but he would not participate in the questioning. The patient had no objections.

Dr. Albert approached him and said, "Tom—I'm sorry, *Rahul*, or whoever you are—can you tell me more about you?"

"Such as what, Doctor?"

"Whatever comes to your mind. You can tell us about where you were born, your childhood, school, job, your family, and etc."

"You are trying to determine if what I am saying is true or not? All right, I will work with you." He said with a smile, "You all know that I was born in India." Then he continued to talk about his parents, his school days in Boston, and college days in Houston.

"So how do you feel about your mom and dad?" asked Robert.

"My mom died a few months ago. God bless her soul! She was a fine person. She loved my daughter very much and called her *Titlee*, a butterfly. I adored her. You saw my dad yesterday. He should have been here by now."

"He is here. But you can't see him."

"Well, they loved each other. My dad was more practical. My mom was a docile and somewhat conservative Hindu, but a very loving person." And he continued to talk about them, and how his father had gotten into MIT and had earned his PhD. His mother had always taken Rahul to a temple on Sundays and holidays. They had wonderful trips to India, etc.

"So how do you feel about Joyce and Jessica?" Robert asked.

"Joyce? Who? Mrs. Spencer?" the patient asked incredulously. "Come on, Dr. Spencer! You are trying to trick me into answering your question. I did not know her well, but I can tell you how Tom felt about her."

Dr. Spencer said, "Never mind! Sorry about that, Dr. Albert."

There were questions about his school and college days and his friends, which, of course, included Tom.

"So the staff tells me that you have turned vegetarian. Is that so?"

"I've been vegetarian all my life. I don't use drugs. And I am not a compulsive gambler either. Excuse me, Dr. Spencer, for spilling it out."

Dr. Spencer simply nodded.

"You are not just saying these things to misdirect us, are you, Rahul?" Dr. Albert asked, trying to get answers from him. "You know we can't prove anything about what you just said. Anyway, we will assume that you are telling us the truth. Please, continue."

The details from Rahul's past checked out. But the diagnosis could not be based only on these simple conversations. They needed more supportive evidence, and the doctors convened to decide on their next course of action. As soon as Vasu entered the examination room, Tom (or Rahul) asked him about his wife and daughter.

"They are fine, son," Vasu replied. "Unfortunately, Julie is not willing to see you in this condition. You know how she felt about Tom, and since you don't appear to be Rahul, she may not support your claim to be her husband. It will take time for us to convince her. We are waiting to hear from the doctors, who will hopefully be able to uphold your claim."

Rahul exhibited anguish on his face and continued, "You know they're my family, my love, and my life. I want to see Julie, with or without Rachel. I just want to talk to her and convince her that I am still her husband, Rahul. Please help me, Dad!" After he stopped sobbing, he said, "I never meant any harm to anyone in my life. I've been very compassionate to my fellow human beings. I helped people, and I never hurt anybody. You know that. So why am I being punished and kept in isolation?"

Dr. Albert sat by his side and told him gently, "Listen, I would like to lay down the facts in front of you. You went to help your friend Tom the other night when you had an accident. As I understand from Dr. Sharma, Julie never liked Tom. Is this correct?"

"Yes, but he was my friend," the patient responded. "I kept the relationship very tepid after a few altercations with Julie."

"Precisely—that is my point. Unfortunately, Tom had terrible vices. He was a compulsive gambler, used illicit drugs, had bad drinking habits, was unreliable at work, and was generally an irresponsible individual. Yet, he was your friend. Tom made more enemies than friends, and your wife was one of the people who despised him. She feels strongly that Tom was responsible for this mess. Now you are telling me that while you look like Tom, you still want to reconcile with Julie. How are we going to accomplish that?"

Vasu realized that the patient was miserable and hurting. Yet, he did not have any way to convince Julie either. The only person who could make her change her mind was Rahul himself. A meeting was very difficult, if not impossible. He refrained from insisting upon it with Julie only because he was almost certain that he would lose contact with his daughter-in-law for a long time, if not forever, which he could not afford to do. The best way to solve this problem was to develop a plan where Rahul's and Julie's friends could credibly affirm his identity.

Vasu thought of many people who could shed light on this riddle. Asha's sister had been planning a trip to the United States, but after her sister's death, she had postponed her trip indefinitely. Rahul and Tom's friends Joey and Renee could provide some proof. Mark was another person who could assist. Julie trusted their friend Madhu, so he might yield a valuable answer, as well. But he wasn't due to visit Houston anytime soon. Locally, the friends might say what they felt like, but it still would not give her any assurance. However, all these rendezvous needed his doctor's approval, the purpose of which would have to remain absolutely secret so that Julie would not feel like there was collusion against her.

But there was a ray of hope for Rahul. Rahul's cousin Vic and his wife, Diya, were scheduled to arrive in Houston, a visit planned long before the accident. Rahul trusted him, and Julie was very comfortable with him; thus Vasu saw their visit as an opportunity for reconciliation between Rahul and Julie. Vasu thought if he could possibly identify that the patient was, in fact, Rahul, he could perhaps influence Julie to believe it too.

The arrival of Vic and Diya in Houston was an awkward time for both of them, but they managed it well. Rahul's father hoped that Vic and his wife would stay long enough to comfort Julie and refute her fears.

Vic was eager to see his cousin Rahul and wished they could be of further help to Rahul's father. Vic was very fond of Julie, but he was shocked to see such a dynamic and vibrant young woman crumbling under the pressure of uncertainty.

Julie's weariness usually disappeared in the presence of young Rachel, who was an absolute doll. She was playful but constantly reminded her mother of her missing dad. She was the only true link between Rahul and Julie at that time.

CHAPTER 46

When Vic and Diya arrived at Rahul's room with Vasu, the doctor was out on his routine check.

Rahul saw his cousin and screamed with joy. "Hi, Vic! Hi, Diya! You are here. How wonderful! Is Sonja with you? How is Auntie? Dad, why didn't you tell me Vic and Diya were coming to Houston?"

Vic said, "Sonja wanted to come, but she didn't have the time off. And you remember Diya."

Vic could not believe his eyes. Vic had met Tom very briefly, whereas Diya never did. Besides, he had met Tom at the wedding, but among so many guests, Vic never came to know him closely. *The patient must be Rahul*, Vic thought. They talked about family details, times they had spent together, and when and how Rahul met Julie.

"Vic," Rahul said, "you don't believe this, do you? It is inconceivable what I am going through. Rahul is alive, but no one realizes it. Even Julie is having a difficult time coping with my situation. You remember how you indirectly helped me talk to Julie? You did a phenomenal job, and that was a paramount moment for us. Now you have one more challenge. Please convince Julie that it is me, Rahul. I may not look like him, but I am still her husband. Can you please help me? I beg you. You and Madhu are my only hope."

"I do sympathize with you, and I can call you Rahul," Vic said. "But what about everyone else? Your appearance is not the same as the Rahul we know. It is going to be an uphill battle for you."

"I don't care about the others."

"I will try my level best to help you. But I can't promise anything. We will see you later," Vic said and left.

In the meantime, Robert Spencer made an unexpected visit to Rahul and told him he was leaving for Boston. "I know you are in good hands with Dr. Albert. I have to leave. I can't ignore my patients. We cannot come to any medical conclusion yet, but we will. What I was going to talk to you about is that your—oh, sorry, *Tom's*—grandfather had left Tom money before he passed away. It's now a little over one hundred thousand dollars. I feel it is only proper for me to hand it over to you. What do you think?"

"Thank you very much," Rahul said. "It's logical and legal for me to accept it. But it isn't prudent, because it's not mine. Dr. Spencer, I don't know what to say, but please do what you think is best for Tom and what would have made him happy."

Robert shook his head and said, "Very well, young man. I will leave, and perhaps I will see you in a few weeks."

After shaking hands with the patient, Robert left to see Dr. Albert. While talking about the conversation he'd had with the patient, Robert said, "Dr. Albert, I have never come across such a case in my life. It's mind-boggling. I have no suggestion for any treatment. I hope you will come up with something. Please keep me posted. By the way, he refuses to accept the inheritance from my father. This is not like Tom. There was never enough money for him. I can't use it, so I don't know what to do with it." After a pause, he said, "Obviously, this looks like a case of resuscitation. But the personalities have changed. I am puzzled."

Dr. Albert thought for a moment and asked, "Are you then convinced that this young man is Rahul and not Tom?"

"After his incontrovertible answers, I am leaning toward it. But I don't understand it. There is no reference to such a precedent in any book that I have ever referred to. It's an interesting case, but very sad for the family members. Have we overlooked anything else, Doctor?"

"I don't think so," Dr. Albert replied. "I am proposing hypnotherapy to see what we can find out. As you rightly said, it may reveal some innermost secrets, but I doubt it. I have no other alternative though. I would like you to be present. Can you make it?"

"When do you plan to perform it? I can make myself available if you give me enough advanced notice. I am very interested in observing these symptoms."

"I still have to get the patient's permission to perform the treatment. Without his willful consent, the tests may not yield any useful results. I'll call you as soon as I find out."

Early the next morning after Julie had left for work, Vasu, Vic, and Diya were sitting at the dining table for breakfast. Vic brought up that he would like to talk to the patient and get into his mind for finer details, to see if he remembered them.

"It's fine with me if it's okay with the doctors," Vasu said. "When do you want to go there? He loves your company, and it surely will cheer him up."

"Can we take Rachel with us?" Vic interjected.

Everybody looked at him, mystified.

"Not without Julie's permission!" Diya said. "And what are you trying to prove? There is no reason to do that, other than cheering up the patient. Rachel cannot recognize how her dad looks now."

"Maybe you're right," Vic said. "Forget it. I don't think Julie will like it."

~~~

Dr. Albert picked up his phone and called Robert Spencer. When he got Robert on the phone, he said, "Dr. Spencer, this is Dr. Albert from Houston. How are you?"

"Very well. Thanks. What can I do for you?"

"I think the patient is ready for the next test, and it would be great if you are present during the procedure."

"I'd like to. Let me see here. What dates do you have in mind?"

"Next Wednesday is the fifteenth and is suitable for me. Can you make it?"

"That would work fine for me. I will see you in the morning of the fifteenth. Any improvement to the patient?"

"Some minor but nothing substantial. We'll see you."

~~~

On the fifteenth the doctors met in Dr. Albert's office. They had invited Vasu too, strictly as an observer.

Dr. Albert said, "I have discussed with the patient about the test and got his approval after suggesting that their diagnosis could achieve positive results—results which might enable them to arrive at reasonable credibility. Dr. Spencer, I'm glad you're here. I propose to conduct Freudian hypnoanalysis. I may touch on pseudoscientific approaches. A hypnotic regression might reveal more information about a patient like this. What do you think?"

Dr. Spencer said, "It's your show. I'm here to observe. You know I follow Freudian techniques, but I'm not ruling out Ericksonian hypnotherapy either."

"All right, young man. Are you ready to begin?" Dr. Albert asked the patient. "Dr. Spencer and Dr. Sharma are here to observe you. Dr. Spencer will assist me in the therapy, and Dr. Sharma will strictly observe it from the gallery. The test should not take long, and I'll show you the results after consulting with my colleagues. Okay?"

The patient was seated in a reclining chair, while Dr. Albert held his hand. "Hello, Dr. Spencer. Hi, Dad! I'm ready when you are, Dr. Albert."

The nurse gave him some tablets, which he swallowed. He was then asked to relax. They injected other medicine through intravenous tubes.

"Okay, when I tell you, you will concentrate, feeling heavier and heavier, until you fall asleep."

Within a few moments, he closed his eyes and went into a hypnagogic state.

"Can you hear me, son?" asked Dr. Albert. "If you can, open your eyes. You will go to your past and answer the questions I ask you, okay?"

He nodded and showed his willingness to cooperate.

They talked about his school and college days, work, his visits to India, and meeting his wife, Julie. His face lit up at the mention of her name, and he told them each and every detail, including meeting his wife. They did not ask him any personal or intimate questions that would embarrass him and others. Those questions also might not produce any fruitful results, except to possibly convince Julie of the truth of Rahul's claims. However, they still preferred not to ask these invasive questions.

"So how long have you known Tom? When did you find out that he was gay?"

"Tom and I went to school together in Boston. He was my close friend. He told us that he was bisexual. We were in Fort Lauderdale one spring. Renee didn't come with us. There were four of us, Tom, Joey, Andre, and me. Joey's aunt, Mrs. Lowenthal, had a handyman, Juan, who took us to Disney World. There, he told us that Tom and Andre were gay. But later on, Tom admitted to all of us that he was bisexual."

Robert's face showed his displeasure, but he did not say anything.

"Good! That's very good," Dr. Albert said. "Please go back to your childhood and tell me what you remember."

He shook his head in affirmation and said that he grew up in Cambridge, Massachusetts, learned to bike, etc.

"So please tell me about your grandmother and other relatives. Did you enjoy visiting them?"

He narrated visiting his grammy to attend his aunt's wedding and get her permission for marriage.

"And when did you have your appendectomy?" Dr. Albert asked.

"Appendectomy? I've never had a surgery."

Dr. Albert was puzzled and looked at Vasu. Then he realized that the scar that he saw was actually on Tom's body, not Rahul's.

"Rahul, I'd like you to come back from your childhood. Now you are a grown-up. You are in Houston and are recuperating from your accident."

The patient's facial expression showed the signs of growing up in a hurry.

"Very good! Tell me about your family, especially your wife and daughter." Dr. Albert was trying to get him engaged in more conversation.

"My wife doesn't believe that I am Rahul. I love her and my daughter very dearly. My life will have no purpose without them and their love." At this point, he showed distinct displeasure and became restless.

Robert indicated to Dr. Albert that the session was going well, but it had to end soon to avoid any unnecessary mental stress and damage to the patient. Dr. Albert agreed.

They asked many other questions that were irrelevant to his life and memory, but they were important for psychological analysis. They finally had enough information from the therapy.

Dr. Albert told the patient to count backward, from ten to one. Then he tapped him lightly on his shoulder to wake him up.

When Rahul opened his eyes, he asked the doctor, "So shall we begin?"

"We are done, son. You take a rest. You can walk if you like, and the nurse will take the IV needle out of your arm. I'll be back soon. Relax!" With that, Dr. Albert left the room with the two fathers—one who had lost his son, and another who had just gained one.

In the office of Dr. Albert, Robert did not show any expression, whereas Vasu looked relieved from the day's experiences.

"So where do we go from here, Doctor?" Vasu asked.

"First of all, Dr. Sharma, let me tell you that the procedure may not look like any more than just the few questions we have asked him," Dr. Albert said. "But they revealed to us many clues. His body movements and his mental stress may also give us many answers, but we still have to analyze them. But let me hear what Dr. Spencer has to say."

Robert was trying to interpret the results of the test. "I think I may safely express my opinion today and say that he is not Tom. But then again, I never knew my son intimately anyway. On the other hand, I am not inclined to assume that he is your son Rahul either, Vasu. You have to encourage him to disclose more evidence to you. The reason is simple—his dreams, his past, and his current behavior can be manipulated by any bright and intelligent individual. But that does not seem to be true in his case. Now let's suppose that you don't support his claim— he could withdraw and have a tragic ending. It is a very delicate matter, and I strongly advise you to handle it with the utmost diligence."

"Robert, I am drowning in a bittersweet reality," said Vasu. "I don't know what to believe. A few weeks ago, I cremated my son at the crematorium in a very somber mood. His wife and I are coping with the loss. What he said in therapy appears to be true. The appendicitis scar, which you saw on Tom's body, is not really his. He was right that, as Rahul, he had no such surgery. Nevertheless, it is very hard for me to grasp this situation. His wife is also on an emotional roller coaster, and you can understand that. She is physically fit but very weak emotionally. How in the world am I going to explain to her what we experienced today? She is very adamant about her views, and I don't even know how to even bring her up to date. Without her support, nothing can be achieved. Sorry, Robert, I am not in a position to talk further about this."

Dr. Albert said, "I am afraid, gentlemen, that the patient, whoever he may be, could continue to behave radically. I can't say for sure, but if his wife listens to either of you, the situation may improve dramatically."

"Robert, you know her, and she knows of you," said Vasu. "Why don't you try to talk to her?"

Dr. Spencer said, "I don't recall that we have ever met, except briefly in an elevator. But we do know of each other, so I can give it a shot. I can't promise you anything. But I owe it to your son, Vasu."

With that, they all dispersed.

Later in the evening, Julie answered a phone call. "Hello, may I help you?"

"May I talk to Mrs. Sharma?"

"This is she. Who am I speaking to?"

"Mrs. Sharma, this is Dr. Robert Spencer, Tom's father. How are you?"

"Call me Julie, Dr. Spencer. I am fine. I heard a lot about you from my husband, Rahul. He had great respect for you. But I don't believe this is a social call. What's on your mind, Doctor?"

"Thank you, Julie. I was wondering if you and I could have a meeting. Being a psychiatrist, I have some information which may be useful for you to hear. In any case, I am not trying to tell you what you should and shouldn't do. My son has always spoken very highly of you, and I want an opportunity to talk to you in person, if I may."

Julie waited for a moment before responding. "Rachel has a pediatrician's appointment tomorrow morning. After I drop my daughter back at home, we can meet at eleven in the morning. I would prefer to meet somewhere close to the Galleria mall."

"That's fine, Julie, I'll see you at eleven tomorrow at the café across from the Galleria. I believe it's a Starbucks."

"I know where it is, Dr. Spencer."

She was apparently showing her lack of desire to meet with him.

At about eleven, Julie approached Dr. Spencer, who was seated at a table in the corner of the café. Although he had briefly met her in Boston, he greeted her, asking her if she was Mrs. Julie Sharma. They were seated at the table.

"Thanks for coming, Julie. I'm glad to see you at last. Your husband and Tom both spoke highly of you, and I can understand why."

Julie recognized Robert, who had a slight facial resemblance to Tom. He was as tall as Tom and well built, with bushy, reddish brown hair that showed patches of gray. He had a likable personality and charisma that attracted people to him.

How could this man be Tom's father? she thought to herself. Her animosity toward Tom's father was waning, and she wanted to hear what he had to say. After ordering herself a decaffeinated coffee, she tried to get more comfortable.

"So I understand you are an attorney," Dr. Spencer said.

"Yes, I am a junior partner with Monk and Abernathy," Julie replied. "And I like it there." She told him briefly about her work.

"You may have guessed why we are here," Robert said.

She showed her uneasiness about the comment, but she kept quiet and looked at him with polite interest.

"You know that I am a psychiatrist. I've practiced for over twenty-five years. I have published many papers and several books on the subject." With a sigh, he continued, "That's very satisfying, but terribly costly. I forgot the most important mission in my life: to raise my family. I had that responsibility, and I ran away from it." He took a sip of coffee and continued, "My son never forgave me for that. Tom was a good kid, but he did not have good values in life and abandoned the common goals of society. Please remember that he grew up without the total support of his parents. After my wife and I separated and divorced, I met him every now and then, and on occasion, he was obnoxious. I don't believe that he meant it though.

"Julie, what I have to say may not come easy for me. A few weeks ago, your husband and Tom were in an accident—fatal for one of them, leaving the other in turmoil. I am sorry that I have to bring up the details, which are very shocking for both of us. At first everyone thought that your husband was killed, whereas my son survived. When he woke up, the patient claimed to be your husband, and he had detailed knowledge of Rahul's life. Dr. Albert, who is an expert fellow psychiatrist, concurs with me. Thus, we ran extensive tests to prove what the patient says, and we have concluded that he is *not* Tom. But to determine if he is Rahul, we need your help. Your father-in-law was present during these investigations, and I hope he has mentioned it to you."

When Julie stared at him and did not respond, he went on. "Julie, it's very hard for a father to lose his son. I have practically lost my whole family as I clung to my work. Although Tom and I did not see eye to eye, he still was my son, and I loved him dearly. It is very difficult for me to give up my son. I can't tell you who the patient is, but the fact remains that he is not my son, Tom, even though he looks like him. This is not a sinister plot to convince you of the contrary. But if my son has survived as Rahul, I would be the last one to object. Your husband was a fine, decent, and caring human being. I don't have medical evidence to prove his claim to be Rahul, but it is my intuition. The rest is up to you, and therefore, I came here to talk to you for your support. Please help us!"

Holding back her tears, she said with a grim face, "Dr. Spencer, I appreciate your talking to me. I don't know how much you know about me. I was married before I married Rahul. My former husband was apparently killed in action—and now this!

"One lonely and dreadful evening, he left me, and my life came to an abrupt halt. All of a sudden, my life became insignificant. It had no purpose anymore. I could not bear his parting. My ultimate wish was to die in his arms, but he was gone. But a message came though, telling me to be strong. He left something for me to nurture, and that was our daughter. I cannot avoid my responsibility, and will continue to drag on through this tragic life. I have to bring up our child, as he would have done. Our enduring love will continue through her.

"All of my life, I've given up everything for a piece of happiness. I've lost two of my most priceless possessions. I have nothing more to offer. My life is almost empty. Other than my daughter, all I have left is my husband's memory, which I will cherish to eternity. So why do you want to take it away from me?" She could not talk any further.

"I'm sorry," said Dr. Spencer. "I did not want to cause you any more pain. All I am saying is that your life need not be empty. Your husband may—I repeat, *may*—be alive, and that is the greatest gift you will ever receive. As I said earlier, I cannot prove anything, but let's suppose that if, miraculously, he survived to be your husband; are you prepared to lose him again? I am not trying to delude you. It is only you who can determine the facts. Please give it a chance."

Handing over his business card to her, he said, "Julie, I'll be leaving early tomorrow morning. I'm staying at the Marriott, a few blocks from here. If you need me for anything, please call me at the hotel or in Boston. You are a brave girl. I hope you and your daughter will be happy to meet him." Julie and Robert left the café at the same time and headed toward their separate destinations.

Back at her home, Julie told Vasu and Vic about her meeting with Dr. Spencer.

Vic said, "I'd like to believe that there may be merit to his belief. Why don't you talk with Dr. Albert before you meet the patient? It's possible that he has been reincarnated as Rahul."

To this Julie asserted, "Vic, you are a Hindu, like Rahul. I am a Christian. Without any offense to you, I don't believe in reincarnation. Secondly, I can't believe that the patient may be my Rahul. That is absurd. What I need is irrefutable evidence to prove that he is my husband. Do you think I'll get that by meeting with him?

"He looks like the one I hate. What good does it do? Even if he is who he claims to be, how can I face anyone who looks like Tom? He isn't welcome in this house, in my life, or to play with my daughter. Please don't worsen the problems I am going through."

"I am sorry, Julie," Vic said. "I understand your feelings. There is no harm in trying though. I'll go with you, if you want me to."

Julie mellowed down and found his suggestion somewhat sensible. She made an appointment with Dr. Albert before she decided to meet with the patient. She respected Vic's views, but, after all, he was one of Rahul's relatives, and he could be prejudiced.

At the office, Julie was busy with her work. She found time to send an e-mail message to her friend and confidant, Madhu, requesting his help to resolve her situation.

CHAPTER 47

Mark Garcia at Robotechnique did not know how to fill the vacant position that Rahul had once occupied. Rahul was proficient at what he did and had eventually become irreplaceable. The only other person who had good knowledge of what Rahul did was Madhu. Mark went to the chief's office and explained that Madhu was the only right candidate to take Rahul's place. The chief always respected Mark's views and suggested that he talk to his counterpart in India first, and then to Madhu. Hence, Mark arranged for Madhu to come to Houston and meet with him and the chief.

Vasu Sharma saw no reason to stay in Houston. He was tormented by this development. He had lost his wife a few years ago and apparently now his son too. It was extremely traumatic for him as a parent to lose his child. He asked for Julie's permission to leave, with the promise to return whenever she needed him. There was a sense of loneliness in her house after his departure.

Julie decided to see Dr. Albert, who disclosed the patient's nightmare to Julie, an additional piece of data that supported the patient's claim that he was Rahul. Even through the hypnotherapy, the patient revealed his true identity.

Julie said, "Dr. Albert, Tom has a history of manipulating people. How can I trust his statements, as well as what he told you?"

"Mrs. Sharma, you do trust Dr. Spencer. Do you feel that he could have any malicious intent?"

"No, Doctor, I didn't mean to imply that. I was merely suggesting that you check to see if you have overlooked anything. Tom may be playing a mind game."

"He could be. But he would have to be extremely brilliant and successful in his endeavor. We have taken all precautions in this regard. It is still possible, but highly unlikely. We have many professionals who would have noticed a slight variation in his behavior pattern. Besides, I've administered sodium pentathol on a couple of tests, with his approval, of course. This medicine is commonly known as the 'truth serum.' Not that it is a foolproof drug, but it is very potent for this purpose. Besides, he is physically very fit. As soon as he shows further improvement in his mental stability, I'll have to release him."

"You are advising me to see him and talk to him?"

"Yes, if you want to. It would be very encouraging for the patient. I have to warn you though. I'll only allow you to do so if you are receptive and ready to accept what he says. I don't want him to become upset or further disturbed."

"All right, I will be calm. But what should I do if I become nervous and can't continue?"

"I'll show you a button. If you push it, we will terminate the meeting. We do have a nurse on standby."

Her heart was pounding hard, and she wondered if anyone could hear it. She was trembling from her nervousness.

"I don't wish to put you though mental stress of this kind," Dr. Albert said. "But sooner or later, you may have to face it, and I'm sure it's better to do so now rather than later."

"No, I'll be fine. I need something to drink first though."

"Should I get you a can of Coke or Sprite, Julie?" asked Vic.

"No, water is fine."

A nurse gave her a glass of water, and she was as ready as she could ever be.

"I'll go with you, and then I'll leave. I recommend that you see him alone," said Dr. Albert.

"That's fine. Rahul's cousin Vic will go in with me for a moment. Is that okay?"

"Yes," said Dr. Albert.

They entered the room together. The patient was reading a paper and saw Dr. Albert and Julie coming toward him. He almost got up on his feet with an outburst of exultation.

Julie, on the other hand, was engulfed with rage to see the person who apparently had gotten her husband killed. But she stayed calm and focused.

"Look who has come to visit you," Dr. Albert said to Rahul.

She kept her composure and sat on a chair next to his bed. Dr. Albert checked him for a minute and left, saying that he would be back. Vic also left the room to give both of them some privacy.

"So how are you?" Julie was not sure whether to call him "Rahul" or "Tom."

"I'm fine. I'm so glad you came. It's nice to see familiar faces around here. How's *Titlee*? Are you all right? You look pale and tired. You'd better take care of yourself." She did not say anything.

Titlee? How did he know that name? she thought to herself. *Did Rahul tell Tom about it?*

"When I didn't see you for a while, I thought you were still mad at me. I shouldn't have left the other night to pick Tom up and leave him at his apartment without telling you what had actually happened. Let me tell—"

She interrupted him. "No need to. They spoke to me about it in detail."

Her laconic response bothered Rahul, but he kept the conversation going. "I don't understand why Mark has not come to see me yet. Looks like he isn't in town. You all are confused about how I look, aren't you? After the accident, I left my body behind and came back in Tom's. It's incredible, but it's true. The doctors ran all the tests to prove who I am, and they're convinced about what I've said all along. Did they tell you what actually happened to me?"

She nodded.

"But you do trust me, don't you? It doesn't matter if anyone else believes me or not. I have you, and you have me. We've known each other so intimately that we should be able to confide in each other without any deception. Let me tell you what I remember." He told her a detailed account of their first encounter in Mumbai and their trip to the Elephanta Caves.

She was very sad as he told the story of these memorable events. She didn't understand what was real and what was not.

"Don't be sad," Rahul said. "You know I can't see you like this. Your being miserable can't help me to recover. Don't you believe that I'm Rahul? Vic says that no one will believe me. But I don't care about anyone else, if you believe it."

Julie said, "It doesn't matter what I believe. If you like, I'll call you Rahul. But how am I going to convince our relatives and friends? How am I going to convince Rachel that you are her dad? How am I going to tell her and many others that you may have transformed from Tom to Rahul? They may listen to me, but could just as well laugh at me for saying so."

"So what do we do?"

"I don't know. I don't have any answers. If you have one, please tell me."

As soon as the door opened, she saw Dr. Albert coming. She stopped talking and remained calm as she got up to leave.

"When will I see you again?" Rahul asked.

"I'll be back as soon as time permits. Rachel takes up much of my time. I'll leave now, okay?" She left with Dr. Albert.

"So what do you think, Mrs. Sharma?" asked Dr. Albert.

"I am honestly confused. He does not look anything like Rahul, but he has recollection of times we spent together, some with intimate details. I need more time to grasp it. I'll be back as soon as I feel mentally and emotionally strong enough."

"Please remember that we will be releasing him soon. Dr. Spencer and I strongly believe that mentally, he does not seem to be Tom, but all the physical tests show that he is not your husband Rahul either. Bizarre, isn't it? Honestly, we cannot conclude *who* the patient is. But by his appearance, we might as well call him Tom Spencer, as he is noted on the medical chart. However, your help will still be very valuable."

"I understood that Dr. Spencer is not sure who the patient is," said Julie. "Maybe he is, but he didn't tell me."

"Dr. Spencer is a fine man and is very reputable," Dr. Albert stated. "He may have confided in you that the patient is not his son. But he would not advocate any probable identity of the patient. Furthermore, you might be delighted to hear that he wanted to donate a portion of money from Tom's inheritance for your daughter's education, but the patient and Dr. Sharma, your father-in-law, refused to accept it. Hence, he is inclined to give it to the National Coalition Against Legalized Gambling and college funds for his niece and daughter. The money belonged to Tom, and it came from his grandfather's estate. Dr. Spencer believes it is unlike Tom to refuse any money."

Julie appeared to be hesitant to have Rahul, or whoever he might be, ever present at her home without at least having a chance to confirm his story.

Vic noticed this and realized that Julie needed more time. He also saw that Rahul was ecstatic over Julie's visit, and knew that Rahul could not wait to see her again. He didn't say anything to Rahul about her at this time, but he decided that he would reason with the patient later about her reluctance.

Julie, on the contrary, was spiraling into a web of skepticism. Was he really her husband? If so, she had mixed emotions. The patient looked like the one she had despised all this time. On the other hand, he sounded like her lover and life partner, Rahul. She needed help. But who could help? She thought of Madhu once more, and since he was critical of Tom, he would not knowingly let her follow the path of deceit.

Later in the evening, Julie, Vic, and Diya sat down to dinner without anyone saying a word. But food was the last thing on Julie's mind. They ate dinner and then retired for the evening. She switched on her television but did not pay attention to what was going on. Suddenly, the phone rang. It was Rahul from the hospital. She talked to him briefly but managed to end the call. When he called again later in the evening, she chatted with slight irritation and eventually hung up the phone, telling him that she needed rest.

The next day, Julie's boss and mentor at work, Joann, was not too sympathetic about Julie's analysis of the patient. As a precaution, she advised Julie to change her phone number. Julie had to stop her when she was about to file a petition for a restraining order to prevent him from calling or possibly visiting Julie.

"You are making a mistake, girl," Joann said.

"Joann, I know what I am up against," Julie answered patiently. "But what if he really is Rahul? I've lost my husband once before. I don't want to do it again through my own wrongdoing. It's just a matter of time until he exposes his true inner self, one way or the other."

"Okay. But be careful!" Joann warned. "If he turns out to be Tom and is playing games with you, we will hunt him down like a mad dog. Believe me! He will not know what hit him."

Julie retreated to her office. Checking her e-mail, she found a message from Madhu, saying that he was arriving in a few weeks. He also mentioned that Julie's mother was fine but was still in a state of shock and was worried about her daughter's health.

Jason Brookfield came in and chatted with Julie. He offered his help to guide her through her difficult ordeal. Over time, they had become very good friends, and even more so after Rahul's accident. Jason was a decent human being. But she kept him at arm's length, since Rahul had not approved of their friendship. Undoubtedly, Rahul was not a jealous person, but after all the diabolical lies that Tom might have told Rahul, she was very careful.

~~~

While Julie was at work, Vic and Diya went to see Rahul at the hospital.

"How are you?" Vic asked.

"Fine. I'm going to be released today or tomorrow. This may be the first chance I get to see my daughter. I miss her very much. I'm sure she misses me too."

"Listen, I have a suggestion," Vic said, looking at his wife, Diya. "You may or may not want to listen to me. Julie is still not comfortable with you, especially with how you appear. Furthermore, the last thing you want is to make her and Rachel uncomfortable and sad. Rachel knows that her dad is dead. Of course, she cried a lot and was utterly sad, but she's beginning to come around. Let me be frank with you. If we tell her that you are her dad, she will resent it and not recognize you as such, not for a while, anyway. It will probably take a long time before Julie and Rachel are convinced otherwise. You need to give them some more time to be receptive and more familiar with you."

"So what do you suggest?" Rahul asked.

"Diya and I believe that it would be in the best interest of all if you moved into your friend Tom's apartment for the time being."

This was the last thing Rahul wanted to hear, and he was silent for a moment. Then his face drooped, and he asked in a sad tone, "Did Julie ask you to convey that message to me?"

"No, she doesn't even know we are with you now. But you can understand her anxiety and nervousness. Moreover, Diya and I are leaving in a couple of days for Los Angeles, and then on to Mumbai. Our earnest wish is for both of you to get back together. But you will have to act very cautiously. You know that she is a very stern woman. She would do anything to protect her family and her love for Rahul."

"Do you think my moving into Tom's apartment would work better for all of us?"

"It can't hurt. You should tell her that you decided to move into Tom's apartment for the time being to give her more time to think about things and for you to establish your true identity."

When Rahul thought about it, he realized that Vic was right and accepted his recommendation, albeit unwillingly. Unfortunately, he was not a part of Julie's life, at least not yet.

When Dr. Albert called Julie about Rahul's release from the hospital, Vic and Diya went to the hospital to drop Rahul off at Tom's apartment. Then they called a cab.

Rahul hadn't seen much of the outdoors lately. The last thing he remembered was being out on a dark and rainy night. Now the weather was bright and sunny, but there was still darkness in his future. His wife was a stranger. His father remained away from him to avoid any more mental stress and confusion. His cousin and his wife were his best friends, but even they were still skeptical. Yet, this was his family. Not that they had abandoned him, but they treated him like some kind of alien. The intimacy had vanished. His relationships were casual, and the past had been erased. But he was a fighter, and when he was given a second chance, he was going to make the most of it.

The apartment was clean and neat, as if it had a feminine touch. It was unlikely that Tom had maintained his apartment to this level of cleanliness. But Rahul then remembered a visit by Dominique and realized that she had probably cleaned the place and made it more livable.

Tom's car was in his carport. He called Julie to get her permission to come by the house to see Rachel. When she showed no objection, Rahul requested that Vic stay behind, and he drove Tom's car to the house.

Rachel was the same as he remembered her.

"Hi, Tom," Rachel said. "How are you? My mom tells me that you were sick. Are you okay now?"

Rachel addressing him as "Tom" tormented him. But in reality, he *was* Tom—in appearance, anyway.

"I am very well. Thank you. How are you? How is school?"

They chatted and played for a while, without any reference to Rahul.

Julie came home from work and saw her guest. She greeted him politely and asked Lupe to give Rachel her bath and get her ready for bed.

"How are you, Julie? Aren't you glad to see that I'm out of the hospital and can return to my normal life? *Titlee* now calls me 'Tom.' If you don't address me as Rahul, we will have a hard time convincing *Titlee* to do so. It seems you still have doubts in your mind."

"I do. I'm confused—very confused. Let's talk about reality. To the rest of the world, you are Tom. Don't you realize it? You have to fight this war by yourself. I sympathize with you, but I am helpless. For you to return to this home, I would have to announce that I am marrying Tom. I could never love you as I loved Rahul, even though you may actually *be* Rahul."

"I've heard that some people become stateless," he said. "But I am homeless, even though I have a family and a home. Very well, let's see how it goes." He paused. "I hear that Madhu is coming to Houston in a few days. Is that true?"

"Yes. He is arriving within a couple of weeks."

"Good. He may help you and me both—I hope. Where is *Titlee*? Has she gone to bed already?"

"She might be sleeping," Julie said. "Lupe is in her room."

It was getting late in the evening, so Rahul left to go to Tom's apartment.

CHAPTER 48

A neon sign that read "Billy's Bar" was flashing brightly across the apartment complex. Rahul had never seen the sign or the place of the business before. A few customers gathered outside, making lewd remarks and having indecent conversations among themselves without any consideration for their neighbors.

A few people saw Rahul getting out of Tom's car at the apartment complex. Bobby, one of Tom's friends, approached him.

"Hi, Tom, buddy! I haven't seen you in a while. What have you been up to lately? Let's go to the bar and have a drink!"

Rahul didn't recognize Tom's friend. "No, I'm tired. I'm going to hit the hay."

"What? Come on, Tom! You're never tired, and you've never refused to drink. Are you all right? Are you sick or something?"

"I'm okay," Rahul said. "But not today." He started to walk toward Tom's apartment. Rahul felt nauseous at the sight of the bar, which was visible from the residence.

They all looked at him with curiosity as he walked away. At the same time, Jack, Tom's landlord, walked by.

"Hey, Jack, Tommy is back," Bobby said. "I have his CD. Give it back to him for me—it doesn't work. Have you talked to him recently?"

"No, I haven't," Jack answered. "I'll do it later."

On his way up, Jack saw Rahul and said, "Hi, Tommy, are you all right now? You know you got a bunch of mail. Hey, you owe me a month's rent. Your cuz paid me the balance. She was kinda cute!"

Rahul remembered him. Jack was a big, burly guy who usually had a cigarette between his lips. His sleeveless shirt revealed large tattoos on his upper arms.

"Thanks, Jack," Rahul said. "I'll write you a check tomorrow. Can I collect my mail now?"

"Yeah, okay. Come on in."

"Hey, Jack, I haven't seen this bar before. Is it something new?" Rahul realized that Houston didn't have strict zoning ordinances.

"Isn't it great?" Jack answered, disregarding Rahul's concern. "It opened just about two weeks ago. We don't have to go far for a drink."

Jack's apartment was disorderly, filled with ashtrays overflowing with cigarette butts. Empty beer cans were on his coffee and night tables. A peculiar, pungent odor blew Rahul's mind, but he couldn't recognize the smell.

"Can I get you a beer or something?" Jack asked. "You know, Tom, we had some wild parties here. You wanna smoke? I got some nice stuff, you know."

Rahul realized what he meant. "No, not today. Thanks for the mail."

"Hey, don't be too formal, man," Jack said. "You know that cousin of yours paid your telephone and electric bills. She asked me to send your bills to her. I hope it was okay."

"That's fine," Rahul said. "Thanks, Jack. I'll take care of it."

"What is all this 'thank you' shit? You're my buddy, you know."

The last thing Rahul wanted was for him to be his buddy, or anyone else's, for that matter. He felt suffocated around these people. *What did I do to deserve this?* Rahul asked himself. *I have to take charge of my life and change all this. I need to go back to Julie and Rachel. How? I am sure Madhu will have a positive influence on her. I am sure Julie is stubborn and uncompromising, but she will listen to him.*

After he entered Tom's apartment, he sat on a chair, gazing apathetically at the wall and watching TV. Sad and dejected, he crawled into bed without switching off the light.

Police sirens woke him up in the middle of the night, around three o'clock. He peeked through his window curtain and saw police officers struggling to put handcuffs on a man at the bar across the street. He didn't recognize the person who was being arrested—and he didn't care.

Although he tried to go back to sleep after the brouhaha at the bar, he was unable to do so. As he thought about taking charge of his life, whatever it held for him, he realized that he must stay close to Julie and Rachel in the hope that things might change. Someday, with any luck, he would be accepted back into his own family.

The next morning, he called Mark and told him that he had been discharged from the hospital and was staying at Tom's apartment. He asked him if they could meet. Mark suggested that they meet at a particular coffee shop that was very secluded. Rahul was surprised that he was asked to go to such a dingy place, but he didn't mind. *Mark probably has some good reasons for it*, he thought.

Rahul didn't have any friends he could talk to. His father had gone to India on an extended vacation. He didn't want to disturb Julie at work. Rahul had many friends in Houston, but he didn't know how they would react while he wore Tom's face. Tom had many friends, but Rahul didn't care for any of them. All of a sudden, he felt extremely lonely. The most fruitful thing for

Rahul to do was to wait for Madhu's arrival. Madhu was his best friend and could offer Rahul some concrete advice.

Rahul reached the coffee shop by noon. He saw Mark seated at a table in an inconspicuous corner. The smell of spilled beer and smoke filled the room. A cook with a cigarette in his mouth was turning burger patties. When the waitress came over to take their order, she wiped down the table with an already shabby napkin. It was unlikely that they would have an appetite for food, but they ordered two sandwiches and soda.

Rahul asked sarcastically, "Mark, what's the reason for such a treat?"

"You'll have to excuse me, Rahul. I can't be seen with you until the dust settles. I need some time to clear up your situation. Your appearance as Tom may impede my position at Robotechnique. Anyway, what's on your mind?"

Rahul thought for a moment. "I don't know how to ask you for this particular favor. Right now, you can't be seen with me, and I was looking to find a place to work—possibly my old job back." He paused. "You know, Mark, there is no one who can continue my assignment. I know that you've asked Madhu to help you. While he is a very bright person, he was never close to my project."

Reluctantly, Mark said, "Your job at Robotechnique is out of the question. The chief would fire me on the spot. I've been thinking about all of this. What if you had plastic surgery to hide Tom's face? They do wonders in that field nowadays."

Rahul said in a sad tone, "Yes, I thought of that alternative, but what am I going to prove? Julie knows who and what I am. Minor reconstruction may be possible, but a lot of our bone structure, face pads, etc., will not match. Besides, as far as Robotechnique is concerned, please don't forget they do have a strong biometric security. I can't even enter your office complex. How am I going to get to my old room through this security? No, Mark, that's no solution. I have to live with what I am, and hopefully I can convince people that I am not Tom."

Mark sighed and said, "God help you, Rahul. You know that I'll try my best to help you get over your problems. The presence of Madhu might help. I can eventually convince the chief, but the Department of Defense is another matter."

After they had eaten, Mark said, "Rahul, I have to run. Stay in touch. Here is my private number—call me anytime. I know you're staying at Tom's old apartment. I'll call you when Madhu arrives."

For Rahul, Tom's apartment came to haunt him. The apartment was livable, but it lacked the warmth of a home. He called Julie and asked her permission to pick up his old computer. Then he set it up and ordered Internet service. Surfing the Web and checking his e-mail messages on the previous server presented no issues. There was a maze of messages, but none of them were useful. He sent a message to Madhu and asked him when he was coming to town. Then he sent another message to Mark, asking if he could help him and work from home. This would help keep his wandering mind busy, and he could earn some money at the same time.

He got his first e-mail message from Madhu, saying that he was coming to Houston within a week's time. There was also a reply from Mark, saying that while he very much wanted Rahul's help, he was unsure about how he could effectively utilize Rahul's talents under the circumstances. He suggested that Rahul wait for Madhu's arrival.

Rahul was very skilled in computer science technology. He approached Tom's professor at the University of Houston and asked him if he could help him to find a job opening. Rahul realized that the professor did not believe Tom was sincere in his efforts to work diligently, but he got him an entry-level job at a small technical service company. Rahul demeaned himself by accepting the job. He didn't like it, but he was probably unable to get anything better. However, his expertise in his work received enormous praise from his superiors. But then again, Rahul was not Tom, and he could not and did not want to prove otherwise.

When Rahul returned from work on Friday, he had a message on his answering machine from Mark, informing him that Madhu had arrived in Houston and was staying at the hotel.

It was a strange feeling for Madhu to show affection when he met Rahul, now in Tom's body.

"*Rahul?* Is it really you?" Madhu was startled to see Rahul in Tom's body.

"Yes, it is me, Rahul. You dumbass!" And he jumped up to give him a hug.

When Rahul told him his story in detail, Madhu had a great deal of apprehension. But slowly, Madhu started to believe Rahul as he unveiled more details of his life-after-death experience. Madhu knew about Rahul's condition because of Julie and Mark, but he didn't know Rahul's life had been going so poorly.

Madhu saw that Rahul was pleading for his help in getting his life back. Until Madhu was fully convinced of Rahul's story, he wasn't ready to convey his thoughts and beliefs to Julie and Mark. There were a few very convincing stories about which only Rahul could have known the details. But Madhu was cautious about passing any judgments regarding his friend.

After Madhu left, Rahul breathed a sigh of relief that his friend came to his rescue, despite his skepticism. And he was right. If there was anyone who could straighten out his life, it was Madhu.

~~~

A phone call late in the night woke him up.

"Hello?" he answered.

"Hi, Tommy! How are you, buddy? I haven't talked to you in a while. This is Andy, *Andy Waters,* from Las Vegas. Remember? I heard you had an accident. Are you okay?"

"I'm fine," Rahul said. "Who is this? Andy? I don't recall meeting any Andy before."

"What's wrong with you?" he said. "I'm Andy, your croupier friend from the casino. You remember that I helped you to get the loan from our friend Ismail, *Ismail Peshawari?* Hey, how could you forget that? I'm in Houston, and I'm coming to see you tomorrow. What time will you be home?"

Rahul was puzzled. "Listen, Andy. It is Andy, right? After the accident, I've been totally in disarray. I need to put my life back together. Is it really necessary to meet in person? I can probably clear up the matter over the phone. What do you want?"

"No, no, man! I have to see you. Don't be a hard-ass and play hard to get. They will find you anyway. It's better that I talk to you before they do."

"Who are they? Are you trying to scare me?"

"Look, man, I can't talk to you on the phone. I'll have to explain it all to you in person. I'll see you tomorrow at ten in the morning. I know where you live. I'll see you then." Then Andy hung up the phone.

This was a new twist in Rahul's life. He realized that there were many surprises to being Tom, but nothing was more eye-opening than this. He had a hard time going back to bed, but he was able to get some sleep early that morning. Being a weekend day, there was no rush for him to wake up and go to work.

When the doorbell rang, Rahul answered it nervously. Andy was a tall person, with a dark goatee and a distinct personality. He was wearing a baseball cap, and he looked like a troublemaker.

As he entered the apartment, he hugged Rahul and said, "Hey, Tommy! How have you been? Got anything to drink?"

Rahul stood there watching as Andy came in and settled into a chair.

"I've got coffee or soda," Rahul replied. "What will you have?"

"Anything like beer or something?"

"No, I haven't had any time to get some."

"All right, give me a Coke."

Andy kept talking about the good old days in Vegas and the casino.

"Remember these guys?" Andy asked, showing Rahul a picture of Ismail Peshawari and his friends.

"Who are they?"

"Man, you are in deep shit, you know?" Andy said. "Listen! Get serious, man! You give them what they want. They busted you up last time. This time, they will hurt you bad."

To get the facts about what Tom had done, Rahul said, "Look here! After the accident, I lost some memory. Tell me, what did he—I mean *I*—promise?"

"Don't be a smart-ass, Tommy. We know that you went to your dead Indian friend's house, you met your former boss for lunch, and just yesterday, your friend came to see you. These guys are keeping an eye on you, man.

"Anyway, I'll tell you your own story," Andy continued. "I could not care less if you hadn't gotten me involved." Pointing at the picture, he said, "These guys lent you a heap of money, and in return you promised to do them a favor. You've been giving them some stuff through me. You gave me some CDs, and I gave them to our buddies. Man, for the last time, give them what they want—*now*. I am scared, and you ought to be too. These guys are dangerous and can do anything to get what they want. I have nothing to do with your macho stuff. Once you're done with them, leave me out of it."

Rahul was still bewildered and said, "What am I supposed to do? What do they want?"

"I'm no expert. But you promised to give them some CDs with your company secrets. I don't know any more. Hey, listen, I came to warn you, and I'm leaving, man." And he did.

Rahul was shaking from Andy's threats. He wanted to run away from here and hide somewhere. *But where? These criminals will find me anywhere,* he thought. He was terrified for his life and more so he was fearful for Julie's and Rachel's safety. He then looked everywhere in the apartment to find any clue to the puzzle.

A knock on his door frightened him, and he looked timidly through the peephole. It was Madhu. As soon as Madhu entered the apartment, he told him about the visit from the Vegas man. Rahul asked him if he knew if Tom had any problems at the office.

"You don't know?" Madhu asked. "First of all, did anyone tell you why Tom was running, and who was he running from, or why he called you to give him a lift?"

"No, I don't know anything about it," Rahul answered. "The last thing I remember is that his car had broken down, and he needed a lift. He was in a rush to get back to his apartment." Rahul paused. "Then I remember that there was a car chasing us on the freeway, and I suddenly lost control and smashed into a barrier."

Madhu said, "Now listen carefully! Tom wanted to steal the design and architecture of a product named ZRQ."

"*What?*" Rahul said loudly. "That's impossible! It's guarded with the utmost security, and I was one of the principals that designed the codes. No one except me was able to work on it, and I was the only one who was allowed to access it. I had special permission from the chief and the DOD."

"And they probably thought that Tom could copy the project onto CDs?" Madhu asked.

"The codes and drawings cannot be copied without proper security codes. Of course, Tom worked in my department, but he wasn't allowed to enter the secured area." Rahul paused, thinking. "Oh, I see. Tom may have thought that I would allow *him* to copy the codes or that I would do it for him. No way! Even if I wanted to do it, I couldn't. Mark knows that. Tom knew it too. Why did he make promises to these guys? Besides, not many people knew about the project anyway."

Madhu said, "Now let me finish my story. These buddies of his are Middle Eastern criminals and terrorists, and they lent him over half a million dollars for his gambling debt and pleasure. They would have paid a lot more. These terrorists wanted the design of ZRQ very badly, and they told Tom to get the details on a CD and give it to them. These goons thought Tom had equal access, as you did. But they probably didn't know that Tom is dead, and the person who looks like Tom is actually you.

"Coming back to Tom, they cornered him in a bar the night of your accident. He was very frightened, and he had good reason to be. He fled from that place. But we're puzzled about why he wanted to rush to his apartment that night. I strongly believe that

Tom might have hidden some documents or details of the project here."

"I'm surprised that Mark believed his story," Rahul said. "It's totally absurd."

"That's nothing. Let me tell you the full story. I have a friend in the Indian CBI who warned me about a security leak at Robotechnique. I had mentioned this to Mark, since we work closely with them. They had kept it low-key before they found out the real culprit."

"Oh, yes," Rahul said. "Mark had told me that. But I had forgotten about it."

"Now comes the juicy part," Madhu said. "You remember how I asked you about your cousin Suri?"

"Yes, what about him?"

"He is none other than Aftab Ali, a notorious criminal and wanted by the CBI."

"*What?*"

"Suri—a.k.a. Aftab—this guy Andy, three other criminals, and Peshawari and his goons all work together. They trapped Tom with his gambling in Las Vegas. Tom had been feeding them small secrets."

"You mean to tell me that Suri came to Las Vegas and never called me?"

"Aren't you the lucky one? He didn't come just once, but several times."

"So where is he now?"

"Well, the CBI nabbed him at the Mumbai Airport recently, and he is currently in their custody. His friend Peshawari put him there. So you see? You are dealing with dangerous criminals. It was a well-planned operation. They were devising this plan ever since you were in Mumbai. Remember when you had lunch with him? The car he gave you to use at your wedding, the Patek Philippe watch, and his other favors were all parts of his plan."

"Julie and I got a housewarming present from him—a set of Tiffany floor lamps. I sensed something unusual about the gift."

"One other thing. Did you line up with any hooker in Las Vegas?"

Rahul's face turned red. He was shocked. "How did you know?"

"Suri had arranged that with Andy to trap you, and he had Andy spike your drink. You are not going to like this."

"What?"

"They took some revealing pictures of you and the hooker in your hotel room. They also had a plan to blackmail you, in case Tom was unable to perform his task."

"My God! Why would Suri turn on me? I am his kin. These goons could have killed me in the process—*did* kill me, as far as they're concerned."

"It's all for money. Ismail had promised Suri that they would not physically harm you. But you can't trust them, obviously."

Rahul was terrified about what Madhu had disclosed to him. "So Suri has really turned into a full-blown criminal. He pulled a prank on me in Kanpur about twenty years ago, and I was almost lost in downtown Kanpur. This time, he pulled one again, and I practically lost my life. Good thinking, Suri!"

"Let me give you a very important piece of advice," Madhu said. "Never mention to anyone that Suri, or Aftab, is your cousin. Not even to Julie! Forget him now. Let's concentrate on what we face here." Madhu looked around. "Have you looked at everything in his apartment? I am sure that the police and the FBI must have done the same."

"I thought so too," said Rahul. "But I looked everywhere in this place and didn't find anything remotely similar that could make any sense. Come to think of it, Tom could have copied some preliminary drawings or codes off my laptop. He may have shown these to people, and they believed that he had access to ZRQ.

"He was always in trouble with the law. So when the police came to look in his apartment, no one suspected anything. I am surprised that these hoods didn't completely ransack his apartment."

"Mark believes that they went into hiding after the accident," Madhu said. "So if you told me that you had a visitor who came to warn you, it means only one thing. These goons are back, and they mean business. I think you should talk to Agent Turner."

"Agent who?"

"Oh, I forgot," Madhu said. "He is an FBI agent who came to see you in the hospital, believing you were Tom. And when the doctors told him the bizarre story, he told them to keep it quiet. He did not want to put your life in jeopardy, whoever you may have been. I strongly urge you to meet with him. I'll get you his contact information."

"That's great. But I never met them. Why would they see me?" Rahul asked.

"Oh, I will have Mark call him, and I'll go with you so you feel more comfortable. I'm sure these criminals are back in business, and your life could be in danger. Tom knew these guys, but you don't even know who is who. Can you recognize any of these people?"

"Andy showed me the picture," Rahul said. "No, I didn't recognize any of them. But I can't forget their faces—they were very frightening."

"Okay, that settles it," Madhu said. "I'll go with you when you get an appointment with Turner. Listen, I came to tell you something. I've been asked to work at Robotechnique on your project as soon as I get special clearance from the chief and the DOD. But I can use all the help I can get. They will never give you security clearance as Tom. Mark was very willing to talk to the chief, but after today's incident, there is only a slim chance. We will meet with Turner, and then we will talk to Mark."

"Listen, not to change the subject," Rahul said, "but I'd like to talk to you about Julie and Rachel."

"What's on your mind?" Madhu asked. "You know that you and I are very good friends, and I'll help you as much as I can. But let me remind you that Julie is of an independent mind, if you haven't figured that out yet." He smiled.

"I know that," Rahul said. "And that's making it hard for me to convince her otherwise. There is nothing more important in my life than my love for Julie and Rachel. Madhu, how can I get my life back?"

Madhu thought for a moment. "I'll do all I can to get you back with your family. Julie needs some incontrovertible proof and more time. I'll try my best to influence her and see where you both stand. I'm going to see her tonight, and I'll bring it up—but I can't promise anything."

Rahul nodded. "I understand."

"Listen, I hate to leave you so soon, but Mark has asked me to see him at the office to discuss the project. I'll call you and give you Agent Turner's number. Please call him and get an appointment as soon as you can."

Madhu prepared to leave Tom's apartment when a knock on his door drew Rahul's attention, and he got up to open it. It was Jack, his landlord.

"Hi, Tommy. Here's your CD. It doesn't work. Bobby tried it too. Something's wrong with it."

Confused, Rahul took the CD. "Um, thanks, Jack."

"You know, when you were in the hospital, the Feds came by to talk to me," Jack said. "With all the rubbish, they also told me that you're gay. Are they kidding? We had lots of fun in Vegas. That barmaid—what's her name? Lisa, yeah, right! She was hot, man. Anyway, I didn't tell them nothing! I don't tell no secrets about my friends to any Feds or cops." He paused. "Tommy, come to think of it, that Lisa was here looking for you. But she left quickly when she saw cops snooping around your apartment. Listen, I'm off to San Tone.[4] Will be back on Monday. Take care!"

"What in the world was that all about?" Madhu asked. "Did you know about Tom's personal life?"

"Yes, I knew, and I don't care." Rahul was now frustrated with Tom's ghost hanging around him.

---

[4]   To many, "San Tone" is Texas slang for "San Antonio."

Madhu was still skeptical about Tom, but he believed what Jack had said to some extent. Tom was a very deceitful person, and Madhu knew that Rahul was naive to have trusted Tom.

"Let's see what's on the CD," Madhu said.

Rahul inserted the CD into his laptop, and after a while he said, "Oh, my God! I can't believe it."

"What are all those drawings and data?" Madhu asked.

"It details the ZRQ project!" Rahul cried. "Oh, my God!" He stared at the information, dumbfounded. "Sometimes Mark and I made a backup copy of the project programs and vital data for safety. Mark would then put this CD in the company's safe. How in the world it got copied is totally unclear to me." Rahul thought for a moment. "I should talk to Mark immediately. You know what this means, Madhu? This is espionage—and it's a federal offense."

"Wait just a minute! God damn it!" Madhu snapped. "Let me think! Okay, so Tom worked under you. And you and Mark made this copy together. So both you and Mark could be suspects, in addition to Tom. Just think, you might put both of yourselves in jeopardy."

"So what should I do?" Rahul asked. "I'm not keeping this CD here. It's dangerous and wrong for me to do so."

"Okay, let me ask Mark to meet us someplace private."

"Please do it soon. I'm scared to have this in my possession."

In spite of the fact that it was the weekend, Mark came to see them in a hurry. When they met in Madhu's hotel room, Rahul handed over the CD to Mark and explained what had happened.

"Oh, my God," Mark said. "I need to talk to the chief. What do you suggest, guys?"

Madhu said, "Mark, lay off your talk to the chief. It may backfire on you, and many innocent people may get hurt. Why don't you destroy this copy or put it in the safe too? No harm is done yet, and nothing *will* be done if you guys act wisely."

"That's a good suggestion," Mark agreed. "Let's go."

CHAPTER 49

"Lupe, could you please see who is at the door?" Julie asked her nanny while she was in the kitchen, preparing dinner.

It was Madhu. "Hi, Julie. How are you?" he asked after Lupe let him in. Julie ran over to him, hugging him very affectionately. "What took you so long to come and see me? I've been in hell for the past few months. Madhu, you know what has happened. I am totally lost. Please help me!"

"How about a 'Good evening' first?" Madhu joked.

"Good evening!" Julie repeated. "Nice to see you, Madhu. I'm glad you're back in town. I could always use some moral support after the terrible experience I've faced."

"I came here to take you and Rachel out to dinner," Madhu said.

"Well, I've prepared a dinner for us. We can eat at home. Rachel has gone to bed, and Lupe is going out for the night."

"That's fine," Madhu replied.

After they had finished the meal, Madhu said, "Lovely dinner."

"Coffee?" Julie asked.

"Yes, I could use some. Julie, I went to see our friend Rahul. You know I've had my doubts, but they have waned after I talked to him for a while."

"So . . . you too? You are among the best friends that I have. Why do you side with everyone but me?"

"You surprise me," Madhu said. "I am always on your side, but I thought you might like to know the truth."

"All right, I'll keep an open mind."

"I had a long chat with Rahul, or Tom, or whatever you wish to call him. If he is, in fact, Rahul, then he is missing his family very much. Is there any chance you will allow him to visit and play with Rachel?"

Julie sat silently in her chair for a while before speaking. "This comes as a surprise to me. You have to be pretty much convinced that Tom is actually Rahul. How can it be?" She paused. "Let me think about it. As far as I'm concerned, my husband is already dead. I am not a devout Catholic, but I do believe in one thing—people do not just rise from the dead."

Madhu nodded.

"Madhu, I loved both of my husbands. I've been a good wife. People say that when I married Vikram, I was an immature person. But when I met Rahul, I thought about our relationship very carefully. Everyone wanted me to move forward with my life, and I did. I got involved and married him. Then I lost him." Suddenly, Julie had tears in her eyes.

Madhu moved close to her and tried to console her. "Julie, please don't think of the past. Look at what you have accomplished and everything you do. Listen to what Confucius said: 'Life is really simple, but we insist on making it complicated.'"

Julie smiled bleakly and said, "It's easier said than done, my friend."

"Coming back to the issue at hand, what should I tell our friend Rahul?"

Julie immediately snapped, "*Don't* call him by Rahul's name! Unless, of course, you do strongly believe that he *is* Rahul."

"Calm down, Julie," Madhu replied. "I am with you. Don't worry."

"Okay, I'll cooperate. He can come and visit Rachel. When I come home from work, I hope he is gone. I don't want to be on an emotional roller-coaster ride again. I'll tell Lupe to expect him."

"By the way, do you recall any Las Vegas incident?" Madhu asked.

Julie said, "I knew that Rahul had an encounter with a prostitute in Las Vegas. He told me that someone spiked his drink, but that it was not Tom. But I have my doubts."

"Rahul was right," Madhu said. "It wasn't Tom, but his cousin Suri from India."

"What? I don't believe it. Why would he do that?"

"It's a long story, and I'll have to tell it to you in full detail, but not today."

"Okay, let's not waste our time on something unimportant," Julie said. "Please convince me that this Tom is actually Rahul."

"I can't prove it beyond the shadow of a doubt. But his speech, sincerity, and thinking are very similar to Rahul's. Besides, he shows no sign of Tom's irrational, conniving, and deceitful behavior. But there's one thing that is perfectly clear— Tom had lots of respect and love for his friend Rahul."

Julie nodded.

"Julie, let sleeping dogs lie. There is no point in discussing Tom any further. But as far as our friend is concerned, I am more inclined to believe that he could very well be Rahul. I'll find out other details when I see him a few more times."

Chapter 50

"May I talk to Mr. Stuart Turner, please?" Rahul asked the operator when he called for the FBI agent.

"May I ask who is calling?"

"My name is Rahul Sharma. I have a feeling that I am being followed by some criminals, and I am fearful for my life."

"Sir, such cases are handled by your local police department. Why don't you call them first?"

"I've been advised to call Agent Turner by my colleagues. He had previously instructed them that I should call him as soon as I was fit to talk. This is in reference to Tom Spencer."

"Could you please hold for one minute? Thanks."

After a while, the secretary came back on the phone and said, "Sir, Mr. Turner will see you next week on Tuesday at 10:00 a.m. Is it all right?"

"I'll be there," said Rahul.

Agent Turner's office was in downtown Houston. The office was simple, without any stringent security. A presidential portrait was on the wall at the entrance, where an American flag stood in the corner. The receptionist signed him and Madhu in and gave them badges in order to meet with Agent Turner. As soon as she called his extension, a young man came to escort them to Turner's office.

Turner was on the phone, but he signaled them to sit in chairs in front of his desk, which was neat and orderly.

Turner appeared to be a tall, well-dressed, and well-built man in his midforties who was sporting a crew cut. As soon as he finished talking on the phone, he said, "Gentlemen, my name is Stuart Turner. This is my associate, Salim Khan." Looking at Rahul, he said, "You look like Tom Spencer. But on the phone, you said your name was something different . . . let me see here . . ." He looked down at the message slip. "You said you were 'Rahul Sharma.'"

Rahul said, "The answer is yes and no. First of all, this is my friend Madhu Marve. He works at Robotechnique. I don't know how much you know about me and my case. But let me tell you, if you don't mind.

"You may recall that Tom Spencer and I had a bad car accident. One of the passengers was killed. The person who survived is me. However, something strange happened—I switched bodies with Tom. Even though I look like Tom, I am actually Rahul Sharma."

With an incredulous smile at Salim Khan, Turner said, "Do you expect me to actually believe this? Do you think that we're running a fantasy camp here? Listen, fellows, I don't have time for this."

Salim whispered something in Turner's ear, and then Turner said, "Let me see here."

Turner opened a thick file full of notes and pictures and read it for a while. "I am familiar with your case," he said. "So what do you want us to do? This is a very bizarre case, and I'm not sure I believe your claims. But let's assume that it really happened."

Rahul said, "After I was released from the hospital, I tried to put the pieces of my life together. But there were more hurdles than I anticipated. My friend here is trying to help me get oriented so that I can move in the proper direction.

"Tom Spencer was my best friend," Rahul continued. "But I didn't know that his life was filled with all these aberrations. His personal life, his compulsive habits, and his associates are all unknown to me."

Rahul took a deep breath. "Just a couple of days ago, I had a visit from one of his friends from Vegas. He said that Tom owed a chunk of money to some Middle Eastern businessmen. And now they're here, and they want the CD of data that Tom had promised them. I have no clue what to do. The product which they're referring to was developed by me, but I cannot pass on any of its secrets to anyone. Besides, I have absolutely no access to the lab any longer."

Showing Rahul one of the photos from his file, Turner asked, "Do you know anyone here?"

Rahul pointed to Andy Waters. He also pointed to Ismail Peshawari and his associates.

Turner slammed his fist on his desk and asked his assistant, Kaminski, "How come *we* don't know that these assholes are back in the country? Go and find out." He turned back to Rahul. "Boy, you are in big trouble. The department can help you, but you ought to be very careful. You never know when or how these people will strike."

Kaminski returned with a note in his hand. "We have no record of these guys back in action in the US."

"I don't fully trust our border patrol," Turner said. "They could sneak in through many channels. In Houston, they could hide forever, and it would be very difficult to find them."

"How can these criminals cross the border so easily?" Rahul asked.

"That's easy," Khan replied. "Terrorism is so transparent that they exist among us, and we don't even see them. This country is so vast, and multitudes of nationalities live here. They can easily infiltrate our security, military, government, and businesses without our knowledge. How can you safeguard against them?"

Rahul said, "My friend and I think you could help me change my identity, maybe with plastic surgery."

Turner laughed. "Plastic surgery may be a good alternative. It's worth a try. It does take time to organize the logistics and prepare for it medically. Moreover, it's not an overnight process.

"I suggested that Tom enter our witness protection program," Agent Turner continued. "But we didn't find it necessary, because we genuinely believed that we had put an end to this case. Now you popped up as Tom. The difficult part is that you do look like Tom, but you have no knowledge of his secret activities. How are you going to safeguard yourself from Tom's wrongdoings? Most importantly, how are you going to explain to a third party that you are *not* Tom? We can offer you the witness relocation program too and prepare you for minor plastic surgery if you care to go through that process. Let me explore this with my boss."

Rahul nodded as he struggled to absorb all this information.

"Okay, gentlemen, sit tight," Agent Turner said. "We'll be in touch. Here is my card and a number to reach me, day and night."

~~~

While deep in thought, Turner said, "Ira, can you ask Khan to come to my office, please?"

"Yes, sir."

After a while, Khan entered Turner's office. "You wanted to talk to me, Stuart?"

"Khan, did you hear what that guy Tom Spencer told us?" he asked while his assistant, Ira Kaminski, listened.

"Yes, but do you believe it?" Khan asked. "It's ludicrous."

"It doesn't matter whether we do or we don't," Turner replied. "What's important is whether or not these criminals believe it. Let's suppose everything happened exactly the way he said. This guy was not aware of the trouble that Tom was in. Peshawari and his associates are ruthless criminals. They will be after him, not realizing that he is *not* Tom. What can we do to protect him?"

Turner handed Khan a printed sheet of paper. "Look at this message from the Indian CBI. These criminals devised this plan in India. They were working on Tom right from the beginning. Since Rahul was not corruptible, they grabbed Tom to do their dirty work. Tom was an easy target since he had bad vices, so they worked on him."

"Why didn't you tell Rahul about his cousin and the plan?" Khan asked.

"It's unimportant now," Turner replied. "Aftab Ali is in CBI custody. Moreover, it may scare Rahul beyond comprehension, and he may stop cooperating. He doesn't know the rest of the guys anyway." He paused, thinking. "Let's see . . . if we act smart, we might nab these criminals."

"Are you sure that we're not prevaricating?" Khan asked. "Even if he knew, I hardly believe it would harm him."

"Khan, Rahul Sharma is dead, as far as they're concerned."

"I hate to make him a scapegoat though."

"We aren't," Turner replied. "With or without our involvement, they will be after Rahul, who now looks like Tom. All we can do is protect him, whoever he may be."

CHAPTER 51

At the Robotechnique office, Madhu asked Mark if Rahul could help get the project moving in some sensible direction. After all, this was Rahul's pet project, and there was no one more knowledgeable and qualified to do so.

"Let me talk to the chief," Mark said. "I'll be right back."

Half an hour later, Mark returned to his office. "Well, the chief can be convinced, but without the DOD's permission we can't do anything. And he strongly believes that the DOD will not permit that, under any circumstances. In fact, the chief does not want Rahul to visit our premises at all."

"Unfortunately, people have the impression that Tom is a malicious person," Madhu replied. "I know he was Rahul's best friend, and that hurts me. Look how Tom's association has ruined Rahul's life. He lost his life, his family, and all his friends."

"What do you want me to do?" Mark asked. "I can't and won't go over the chief's head. Let's see if the DOD allows us to give him special or restricted permission in order to salvage the project."

Madhu responded in a discouraged tone, "I understand. Let's wait for the DOD's reaction."

Dejected, Madhu left Mark's room and called Rahul with the company's decision. It did not surprise Rahul at all. Although he was disappointed, his main concern was the project and its continuation.

About a week later, the DOD gave Rahul very limited access to the project. But he would have to be supervised by DOD personnel at all times. Upon leaving the office premises, he was practically strip-searched. Rahul accepted the humiliation for the sake of the project and his personal satisfaction. If he proved that he could finish the project gracefully without any incidents, they might look upon him favorably.

Rahul was excited to see Rachel whenever he could. Spending time with her was the greatest thrill of all. He very much wanted to tell Rachel that he indeed was her dad and not her dad's friend Tom. But he didn't, since those were Julie's strict instructions.

Nevertheless, he thanked Madhu for getting Julie's permission to spend time with his own daughter. A lot of work would have to be done in order to prove his identity and get his life back. He knew it very well that Julie was stern and her innermost feelings for her husband *Rahul* were still overwhelming. He believed that given time, he could still win her over.

The FBI had put their surveillance on the back burner, partly because of a lack of personnel. Turner objected to the termination of the surveillance, but the decision was overruled by his superiors.

~~~

A knock on Rahul's apartment door drew his attention. He was busy on his laptop, working on his project. As soon as he opened the door, a couple of guys pushed their way in. Andy was one of them. There was a dreadful-looking man who Rahul recognized from a picture as Ismail Peshawari. Within a split second, he was standing in front of Rahul, giving him no time to react.

"Hi, Tom," Ismail said. "We meet again."

"Who are you?" Rahul asked nervously. "What do you want?"

"So you want to play games, you asshole?" Ismail demanded. "I am serious. We know you went to your dead friend's house to visit his wife and kid. Didn't you?"

Rahul started shivering when he heard the man's strong and forceful voice.

"You like them," Ismail said. "You don't want anything to happen to them, do you?"

Rahul got up and grabbed Ismail by the shirt. "You keep away from them. You understand?"

One of Ismail's henchmen came over to Rahul and pointed a gun to his head.

"No! No, Abdul," Ismail instructed the henchman. "We don't want him hurt. Not yet, anyway." He turned his attention back to Rahul. "Is anything going on between you and that Indian woman?"

"No, of course not!" he protested.

Ismail and his gang ransacked the apartment in search of the CD that they were after, but they didn't find anything remotely similar to it.

Ismail walked back over to Rahul and hit him hard in the gut. He held a large knife to Rahul's throat. "Where is my CD?" he demanded. "I could kill you for that."

Rahul shivered. "Honestly, I don't know," he replied anxiously.

Andy came over to Ismail. "Hey, man, I don't want anything to do with this macho shit," he said. "I'm leaving, Ismail. I'll be quiet. Please let me go!"

Two other guys held Andy tight, and Ismail put his arm around him. "Hey, Andy. We are your friends. Don't worry. We won't hurt you. But you won't talk to anyone, will you?"

In a terrified voice, Andy replied, "No, Ismail. Of course not! Listen, I'm not leaving. Don't hurt me, please."

"Come on, Andy," Ismail hissed. "You don't have to worry about anything. Just make sure your friend here delivers my merchandise."

Addressing Abdul, he said, "Pick up all the CDs and paperwork." While pointing Abdul's gun to Rahul's head, Ismail said, "I want my merchandise, so don't do anything foolish. This isn't over yet. We will meet again. Think about the sweet little girl and her mother. We will be watching you, Tommy."

Rahul breathed a sigh of relief as soon as the men left. After quickly locking the door, he placed a chair against the bolt to help prevent a forced entry. Not knowing what to do next, he turned on the television set and watched it without paying attention. His mind was still wandering, trying to figure out what he should do next and how to do it without hurting the people he loved. After brainstorming for a while, he finally dozed off in his chair.

When he woke up, the local news broadcast was on television. The anchorperson was talking about the local news, weather, and sports. Suddenly, there was a special bulletin flashing on the screen. "A dead body has been found along a side street behind the Galleria mall," the anchorman said. "Police have not yet been able to identify the body of a white male in his thirties, shot twice in the head. Stay tuned for more details as they become available."

Then the TV screen flashed the face of the victim.

It was Andy.

CHAPTER 52

Ever since Rahul knew that the dead man was Andy, he was sick to his stomach. He shivered. He was now terribly worried.

When Rahul got up the next morning, he called Agent Turner to explain what had happened at Tom's apartment the night before. As Turner had previously suggested, Rahul did not call the police with this information, as it would only jeopardize his and his family's lives. He told Turner that the dead person was Andy Waters, Tom's croupier friend from Las Vegas.

Turner ran over to his assistant, Kaminski, and said, "Listen, put a tail on this Rahul guy and immediately report to me any suspicious characters that come to see him. Also, book me a flight to Washington ASAP. I need to get to the bottom of this, and I am damned tired of this charade."

As he began to leave, he said, "Oh, and tell Khan to also keep an eye on this guy, okay?"

Ismail and his hoods took a hiatus from chasing Rahul and his family for the time being.

CHAPTER 53

Rahul's life was moving at a steady and monotonous pace. His performance at Robotechnique was excellent, but his rewards were barely tolerable. His family life was shattered, his loving wife was now a stranger, and he lacked intimacy with his friends. His only consolation was his daughter, who adhered to him as her father's friend, a stranger. He dragged on with his life in the hope that one day he might be able to prove that he was the same wonderful husband, father, and friend that his loved ones once knew.

The following week on Friday, as he was engrossed in his work at the office, Madhu interrupted him.

"Hi, Rahul," Madhu asked. "Are you busy?"

"Never too busy for you. What's on your mind?"

"Julie called me. She's in court today. Lupe is sick and has gone to a doctor. Julie asked me if I could pick up Rachel from school. Can you go with me and bring Rachel home?"

Rahul was more than happy to do this, especially because it would give him some extra quality time with his daughter. "Sure," he said. "Let's go."

"My car is in the shop today," Madhu said. "Can you drive?"

"Sure can. No problem." Rachel's pre-K school was approximately ten miles away, and Rahul was familiar with the area.

When they arrived at the school, Rahul said to Madhu, "Why don't you go in and get her? I'll wait in the car."

As soon as Rahul parked his car in the school's parking lot, Madhu left to get Rachel. Rahul did not want to go into the school without Julie's permission, as the school's security was very tight. However, Julie must have informed the authorities that Madhu was going to pick her daughter up, because Rachel's teacher seemed to know who Madhu was. Rachel, however, seemed confused.

"Hi, Madhu," Rachel said. "What happened to Lupe? Why are you picking me up? You have to promise me that you will buy me chocolate ice cream at the Marble Slab."

"Okay, honey," Madhu answered. "Let's go home."

When Rachel saw Rahul, she said, "Hi, Tom. Are you picking me up too?"

"Yes, dear. I am," Rahul answered. "How was school? Is your mommy helping you with your homework?" Rahul asked his questions very affectionately.

Suddenly Rachel said in a slight panic, "Madhu, I need to go back to my class. I forgot to pick up my book from my teacher."

"Honey, please wait in the car," Madhu said. "I'll go and get it for you. I'll be back in a jiffy."

While Rahul and Rachel were waiting and chatting in the car, the car doors jerked open. Two bearded men got in.

"Drive!" one of the men demanded.

"Who are you?" Rahul asked the men, bewildered. "What do you want? Here's my wallet. Take it!" Rahul pleaded with the men, thinking that they were robbing him.

"We don't want your money," one of the men answered. "Drive, I say!"

The person in the front seat was very stern and took out his pistol, pointing it at Rahul's gut.

"Where to?" Rahul asked, shaking.

"Keep driving," the man answered. "I will tell you."

Madhu was returning with Rachel's book when he saw Rahul drive by in his car, along with a couple of men who appeared to be holding Rahul and Rachel hostage.

"Wait!" Madhu shouted. "Rahul, where are you going? What are you doing?"

The reality that Rahul and Rachel had been kidnapped sunk into Madhu's consciousness. To make matters worse, he knew that the kidnappers were probably from the gang of terrorists. Shivering at the thought, he quickly called Julie.

In the meantime, security guards and teachers assembled to see what had happened. One of the security guards called the local police, and police cars immediately appeared, with sirens on and lights flashing.

"Officer, one of our children has been kidnapped," a teacher said.

Madhu and the security guards told the police what happened, and a bulletin was issued to the police headquarters.

An officer radioed his central office or precinct. "We have an Amber Alert and possible carjacking here at the school."

Madhu had Agent Turner's business card in his pocket. He called him immediately to convey the bad news that they had always feared.

Turner told Madhu that he was en route to the scene and asked him to wait for him. He slammed his phone down on his desk and called for Kaminski, instructing him to be on alert. With that, he left in a hurry.

When Julie arrived at the school, she frantically ran over to Madhu. "Where is my baby, Madhu?" she demanded. "I am sure Tom has something to do with this! Why did you have to bring that son of a bitch with you?" She was literally screaming, and her emotions were spiraling out of control.

Madhu held her tight and asked her to compose herself.

As soon as Turner showed up, Madhu ran over to get him. After a while, they both approached Julie.

"What happened?" Turner asked Madhu.

"I think her daughter and Rahul have been kidnapped."

"Do you recognize any of the kidnappers?"

"No, not really. They had their heads covered," Madhu said.

A police officer muttered, "My, my! The Feds are here." He conveyed the message to his sergeant.

"I knew it. I knew it," Julie said in anger. "Tom killed my husband. And now, my daughter's life is in danger because of him. Mr. Turner, please do something! Kill that son of a bitch! He has hurt our family badly, very badly. I hope he dies."

"Mrs. Sharma, the person you are referring to may not actually *be* Tom," Agent Turner replied. "At least, we are led to believe that. We will get your daughter back. They only want the man they *believe* is Tom. Once they realize that he actually isn't Tom, they might let them go."

Julie was sobbing.

"Ma'am, after I gather some more information here, I need to run," Agent Turner said. As he walked away from her, he murmured, "God help them."

Turner talked to Madhu some more and then spoke to the security guards and police officers. A message came in on his cell phone. It was Ira Kaminski, his assistant.

"Sir, police have found Tom's abandoned car on the road," Kaminski said.

"Give me the address. I'm heading out there. Have you heard anything from Khan?"

"No, sir."

"Find out where he is and what he's doing to locate these guys' hideouts," Turner said. "Call me back immediately when you know something." He hung up and went back over to Madhu and Julie, informing them that the police had found the car. He told them that he would go to the site and investigate further.

"I want to go with you," Madhu said. "May I?"

"No, sir. That's highly irregular," Turner replied. "We are in an emergency, and I can't have any civilian with me in this situation."

Turner raced to go to the site where the car had been abandoned. In the meantime, Turner's phone rang once more.

"Yes, Khan," he answered. "What do you have?" Turner listened and said, "Yes, yes. I know exactly where it is. I'll meet you there shortly. What? Okay, then I'll meet you inside the McDonald's. Don't rouse any suspicion. We have a hostage situation. We'll need backup. Call Ira and arrange for it."

As soon as Turner hung up the phone, he got yet another call. "Yes?"

The voice at the other end said, "This is Sergeant O'Malley of the Houston Police Department. We understand that your men are following the possible child abduction case at the school. You know that the case falls under local police jurisdiction."

"Yes, Sergeant, I know," Turner replied. "But this is not a mere case of kidnapping. It's our understanding that there is a hostage situation, and we are dealing with deadly criminals and terrorists here. They are dangerous, and we hope to get the child back unharmed."

Turner paused for a moment. "We met at the hospital a few months ago while you were investigating an auto accident where one man was killed. The girl who has been kidnapped is the daughter of the deceased. And they have abducted the other person involved in that accident too.

"Espionage and terrorist activity is a federal offense, and we fully intend to follow it up. We have our team on immediate response. We are in an emergency situation, and we need to run. Good day, sir."

After Turner parked his car at the back of the McDonald's restaurant, he went in through the side door. There, he saw Khan and a few men talking to each other, planning an attack. Agents put on their bulletproof vests, checked their machine guns, and packed revolvers into their holsters. The FBI logo was displayed prominently on their vests.

"Hello, Khan. What is the situation?"

"They are holding Rahul and the kid next door in the restaurant. It is open, and there are a few customers inside. It's an Indian-Pakistani restaurant, and I know the owner. It's now past three o'clock, and they will soon close to prepare for dinner," Khan said.

"I tried to communicate with the owner of the restaurant but cannot."

"I'm familiar with the layout of the facility," Khan continued. "They have a large storage room with a wash area at the back of the restaurant, which leads to the kitchen, and from there, one can enter the dining area and bar. There is an additional door at the back, but it opens from the inside and is usually locked. Even though the back door is always secured, they use it for delivery and trash. I know their suppliers. If someone from the restaurant calls for supplies, the delivery van is able to gain access through the back door."

"Did you call for a delivery van?" he asked Khan. "What if the restaurant isn't expecting any supplies today?"

Khan assured him, "They get meat, fish, and poultry delivered regularly before they start the dinner preparation, and I have asked the delivery company for a van to be delivered to us."

"Good work! By the way, how did you locate the hideout?"

"You remember we had planted a GPS in Rahul's car, which brought us to his abandoned car. We have an eyewitness who described the van and a logo on it. Van belongs to a courier company. They say that they haven't heard from the driver for over two hours."

"What happened to the driver?"

"We don't know yet. I hope these bastards haven't killed him."

"What else?"

One of the other agents turned to speak to them. "I have a report that there are two men with AK-47s guarding the back entrance."

"Why am I not surprised?" Turner said in frustration.

"Okay, let's get the ball rolling," Turner said.

CHAPTER 54

Madhu and Julie waited at the school and talked to the teacher and the police officers, when they saw Sergeant O'Malley arriving in an unmarked police car.

"What's happening here?" he asked one of his officers.

He described the kidnapping and Turner, who came in and left after talking with Madhu and Julie.

As he approached them, he asked, "What is going on here?"

"They took my baby, Sergeant O'Malley. I want to know where they have taken her and what is happening! Please help me." Julie was hysterical.

"All right! Let me find out." O'Malley assured her and left for his car to make calls.

Putting a small note of address in Madhu's hand, he said, "I am going there. You can go there by yourself. But be very inconspicuous. It may be a life-or-death situation."

And he sped away.

CHAPTER 55

Earlier on, the van holding the hostages had sneaked Rahul and Rachel into the storage area of the restaurant through the back door. Rahul saw a couple of bearded men holding AK-47 rifles in their hands.

Ismail Peshawari came over to Rahul and said, "Hey, Tom. Nice to see you again. Andy and I came to talk to you, and you know what you do? You go to the FBI. That's bad. We trusted you. You betrayed us. What shall we do with you?" he sneered. "I think you should meet your Indian friend and Andy soon. I can arrange that." He hit Rahul's jaw with the handle of the AK-47.

Spitting blood, Rahul said, "I've told your friend Andy before, and I am telling you that I am not Tom. My name is Rahul Sharma. After my accident, I just *look* like him. I have no idea what you are talking about."

Ismail Peshawari fleered. "That's a good one, Tom," he replied. "Are you now trying to piss me off?"

"Leave him alone. Don't hurt him." Rachel started to scream, clinging to Tom, and started to wipe the blood off his mouth.

Ismail looked at one of his henchmen and instructed him in Urdu to take the girl into the small room next door and close the door.

He signaled to two of his goons to rough Rahul up. "Tom, this may jog your memory."

Now Rahul was screaming with pain and also bleeding. Ismail came up to Rahul and jerked his head back by his hair. "Remember anything yet?" he whispered mockingly.

Rahul said nothing.

"We paid you a lot of money," Ismail said. "Where is my merchandise? Abdul will go and collect my CD from your apartment. Where are you hiding it? Tell me. Otherwise both of you are going out of here in body bags."

Rahul pleaded, "I don't have it. Please, let us go. I'll pay you back every penny."

"I don't want your fucking money," Ismail said in anger. "I want my disk. Where is it?" He told one of his men, "Bring him over here."

They put a towel over his face and started to pour water to gag him. Rahul was in excruciating pain and moved his arms around, grasping for a breath.

After ten minutes or so, they removed the towel and let him take a deep breath.

"Bastards, are you trying to kill me?" Rahul yelled.

"That's the general idea if you do not cooperate," Ismail said.

"I don't know anything," Rahul pleaded.

"Well, in that case we don't need you. We might as well kill you."

Rahul looked at the men with fear and agony. Ismail was sipping hot tea.

"Give him some tea, Abdul," Ismail said.

Abdul, one of his goons, started to pour tea into a cup.

"Not that way," Ismail snapped. "Where is your hospitality? Give him the whole *kettle* full of tea." He walked over and grabbed the kettle. "Like *this*." Ismail poured the whole kettle of piping hot tea over Rahul's head.

Rahul screamed loud again in pain. He was completely drenched with it. He was shaking with pain and fear, and he realized that these rogues meant business. They would never let him go unless he gave them what they wanted. Although he didn't care about his own life, he was terrified about Rachel's well-being.

"If you don't cooperate, you know what?" Ismail asked. "We will take this little darling with us and add her to my harem. What do you think?"

"You . . . you . . . *fucking* maniac!" Rahul yelled. "Why don't you leave her alone? I can kill you with my bare hands."

Ismail laughed loudly. "We are *Jihadis*. We are not afraid of dying, like you assholes."

Rahul was telling them the truth about his identity, but nobody believed him. He brainstormed how to get out of this mess, by any means necessary, but he couldn't come up with any plan that would work.

Ismail came back to him and said, "So . . . you're not going to listen to me, are you?"

Rahul remained silent.

"Abdul, get that kitchen cart!" Ismail yelled. "Put it here."

A table was placed in front of Rahul. Bewildered, he looked at it. His hands were tied behind his chair so he could not move easily.

Ismail cut the ties on Rahul's wrists, freeing his hands. "That better?" he asked.

Rahul shook and rubbed his hands to get the blood circulation back.

Ismail signaled Abdul to force Rahul's hand on the table. "Let's play a game of memory," he said. "I will cut your fingers off, one by one, until you cooperate."

"*I don't know anything!*" Rahul protested loudly. "I am telling you. I am *not Tom*."

"You think I am an idiot, you . . ." Ismail uttered a word of profanity in Urdu.

Rahul did not understand the language very well, but he knew enough to understand what this guy meant. He also realized that Ismail was now raving mad.

Ismail said something to Abdul in Urdu, and Abdul opened his big knife.

"So which finger shall we cut, Abdul?" Ismail asked.

"Er . . . the first one?" Abdul replied.

"No, that's not an important one. Let's cut the middle finger. He has been waving it at us for quite some time."

Rahul's hand was spread on the table, waiting for Ismail's signal.

~~~

In the meantime, a delivery van rolled to the back door of the Indian restaurant. There was a guard standing at the door, watching. He asked the driver to stop the van. A person at the door came to an alert position and got ready with a charged magazine.

"Open it!" he commanded the driver while pointing an AK-47 at his head. The driver got out of the van and complied.

As soon as the driver opened the van, Khan opened fire at the guard with a handgun attached with a silencer. The other guard's throat was slashed by another FBI commando. Both fell to the ground and were put in the van.

All agents stormed out of the storage room of the restaurant. Everyone panicked when they heard the shoot-out, and a few terrorists fell to the ground, as well as a couple of agents.

Rahul was still on the floor, hiding behind the table during the shooting. He was happy to see Turner and signaled him to where Ismail was. Jumping to his feet, he ran over to the room to save his daughter from these vicious criminals.

Ismail signaled to Abdul to go to the other room and grab the child. Heedless of the danger to his life, Rahul shielded Rachel with his own body. A bullet from Abdul's gun hit Rahul, and he fell to the ground in front of his daughter. Realizing that the child was being attacked, Khan fired at Abdul, but missed.

The agents could not account for all the terrorists. Suddenly, one of them came out of the kitchen and shot Khan in the back. Turner fired at the shooter, killing him instantly. He quickly ran into the room where Rahul and his daughter were, and he saw that Rahul was bleeding badly from a bullet wound. Looking out the door, Turner saw Ismail hiding behind a rack. Turner and Ismail exchanged fire, and a bullet hit Ismail in the shoulder blade, forcing him to the ground in pain. Ismail then hit Turner in his left thigh, disabling him.

Struggling to his feet, Ismail fired at the lock on the other back door to open it. With a single kick, he broke the door open and saw his car parked nearby.

"Hey Abdul, get the child and let's go."

Abdul grabbed Rachel and ran toward his car. Rahul was hurting badly, but he jumped up, ran toward the car, and grabbed Abdul. Julie was outside with Madhu and saw Rahul struggling with the criminals. Sergeant O'Malley tried to hold her back, but she ran over to get her daughter. Violently, Ismail pushed her into the backseat of the car.

Abdul, freeing himself from Rahul, opened the front passenger door and got in. He dropped Rachel into the backseat, and Julie and her daughter clung to each other.

Rahul was on the ground. Suddenly his strong instincts rose to the rescue. He got up, fiercely yanked the passenger door open, and pushed Abdul out of the car. Rahul did not realize how mightily strong he was, but he was in Tom's body.

Ismail saw this, put his car in reverse, and drove at high speed to get out of the parking lot, as well as to shake off Rahul, who was trying to get inside. The open passenger door slammed into another car and detached from the vehicle. Rahul leaped into the car's front seat, in spite of Ismail's attempts to push him out of the car.

Ismail's right shoulder was disabled from the gunshot wound, so he was driving with his left hand and holding a gun with his right. He fired at Rahul twice but missed him.

The car was now on the road and racing at a very high speed. Police cars were chasing it, their sirens loud. Rahul was wild with anger, hitting and kicking Ismail.

"Stop the car, you asshole! I am going to kill you with my bare hands!" Rahul shouted at Ismail. They he yelled at Julie, "Get down! Get down to the floor of the car. Hold *Titlee* tight! I am going to stop this maniac."

The car was out of control, swerving from side to side, and hitting small obstacles on the road. Ismail shot back a couple of times, attempting to hit Julie and Rachel.

"Don't you shoot at them, you mother—" Rahul stopped short of swearing in the presence of his daughter. "Give me your gun!" He grabbed Ismail's arm in anger, and he tried to twist the gun from his hand. Instead, the gun fired, shooting Ismail in the head and killing him.

Without a driver at the wheel, the car careened out of control. Rahul was now barely hanging on to the armrest, holding on for dear life. The car finally hit a large tree, bounced back violently, and turned around almost 180 degrees.

Rahul hit the dashboard and was thrown out of the car. He got up, hurting badly, and ran back over to the car. He tried to open the rear doors with all his force, but the doors were jammed.

"Kick the door open. It's on fire. It might explode," he shrieked. When they couldn't push the door open, he asked Julie from the front seat of the car, "Toss *Titlee* to me. Hurry!" Putting Rachel to safety out of the car, he told Julie again, "Give me your hand. You will have to jump into the front seat. I will catch you. Quick. Quick!"

"I can't. My pants are jammed."

"Rip them off. Hurry."

"Can't."

"Okay, take them off and get out. I will help you tear them so you are free."

With his bare hands, he vigorously yanked off her pants and pulled her from the backseat. She was free and maneuvered out of the car, and they all quickly ran to hide behind a truck parked on the opposite side of the road.

Suddenly, an explosion ripped through the glass of the truck and a couple of parked cars. Ismail's car was now on fire—the place they had been just moments before. Firefighters arrived shortly thereafter and tried to put out the fire.

Rahul was happy to see that Ismail was killed at last—burned to ashes.

Severely bleeding from the gunshot wound and the accident, Rahul collapsed behind the truck, with Julie and Rachel safely beside him. The medics ran over to him and then put him in an ambulance to drive him to the hospital.

In the meantime, Madhu came and sat by them. Rachel ran to him and hugged him. He held her tight.

The paramedics checked Julie and Rachel to see if they were hurt. Rachel had minor cuts and bruises, but Julie was bleeding badly.

"My arm also hurts." The paramedics put the bandages on her to stop the bleeding and looked at her arm.

"Madam, I am taking you to the emergency room. It seems that your left arm may be broken or severely bruised."

"Go ahead, Julie. Rachel and I will follow you," Madhu said.

~~~

Afterward, at the restaurant, Agent Turner asked Kaminski about Ismail and Rahul. He explained the entire episode to Turner.

"Where is Ismail?" Turner asked. "Do we have him?"

"No need to," Kaminski replied. "He's dead."

Turner breathed a sigh of relief. "Are the woman and child all right?"

Kaminski said, "Yes, sir. They are. Paramedics looked at them. Not sure yet, but they need to be seen by the doctors. They are on their way to the ER."

"I believe if it had not been for Rahul, these criminals would have gotten away with the hostages and would have been out of the country by now," Kaminski said. "We tried to apprehend a small plane and its pilot at the private airport on the west side, but he escaped. I'm sure we'll catch him before he crosses the border."

"We have three of these terrorists in custody, and the others are presumably dead," Kaminski continued. "I guess they tried waterboarding Rahul. Look at that water spill and wet towel."

Turner could barely get up. "Any casualties on our side?"

"I am sorry to report that Agent Khan is badly hurt. We haven't surveyed everything yet, and the local police have come in."

"Are you going to live, Turner?" O'Malley asked as he came in.

"Of course. I'll sleep well too. What brings *you* here, Sergeant?" he joked with O'Malley.

O'Malley said, "They tell me that you lost a couple of good men. Your associate Khan is one of them."

Turner lowered his face in agony and said, "Damn!"

"Khan was one of our best men," Turner replied. "We can't recruit enough of them."

Then the paramedics quickly whisked him away in an ambulance and disappeared in the traffic going toward the hospital.

CHAPTER 56

Madhu held Rachel for some time before he put her in Julie's car. They were on the way to the hospital to check on Julie and Rahul.

"Madhu, what happened? Where is Mom? Where is Tom?" Rachel asked.

"Honey, your dad, er . . . *Tom* was trying to rescue you from these bad . . . very bad people. He got hurt, and so did your mom. They are at the hospital for a checkup. We are going to see them soon."

"Who were these bad people?"

"It's a long story. Your mom will tell you one day when you are old enough. But now don't you worry! The police got them."

The emergency area at the hospital was overcrowded and as busy as ever. Madhu was holding Rachel, who was asleep on his shoulder. Julie was waiting for the doctors to finish treating her. The doctors had put a soft cast on her left forearm, and it was in a sling. She came to Madhu and Rachel and patted her very gently.

After checking on Rahul's whereabouts, they were told that Rahul was in the ICU, where they did not allow any visitors. A few federal agents and police staff were visible.

Suddenly Sergeant O'Malley appeared. Madhu went over to him and asked if there was any chance that they could visit Rahul.

"I don't think they'll let anyone visit him at this time," O'Malley said.

"He is my husband," Julie said quickly. "Sergeant, I can see him, can't I?"

Surprised, both O'Malley and Madhu looked at Julie.

"Let me check," O'Malley said. "I'll be back in a moment."

He returned five minutes later with an attending surgeon on duty, with a surgical mask still around his neck.

"Doctor," O'Malley said, pointing at Julie, "she is the patient's wife. She would like to see him. Is that okay?"

"Well, his condition is still critical, but if he is a fighter, he should make it all right," the doctor replied. "We have removed a bullet from his chest. He may be fast asleep. I will allow you for five to ten minutes."

The doctor signaled the nurse, who took Julie to meet Rahul.

Rahul's appearance was frightening. Tubes were inserted into his body, and there was an oxygen tube in his nose. Large bandages were on his left hand and around his chest, stomach, and back. He was heavily sedated and resting.

Julie stayed with him for only five minutes and left.

"Hi, Mom." Rachel got up and wanted to go to Julie and give her a hug.

"Honey, I can't lift you. I have a broken arm," Julie said affectionately, showing her arm with the cast to her daughter.

"How is he doing?" asked Madhu.

"He looks bad, but I think he will make it."

Julie thought that it had been a trying day for all, so she dropped Madhu off and returned home for a quiet evening with her daughter. After Rachel went to bed, she sat stoically on the sofa, with pensive thoughts on Rahul. *I think he is my husband. He put his own life in danger to save me and Rachel. What should I do? I think the only fair thing for me to do is accept him as my beloved husband. Madhu and everyone around me think the same. I do not want to lose him again.* With these thoughts, she went to sleep.

Over the next few days, she went to see Rahul and found out that he was recuperating slowly. He was getting more alert day by day.

Over the weekend, when she went to the hospital to check on Rahul, she could go to his room and talk to him. Rahul appeared to her in much better condition than when she saw him earlier. He still had bandages on his face.

"You are doing all right, Rahul," Julie said. Addressing him as *Rahul* put him in a state of ebullience.

"How is our *Titlee* doing?"

"She is home and asks many questions. I am waiting for you to come home and respond to her."

"I will, I will. But what will I say if she asks me why I still look like Tom and not like Rahul?"

"We have an uphill battle with that. But we will have to manage."

In the meantime, another physician came in and wanted to talk to both.

After carefully looking at his chart and identification on his arm, he asked, "Are you Rahul Sharma?"

"It's a long story. But I can say yes."

"Yes, I know. The FBI has briefed me about it.

"Anyway, my name is Dr. Ackerman. I am a plastic surgeon. You have serious burns and scars on your face. They say it is from hot water or tea. Well, in short, we have to reconstruct your face by grafting some tissues."

He continued, "Well, there is one problem. You are not going to look the same as before. I hope you do not have any objection to that."

Julie murmured, "Thank you," and then said audibly, "Oh, no. I—we—do not have any objection to that. Right, Rahul?"

"Yes, sir!" he said jubilantly. "How long will it take?"

"I can't say for sure. It's a major surgery but not too complicated. Let me check with the staff. If you are agreeable, then you both have to sign these papers."

The doctor left the papers with Julie and left.

"Can't they make you look like Rahul?" Julie asked.

"That may not be possible. But you may ask the doctor," Rahul said. "But that does not matter. I am still Rahul with a different appearance. At least I may not look like Tom though."

CHAPTER 57

About two weeks after Rahul's surgery, Madhu and Julie went to the hospital to bring Rahul home. After he was discharged, Rahul came out in a wheelchair.

Julie had seen him when they removed his bandages. For Madhu, it was somewhat of a shock to see his unfamiliar face.

"It's me, dummy!" Rahul told Madhu, whereas Julie simply smiled.

"You don't look like anyone I would recognize. Well, it's good for you. Finally, you got rid of Tom's ghost."

"Let's go home," Julie said.

~~~

"Dad is home!" Julie shouted as soon as they entered their home.

Rachel came running and stood aghast in front of Rahul.

"This is your dad, Rachel."

"No, he is not!" Rachel clung to her mother.

Rahul extended his hand and said, "Come here. Let me tell you something. Some very bad men took me to their place. They wanted me to do something terrible. I wouldn't do it. So they bruised my face and arm. They also hurt your mom and tried to take you away in the car. I came rushing and rescued you."

"But it was Tom."

"No, honey, they had killed Tom. It was me, and they changed my face to look like him."

"But why?"

"I don't know, honey. There are some bad people who hurt innocent people, and we have to be very careful about it. Can I now call you *Titlee*?"

"Okay."

"Come here and hug your dad."

EPILOGUE

Rahul said, "Julie, one of these days, I need to go to Tom's apartment with Madhu to get rid of it." He then added, "By the way, while I was in the hospital, the FBI came to see me. They offered us a deal to enter a witness protection program and help to get me a job with the Defense department. It probably will not be in Houston."

"That means that we have to relocate? Where?" Julie asked.

"Yes. The location will not be known till we get there. A US marshal will escort us to our new location. We will have a new identity. Julie, I am scared to go through the same ordeal again. Tom had many vices, and I am afraid to face any of them."

"Well, okay, if you say so."

"I have hardened myself from the last situation. However, I hate to see something happen to you or our daughter. Please, do not talk to anyone as of yet. Not even to Madhu, your mom, or my dad if he calls."

"No, I won't. I meant to ask you, what did we learn from all this?" Julie asked.

"A great deal! But I recall a quote from Ralph Waldo Emerson: 'What lies behind you and what lies in front of you, pales in comparison to what lies inside of you.'"

After a brief pause, Rahul continued, "I have to tell you something. While I was in the hospital, I opted to have a vasectomy. I do not want to sire any children who may have Tom's genes."

"That's a strange revelation. But I thank you for your thoughtfulness."

She came close to Rahul, sexually arousing him. He was waiting for this moment to get close to Julie, but not without her acceptance. Their lovemaking was passionate and ecstatic.

~~~

The family was united. They paid the price for Tom's bad influence and company. Even though Rahul and Julie were still cynical about their fate, they were always hoping to find the rainbow of happiness and contentment.